The Seamy Side of History

"IN THE NAME OF JESUS, I FORGIVE YOU"

The Seamy Side of History

THE COMEDY OF HUMAN LIFE, VOLUME XXXII

Honoré de Balzac

NONSUCH

First published in this translation 1901

Nonsuch Publishing Limited
The Mill, Brimscombe Port, Stroud, Gloucestershire, GL5 2QG
www.nonsuch-publishing.com

British Library Cataloguing in Publication Data.
A catalogue record for this book is available from the British Library.

ISBN 1-84588-052-8

Typesetting and origination by Nonsuch Publishing Limited
Printed in Great Britain by Oaklands Book Services Limited

CONTENTS

Introduction to the Modern Edition

ON 20 August 1850, at the Père Lachaise cemetery in Paris, Victor Hugo delivered an impassioned funeral oration over the grave of his friend Honoré de Balzac. Among the many compliments he lavished on his fellow-novelist was this stirring summary of Balzac's literary output: "All his volumes form but a single book, wherein our contemporary civilization is seen to move with a certain terrible weirdness and reality – a marvellous book which the maker of it entitled a comedy and which he might have entitled a history." Hugo was of course referring to *La Comédie Humaine*, the collection of linked stories and novels which Balzac produced between 1830 and 1850 and in which he attempted to hold up a mirror to contemporary French society and capture it in all its many guises: the virtuous, the venal, and the downright vicious.

The eight stories which make up *The Seamy Side of Life*, most of them written in the final decade of Balzac's life, serve to illustrate the extraordinary range of his imaginative sympathy. The title story follows the redemptive adventures of a disillusioned young man, Godefroid, when he comes into contact with a mysterious charitable organisation known as the Brothers of Consolation. From this study of forgiveness and compassion, the reader is plunged into the dissolute world of the fallen aristocracy in "The Prince of Bohemia", a world which revolves around the theatre and the *salon*, where wit and nonchalance are the only valid currency and any kind of cruelty can be justified as long as it is carried out with due style. As the narrator explains, "'Bohemia has nothing and lives upon itself. Hope is its religion; faith (in oneself) its creed; and charity is supposed to be its budget.'" The contrasting moral tone of these two opening stories gives some idea of the depth and complexity of the Balzacian universe.

This complexity becomes understandable when we consider that Balzac's lifespan corresponded almost exactly with the first half of the nineteenth century, a time of intense social and political upheaval in France. He grew up under Napoleon, saw the monarchy restored, lived through the reigns of Louis XVIII and Charles X, witnessed the establishment of Louis Philippe in the July Revolution of 1830, and was even present in Paris during the first days of the 1848 revolution. No other period of French history, perhaps, could have provided a novelist with such a dazzling range of subject matter. In Balzac's Paris, all the old certainties had vanished, and this sense of displacement and disorder runs all through *The Seamy Side of Life*: aristocrats mingle with the *demi-monde*; would-be statesmen starve in garrets; a former judge is powerless to protect himself against his scheming landlord. But despite Balzac's horror at the acquisitiveness of bourgeois society, and his undoubtedly conservative religious views, he was also fascinated – and liberated as a writer – by the chaos he saw around him. In the opening passage of the story "Facino Cane", the narrator describes his habit of wandering the Paris streets at night, listening to the passers-by and gathering scraps of information about their lives; he calls this activity "a kind of intoxication". For Balzac, too, Paris was a seething mass of secrets, stories, ironies, conflicts, coincidences: ugly, yes, and brutal, but also breathtaking in its variety and energy.

La Comedie Humaine was a vastly ambitious undertaking. The very title, with its echoes of Dante, evokes a precedent which would have daunted most novelists. But perhaps an enterprise on this scale was the only way Balzac could respond to a society which was steadily eating away at human values and expectations. The modern bureaucratic state, he wrote, was a "pouvoir gigantesque mis en mouvement par des nains" ["a giant power wielded by pygmies"]. For one man to create a work of art as elaborate and as all-encompassing as *La Comedie Humaine* was a testament to the abiding strength of the individual imagination.

Most English readers, if they encounter Balzac at all, read *Eugénie Grandet* or *Le Père Goriot*. But if Victor Hugo was right, and all of Balzac's writing comprises one remarkable, indivisible work, then these lesser-known stories are essential to an understanding of the author's great project.

The introduction to follow is the work of George Saintsbury (1845–1933), academic and literary critic. A prolific author in his own right, Saintsbury was also regarded as the foremost authority on French literature of his time.

INTRODUCTION

IT would be difficult to find another book, composed of two parts by the same author, which offers more remarkable variations and contrasts than the volume which contains *L'Envers de l'Histoire Contemporaine* and *Z. Marcas*. And in certain respects it must be said that the contrast of the longer and later story with the earlier and shorter one is not such as to inspire us with any great certainty that, had Balzac's comparatively short life been prolonged, we should have had many more masterpieces. It is true that, considering the remarkable excellence of the work (*Les Parents Pauvres*) which immediately preceded *L'Envers de l'Histoire*, it is not possible to say with confidence that the inferiority of the present book is anything more than one of the usual phenomena of *maxima* and *minima*—of ups and downs—which present themselves in all human affairs.

At the same time, there is in *L'Envers de l'Histoire Contemporaine* an ominous atmosphere of flagging, combined with a not less ominous return to a weaker handling of ideas and schemes which the author had handled more strongly earlier. We have seen that the secret-society craze—a favorite one with most Frenchmen, and closely connected with their famous panic-terror of being "betrayed" in war and politics—had an especially strong hold on this most typical of French novelists. He had almost begun his true career with the notion of a league of *Dévorants*, of persons banded, if not exactly against society, at any rate for the gratifying of their own desires and the avenging of their own wrongs, with an utter indifference to social laws and arrangements. He ended it, or nearly so, with the idea of a contrary league of Consolation, which should employ money, time, pains, and combination to supply the wants and heal the wounds which Society either directly causes or more or less callously neglects.

The later idea is, of course, a far nobler one than the earlier; it shows a saner, healthier, happier state of imagination; it coincides rather remarkably with an increasing tendency of the age ever since Balzac's time. Nay, more, the working out of it contains none of those improbabilities and childishnesses which, to any but very youthful tastes and judgments, mar the *Histoire des Treize*. And it is also better written. Balzac, with that extraordinary "long development" of his, as they say of wines, constantly improved in this particular; and whatever may be the doubts on the point referred to above, we may say with some confidence that had he lived, he would have written, in the mere sense of writing, even better and better. Yet again, we catch quaint and pleasant echoes of youth in these pages, and are carried back nearly fifty years in nominal date, and more than twenty in dates of actual invention, by such names as Montauran and Pille-Miche and Marche-à-Terre.

But when all this is said, it cannot, I think, be denied that a certain dulness, a heaviness, does rest on Madame de la Chanterie and L'Initié. The very reference to the *Médecin de Campagne,* which Balzac with his systematizing mania brings in, calls up another unlucky contrast. There, too, the benevolence and the goodness were something fanciful, not to say fantastic; but there was an inspiration, a vigor, to speak vulgarly, a "go," which we do not find here. Balzac's awkward and inveterate habit of parenthetic and episodic narratives and glances backward is not more obvious here than in many other pieces; but there is not, as in some at least of these other pieces, strength enough of main interest to carry it off. The light is clear, it is religious and touching in its dimness; but the lamp burns low.

Z. Marcas, on the other hand, written a good deal earlier in the author's public career, at that quaint and tumbledown residence of Les Jardies, where he did some of his very best work, has all the verve and vigor which its companion or companions lack. Numerous and often good as are the stories by all manner of hands, eminent and other, of the strange neighbors and acquaintance which the French habit of living in apartments brings about, this may vie with almost the best of them for individuality and force. Of course, it may be said that its brevity demanded no very great effort; and also, a more worthy criticism, that Balzac has not made it so very clear after all why the political ingratitude of those for whom Marcas labored made it impossible for him to gain a living more amply and comfortably than by copying. The former carp needs no answer; the sonnet *is* the equal of the long poem if it is a perfect sonnet. The latter, more respectable, is also more damaging. But it is a fair, if not quite a full, defence to say that Balzac is here once more exemplifying his favorite notion of the *maniaque* in the French sense—of the man with one idea, who is incapable not only of making a dishonorable surrender of that idea, but of entering into even the most honorable armistice in his fight for it. Not only will such a man not bow in the House of Rimmon, but the fullest liberty to stay outside will not content him—he must force himself in and be at the idol. The external as well as the internal portraiture of *Z. Marcas* is also as good as it can be: and it cannot but add legitimate interest to the sketch to remember, first, that Balzac attributes to Marcas his own favorite habits and times of work; and secondly, that, like some other men of letters, he himself was an untiring, and would fain have been an influential, politician.

"*Un Episode sous la Terreur* is one of the brilliant things in a small way, which the author did not attempt afterwards to expand at the obvious risk of weakening. It is compressed into compass commensurate with its artistic limits, and, thus preserved, it displays all the strength and vivacity which the plot demands. When Balzac was thus content to leave a 'skit' of this sort, or when he condensed as only Balzac could condense—as in the case of *La Maison du Chat-qui-Pelote*—the result was a story the like of which could scarcely be duplicated in the whole range of French literature. As for the sinister side of *Un Episode sous la Terreur*, it is well known how great was the attraction with the author for things of this kind. And that he treated them vigorously and well, this story will witness."

Un Episode sous la Terreur, together with the two stories just noted, forms a part of the limited *Scènes de la Vie Politique.*

L'Envers de l'Histoire Contemporaine, as above stated, was, in part, one of the very latest of Balzac's works, and was actually finished during his residence at Vierzschovnia. *Madame de la Chanterie*, however, was somewhat earlier, part of it having been written in 1842. It appeared in a fragmentary and rather topsy-turvy fashion, with separate titles, in the *Musée des Familles*, from September in the year just named to November 1844, and was only united together in the first edition of the *Comédie* two years later, though even after this it had a separate appearance with some others of its author's works in 1847. *L'Initié*, or, as it was first entitled, *Les Frères de la Consolation*, was not written till this latter year, and appeared in 1848 in the *Spectateur Republicain*, but not as a book till after the author's death. In both cases there was the usual alternation of chapter divisions, with headings and none.

Z. Marcas, written in 1840, appeared in the *Revue Parisienne* for July of that year, made its first book appearance in a miscellany by different hands called *Le Fruit Défendu* (1841), and five years later took rank in the *Comédie.*

The other stories included here for the sake of convenience may be located readily by reference to the Balzacian scheme, all being from *Scènes de la Vie Parisienne.*

A Prince of Bohemia, the first of the short stories which Balzac originally chose as make-weights to associate with the long drama of *Splendeurs et Misères des Courtisanes*, is one of the few things that, both in whole and in part, one would much rather he had not written. Its dedication to Heine only brings out its shortcomings. For Heine, though he would certainly be as spiteful and unjust as Balzac here shows himself, never failed to carry the laugh on his side. You may wish him, in his lampoons, better morals and better taste, but you can seldom wish him better literature. Had he made this attack on Sainte-Beuve, we should certainly not have yawned over it; and it is rather amusing to think of the sardonic smile with which the dedicatee must have read Balzac's comfortable assurance that he, Heinrich Heine, would understand the *plaisanterie* and the *critique* which *Un Prince de la Bohème* contains. Heine "understood" most things; but if understanding, as is probable, here includes sympathetic enjoyment, we may doubt.

It was written at the same time, or very nearly so, as the more serious attack on Sainte-Beuve in August 1840, and, like that, appeared in Balzac's own *Revue Parisienne*, though it was somewhat later. The thread, such as there is, of interest is two-fold—the description of the Bohemian *grand seigneur* Rusticoli or La Palférine, and the would-be satire on Sainte-Beuve. It is difficult to say which is least well done. Both required an exceedingly light hand, and Balzac's hand was at no time light. Moreover, in the sketch of La Palférine he commits the error—nearly as great in a book as on the stage, where I am told it is absolutely fatal—of delineating his hero with a sort of sneaking kindness which is neither dramatic impartiality nor satiric raillery. La Palférine as portrayed is a "raff," with a touch of no aristocratic quality except insolence. He might have been depicted with cynically concealed savagery, as Swift would have done it; with humorous ridicule, as Gautier or Charles de Bernard would have done it; but there was hardly a third way. As it is, the sneaking kindness above referred to is one of the weapons in the hands of those who—unjustly if it be done without a great deal of limitation—contend that Balzac's ideal of a gentleman was low, and that he had a touch of snobbish admiration for mere insolence.

Here, however, it is possible for a good-natured critic to put in the apology that the artist has tried something unto which he was not born, and failing therein, has apparently committed faults greater than his real ones. This kindness is impossible in the case of the parodies, which are no parodies, of Sainte-Beuve.

From the strictly literary point of view, it is disastrous to give as a parody of a man's work, with an intention of casting ridicule thereon, something which is not in the least like that work, and which in consequence only casts ridicule on its author. To the criticism which takes in life as well as literature, it is a disaster to get in childish rages with people because they do not think your work as good as you think it yourself. And it is not known that Balzac had to complain of Sainte-Beuve in any other way than this, though he no doubt read into what Sainte-Beuve wrote a great deal more than Sainte-Beuve did say. There is a story (I think unpublished) that a certain very great English poet of our times once met an excellent critic who was his old friend (they are both dead now). "What do you mean by calling — vulgar?" growled the poet.—"I didn't call it vulgar," said the critic.—"No; but you meant it," rejoined the bard. On this system of interpretation it is of course possible to accumulate crimes with great rapidity on a censor's head. But it cannot be said to be a critical or rational proceeding. And it must be said that if an author does reply, against the advice of Bacon and all wise people, he should reply by something better than the spluttering abuse of the *Revue Parisienne* article or the inept and irrelevant parody of this story.

Un Homme d'Affaires, relieved of this unlucky weight, is better, but it also, in the eyes of some readers, does not stand very high. La Palférine reappears, and that more exalted La Palférine Maxime de Trailles, "Balzac's pet scoundrel," as some one has called him, though not present, is the hero of the tale, which is artificial and slight enough.

Gaudissart II is much better. Of course, it is very slight, and the "Anglaise" is not much more like a human being than most "Anglaises" in French novels till quite recently. But the anecdote is amusing enough, and it is well and smartly told.

Sarrasine presents two points of divergence from other Balzacian stories: It contains no feminine characters, although the pro- and epilogue introduce two of the 'stock' women personages of the *Comédie.* It is a story within a story, which is no infrequent thing, but, unlike others, the conteur is unknown. While not dealing with a theme the most pleasant, *Sarrasine* will appeal by its clear-cut style; it is one of the cleverest of the shorter tales. Considering the species of singer referred to, the personnel of the Italian operatic stage was well known as far back as the days of Addison and Steele. In France also its customs were freely discussed. Granted, however, that such was the case, the story is open to criticism on this account. It seems hardly possible that a well-informed man of the time should have been entirely ignorant of the fact that the Italians allowed no women to sing in public; and that this man, a sculptor by profession, should have been deceived by the figure of a eunuch so frankly displayed in the glare of the footlights. He studied every line of every limb. He noted the well-formed shoulders and the poise of the head. He reproduced the contour of the form in marble. Yet he was deluded openly and hoaxed without mercy. But, aside from this possible defect in plot, the story presents a striking contrast in the figures of the passionate, obstinate, hot-headed man, and the shrinking, irresolute, sexless creature.

Facino Cane did not originally rank in the Parisian Scenes at all, but was a *Conte Philosophique*. It is slight and rather fanciful, the chief interest lying in Balzac's unfailing fellow-feeling for all those who dream of millions, as he himself did all his life long, only to exemplify the moral of his own *Peau de Chagrin*.

Un Prince de la Bohème, in its *Revue Parisienne* appearance, bore the title of *Les Fantaisies de Claudine*, but when, four years later, it followed *Honorine* in book form, it took the present label. The *Comédie* received it two years later. *Gaudissart II* was written for a miscellany called *Le Diable à Paris*; but as this delayed its appearance, it was first inserted in the *Presse* for October 12, 1844, under a slightly different title, which it kept in the *Diable*. Almost immediately, however, it joined the *Comédie* under its actual heading. *Un Homme d'Affaires* appeared in the *Siècle* for September 10, 1845, and was then called *Les Roueries d'un Créancier*. It entered the *Comédie* almost at once, but made an excursion therefrom to join, in 1847, *Ou mènent les mauvais chemins* and others as *Un Drame dans les Prisons.*

Facino Cane is earlier than these, having first seen the light in the *Chronique de Paris* of March 17, 1836. Next year it became an *Étude Philosophique*. It had another grouped appearance (with *La Muse du Département* and *Albert Savarus*) in 1843, and entered the *Comédie* the year after.

Sarrasine was published by Werdet in October 1838, being included in a volume with *Les Secrets de la Princesse de Cadignan*, *Les Employés*, *Facino Cane* and *La Maison Nucingen*, the latter of which was the title story. It was included in its present place in the *Comédie* in 1844.

G. S.

THE SEAMY SIDE OF HISTORY

FIRST EPISODE: MADAME DE LA CHANTERIE

ONE fine September evening, in the year 1836, a man of about thirty was leaning over the parapet of the quay at a point whence the Seine may be surveyed up stream from the Jardin des Plantes to Notre-Dame, and down in grand perspective to the Louvre.

There is no such view elsewhere in the Capital of Ideas (Paris). You are standing, as it were, on the poop of a vessel that has grown to vast proportions. You may dream there of Paris from Roman times to the days of the Franks, from the Normans to the Burgundians, through the Middle Ages to the Valois, Henri IV, Napoleon, and Louis Philippe. There is some vestige or building of each period to bring it to mind. The dome of Sainte-Geneviève shelters the *Quartier Latin*. Behind you rises the magnificent east end of the Cathedral. The Hôtel de Ville speaks of all the revolutions, the Hôtel Dieu of all the miseries of Paris. After glancing at the splendours of the Louvre, take a few steps, and you can see the rags that hang out from the squalid crowd of houses that huddle between the Quai de la Tournelle and the Hôtel Dieu; the authorities are, however, about to clear them away.

In 1836 this astonishing picture inculcated yet another lesson. Between the gentleman who leaned over the parapet and the cathedral, the deserted plot, known of old as le Terrain, was still strewn with the ruins of the Archbishop's palace. As we gaze there on so many suggestive objects, as the mind takes in the past and the present of the city of Paris, Religion seems to have established herself there that she might lay her hands on the sorrows on both sides of the river, from the Faubourg Saint-Antoine to the Faubourg Saint-Marceau.

It is to be hoped that these sublime harmonies may be completed by the construction of an Episcopal palace in a Gothic style to fill the place of the meaningless buildings that now stand between the Island, the Rue d'Arcole, and the Quai de la Cité.

This spot, the very heart of old Paris, is beyond anything deserted and melancholy. The waters of the Seine break against the wall with a loud noise, the Cathedral throws its shadow there at sunset. It is not strange that vast thoughts should brood there in a brain-sick man. Attracted perhaps by an accordance between his own feelings at the moment and those to which such a varied prospect must give rise, the loiterer folded his hands over the parapet, lost in the twofold contemplation of Paris and of himself! The shadows spread, lights twinkled into being, and still he did not stir; carried on as he was by the flow of a mood of thought, big with the future, and made solemn by the past.

At this instant he heard two persons approaching, whose voices had been audible on the stone bridge where they had crossed from the Island of the Cité to the Quai de la Tournelle. The two speakers no doubt believed themselves to be alone, and talked somewhat louder than they would have done in a more frequented place, or if they had noticed the propinquity of a stranger. From the bridge their tones betrayed an eager discussion, bearing, as it seemed, from a few words that reached the involuntary listener, on a loan of money. As they came closer, one of the speakers, dressed as a working man, turned from the other with a gesture of despair. His companion looked round, called the man back, and said:

"You have not a sou to pay the bridge-toll. Here!"—and he gave him a coin— "and remember, my friend, it is God Himself who speaks to us when a good thought occurs to us."

The last words startled the dreamer. The man who spoke had no suspicion that, to use a proverbial expression, he was killing two birds with one stone; that he spoke to two unhappy creatures—a workman at his wits' end, and a soul without a compass; a victim of what Panurge's sheep call Progress, and a victim of what France calls equality.

These words, simple enough in themselves, acquired grandeur from the tone of the speaker, whose voice had a sort of magical charm. Are there not such voices, calm and sweet, affecting us like a view of the distant ocean?

The speaker's costume showed him to be a priest, and his face, in the last gleam of twilight, was pale, and dignified, though worn. The sight of a priest coming out of the grand Cathedral of Saint Stephen at Vienna to carry extreme unction to a dying man, persuaded Werner, the famous tragic poet, to become a Catholic. The effect was much the same on our Parisian when he saw the man who, without intending it, had brought him consolation; he discerned on the dark line of his horizon in the future a long streak of light where the blue of heaven was shining, and he followed the path of light, as the shepherds of the Gospel followed the voice that called to them from on high, "Christ the Lord is born!"

The man of healing speech walked on under the cathedral, and by favour of Chance—which is sometimes consistent—made his way towards the street from which the loiterer had come, and whither he was returning, led there by his own mistakes in life.

This young man's name was Godefroid. As this narrative proceeds, the reader will understand the reasons for giving to the actors in it only their Christian names.

And this is the reason why Godefroid, who lived near the Chausée d'Antin, was lingering at such an hour under the shadow of Notre-Dame.

He was the son of a retail dealer, who, by economy, had made some little fortune, and in him centred all the ambitions of his parents, who dreamed of seeing him a notary in Paris. At the early age of seven he had been sent to a school, kept by the Abbé Liautard, where he was thrown together with the children of certain families of distinction, who had selected this establishment for the education of their sons, out of attachment to religion, which, under the emperor, was somewhat too much neglected in the Lycées, or public schools. At that age social inequalities are not recognised between school-fellows; but in 1821, when his studies were finished, Godefroid, articled to a notary, was not slow to perceive the distance that divided him from those with whom he had hitherto lived on terms of intimacy.

While studying the law, he found himself lost in the crowd of young men of the citizen class, who, having neither a ready-made fortune nor hereditary rank, had nothing to look to but their personal worth or persistent industry. The hopes built upon him by his father and mother, who had now retired from business, stimulated his conceit without giving him pride. His parents lived as simply as Dutch folks, not spending more than a quarter of their income of twelve thousand francs; they intended to devote their savings, with half their capital, to the purchase of a connection for their son. Godefroid, reduced also to live under the conditions of this domestic thrift, regarded them as so much out of proportion to his parents' dreams and his own, that he felt disheartened. In weak characters such discouragement leads to envy. While many other men, in whom necessity, determination, and good sense were more marked than talent, went straight and steadfastly onward in the path laid down for modest ambitions, Godefroid waxed rebellious, longed to shine, insisted on facing the brightest light, and so dazzled his eyes. He tried to "get on," but all his efforts ended in demonstrating his incapacity. At last, clearly perceiving too great a discrepancy between his desires and his prospects, he conceived a hatred of social superiority; he became a Liberal, and tried to make himself famous by a book; but he learned, to his cost, to regard talent much as he regarded rank. Having tried by turns the profession of notary, the bar, and literature, he now aimed at the higher branch of the law.

At this juncture his father died. His mother, content in her old age with two thousand francs a year, gave up almost her whole fortune to his use. Possessor now, at five-and-twenty, of ten thousand francs a year, he thought himself rich, and he was so as compared with the past. Hitherto his life had been a series of acts with no will behind them, or of impotent willing; so, to keep pace with the age, to act, to become a personage, he tried to get into some circle of society by the help of his money.

At first he fell in with journalism, which has always an open hand for any capital that comes in its way. Now, to own a newspaper is to be a Personage; it means employing talent and sharing its successes without dividing its labours. Nothing is more tempting to second-rate men than thus to rise by the brains of others. Paris has had a few *parvenus* of this type, whose success is a disgrace both to the age and to those who have lent a lifting shoulder.

In this class of society Godefroid was soon cut out by the vulgar cunning of some and the extravagance of others, by the money of ambitious capitalists or the manoeuvring of editors; then he was dragged into the dissipations that a literary or political life entails, the habits of critics behind the scenes, and the amusements needed by men who work their brains hard. Thus he fell into bad company; but he there learned that he was an insignificant-looking person, and that he had one shoulder higher than the other without redeeming this malformation by any distinguished ill-nature or wit. Bad manners are a form of self-payment which actors snatch by telling the truth.

Short, badly made, devoid of wit or of any strong bent, all seemed at an end for a young man at a time when for success in any career the highest gifts of mind are as nothing without luck, or the tenacity which commands luck.

The revolution of 1830 poured oil on Godefroid's wounds; he found the courage of hope, which is as good as that of despair. Like many another obscure journalist, he got an appointment where his Liberal ideas, at loggerheads with the demands of a newly-established power, made him but a refractory instrument. Veneered only with Liberalism, he did not know, as superior men did, how to hold his own. To obey the Ministry was to him to surrender his opinions. And the Government itself seemed to him false to the laws that had given rise to it. Godefroid declared in favour of movement when what was needed was tenacity; he came back to Paris almost poor, but faithful to the doctrines of the opposition.

Alarmed by the licentiousness of the press, and yet more by the audacity of the republican party, he sought in retirement the only life suited to a being of incomplete faculties, devoid of such force as might defy the rough jolting of political life, weary too of repeated failures, of suffering and struggles which had won him no glory; and friendless, because friendship needs conspicuous qualities or defects, while possessing feelings that were sentimental rather than deep. Was it not, in fact, the only prospect open to a young man who had already been several times cheated by pleasure, and who had grown prematurely old from friction in a social circle that never rests nor lets others rest?

His mother, who was quietly dying in the peaceful village of Auteuil, sent to her son to come to her, as much for the sake of having him with her as to start him in the road where he might find the calm and simple happiness that befits such souls. She had at last taken Godefroid's measure when she saw that at eight-and-twenty he had reduced his whole fortune to four thousand francs a year; his desires blunted, his fancied talents extinct, his energy nullified, his ambition crushed, and his hatred for every one who rose by legitimate effort increased by his many disappointments.

She tried to arrange a marriage for Godefroid with the only daughter of a retired merchant, thinking that a wife might be a guardian to his distressful mind, but the old father brought the mercenary spirit that abides in those who have been engaged in trade to bear on the question of settlements. At the end of a year of attentions and intimacy, Godefroid's suit was rejected. In the first place, in the opinion of these case-hardened traders, the young man must necessarily have retained a deep-dyed immorality from his former pursuits; and then, even during this past year, he had drawn upon his capital both to dazzle the parents and to attract the daughter. This not unpardonable vanity gave the finishing touch; the family had a horror of unthrift; and their refusal was final when they heard that Godefroid had sacrificed in six years a hundred and fifty thousand francs of his capital.

The blow fell all the harder on his aching heart because the girl was not at all good-looking. Still, under his mother's influence, Godefroid had credited the object of his addresses with a sterling character and the superior advantages of a sound judgment; he was accustomed to her face, he had studied its expression, he liked the young lady's voice, manners, and look. Thus, after staking the last hope of his life on this attachment, he felt the bitterest despair.

His mother dying, he found himself—he whose requirements had always followed the tide of fashion—with five thousand francs for his whole fortune, and the certainty of never being able to repair any future loss, since he saw himself incapable of the energy which is imperatively demanded for the grim task of *making a fortune.*

But a man who is weak, aggrieved, and irritable cannot submit to be extinguished at a blow. While still in mourning, Godefroid wandered through Paris in search of something to "turn up"; he dined in public rooms, he rashly introduced himself to strangers, he mingled in society, and met with nothing but opportunities for expenditure. As he wandered about the Boulevards, he was so miserable that the sight of a mother with a young daughter to marry gave him as keen a pang as that of a young man going on horseback to the Bois, of a *parvenu* in a smart carriage, or of an official with a ribbon in his buttonhole. The sense of his own inadequacy told him that he could not pretend even to the more respectable of second-class positions, nor to the easiest form of office-work. And he had spirit enough to be constantly vexed, and sense enough to bewail himself in bitter self-accusation.

Incapable of contending with life, conscious of certain superior gifts, but devoid of the will that brings them into play, feeling himself incomplete, lacking force to undertake any great work, or to resist the temptations of those tastes he had acquired from education or recklessness in his past life, he was a victim to three maladies, any one of them enough to disgust a man with life when he has ceased to exercise his religious faith. Indeed, Godefroid wore the expression so common now among men, that it has become the Parisian type: it bears the stamp of disappointed or smothered ambitions, of mental distress, of hatred lulled by the apathy of a life amply filled up by the superficial and daily spectacle of Paris, of satiety seeking stimulants, of repining without talent, of the affectation of force; the venom of past failure which makes a man smile at scoffing, and scorn all that is elevating, misprize the most necessary authorities, enjoy their dilemmas, and disdain all social forms.

This Parisian disease is to the active and persistent coalition of energetic malcontents what the soft wood is to the sap of a tree; it preserves it, covers it, and hides it.

Weary of himself, Godefroid one morning resolved to give himself some reason for living. He had met a former school-fellow, who had proved to be the tortoise of the fable while he himself had been the hare. In the course of such a conversation as is natural to old companions while walking in the sunshine on the Boulevard des Italiens, he was amazed to find that success had attended this man, who, apparently far less gifted than himself with talent and fortune, had simply resolved each day to do as he had resolved the day before. The brain-sick man determined to imitate this simplicity of purpose.

"Life in the world is like the earth," his friend had said; "it yields in proportion to our labours."

Godefroid was in debt. As his first penance, his first duty, he required himself to live in seclusion and pay his debts out of his income. For a man who was in the habit of spending six thousand francs when he had five, it was no light thing to reduce his expenses to two thousand francs. He read the advertisement-sheets every morning, hoping to find a place of refuge where he might live on a fixed sum, and where he might enjoy the solitude necessary to a man who wanted to study and examine himself, and discern a vocation. The manners and customs of the boarding-houses in the *Quartier Latin* were an offence to his taste; a private asylum, he thought, would be unhealthy; and he was fast drifting back into the fatal uncertainty of a will-less man, when the following advertisement caught his eye:

> "Small apartments, at seventy francs a month; might suit a clerk in orders. Quiet habits expected. Board included; and the rooms will be inexpensively furnished on mutual agreement. Inquire of M. Millet, grocer, Rue Chanoinesse, by Notre-Dame, for all further particulars."

Attracted by the artless style of this paragraph, and the aroma of simplicity it seemed to bear, Godefroid presented himself at the grocer's shop at about four in the afternoon, and was told that at that hour Madame de la Chanterie was dining, and could see no one at meal-times. The lady would be visible in the evening after seven, or between ten and twelve in the morning. While he talked, Monsieur Millet took stock of Godefroid, and proceeded to put him through his first examination— "Was monsieur single? Madame wished for a lodger of regular habits. The house was locked up by eleven at latest."

"Well," said he in conclusion, "you seem to me, monsieur, to be of an age to suit Madame de la Chanterie's views."

"What age do you suppose I am?" asked Godefroid.

"Somewhere about forty," replied the grocer.

This plain answer cast Godefroid into the depths of misanthropy and dejection. He went to dine on the Quai de la Tournelle, and returned to gaze at Notre-Dame just as the fires of the setting sun were rippling and breaking in wavelets on the buttresses of the great nave. The quay was already in shadow, while the towers still glittered in the glow, and the contrast struck Godefroid as he tasted all the bitterness which the grocer's brutal simplicity had stirred within him. Thus the young man was oscillating between the whisperings of despair and the appealing tones of religious harmony aroused in his mind by the cathedral bells, when, in the darkness, and silence, and calm moonshine, the priest's speech fell on his ear. Though far from devout—like most men of the century—his feelings were touched by these words, and he went back to the Rue Chanoinesse, where he had but just decided not to go.

The priest and Godefroid were equally surprised on turning into the Rue Massillon, opposite the north door of the cathedral, at the spot where it ends by the Rue de la Colombe, and is called Rue des Marmousets. When Godefroid stopped under the arched doorway of the house where Madame de la Chanterie lived, the priest turned round to examine him by the light of a hanging oil-lamp, which will, very likely, be one of the last to disappear in the heart of old Paris.

"Do you wish to see Madame de la Chanterie, monsieur?" asked the priest.

"Yes," replied Godefroid. "The words I have just heard you utter to that workman prove to me that this house, if you dwell in it, must be good for the soul."

"Then you witnessed my failure," said the priest, lifting the knocker, "for I did not succeed."

"It seems to me that it was the workman who failed. He had begged sturdily enough for money."

"Alas!" said the priest, "one of the greatest misfortunes attending revolutions in France is that each, in its turn, offers a fresh premium to the ambitions of the lower classes. To rise above his status and make a fortune, which, in these days, is considered the social guarantee, the workman throws himself into monstrous plots, which, if they fail, must bring those who dabble in them before the bar of human justice. This is what good-nature sometimes ends in."

The porter now opened a heavy gate, and the priest said to Godefroid:

"Then you have come about the rooms to let?"

"Yes, monsieur."

The priest and Godefroid then crossed a fairly wide courtyard, beyond which stood the black mass of a tall house, flanked by a square tower even higher than the roof, and amazingly old. Those who know the history of Paris are aware that the old soil has risen so much round the cathedral, that there is not a trace to be seen of the twelve steps which originally led up to it. Hence what was the ground floor of this house must now form the cellars. There is a short flight of outer steps to the door of the tower, and inside it an ancient *Vise* or stairs, winding in a spiral round a newell carved to imitate a vine-stock. This style, resembling that of the Louis XII staircases at Blois, dates as far back as the fourteenth century.

Struck by these various signs of antiquity, Godefroid could not help exclaiming:

"This tower was not built yesterday!"

"It is said to have withstood the attacks of the Normans and to have formed part of a primeval palace of the kings of Paris; but according to more probable traditions, it was the residence of Fulbert, the famous Canon, and the uncle of Héloïse."

As he spoke the priest opened the door of the apartment, which seemed to be the ground floor, and which, in fact, is now but just above the ground of both the outer and the inner courtyard—for there is a small second court.

In the first room a servant sat knitting by the light of a small lamp; she wore a cap devoid of any ornament but its goffered cambric frills. She stuck one of the needles through her hair, but did not lay down her knitting as she rose to open the door of a drawing-room looking out on the inner court. This room was lighted up. The woman's dress suggested to Godefroid that of some Grey Sister.

"Madame, I have found you a tenant," said the priest, showing in Godefroid, who saw in the room three men, sitting in armchairs near Madame de la Chanterie.

The three gentlemen rose; the mistress of the house also; and when the priest had pushed forward a chair for the stranger, and he had sat down in obedience to a sign from Madame de la Chanterie and an old-fashioned bidding to "Be seated," the Parisian felt as if he were far indeed from Paris, in remote Brittany, or the backwoods of Canada.

There are, perhaps, degrees of silence. Godefroid, struck already by the tranquillity of the Rue Massillon and Rue Chanoinesse, where a vehicle passes perhaps twice in a month, struck too by the stillness of the courtyard and the tower, may have felt himself at the very heart of silence, in this drawing-room, hedged round by so many old streets, old courtyards, and old walls.

This part of the Island, called the Cloister, preserves the character common to all cloisters; it is damp, and cold, and monastic; silence reigns there unbroken, even during the noisiest hours of the day. It may also be remarked that this part of the Cité, lying between the body of the Cathedral and the river, is to the north and under the shadow of Notre-Dame. The east wind loses itself there, unchecked by any obstacle, and the fogs from the Seine are to some extent entrapped by the blackened walls of the ancient metropolitan church.

So no one will be surprised at the feeling that came over Godefroid on finding himself in this ancient abode, and in the presence of four persons as silent and as solemn as everything around them. He did not look about him; his curiosity centred in Madame de la Chanterie, whose name even had already puzzled him.

This lady was evidently a survival from another century, not to say another world. She had a rather sweet face, with a soft, coldly-coloured complexion, an aquiline nose, a benign brow, hazel eyes, and a double chin, the whole framed in curls of silver hair. Her dress could only be described by the old name of *fourreau* (literally, a sheath, a tightly-fitting dress), so literally was she cased in it, in the fashion of the eighteenth century. The material—silk of carmelite grey, finely and closely striped with green—seemed to have come down from the same date; the body, cut low, was hidden under a mantilla of richer silk, flounced with black lace, and fastened at the bosom with a brooch containing a miniature. Her feet, shod in black velvet boots, rested on a little stool. Madame de la Chanterie, like her maid-servant, was knitting stockings, and had a knitting pin stuck through her waving hair under her lace cap.

"Have you seen Monsieur Millet?" she asked Godefroid in the head voice peculiar to dowagers of the Faubourg Saint-Germain, as if to invite him to speak, seeing that he was almost thunderstruck.

"Yes, madame."

"I am afraid the rooms will hardly suit you," she went on, observing that her proposed tenant was dressed with elegance in clothes that were new and smart.

Godefroid, in fact, was wearing patent leather boots, yellow gloves, handsome shirt-studs, and a neat watch chain passed through the buttonhole of a black silk waistcoat sprigged with blue.

Madame de la Chanterie took a small silver whistle out of her pocket and blew it. The woman servant came in.

"Manon, child, show this gentleman the rooms. Will you, my dear friend, accompany him?" she said to the priest. "And if by any chance the rooms should suit you," she added, rising, and looking at Godefroid, "we will afterwards discuss the terms."

Godefroid bowed and went out. He heard the iron rattle of a bunch of keys which Manon took out of a drawer, and saw her light a candle in a large brass candlestick.

Manon led the way without speaking a word. When he found himself on the stairs again, climbing to the upper floors, he doubted the reality of things; he felt dreaming though awake, and saw the whole world of fantastic romance such as he had read of in his hours of idleness. And any Parisian dropped here, as he was, out of the modern city with its luxurious houses and furniture, its glittering restaurants and theatres, and all the stirring heart of Paris, would have felt as he did. The single candle carried by the servant lighted the winding stair but dimly; spiders had hung it with their dusty webs.

Manon's dress consisted of a skirt broadly pleated and made of coarse woollen stuff; the bodice was cut square at the neck, behind and before, and all her clothes seemed to move in a piece. Having reached the second floor, which had been the third, Manon stopped, turned the springs of an antique lock, and opened a door painted in coarse imitation of knotted mahogany.

"There!" said she, leading the way.

Who had lived in these rooms? A miser, an artist who had died of want, a cynic indifferent to the world, or a pious man who was alien to it? Any one of the four seemed possible, as the visitor smelt the very odour of poverty, saw the greasy stains on wall-papers covered with a layer of smoke, the blackened ceilings, the windows with their small dusty panes, the brown-tiled floor, the wainscot sticky with a deposit of fog. A damp chill came down the fireplaces, faced with carved stonework that had been painted, and with mirrors framed in the seventeenth century. The rooms were at the angle of a square, as the house stood, enclosing the inner courtyard, but this Godefroid could not see, as it was dark.

"Who used to live here?" Godefroid asked of the priest.

"A Councillor to the Parlement, Madame's grand-uncle, a Monsieur de Boisfrelon. He had been quite childish ever since the Revolution, and died in 1832 at the age of ninety-six; Madame could not bear the idea of seeing a stranger in the rooms so soon; still, she cannot endure the loss of rent ..."

"Oh, and Madame will have the place cleaned and furnished, to be all monsieur could wish," added Manon.

"It will only depend on how you wish to arrange the rooms," said the priest. "They can be made into a nice sitting-room and a large bedroom and dressing-room, and the two small rooms round the corner are large enough for a spacious study. That is how my rooms are arranged below this, and those on the next floor."

"Yes," said Manon; "Monsieur Alain's rooms are just like these, only that they look out on the tower."

"I think I had better see the rooms again by daylight," said Godefroid shyly.

"Perhaps so," said Manon.

The priest and Godefroid went downstairs again, leaving Manon to lock up, and she then followed to light them down. Then, when he was in the drawing-room, Godefroid, having recovered himself, could, while talking to Madame de la Chanterie, study the place, the personages, and the surroundings.

The window-curtains of this drawing-room were of old red satin; there was a cornice-valance, and the curtains were looped with silk cord; the red tiles of the floor showed beyond an ancient tapestry carpet that was too small to cover it entirely. The woodwork was painted stone-colour. The ceiling, divided down the middle by a joist starting from the chimney, looked like an addition lately conceded to modern luxury; the easy-chairs were of wood painted white, with tapestry seats. A shabby clock, standing between two gilt candlesticks, adorned the chimney-shelf. An old table with stag's feet stood by Madame de la Chanterie, and on it were her balls of wool in a wicker basket. A clockwork lamp threw light on the picture.

The three men, sitting as rigid, motionless, and speechless as Bonzes, had, like Madame de la Chanterie, evidently ceased speaking on hearing the stranger return. Their faces were perfectly cold and reserved, as befitted the room, the house, and the neighbourhood.

Madame de la Chanterie agreed that Godefroid's observations were just, and said that she had postponed doing anything till she was informed of the intentions of her lodger, or rather of her boarder; for if the lodger could conform to the ways of the household, he was to board with them—but their ways were so unlike those of Paris life! Here, in the Rue Chanoinesse, they kept country hours; every one, as a rule, had to be in by ten at night; noise was not to be endured; neither women nor children were admitted, so that their regular habits might not be interfered with. No one, perhaps, but a priest could agree to such a rule. At any rate, Madame de la Chanterie wished for some one who liked plain living and had few requirements; she could only afford the most necessary furniture in the rooms. Monsieur Alain was satisfied, however—and she bowed to one of the gentlemen—and she would do the same for the new lodger as for the old.

"But," said the priest, "I do not think that monsieur is quite inclined to come and join us in our convent."

"Indeed; why not?" said Monsieur Alain. "We are all quite content, and we all get on very well."

"Madame," said Godefroid, rising, "I will have the honour of calling on you again to-morrow."

Though he was but a young man, the four old gentlemen and Madame de la Chanterie stood up, and the priest escorted him to the outer steps. A whistle sounded, and at the signal the porter appeared, lantern in hand, to conduct Godefroid to the street; then he closed the yellow gate, as heavy as that of a prison, and covered with arabesque ironwork, so old that it would be hard to determine its date.

When Godefroid found himself sitting in a hackney cab and being carried to the living regions of Paris, where light and warmth reigned, all he had just seen seemed like a dream; and as he walked along the Boulevard des Italiens, his impressions already seemed as remote as a memory. He could not help saying to himself:

"Shall I find those people there to-morrow, I wonder?"

On the following day, when he woke in the midst of the elegance of modern luxury and the refinements of English comfort, Godefroid recalled all the details of his visit to the Cloister of Notre-Dame, and came to some conclusions in his mind as to the things he had seen there. The three gentlemen, whose appearance, attitude, and silence had left an impression on him, were no doubt boarders, as well as the priest. Madame de la Chanterie's gravity seemed to him to be the result of the reserved dignity with which she had endured some great sorrows. And yet, in spite of the explanations he gave himself, Godefroid could not help feeling that there was an air of mystery in these uncommunicative faces. He cast a glance at his furniture to choose what he could keep, what he thought indispensable; but, transporting them in fancy to the horrible rooms in the Rue Chanoinesse, he could not help laughing at the grotesque contrast they would make there, and determined to sell everything, and pay away so much as they might bring; leaving the furnishing of the rooms to Madame de la Chanterie. He longed for a new life, and the objects that could recall his old existence must be bad for him. In his craving for transformation—for his was one of those natures which rush forward at once with a bound, instead of approaching a situation step by step as others do—he was seized, as he sat at breakfast, by an idea: he would realise his fortune, pay his debts, and place the surplus with the banking firm his father had done business with.

This banking house was that of Mongenod and Co., established in Paris since 1816 or 1817, a firm whose reputation had never been blown on in the midst of the commercial depravity which at this time had blighted, more or less, several great Paris houses. Thus, in spite of their immense wealth, the houses of Nucingen and du Tillet, of Keller Brothers, of Palma and Co., suffer under a secret disesteem whispered, as it were, between lip and ear. Hideous transactions had led to such splendid results; and political successes, nay, monarchical principles, had overgrown such foul beginnings, that no one in 1834 thought for a moment of the mud in which the roots were set of such majestic trees—the upholders of the State. At the same time, there was not one of these bankers that did not feel aggrieved by praises of the house of Mongenod.

The Mongenods, following the example of English bankers, make no display of wealth; they do everything quite quietly, and carry on their business with such prudence, shrewdness, and honesty as allow them to operate with certainty from one end of the world to the other.

The present head of the house, Frédéric Mongenod, is brother-in-law to the Vicomte de Fontaine. Thus his numerous family is connected, through the Baron de Fontaine, with Monsieur Grossetête, the Receiver-General (brother to the Grossetête and Co. of Limoges), with the Vandenesses, and with Planat de Baudry, another Receiver-General. This relationship, after being of the greatest service to the late Mongenod *senior* in his financial operations at the time of the Restoration, had gained him the confidence of many of the old nobility, whose capital and vast savings were intrusted to his bank. Far from aiming at the peerage, like Keller, Nucingen, and du Tillet, the Mongenods kept out of political life, and knew no more of it than was needed for banking business.

Mongenod's bank occupies a magnificent house in the Rue de la Victoire, with a garden behind and a courtyard in front, where Madame Mongenod resided with her two sons, with whom she was in partnership. Madame la Vicomtesse de Fontaine had taken out her share on the death of the elder Mongenod in 1827. Frédéric Mongenod, a handsome fellow of about five-and-thirty, with a cold manner, as silent and reserved as a Genevese, and as neat as an Englishman, had acquired under his father all the qualifications needed in his difficult business. He was more cultivated than most bankers, for his education had given him the general knowledge which forms the curriculum of the École Polytechnique; and, like many bankers, he had an occupation, a taste, outside his regular business, a love of physics and chemistry. Mongenod *junior*, ten years younger than Frédéric, filled the place, under his elder brother, that a head-clerk holds under a lawyer or a notary; Frédéric was training him, as he himself had been trained by his father, in the scientific side of banking, for a banker is to money what a writer is to ideas—they both ought to know everything.

Godefroid, as he mentioned his family name, could see how highly his father had been respected, for he was shown through the offices at once to that next to Mongenod's private room. This room was shut in by glass doors, so that, in spite of his wish not to listen, Godefroid overheard the conversation going on within.

"Madame, your account shows sixteen hundred thousand francs on both sides of the balance sheet," Mongenod the younger was saying. "I know not what my brother's views may be; he alone can decide whether an advance of a hundred thousand francs is possible. You lacked prudence. It is not wise to put sixteen hundred thousand francs into a business—"

"Too loud, Louis!" said a woman's voice. "Your brother's advice is never to speak but in an undertone. There may be some one in the little waiting-room."

At this instant Frédéric Mongenod opened the door from his living rooms to his private office; he saw Godefroid, and went through to the inner room, where he bowed respectfully to the lady who was talking to his brother.

He showed Godefroid in first, saying as he did so, "And whom have I the honour of addressing?"

As soon as Godefroid had announced himself, Frédéric offered him a chair; and while the banker was opening his desk, Louis Mongenod and the lady, who was none else than Madame de la Chanterie, rose and went up to Frédéric. Then they all three went into a window recess, where they stood talking to Madame Mongenod, who was in all the secrets of the business. For thirty years past this clever woman had given ample proofs of her capacity, to her husband first, now to her sons, and she was, in fact, an active partner in the house, signing for it as they did. Godefroid saw in a pigeonhole a number of boxes labeled "La Chanterie," and numbered 1 to 7.

When the conference was ended by a word from the Senior to his brother, "Well, then, go to the cashier," Madame de la Chanterie turned round, saw Godefroid, restrained a start of surprise, and then asked a few whispered questions of Mongenod, who replied briefly, also in a low voice.

Madame de la Chanterie wore thin prunella shoes and grey silk stockings; she had on the same dress as before, and was wrapped in the Venetian cloak that was just coming into fashion again. Her drawn bonnet of green silk, *à la bonne femme*, was lined with white, and her face was framed in flowing lace. She stood very erect, in an attitude which bore witness, if not to high birth, at any rate to aristocratic habits. But for her extreme affability, she would perhaps have seemed proud. In short, she was very imposing.

"It is not so much good luck as a dispensation of Providence that has brought us together here, monsieur," said she to Godefroid. "I was on the point of declining a boarder whose habits, as I fancied, were ill suited to those of my household; but Monsieur Mongenod has just given me some information as to your family which is—"

"Indeed, madame—monsieur—" said Godefroid, addressing the lady and the banker together, "I have no longer any family, and I came to ask advice of my late father's banker to arrange my affairs in accordance with a new plan of life."

Godefroid told his story in a few words, and expressed his desire of leading a new life.

"Formerly," said he, "a man in my position would have turned monk; but there are now no religious Orders—"

"Go to live with Madame, if she will accept you as a boarder," said Frédéric Mongenod, after exchanging glances with Madame de la Chanterie, "and do not sell your investments; leave them in my hands. Give me the schedule of your debts; I will fix dates of payment with your creditors, and you can draw for your own use a hundred and fifty francs a month. It will take about two years to pay everything off. During those two years, in the home you are going to, you will have ample leisure to think of a career, especially as the people you will be living with can give you good advice."

Louis Mongenod came back with a hundred thousand-franc notes, which he gave to Madame de la Chanterie. Godefroid offered his arm to his future landlady, and took her to her hackney-coach.

"Then we shall meet again presently," said she in a kind tone.

"At what hour shall you be at home, madame?" said Godefroid.

"In two hours' time."

"I have time to get rid of my furniture," said he, with a bow.

During the few minutes while Madame de la Chanterie's arm had lain on his as they walked side by side, Godefroid could not see beyond the halo cast about this woman by the words, "Your account stands at sixteen hundred thousand francs," spoken by Louis Mongenod to a lady who buried her life in the depths of the Cloister of Notre-Dame.

This idea, "She must be rich!" had entirely changed his view of things. "How old is she, I wonder?"

And he had a vision of a romance in his residence in the Rue Chanoinesse.

"She looks like an aristocrat; does she dabble in banking affairs?" he asked himself.

And in our day nine hundred and ninety-nine men out of a thousand would have thought of the possibility of marrying this woman.

A furniture-dealer, who was also a decorator, but chiefly an agent for furnished flats, gave about three thousand francs for all that Godefroid wished to dispose of, leaving the things in his rooms for the few days needed to clean and arrange the dreadful rooms in the Rue Chanoinesse.

Thither the brain-sick youth at once repaired; he called in a painter, recommended by Madame de la Chanterie, who undertook for a moderate sum to whitewash the ceilings, clean the windows, paint the wainscoting like grey maple, and colour the floors, within a week. Godefroid measured the rooms to carpet them all alike with green drugget of the cheapest description. He wished everything to be uniform and as simple as possible in his cell.

Madame de la Chanterie approved of this. With Manon's assistance she calculated how much white dimity would be needed for the window curtains and for a simple iron bedstead; then she undertook to procure the stuff and to have them made for a price so small as to amaze Godefroid. With the new furniture he would send in, his apartments would not cost him more than six hundred francs.

"So I can take about a thousand to Monsieur Mongenod."

"We here lead a Christian life," said Madame de la Chanterie, "which is, as you know, quite out of keeping with much superfluity, and I fear you still preserve too many."

As she gave her new boarder this piece of advice, she glanced at the diamond that sparkled in a ring through which the ends of Godefroid's blue necktie were drawn.

"I only mention this," she added, "because I perceive that you are preparing to break with the dissipated life of which you spoke with regret to Monsieur Mongenod."

Godefroid gazed at Madame de la Chanterie, listening with delight to the harmony of her clear voice; he studied her face, which was perfectly colourless, worthy to be that of one of the grave cold Dutch women so faithfully depicted by the painters of the Flemish school, faces on which a wrinkle would be impossible.

"Plump and fair!" thought he, as he went away. "Still, her hair is white—"

Godefroid, like all weak natures, had readily accustomed himself to the idea of a new life, believing it would be perfect happiness, and he was eager to settle in the Rue Chanoinesse; nevertheless, he had a gleam of prudence—or, if you like, of suspicion. Two days before moving in he went again to Monsieur Mongenod to ask for further information concerning the household he was going to join. During the few minutes he had spent now and then in his future home, to see what alterations were being made, he had observed the going and coming of several persons whose appearance and manner, without any air of mystery, suggested that they were busied in the practice of some profession, some secret occupation with the residents in the house. At this time many plots were afoot to help the elder branch of Bourbons to remount the throne, and Godefroid believed there was some conspiracy here.

But when he found himself in the banker's private room and under his searching eye, he was ashamed of himself as he formulated his question and saw a sardonic smile on Frédéric Mongenod's lips.

"Madame la Baronne de la Chanterie," he replied, "is one of the obscurest but one of the most honourable women in Paris. Have you any particular reason for asking for information?"

Godefroid fell back on flat excuses—he was arranging to live a long time with these strangers, and it was as well to know to whom he was tying himself, and the like. But the banker's smile only became more and more ironical, and Godefroid more and more ashamed, till he blushed at the step he had taken, and got nothing by it; for he dared ask no more questions about Madame de la Chanterie or his fellow-boarders.

Two days later, after dining for the last time at the Café Anglais, and seeing the first two pieces at the *Variétés*, at ten o'clock on a Monday night he came to sleep in the Rue Chanoinesse, where Manon lighted him to his room.

Solitude has a charm somewhat akin to that of the wild life of savages, which no European ever gives up after having once tasted it. This may seem strange in an age when every one lives so completely in the sight of others that everybody is inquisitive about everybody else, and that privacy will soon have ceased to exist, so quickly do the eyes of the Press—the modern Argus—increase in boldness and intrusiveness; and yet the statement is supported by the evidence of the first six Christian centuries, when no recluse ever came back to social life again. There are few mental wounds that solitude cannot cure. Thus, in the first instance, Godefroid was struck by the calm and stillness of his new abode, exactly as a tired traveller finds rest in a bath.

On the day after his arrival as a boarder with Madame de la Chanterie, he could not help cross-examining himself on finding himself thus cut off from everything, even from Paris, though he was still under the shadow of its Cathedral. Here, stripped of every social vanity, there would henceforth be no witnesses to his deeds but his conscience and his fellow-boarders. This was leaving the beaten high-road of the world for an unknown track; and whither would the track lead him? To what occupation would he find himself committed?

He had been lost in such reflections for a couple of hours, when Manon, the only servant of the establishment, knocked at his door and told him that the second breakfast was served; they were waiting for him. Twelve was striking.

The new boarder went downstairs at once, prompted by his curiosity to see the five persons with whom he was thenceforth to live. On entering the drawing-room he found all the residents in the house standing up and dressed precisely as they had been on the day when he had first come to make inquiries.

"Did you sleep well?" asked Madame de la Chanterie.

"I did not wake till ten o'clock," said Godefroid, bowing to the four gentlemen, who returned the civility with much gravity.

"We quite expected it," said the old man, known as Monsieur Alain, and he smiled.

"Manon spoke of the second breakfast," Godefroid went on. "I have, I fear, already broken one of your rules without intending it.—At what hour do you rise?"

"We do not get up quite by the rule of the monks of old," replied Madame de la Chanterie graciously, "but, like workmen, at six in winter and at half-past three in summer. We also go to bed by the rule of the sun; we are always asleep by nine in winter, by half-past eleven in summer. We drink some milk, which is brought from our own farm, after prayers, all but Monsieur l'Abbé de Vèze, who performs early Mass at Notre-Dame—at six in summer, at seven in winter—and these gentlemen as well as I, your humble servant, attend that service every day."

Madame de la Chanterie finished this speech at table, where her five guests were now seated.

The dining-room, painted grey throughout, and decorated with carved wood of a design showing the taste of Louis XIV., opened out of the sort of ante-room where Manon sat, and ran parallel with Madame de la Chanterie's room, adjoining the drawing-room, no doubt. There was no ornament but an old clock. The furniture consisted of six chairs, their oval backs upholstered with worsted-work evidently done by Madame de la Chanterie, of two mahogany sideboards, and a table to match, on which Manon placed the breakfast without spreading a cloth. The breakfast, of monastic frugality, consisted of a small turbot with white sauce, potatoes, a salad, and four dishes of fruit: peaches, grapes, strawberries, and green almonds; then, by way of *hors d'oeuvre*, there was honey served in the comb as in Switzerland, besides butter, radishes, cucumber, and sardines. The meal was served in china sprigged with small blue cornflowers and green leaves, a pattern which was no doubt luxuriously fashionable in the time of Louis XVI, but which the increasing demands of the present day have made common.

"It is a fast day!" observed Monsieur Alain. "Since we go to Mass every morning, you may suppose that we yield blindly to all the practices of the Church, even the strictest."

"And you will begin by following our example," added Madame de la Chanterie, with a side-glance at Godefroid, whom she had placed by her side.

Of the four boarders, Godefroid already knew the names of the Abbé de Vèze and Monsieur Alain; but he yet had to learn those of the other two gentlemen. They sat in silence, eating with the absorbed attention that the pious seem to devote to the smallest details of their meals.

"And does this fine fruit also come from your farm, madame?" Godefroid inquired.

"Yes, monsieur," she replied. "We have our little model farm, just as the Government has; it is our country house, about three leagues from hence, on the road to Italy, near Villeneuve-Saint-Georges."

"It is a little estate that belongs to us all, and will be the property of the last survivor," said the worthy Monsieur Alain.

"Oh, it is quite inconsiderable," added Madame de la Chanterie, who seemed afraid lest Godefroid should regard this speech as a bait.

"There are thirty acres of arable land," said one of the men unknown to Godefroid, "six acres of meadow, and an enclosure of about four acres of garden, in the midst of which our house stands; in front of it is the farm."

"But such an estate must be worth above a hundred thousand francs," observed Godefroid.

"Oh, we get nothing out of it but our produce," replied the same speaker.

He was a tall man, thin and grave. At a first glance he seemed to have served in the army; his white hair showed that he was past sixty, and his face revealed great sorrows and religious resignation.

The second stranger, who appeared to be a sort of compound of a master of rhetoric and a man of business, was of middle height, stout but active, and his face bore traces of a joviality peculiar to the notaries and attorneys of Paris.

The dress of all four men was marked by the extreme neatness due to personal care; and Manon's hand was visible in the smallest details of their raiment. Their coats were perhaps ten years old, and preserved, as a priest's clothes are preserved, by the occult powers of a housekeeper and by constant use. These men wore, as it were, the livery of a system of life; they were all the slaves of the same thought, their looks spoke the same word, their faces wore an expression of gentle resignation, of inviting tranquillity.

"Am I indiscreet, madame," said Godefroid, "to ask the names of these gentlemen? I am quite prepared to tell them all about myself; may I not know as much about them as circumstances allow?"

"This," said Madame de la Chanterie, introducing the tall, thin man, "is Monsieur Nicolas; he is a retired Colonel of the Gendarmerie, ranking as a Major-General.—And this gentleman," she went on, turning to the little stout man, "was formerly Councillor to the Bench of the King's Court in Paris; he retired from his functions in August 1830; his name is Monsieur Joseph. Though you joined us but yesterday, I may tell you that in the world Monsieur Nicolas bore the name of Marquis de Montauran, and Monsieur Joseph that of Lecamus, Baron de Tresnes; but to us, as to the outer world, these names no longer exist. These gentlemen have no heirs; they have anticipated the oblivion that must fall on their families; they are simply Monsieur Nicolas and Monsieur Joseph, as you will be simply Monsieur Godefroid."

As he heard these two names—one so famous in the history of Royalism from the disaster which put an end to the rising of the Chouans at the beginning of the Consulate, the other so long respected in the records of the old Parlement—Godefroid could not repress a start of surprise; but when he looked at these survivors from the wreck of the two greatest institutions of the fallen monarchy, he could not detect the slightest movement of feature or change of countenance that betrayed a worldly emotion. These two men did not or would not remember what they once had been. This was Godefroid's first lesson.

"Each name, gentlemen, is a chapter of history," said he respectfully.

"The history of our own time," said Monsieur Joseph, "of mere ruins."

"You are in good company," said Monsieur Alain, smiling. He can be described in two words: he was a middle-class Paris citizen; a worthy man with the face of a calf, dignified by white hairs, but insipid with its eternal smile.

As to the priest, the Abbé de Vèze, his position was all sufficient. The priest who fulfils his mission is recognisable at the first glance when his eyes meet yours.

What chiefly struck Godefroid from the first was the profound respect shown by the boarders to Madame de la Chanterie; all of them, even the priest, notwithstanding the sacred dignity conferred by his functions, behaved to her as to a queen. He also noted the temperance of each guest; they ate solely for the sake of nourishment. Madame de la Chanterie, like the rest, took but a single peach and half a bunch of grapes; but she begged the newcomer not to restrict himself in the same way, offering him every dish in turn.

Godefroid's curiosity was excited to the highest pitch by this beginning. After the meal they returned to the drawing-room, where he was left to himself; Madame de la Chanterie and her four friends held a little privy council in a window recess. This conference, in which no animation was displayed, lasted for about half an hour. They talked in undertones, exchanging remarks which each seemed to have thought out beforehand. Now and again Monsieur Alain and Monsieur Joseph consulted their pocket-books, turning over the leaves.

"You will see to the Faubourg," said Madame de la Chanterie to Monsieur Nicolas, who went away.

These were the first words Godefroid could overhear.

"And you to the Quartier Saint-Marceau," she went on, addressing Monsieur Joseph.

"Will you take the Faubourg Saint-Germain and try to find what we need?" she added to the Abbé de Vèze, who at once went off.— "And you, my dear Alain," she added with a smile, "look into matters.—To-day's business is all settled," said she, returning to Godefroid.

She sat down in her armchair, and took from a little work-table some under-linen, ready cut out, on which she began to sew as if working against time.

Godefroid, lost in conjectures, and seeing in all this a Royalist conspiracy, took the lady's speech as introductory, and, seating himself by her side, watched her closely. He was struck by her singular skill in stitching; while everything about her proclaimed the great lady, she had the peculiar deftness of a paid seamstress; for every one can distinguish, by certain tricks of working, the habits of a professional from those of an amateur.

"You sew," said Godefroid, "as if you were used to the business."

"Alas!" she said, without looking up, "I have done it ere now from necessity—"

Two large tears rose to the old woman's eyes, and rolled down her cheeks on to the work she held.

"Pray, forgive me, madame!" cried Godefroid.

Madame de la Chanterie looked at her new inmate, and saw on his features such an expression of regret, that she nodded to him kindly. Then, after wiping her eyes, she recovered the composure that characterised her face, which was not so much cold as chilled.

"You here find yourself, Monsieur Godefroid—for, as you know already, you will be called only by your Christian name—amid the wreckage from a great storm. We have all been stricken and wounded to the heart through family interests or damaged fortunes, by the forty years' hurricane that overthrew royalty and religion, and scattered to the winds the elements that constituted France as it was of old. Words which seem but trivial bear a sting for us, and that is the reason of the silence that reigns here. We rarely speak of ourselves; we have forgotten what we were, and have found means of substituting a new life for the old life. It was because I fancied, from your revelation to the Mongenods, that there was some resemblance between your situation and our own, that I persuaded my four friends to receive you among us; in fact, we were anxious to find another recluse for our convent. But what do you propose to do? We do not enter on solitude without some stock of moral purpose."

"Madame, as I hear you speak, I shall be too happy to accept you as the arbiter of my destiny."

"That is speaking like a man of the world," said she. "You are trying to flatter me—a woman of sixty!—My dear boy," she went on, "you are, you must know, among people who believe firmly in God, who have all felt His hand, and who have given themselves up to Him almost as completely as do the Trappists. Have you ever observed the assurance of a true priest when he has given himself to the Lord, when he hearkens to His voice and strives to be a docile instrument under the fingers of Providence? He has shed all vanity, all self-consciousness, all the feelings which cause constant offences to the worldly; his quiescence is as complete as that of the fatalist, his resignation enables him to endure all things. The true priest—an Abbé de Vèze—is like a child with his mother; for the Church, my dear sir, is a good mother. Well, a man may be a priest without a tonsure; not all priests are in orders. If we devote ourselves to doing good, we imitate the good priest, we obey God!—I am not preaching to you; I do not want to convert you; I am only explaining our life."

"Instruct me, madame," said Godefroid, quite conquered. "I would wish not to fail in any particular of your rules."

"You would find that too much to do; you will learn by degrees. Above all things, never speak here of your past misfortunes, which are mere child's play as compared with the terrible catastrophes with which God has stricken those with whom you are now living—"

All the time she spoke, Madame de la Chanterie went on pulling her thread through with distracting regularity; but at this full stop, she raised her head and looked at Godefroid; she saw that he was spellbound by the thrilling sweetness of her voice, which had indeed a sort of apostolic unction. The young sufferer was gazing with admiration at the really extraordinary appearance of this woman, whose face was radiant. A faint flush tinged her wax-white cheeks, her eyes sparkled, a youthful soul gave life to the wrinkles that had acquired sweetness, and everything about her invited affection. Godefroid sat measuring the depth of the gulf that parted this woman from vulgar souls; he saw that she had attained to an inaccessible height, whither religion had guided her; and he was still too much of the world not to be stung to the quick, not to long to go down into that gulf and climb to the sharp peak where Madame de la Chanterie stood, and to stand by her side. While he gave himself up to a thorough study of this woman, he related to her all the mortifications of his life, all he could not say at Mongenod's, where his self-betrayal had been limited to a statement of his position.

"Poor child!"

This motherly exclamation, dropping from the lips of Madame de la Chanterie, fell, from time to time, like healing balm, on the young man's heart.

"What can I find to take the place of so many hopes deceived, of so much disappointed affection?" said he at last, looking at the lady, who seemed lost in reverie. "I came here," he went on, "to reflect and make up my mind. I have lost my mother—will you take her place?"

"But," said she, "will you show me a son's obedience?"

"Yes, if you can show me the tenderness that exacts it."

"Very well; we will try," said she.

Godefroid held out his hand to take that which the lady offered him, and raised it reverently to his lips. Madame de la Chanterie's hands were admirably formed—neither wrinkled, nor fat, nor thin; white enough to move a young woman to envy, and of a shape that a sculptor might copy. Godefroid had admired these hands, thinking them in harmony with the enchantment of her voice and the heavenly blue of her eye.

"Wait here," said Madame de la Chanterie, rising and going into her own room.

Godefroid was deeply agitated, and could not think to what he was to attribute the lady's departure: he was not left long in perplexity, for she returned with a book in her hand.

"Here, my dear boy," said she, "are the prescriptions of a great healer of souls. When the things of everyday life have failed to give us the happiness we looked for, we must seek in a higher life, and here is the key to that new world. Read a chapter of this book morning and evening; but give it your whole attention; study every word as if it were some foreign tongue. By the end of a month you will be another man. For twenty years now have I read a chapter every day, and my three friends, Nicolas, Alain, and Joseph, would no more omit it than they would miss going to bed and getting up again; imitate them for the love of God—for my sake—" she said, with divine serenity and dignified confidence.

Godefroid turned the book round and read on the back *Imitation of Jesus Christ*. The old lady's artlessness and. youthful candour, her certainty that she was doing him good, confounded the ex-dandy. Madame de la Chanterie had exactly the manner, the intense satisfaction, of a woman who might offer a hundred thousand francs to a merchant on the verge of bankruptcy.

"I have used this book," she said, "for six-and-twenty years. God grant that its use may prove contagious! Go and buy me another copy, for the hour is at hand when certain persons are coming here who must not be seen."

Godefroid bowed and went up to his rooms, where he tossed the book on a table, exclaiming:

"Poor, dear woman! There—"

The book, like all that are constantly used, fell open at a particular place. Godefroid sat down to arrange his ideas a little, for he had gone through more agitation that morning than he had in the course of the most stormy two months of his life; his curiosity especially had never been so strongly excited. His eyes wandered mechanically, as happens with men when their minds are absorbed in meditation, and fell on the two pages that lay facing him. He read as follows:—

"CHAPTER XII.
"ON THE ROYAL ROAD OF THE HOLY CROSS."

He picked up the volume, and this paragraph of that grand book captivated his eyes as though by words of fire:

> "He has gone before you carrying His cross, and died for you, that you too might have strength to carry your cross, and be willing to die upon the Cross …
>
> "Go where you will, try what you will, you will not find a grander way, or a safer way, than the way of the Holy Cross. Arrange and order all your life as you like or think fit, still you will find that you will always have something to suffer, by your own choice or by necessity; and so you will always find a cross. For either you will have bodily pain to bear, or some trouble of the spirit.
>
> "Sometimes God will leave you to yourself, sometimes you will be vexed by your neighbour, and, what is harder than all, you will often be weary of yourself, and there is no remedy or solace by which you can be delivered or relieved. You will have to bear your trouble as long as God decrees. For He wishes you to learn to suffer trial without consolation, to yield humbly to His will, and to become humbler by means of tribulations."

"What a book!" said Godefroid to himself, as he turned over the pages. And he came upon these words:

> "When you have come to feel all trouble sweet and pleasant for the love of Christ, then indeed you may say that all is well with you; you have made for yourself a heaven on earth."

Irritated by this simplicity, characteristic of strength, and enraged at being vanquished by this book, he shut it; but on the morocco cover he saw this motto, stamped in letters of gold:

"Seek only that which is eternal."

"And have they found it here?" he wondered.

He went out to purchase a handsome copy of the *Imitation of Christ*, remembering that Madame de la Chanterie would want to read a chapter that evening. He went downstairs and into the street. For a minute or two he remained standing near the gate, undecided as to which way he would go, and wondering in what street, and at what bookseller's he might find the book he needed; and he then heard the heavy sound of the outer gate shutting.

Two men had just come out of the Hôtel de la Chanterie—for the reader, if he has understood the character of the old house, will have recognised it as an ancient family mansion. Manon, when she had called Godefroid to breakfast, had asked him how he had slept the first night at the Hôtel de la Chanterie, laughing as she spoke.

Godefroid followed the two men, with no idea of spying on them; and they, taking him for an indifferent passer-by, talked loud enough for him to hear them in those deserted streets. The men turned down the Rue Massillon, along by the side of Notre-Dame, and across the Cathedral Square.

"Well, old man, you see how easy it is to get the coppers out of 'em! You must talk their lingo, that is all."

"But we owe the money."

"Who to?"

"To the lady—"

"I should like to see myself sued for debt by that old image! I would—"

"You would what?—You would pay her, I can tell you."

"You're right there, for if I paid I could get more out of her afterwards than I got to-day."

"But wouldn't it be better to take their advice and set up on the square?"

"Get out!"

"Since she said she could find some one to stand security?"

"But we should have to give up life—"

"I am sick of 'life'—it is not life to be always working in the vineyards—"

"No; but didn't the Abbé throw over old Marin the other day. He wouldn't give him a thing."

"Ay, but old Marin wanted to play such a game as no one can win at that has not thousands at his back."

At this moment the two men, who were dressed like working foremen, suddenly doubled, and retraced their steps to cross the bridge by the Hôtel-Dieu to the Place Maubert; Godefroid stood aside; but seeing that he was following them closely, the men exchanged looks of suspicion, and they were evidently vexed at having spoken out so plainly.

Godefroid was indeed all the more interested in the conversation because it reminded him of the scene between the Abbé de Vèze and the workman on the evening of his first call.

"What goes on at Madame de la Chanterie's?" he asked himself once more.

As he thought over this question, he made his way to a bookshop in the Rue Saint-Jacques, and returned home with a very handsome copy of the best edition of *The Imitation* that has been published in France.

As he walked slowly homewards to be punctual to the dinner-hour, he went over in his mind all his experience of the morning, and found his soul singularly refreshed by it. He was possessed indeed by intense curiosity, but that curiosity paled before an indefinable wish; he was attracted by Madame de la Chanterie, he felt a vehement longing to attach himself to her, to devote himself for her, to please her and deserve her praise; in short, he was aware of a Platonic passion; he felt that there was unfathomed greatness in that soul, and that he must learn to know it thoroughly. He was eager to discover the secrets of the life of these pure-minded Catholics. And then, in this little congregation of the Faithful, practical religion was so intimately allied with all that is most majestic in the Frenchwoman, that he resolved to do his utmost to be admitted to the fold. Such a vein of feeling would have been sudden indeed in a man of busy life; but Godefroid, as we have seen, was in the position of a shipwrecked wretch who clings to the most fragile bough, hoping that it may bear him, and his soul was ploughed land, ready to receive any seed.

He found the four gentlemen in the drawing-room, and he presented the book to Madame de la Chanterie, saying:

"I would not leave you without a copy for this evening."

"God grant," said she, looking at the splendid volume, "that this may be your last fit of elegance!"

And seeing that the four men had reduced the smallest details of their raiment to what was strictly decent and useful, noticing too that this principle was rigorously carried out in every detail of the house, Godefroid understood the purpose of this reproof so delicately expressed.

"Madame," said he, "the men you benefited this morning are monsters. Without intending it, I overheard what they were saying as they went away, and it was full of the blackest ingratitude."

"The two iron-workers from the Rue Mouffetard," said Madame de la Chanterie to Monsieur Nicolas, "that is your concern—"

"The fish gets off the hook more than once before it is caught," said Monsieur Alain, laughing.

Madame de la Chanterie's entire indifference on hearing of the immediate ingratitude of the men to whom she had certainly given money amazed Godefroid, who became thoughtful.

Monsieur Alain and the old lawyer made the dinner a cheerful meal; but the soldier was constantly grave, sad, and cold; his countenance bore the ineradicable stamp of a bitter sorrow, a perennial grief. Madame de la Chanterie was equally attentive to all. Godefroid felt that he was watched by these men, whose prudence was not less than their piety, and vanity led him to imitate their reserve, so he measured his words carefully.

This first day, indeed, was far more lively than those which came after. Godefroid, finding himself shut out from all serious matters, was obliged, during the early morning and the evening when he was alone in his rooms, to read *The Imitation of Christ*, and he finally studied it as we must study a book when we are imprisoned with that one alone. We then feel to the book as we should towards a woman with whom we dwelt in solitude; we must either love or hate the woman; and in the same way we must enter into the spirit of the author or not read ten lines of his work.

Now it is impossible not to be held captive by *The Imitation*, which is to dogma what action is to thought. The Catholic spirit thrills through it, moves and works in it, struggles in it hand to hand with the life of man. That book is a trusty friend. It speaks to every passion, to every difficulty, even to the most worldly; it answers every objection, it is more eloquent than any preacher, for it speaks with your own voice—a voice that rises from your own heart and that you hear with your soul. In short, it is the Gospel interpreted and adapted to all times and seasons, controlling every situation. It is strange indeed that the Church should not have canonised Gerson, for the Holy Spirit certainly guided his pen.

To Godefroid the Hôtel de la Chanterie contained a woman as well as a book; every day he was more and more bewitched by her. In her he found flowers buried under the snow of many winters; he had glimpses of such a sacred friendship as religion sanctions, as the angels smile on—as bound those five, in fact—and against which no evil could prevail. There is a sentiment superior to all others, an affection of soul for soul which resembles those rare blossoms that grow on the loftiest peaks of the earth. One or two examples are shown us in a century; lovers are sometimes united by it; and it accounts for certain faithful attachments which would be inexplicable by the ordinary laws of the world. In such an attachment there are no disappointments, no differences, no vanities, no rivalries, no contrasts even, so intimately fused are two spiritual natures.

It was this immense and infinite feeling, the outcome of Catholic charity, that Godefroid was beginning to dream of. At times he could not believe in the spectacle before his eyes, and he sought to find reasons for the sublime friendships between these five persons, wondering to find true Catholics, Christians of the most primitive type, in Paris, and in 1836.

A week after entering the house, Godefroid had seen such a number of people come and go, he had overheard fragments of conversation in which such serious matters were discussed, that he understood that the existence of this council of five was full of prodigious activity. He noticed that not one of them slept more than six hours at most. Each of them had, as it were, lived through a first day before they met at the second breakfast. Strangers brought in or carried away sums of money, sometimes rather considerable. Mongenod's cashier came very often, always early in the morning, so that his work in the bank should not be interfered with by this business, which was independent of the regular affairs of the House.

One evening Monsieur Mongenod himself called, and Godefroid observed a touch of filial familiarity in his tone to Monsieur Alain, mingled with the deep respect he showed to him, as to Madame de la Chanterie's three other boarders.

That evening the banker only asked Godefroid the most ordinary questions: Was he comfortable? Did he mean to stay? and so forth, advising him to persevere in his determination.

"There is but one thing wanting to make me happy," said Godefroid.

"And what is that?" said the banker.

"An occupation."

"An occupation!" cried the Abbé de Vèze. "Then you have changed your mind; you came to our retreat in search of rest."

"But without prayer, which gives life to the cloister; without meditation, which peoples the desert, rest becomes a disease," said Monsieur Joseph sententiously.

"Learn bookkeeping," said Mongenod, smiling. "In the course of a few months you may be of great use to my friends here—"

"Oh, with the greatest pleasure," exclaimed Godefroid.

The next day was Sunday. Madame de la Chanterie desired her boarder to give her his arm and to escort her to High Mass.

"This," she said, "is the only thing I desire to force upon you. Many a time during the week I have been moved to speak to you of your salvation; but I do not think the time has come. You would have plenty to occupy you if you shared our beliefs, for you would also share our labours."

At Mass, Godefroid observed the fervency of Messieurs Nicolas, Joseph, and Alain. Having, during these few days, convinced himself of the superior intellect of these three men, their perspicacity, extensive learning, and lofty spirit, he concluded that if they could thus abase themselves, the Catholic religion must contain mysteries which had hitherto escaped his ken.

"And, after all," said he to himself, "it is the religion of Bossuet, of Pascal, of Racine, of Saint-Louis, of Louis XVI, of Raphael, Michael Angelo, and Ximenes, of Bayard and du Guesclin—and how should such a poor creature as I compare myself with these great brains, statesmen, poets, warriors—?"

Were it not that a great lesson is to be derived from these trivial details, it would be foolish in such times as these to dwell on them; but they are indispensable to the interest of this narrative, which the readers of our day will, indeed, find it hard to believe, beginning as it does by an almost ridiculous incident—the influence exerted by a woman of sixty over a young man who had tried everything and found it wanting.

"You did not pray," said Madame de la Chanterie to Godefroid as they came out of Notre-Dame. "Not for any one, not even for the peace of your mother's soul!"

Godefroid reddened, but said nothing.

"Do me the pleasure," Madame de la Chanterie went on, "to go to your room, and not to come down to the drawing-room for an hour. And for the love of me, meditate on a chapter of the *Imitation*—the first of the Third Book, entitled 'On Christ Speaking Within The Faithful Soul.' "

Godefroid bowed coolly, and went upstairs.

"The Devil take 'em all!" he exclaimed, now really in a rage. "What the deuce do they want of me here? What game are they playing? Pshaw! Every woman, even the veriest bigot, is full of tricks, and if Madame" (the name the boarders gave their hostess) "does not want me downstairs, it is because they are plotting something against me."

With this notion in his head, he tried to look out of his own window into that of the drawing-room, but the plan of the building did not allow of it. Then he went down one flight, but hastily ran up again; for it struck him that in a house where the principal inhabitants held such strict principles, an act of espionage would lead to his immediate dismissal. Now, to lose the esteem of those five persons seemed to him as serious a matter as public dishonour.

He waited about three-quarters of an hour, resolved to take Madame de la Chanterie by surprise, and to go down a little before the time she had named. He intended to excuse himself by a fib, saying that his watch was in fault, and twenty minutes too fast. He went down cautiously, without a sound, and on reaching the drawing-room door opened it suddenly.

He saw a man, still young but already famous, a poet whom he had often met in society, Victor de Vernisset, kneeling on one knee before Madame de la Chanterie and kissing the hem of her gown. The sky falling in splinters as if it were made of crystal, as the ancients believed, would have amazed Godefroid less than this sight. The most shocking ideas besieged his brain, and the reaction was even more terrible when, just as he was about to utter the first sarcasm that rose to his lips, he saw Monsieur Alain standing in a corner, counting thousand-franc notes.

In an instant Vernisset had started to his feet. Good Monsieur Alain stared in astonishment. Madame de la Chanterie flashed a look that petrified Godefroid, for the doubtful expression in the new boarder's face had not escaped her.

"Monsieur is one of us," she said to the young author, introducing Godefroid.

"You are a happy man, my dear fellow," said Vernisset. "You are saved!—But, madame," he went on, turning to Madame de la Chanterie, "if all Paris could have seen me, I should be delighted. Nothing can ever pay my debt to you. I am your slave for ever! I am yours, body and soul. Command in whatever you will, I will obey; my gratitude knows no bounds. I owe you my life—it is yours."

"Come, come," said the worthy Alain, "do not be rash. Only work; and, above all, never attack religion in your writings.—And remember you are in debt."

He handed him an envelope bulging with the banknotes he had counted out. Victor de Vernisset's eyes filled with tears. He respectfully kissed Madame de la Chanterie's hand, and went away after shaking hands with Monsieur Alain and with Godefroid.

"You did not obey Madame," said the good man solemnly; and his face had an expression of sadness, such as Godefroid had not yet seen on it. "That is a capital crime. If it occurs again, we must part.—It would be very hard on you, after having seemed worthy of our confidence—"

"My dear Alain," said Madame de la Chanterie, "be so good, for my sake, as to say nothing of this act of folly. We must not expect too much of a newcomer who has had no great sorrows, who has no religion—who has nothing, in fact, but great curiosity concerning every vocation, and who as yet does not believe in us."

"Forgive me, madame," replied Godefroid. "From this moment I will be worthy of you; I submit to every test you may think necessary before initiating me into the secret of your labours; and if Monsieur the Abbé will undertake to enlighten me, I give myself up to him, soul and reason."

These words made Madame de la Chanterie so happy that a faint flush rose to her cheeks, she clasped Godefroid's hand and pressed it, saying, with strange emotion, "That is well!"

In the evening, after dinner, Godefroid saw a Vicar-General of the Diocese of Paris, who came to call, two canons, two retired mayors of Paris, and a lady who devoted herself to the poor. There was no gambling; the conversation was general, and cheerful without being futile.

A visitor who greatly surprised Godefroid was the Comtesse de Saint-Cygne, one of the loftiest stars of the aristocratic spheres, whose drawing-room was quite inaccessible to the citizen class and to *parvenus*. The mere presence of this great lady in Madame de la Chanterie's room was sufficiently amazing; but the way in which the two women met and treated each other was to Godefroid quite inexplicable, for it bore witness to an intimacy and constant intercourse which proved the high merit of Madame de la Chanterie. Madame de Saint-Cygne was gracious and friendly to her friend's four friends, and very respectful to Monsieur Nicolas.

As may be seen, social vanity still had a hold on Godefroid, who, hitherto undecided, now determined to yield, with or without conviction, to everything Madame de la Chanterie and her friends might require of him, to succeed in being affiliated by them to their Order, or initiated into their secrets, promising himself that until then he would not definitely commit himself.

On the following day, he went to the bookkeeper recommended by Madame de la Chanterie, agreed with him as to the hours when they were to work together, and so disposed of all his time; for the Abbé de Vèze was to catechise him in the morning, he spent two hours of every day learning book-keeping, and between breakfast and dinner he worked at the exercises and imaginary commercial correspondence set him by his master.

Some few days thus passed, during which Godefroid learned the charm of a life of which every hour has its employment. The recurrence of the same duties at fixed hours, and perfect regularity, sufficiently account for many happy lives, and prove how deeply the founders of religious orders had meditated on human nature. Godefroid, who had made up his mind to learn of the Abbé de Vèze, had already begun to feel qualms as to his future life, and to discover that he was ignorant of the importance of religious matters.

Finally, day by day, Madame de la Chanterie, with whom he always sat for about an hour after the second breakfast, revealed some fresh treasures of her nature; he had never conceived of goodness so complete, so all-embracing. A woman as old as Madame de la Chanterie seemed to be has none of the triviality of a young woman; she is a friend who may offer you every feminine dainty, who displays all the grace and refinement with which Nature inspires woman to please man, but who no longer asks for a return; she may be execrable or exquisite, for all her demands on life are buried beneath the skin—or are dead; and Madame de la Chanterie was exquisite. She seemed never to have been young; her looks never spoke of the past. Far from allaying his curiosity, Godefroid's increased intimacy with this beautiful character, and the discoveries he made day by day, increased his desire to know something of the previous history of the woman he now saw as a saint. Had she ever loved? Had she been married? Had she been a mother? There was nothing in her suggestive of the old maid; she had all the elegance of a woman of birth; and her strong health, and the extraordinary charm of her conversation, seemed to reveal a heavenly life, a sort of ignorance of the world. Excepting the worthy and cheerful Alain, all these persons had known suffering; but Monsieur Nicolas himself seemed to give the palm of martyrdom to Madame de la Chanterie; nevertheless, the memory of her sorrows was so entirely suppressed by Catholic resignation, and her secret occupations, that she seemed to have been always happy.

"You are the life of your friends," said Godefroid to her one day. "You are the bond that unites them; you are the housekeeper, so to speak, of a great work; and as we are all mortal, I cannot but wonder what would become of your association without you."

"Yes, that is what they fear; but Providence—to whom we owe our bookkeeper," said she with a smile—"will doubtless provide. However, I shall think it over—"

"And will your bookkeeper soon find himself at work for your business?" asked Godefroid, laughing.

"That must depend on him," she said with a smile. "If he is sincerely religious, truly pious, has not the smallest conceit, does not trouble his head about the wealth of the establishment, and endeavors to rise superior to petty social considerations by soaring on the wings God has bestowed on us."

'Which are they?"

"Simplicity and purity," replied Madame de la Chanterie.

"Your ignorance proves that you neglect reading your book," she added, laughing at the innocent trap she had laid to discover whether Godefroid read the *Imitation of Christ*. "Soak your mind in Saint Paul's chapter on Charity. It is not you who will be devoted to us, but we to you," she said with a lofty look, "and it will be your part to keep account of the greatest riches ever possessed by any sovereign; you will have the same enjoyment of them as we have; and let me tell you, if you remember the Thousand and One Nights, that the treasures of Aladdin are as nothing in comparison with ours. Indeed, for a year past, we have not known what to do; it was too much for us. We needed a bookkeeper."

As she spoke she studied Godefroid's face; he knew not what to think of this strange confidence; but the scene between Madame de la Chanterie and the elder Madame Mongenod had often recurred to him, and he hesitated between doubt and belief.

"Yes, you would be very fortunate!" said she.

Godefroid was so consumed by curiosity, that from that instant he resolved to undermine the reserve of the four friends, and to ask them about themselves. Now, of all Madame de la Chanterie's boarders, the one who most attracted Godefroid, and who was the most fitted in all ways to invite the sympathy of people of every class, was the kindly, cheerful, and unaffected Monsieur Alain. By what means had Providence guided this simple-minded being to this secular convent, where the votaries lived under rules as strictly observed, in perfect freedom and in the midst of Paris, as though they were under the sternest of Priors? What drama, what catastrophe, had made him turn aside from his road through the world to take a path so hard to tread across the troubles of a great city?

One evening Godefroid determined to call on his neighbour, with the purpose of satisfying a curiosity which was more excited by the incredibility of any catastrophe in such a man's life than it could have been by the expectation of listening to some terrible episode in the life of a pirate.

On hearing the reply, "Come in," in answer to two modest raps on the door, Godefroid turned the key, which was always in the lock, and found Monsieur Alain seated in his chimney corner, reading a chapter of the *Imitation* before going to bed by the light of two wax candles with green shades, such as whist-players use. The worthy man had on his trousers and a dressing-gown of thick grey flannel; his feet were raised to the level of the fire on a hassock worked in cross-stitch—as his slippers were also—by Madame de la Chanterie. His striking old head, with its circlet of white hair, almost resembling that of an old monk, stood out, a lighter spot against the brown background of an immense armchair.

Monsieur Alain quietly laid his book, with its worn corners, on the little table with twisted legs, while with the other hand he waved the young man to the second armchair, removing his glasses, which nipped the end of his nose.

"Are you unwell, that you have come down so late?" he asked.

"Dear Monsieur Alain," Godefroid frankly replied, "I am a prey to curiosity which a single word from you will prove to be very innocent or very indiscreet, and that is enough to show you in what spirit I shall venture to ask a question."

"Oh, ho! and what is it?" said he, with an almost mischievous sparkle in his eye.

"What was the circumstance that induced you to lead the life you lead here? For to embrace such a doctrine of utter renunciation, a man must be disgusted with the world, must have been deeply wounded, or have wounded others."

"Why, why, my boy?" replied the old man, and his full lips parted in one of those smiles which made his ruddy mouth one of the most affectionate that the genius of a painter could conceive of. "May he not feel touched to the deepest pity by the sight of the woes to be seen within the walls of Paris? Did Saint Vincent de Paul need the goad of remorse or of wounded vanity to devote himself to foundling babes?"

"Such an answer shuts my mouth all the more effectually, because if ever a soul was a match for that of the Christian hero, it is yours," replied Godefroid.

In spite of the thickening given by age to his yellow and wrinkled face, the old man coloured crimson, for he might seem to have invited the eulogium, though his well-known modesty forbade the idea that he had thought of it. Godefroid knew full well that Madame de la Chanterie's guests had no taste for this kind of incense. And yet good Monsieur Alain's guilelessness was more distressed by this scruple than a young maid would have been by some evil suggestion.

"Though I am far from resembling him in spirit," replied Monsieur Alain, "I certainly am like him in appearance—"

Godefroid was about to speak, but was checked by a gesture from the old man, whose nose had in fact the bulbous appearance of the Saint's, and whose face, much like that of some old vinedresser, was the very duplicate of the coarse, common countenance of the founder of the Foundling Hospital. "As to that, you are right," he went on; "my vocation to this work was the result of an impulse of repentance in consequence of an adventure—"

"An adventure! You!" said Godefroid softly, who at this word forgot what he had been about to say.

"Oh, the story I have to tell will seem to you a mere trifle, a foolish business; but before the tribunal of conscience it looked different. If, after having heard me, you persist in your wish to join in our labours, you will understand that feelings are in inverse proportion to our strength of soul, and that a matter which would not trouble a Freethinker may greatly weigh on a feeble Christian."

After this prelude, the neophyte's curiosity had risen to an indescribable pitch. What could be the crime of this good soul whom Madame de la Chanterie had nicknamed her *Paschal Lamb*? It was as exciting as a book entitled *The Crimes of a Sheep*. Sheep, perhaps, are ferocious to the grass and flowers. If we listen to one of the mildest republicans of our day, the best creatures living are cruel to something. But good Monsieur Alain! He, who, like Sterne's Uncle Toby, would not crush a fly when it had stung him twenty times! This beautiful soul—tortured by repentance!

These reflections filled up the pause made by the old man after he had said, "Listen, then!" and during which he pushed forward the footstool under Godefroid's feet that they might share it.

"I was a little over thirty," said he; "it was in the year '98, so far as I recollect, a time when young men of thirty had the experience of men of sixty. One morning, a little before my breakfast hour at nine o'clock, my old housekeeper announced one of the few friends left to me by the storms of the Revolution. So my first words were to ask him to breakfast. My friend, whose name was Mongenod, a young fellow of eight-and-twenty, accepted, but with some hesitancy. I had not seen him since 1793—"

"Mongenod!" cried Godefroid, "the—?"

"If you want to know the end of the story before the beginning," the old man put in with a smile, "how am I to tell it?"

Godefroid settled himself with an air that promised perfect silence.

"When Mongenod had seated himself," the good man went on, "I observed that his shoes were dreadfully worn. His spotted stockings had been so often washed, that it was hard to recognise that they were of silk. His knee-breeches were of nankeen-colored kerseymere, so faded as to tell of long wear, emphasised by stains in many places, and their buckles, instead of steel, seemed to me to be of common iron; his shoe-buckles were to match. His flowered white waistcoat, yellow with long use, his shirt with its frayed pleated frill, revealed extreme though decent poverty. Finally, his coat—a *houppe-lande*, as we called such a coat, with a single collar like a very short cape—was enough to assure me that my friend had fallen on bad times. This coat of nut-brown cloth, extremely threadbare, and brushed with excessive care, had a rim of grease or powder round the collar, and buttons off which the plating had worn to the copper. In fact, the whole outfit was so wretched, that I could not bear to look at it. His crush hat—a semicircular structure of beaver, which it was then customary to carry under one arm instead of wearing it on the head—must have survived many changes of government.

"However, my friend had no doubt just spent a few sous to have his head dressed by a barber, for he was freshly shaved, and his hair, fastened into a club with a comb, was luxuriously powdered, and smelled of pomatum. I could see two chains hanging parallel out of his fobs, chains of tarnished steel, but no sign of the watches within. It was winter, but Mongenod had no cloak, for some large drops of melting snow fallen from the eaves under which he had walked for shelter lay on the collar of his coat. When he drew off his rabbit-fur gloves and I saw his right hand, I could perceive the traces of some kind of hard labour.

"Now, his father, an advocate in the higher court, had left him some little fortune—five or six thousand francs a year. I at once understood that Mongenod had come to borrow of me. I had in a certain hiding-place two hundred louis in gold, an enormous sum at that time, when it represented I know not how many hundred thousand francs in paper *assignats.*

"Mongenod and I had been schoolfellows at the Collège des Grassins, and we had been thrown together again in the same lawyer's office—an honest man, the worthy Bordin. When two men have spent their boyhood together and shared the follies of their youth, there is an almost sacred bond of sympathy between them; the man's voice and look stir certain chords in your heart, which never vibrate but to the particular memories that he can rouse. Even if you have some cause to complain of such a comrade, that does not wipe out every claim of friendship, and between us there had not been the slightest quarrel.

"In 1787, when his father died, Mongenod had been a richer man than I and though I had never borrowed from him, I had owed to him certain pleasures which my father's strictness would have prohibited. But for my friend's generosity, I should not have seen the first performance of the *Marriage of Figaro*.

"Mongenod was at that time what was called a finished gentleman, a man about town and attentive to 'the ladies.' I constantly reproved him for his too great facility in making friends and obliging them; his purse was constantly open, he lived largely, he would have stood surety for you after meeting you twice.—Dear me, dear me! You have started me on reminiscences of my youth!" cried Monsieur Alain, with a bright smile at Godefroid as he paused.

"You are not vexed with me?" said Godefroid.

"No, no. And you may judge by the minute details I am giving you how large a place the event filled in my life.—Mongenod, with a good heart and plenty of courage, something of a Voltairean, was inclined to play the fine gentleman," Monsieur Alain went on. "His education at the Grassins, where noblemen's sons were to be met, and his adventures of gallantry, had given him the polish of men of rank, in those days termed Aristocrats. So you may imagine how great was my consternation at observing in Mongenod such signs of poverty as degraded him in my eyes from the elegant young Mongenod I had known in 1787, when my eyes wandered from his face to examine his clothes.

"However, at that time of general public penury, some wily folks assumed an appearance of wretchedness; and as others no doubt had ample reasons for assuming a disguise, I hoped for some explanation, and invited it.

"'What a plight you are in, my dear Mongenod!' said I, accepting a pinch of snuff, which he offered me from a box of imitation gold.

"'Sad enough!' replied he. 'I have but one friend left—and you are that friend. I have done everything in the world to avoid coming to this point, but I have come to ask you to lend me a hundred louis. It is a large sum,' said he, noticing my surprise, 'but if you lend me no more than fifty, I shall never be able to repay you; whereas, if I should fail in what I am undertaking, I shall still have fifty louis to try some other road to fortune, and I do not yet know what inspiration despair may bring me.'

"'Then, have you nothing?' said I.

"'I have,' said he, hiding a tear, 'just five sous left out of my last piece of silver. To call on you, I had my boots cleaned and my head dressed. I have the clothes on my back.—But,' he went on, with a desperate shrug, 'I owe my landlady a thousand crowns in *assignats*, and the man at the cookshop yesterday refused to trust me. So I have nothing—nothing.'

"'And what do you propose to do?' said I, insistently meddling with his private affairs.

"'To enlist if you refuse to help me.'

"'You, a soldier! You—Mongenod!'

"'I will get killed, or I will be General Mongenod.'

"'Well,' said I, really moved, 'eat your breakfast in peace; I have a hundred louis—'

"And here," said the good man, looking slily at Godefroid, "I thought it necessary to tell a little lender's fib.

"'But it is all I have in the world,' I said to Mongenod. 'I was waiting till the funds had gone down to the lowest mark to invest my money, but I will place it in your hands, and you may regard me as your partner; I leave it to your conscience to repay me the whole in due time and place. An honest man's conscience,' I added, 'is the best possible security.'

"Mongenod looked hard at me as I spoke, seeming to stamp my words on his heart. He held out his right hand, I gave him my left, and we clasped hands—I, greatly moved, and he, without restraining two tears which now trickled down his thin cheeks. The sight of those tears wrung my heart; and I was still more unnerved when, forgetful of everything in such a moment, Mongenod, to wipe them away, pulled out a ragged bandana.

"'Wait here,' said I, running off to my hidden store, my heart as full as though I had heard a woman confess that she loved me. I returned with two rolls of fifty louis each.

"'Here—count them.'

"But he would not count them; he looked about him for a writing-table in order, as he said, to give me a receipt. I positively refused to have one.

"'If I were to die,' said I, 'my heirs would worry you. This is a matter between you and me.'

"Finding me so true a friend, Mongenod presently lost the haggard and anxious expression he had worn on entering, and became cheerful. My housekeeper gave us oysters, white wine, an omelette, kidneys *à la brochette*, and the remains of a pâté de Chartres sent me by my mother; a little dessert, coffee, and West Indian liqueur. Mongenod, who had fasted for two days, was the better for it. We sat till three in the afternoon talking over our life before the Revolution, the best friends in the world.

"Mongenod told me how he had lost his fortune. In the first instance, the reduction of the dividends on the Hôtel de Ville had deprived him of two-thirds of his income, for his father had invested the larger part of his fortune in municipal securities; then, after selling his house in the Rue de Savoie, he had been obliged to accept payment in *assignats*; he had then taken it into his head to run a newspaper, *La Sentinelle*, and at the end of six months was forced to fly. At the present moment all his hopes hung on the success of a comic opera called *Les Péruviens*. This last confession made me quake. Mongenod, as an author, having spent his all on the *Sentinelle*, and living no doubt at the theatre, mixed up with Feydeau's singers, with musicians, and the motley world behind the curtain, did not seem to me like the same, like my Mongenod. I shuddered a little. But how could I get back my hundred louis? I could see the two rolls, one in each fob like the barrel of a pistol.

"Mongenod went away. When I found myself alone, no longer face to face with his bitter and cruel poverty, I began to reflect in spite of myself; I was sober again. 'Mongenod,' thought I to myself, 'has no doubt sunk as low as possible; he has acted a little farce for my benefit!' His glee when he saw me calmly hand over so vast a sum now struck me as that of a stage rascal cheating some Géronte. I ended where I ought to have begun, resolved to make some inquiries about my friend Mongenod, who had written his address on the back of a playing-card.

"A feeling of delicacy kept me from going to see him the next day; he might have ascribed my haste to distrust of him. Two days after I found my whole time absorbed by various business; and it was not, in fact, till a fortnight had elapsed that, seeing no more of Mongenod, I made my way from La Croix-Rouge, where I then lived, to the Rue des Moineaux, where he lived.

"Mongenod was lodged in a furnished house of the meanest description; but his landlady was a very decent woman, the widow of a farmer-general who had died on the scaffold. She, completely ruined, had started with a few louis the precarious business of letting rooms. Since then she has rented seven houses in the neighborhood of Saint-Roch and made a fortune.

"'Citizen Mongenod is out,' said she. 'But there is some one at home.'

"This excited my curiosity. I climbed to the fifth floor. A charming young woman opened the door! Oh! A person of exquisite beauty, who, looking at me doubtfully, stood behind the partly opened door.

"'I am Alain,' said I, 'Mongenod's friend.'

"I AM ALAIN, MONGENOD'S FRIEND"

"At once the door was wide open, and I went into a horrible garret, which the young woman had, however, kept scrupulously clean. She pushed forward a chair to the hearth piled with ashes, but with no fire, where in one corner I saw a common earthenware fire-pan. The cold was icy.

"'I am glad indeed, monsieur,' said she, taking my hands and pressing them warmly, 'to be able to express my gratitude, for you are our deliverer. But for you I might never have seen Mongenod again. He would have—God knows—have thrown himself into the river. He was desperate when he set out to see you.'

"As I looked at the young lady I was greatly astonished to see that she had a handkerchief bound about her head; and below its folds at the back and on the temples there was a sort of black shadow. Studying it attentively, I discovered that her head was shaved.

"'Are you ill?' I asked, noticing this strange fact.

"She glanced at herself in a wretched dirty pier-glass, and coloured, while tears rose to her eyes.

"'Yes, monsieur,' said she hastily; 'I had dreadful headaches; I was obliged to cut off my hair, which fell to my heels—'

"'Have I the honour of speaking to Madame Mongenod?' I asked.

"'Yes, monsieur,' said she, with a really heavenly expression.

"I made my bow to the poor little lady, and went downstairs, intending to make the landlady give me some information, but she was gone out. It struck me that the young woman had sold her hair to buy bread. I went off at once to a wood merchant, and sent in half a load of wood, begging the carter and the sawyers to give the lady a receipted bill to the name of Mongenod.

"And there ends the phase of my life which I long called my foolish stage," said Monsieur Alain, clasping his hands and uplifting them a little with a repentant gesture.

Godefroid could not help smiling; but he was, as will be seen, quite wrong to smile.

"Two days later," the good man went on, "I met one of those men who are neither friends nor strangers—persons whom we see from time to time, in short, an acquaintance, as we say—a Monsieur Barillaud, who, as we happened to speak of *Les Péruviens*, proclaimed himself a friend of the author's.

"'Thou know'st Citizen Mongenod?' said I—for at that time we were still required by law to address each other with the familiar *tu*," said he to Godefroid in a parenthesis.

"The citizen looked at me," said Monsieur Alain, resuming the thread of his story, "and exclaimed:

"'I only wish I had never known him, for he has borrowed money of me many a time, and is so much my friend as not to return it. He is a queer fellow! the best old boy alive, but full of illusions?—An imagination of fire.—I will do him justice; he does not mean to be dishonest, only as he is always deceiving himself about a thousand things, he is led into conduct that is not altogether straight.'

"'How much does he owe you?'

"'Oh, a few hundred crowns. He is a regular sieve. No one knows where his money goes, for he perhaps does not know that himself.'

"'Has he any expedients?'

"'Oh, dear, yes!' said Barillaud, laughing. 'At this moment he is talking of buying up land among the wild men in the United States.'

"I went away with this drop of vitriol shed by slander on my heart to turn all my best feelings sour. I went to call on my old master in the law, who was always my counsellor. As soon as I had told him the secret of my loan to Mongenod, and the way in which I had acted:

"'What,' cried he, 'is it a clerk of mine that can behave so? You should have put him off a day and have come to me. Then you would have known that I had shown Mongenod the door. He has already borrowed from me in the course of a year more than a hundred crowns in silver, an enormous sum! And only three days before he went to breakfast with you, he met me in the street and described his misery in such desperate language that I gave him two louis.'

"'Well, if I am the dupe of a clever actor, so much the worse for him rather than for me!' said I. 'But what is to be done?'

"'At any rate, you must try to get some acknowledgment out of him, for a debtor however worthless may recover himself, and then you may be paid.'

"Thereupon Bordin took out of one of the drawers of his table a wrapper on which was written the name of Mongenod; he showed me three acknowledgments, each for a hundred livres.

"'The first time he comes,' said he, 'I shall make him add on the interest and the two louis I gave him, and whatever money he asks for; and then he must sign an acceptance and a statement, saying that interest accrues from the first day of the loan. That, at any rate, will be all in order; I shall have some means of getting paid.'

"'Well, then,' said I to Bordin, 'cannot you put me as much in order as yourself? For you are an honest man, and what you do will be right.'

"'In this way I remain the master of the field,' replied the lawyer. 'When a man behaves as you have done, he is at the mercy of another who may simply make game of him. Now I don't choose to be laughed at. A retired Public Prosecutor of the Châtelet! Bless me, what next!—Every man to whom you lend money as recklessly as you lent it to Mongenod, sooner or later thinks of it as his own. It is no longer your money; it is his money; you are his creditor, a very inconvenient person. The debtor then tries to be quit of you by a compromise with his conscience, and seventy-five out of every hundred will try to avoid meeting you again to the end of his days—'

"'Then you look for no more than twenty-five per cent of honest men?'

"'Did I say so?' said he, with an ironical smile. 'That is a large allowance!'

"A fortnight later I had a note from Bordin desiring me to call on him to fetch my receipt. I went.

"'I tried to snatch back fifty louis for you,' said he.—I had told him all about my conversation with Mongenod.—'But the birds are flown. You may say good-bye to your yellow-boys! Your canary-birds have fled to warmer climes. We have a very cunning rascal to deal with. Did he not assure me that his wife and his father-in-law had set out for the United States with sixty of your louis to buy land, and that he intended to join them there? To make a fortune, as he said, so as to return to pay his debts, of which he handed me the schedule drawn out in due form; for he begged me to keep myself informed as to what became of his creditors. Here is the schedule,' added Bordin, showing me a wrapper on which was noted the total. 'Seventeen thousand francs in hard cash! With such a sum as that a house might be bought worth two thousand crowns a year.'

"After replacing the packet, he gave me a bill of exchange for a sum equivalent to a hundred louis in gold, stated in *assignats*, with a letter in which Mongenod acknowledged the debt with interest on a hundred louis d'or.

"'So now I am all safe?' said I to Bordin.

"'He will not deny the debt,' replied my old master. 'But where there are no effects, the King—that is to say, the Directoire—has no rights.'

"I thereupon left him. Believing myself to have been robbed by a trick that evades the law, I withdrew my esteem from Mongenod, and was very philosophically resigned.

"It is not without a reason that I dwell on these commonplace and apparently unimportant details," the good man went on, looking at Godefroid. "I am trying to show you how I was led to act as most men act, blindly, and in contempt of certain rules which even savages do not disregard in the most trifling matters.

Many men would justify themselves by the authority of Bordin; but at this day I feel that I had no excuse. As soon as we are led to condemn one of our fellows, and to refuse him our esteem for life, we ought to rely solely on our own judgment—and even then!—Ought we to set up our own feelings as a tribunal before which to arraign our neighbour? Where would the law be? What should be our standard of merit? Would not a weakness in me be strength in my neighbour? So many men, so many different circumstances would there be for each deed; for there are no two identical sets of conditions in human existence. Society alone has the right of reproving its members; for I do not grant it that of punishing them. A mere reprimand is sufficient, and brings with it cruelty enough.

"So as I listened to the haphazard opinions of a Parisian, admiring my former teacher's acumen, I condemned Mongenod," the good man went on, after drawing from his narrative this noble moral.

"The performance of *Les Péruviens* was announced. I expected to have a ticket for the first night; I conceived myself in some way his superior. As a result of his indebtedness, my friend seemed to me a vassal who owed me many things besides the interest on my money. We are all alike!

"Not only did Mongenod send me no ticket, but I saw him at a distance coming along the dark passage under the Théâtre Feydeau, well dressed—nay, almost elegant; he affected not to see me; then, when he had passed me, and I thought I would run after him, he had vanished down some cross passage. This irritated me extremely; and my annoyance, far from being transient, increased as time went on.

"This was why. A few days after this incident I wrote to Mongenod much in these words:

> "'My Friend,—You should not regard me as indifferent to anything that can happen to you, whether for good or ill. Does the *Péruviens* come up to your expectations? You forgot me—you had every right to do so—at the first performance, when I should have applauded you heartily! However, I hope, all the same, that you may find Peru in the piece, for I can invest my capital, and I count on you when the bill falls due.—Your friend, Alain.'

"After waiting for a fortnight and receiving no answer, I called in the Rue des Moineaux. The landlady told me that the little wife had, in fact, set out with her father, at the date named by Mongenod to Bordin. Mongenod always left his garret early in the morning, and did not come in till late at night. Another fortnight passed; I wrote another letter in these terms:

> "'MY DEAR MONGENOD,—I see nothing of you; you do not answer my notes; I cannot at all understand your conduct; and if I were to behave so to you, what would you think of me?'

"I did not sign myself 'Your friend.' I wrote 'With best regards.'

"A month slipped by; no news of Mongenod. The *Péruviens* had not obtained so great a success as Mongenod had counted on. I paid for a seat at the twentieth performance, and I found a small house. And yet Madame Scio was very fine in it. I was told in the *foyer* that there would be a few more performances of the piece. I went seven times to call on Mongenod; he was never at home, and each time I left my name with the landlady. So then I wrote again:

> "'Monsieur, if you do not wish to lose my respect after forfeiting my friendship, you will henceforth treat me as a stranger—that is to say, with civility—and you will tell me whether you are prepared to pay me when your note of hand falls due. I shall act in accordance with your reply.—Yours faithfully. ALAIN.'

"No reply. It was now 1799; a year had elapsed all but two months.

"When the bill fell due I went to see Bordin. Bordin took the note of hand, and then took legal proceedings. The reverses experienced by the French armies had had such a depressing effect on the funds that five francs a year could be purchased for seven francs. Thus, for a hundred louis in gold, I might have had nearly fifteen hundred francs a year. Every morning, as I read the paper over my cup of coffee, I would exclaim:

"'Confound that Mongenod! But for him, I could have a thousand crowns a year!'

"Mongenod had become my chronic aversion; I thundered at him even when I was walking in the street.

"'Bordin is after him!' said I to myself. 'He will catch him—and serve him right!'

"My rage expended itself in imprecations; I cursed the man; I believed him capable of any crime. Yes! Monsieur Barillaud was quite right in what he said.

"Well, one morning my debtor walked in, no more disconcerted than if he had not owed me a centime; and I, when I saw him, I felt all the shame that should have been his. I was like a criminal caught in the act; I was quite ill at ease. The 18th of Brumaire was past, everything was going on well, and Bonaparte had set out to fight the battle of Marengo.

"'It is unlucky, monsieur,' said I, 'that I should owe your visit solely to the intervention of a bailiff.'

"Mongenod took a chair and sat down.

"'I have come to tell you,' said he, with the familiar *tu*, 'that I cannot possibly pay you.'

"'You have lost me the chance of investing my money before the arrival of the First Consul—at that time I could have made a little fortune—"

"'I know it, Alain,' said he; 'I know it. But what will you get by prosecuting me for debt and plunging me deeper by loading me with costs? I have letters from my father-in-law and my wife; they have bought some land and sent me the bill for the necessaries of the house; I have had to spend all I had in those purchases. Now, and nobody can hinder me—I mean to sail by a Dutch vessel from Flushing, whither I have sent all my small possessions. Bonaparte has won the battle of Marengo, peace will be signed, and I can join my family without fear—for my dear little wife was expecting a baby.'

"'And so you have sacrificed me to your own interests?' cried I.

"'Yes,' said he; 'I thought you my friend.'

"At that moment I felt small as compared to Mongenod, so sublime did that speech seem to me, so simple and grand.

"'Did I not tell you so,' he went on; 'was I not absolutely frank with you—here, on this very spot? I came to you, Alain, as being the only man who would appreciate me.—Fifty louis would be wasted, I told you; but if you lent me a hundred, I would repay them. I fixed no date, for how can I tell when my long struggle with poverty will come to an end? You were my last friend. All my friends, even our old master Bordin, despised me simply because I wanted to borrow money of them. Oh! Alain, you can never know the dreadful feelings that grip the heart of an honest man fighting misfortune when he goes into another man's house to ask for help!—and all that follows!—I hope you may never know them; they are worse than the anguish of death!

"'You have written me certain letters which, from me under similar circumstances, would have struck you as odious. You expected things of me that were out of my power. You are the only man to whom I attempt to justify myself. In spite of your severity, and though you ceased to be my friend and became only my creditor from the day when Bordin asked me for an acknowledgment of your loan, thus discrediting the handsome agreement we ourselves had come to, here, shaking hands on it with tears in our eyes!—Well, I have forgotten everything but that morning's work.

"'It is in memory of that hour that I have come now to say, "You know not what misfortune is; do not rail at it!—I have not had an hour, not a second, to write to you in reply! Perhaps you would have liked me to come and pay you compliments?—You might as well expect a hare, harassed by dogs and hunters, to rest in a clearing and crop the grass!—I sent you no ticket! No; I had not enough to satisfy those on whom my fate depended. A novice in the theatrical world, I was the prey of musicians, actors, singers, the orchestra. To enable me to join my family over seas, and buy what they need, I sold the *Péruviens* to the manager with two other pieces I had in my desk. I am setting out for Holland without a sou. I shall eat dry bread on my journey till I reach Flushing. I have paid my passage, and have nothing more. But for my landlady's compassion, and her trust in me, I should have had to walk to Flushing with a knapsack on my back. And so, in spite of your doubting me, as, but for you, I could not have sent my father-in-law and my wife to New York, I am entirely grateful."—No, *Monsieur* Alain, I will not forget that the hundred louis you lent me might at this time be yielding you an income of fifteen hundred francs'

"'I would fain believe you, Mongenod,' said I, almost convinced by the tone in which he poured out this explanation.

"'At any rate, you no longer address me as monsieur,' said he eagerly, and looking at me with emotion. 'God knows I should quit France with less regret if I could leave one man behind me in whose eyes I was neither half a rogue, nor a spendthrift, nor a victim to illusions. A man who can love truly, Alain, is never wholly despicable.'

"At these words I held out my hand; he took it and pressed it.

"'Heaven protect you!' said I.

"'We are still friends?' he asked.

"'Yes,' I replied; 'it shall never be said that my schoolfellow, the friend of my youth, set out for America under the ban of my anger!—'

"Mongenod embraced me with tears in his eyes, and rushed off to the door.

"When I met Bordin a few days afterwards, I told him the story of our interview, and he replied with a smile:

"'I only hope it was not all part of the performance!—He did not ask you for anything?'

"'No,' said I.

"'He came to me too, and I was almost as weak as you; but he asked me for something to get food on the way. However, he who lives will see!'

"This remark of Bordin's made me fear lest I had yielded stupidly to an impulse of feeling.

"'Still, he too, the Public Prosecutor, did the same,' said I to myself.

"It is unnecessary, I think, to explain to you how I lost all my fortune excepting the other hundred louis, which I invested in Government securities when prices had risen so high that I had barely five hundred francs a year to live upon by the time I was four-and-thirty. By Bordin's interest I obtained an appointment at eight hundred francs a year in a branch of the *Mont-de-Piété*, Rue des Petits Augustins. I lived in the humblest way; I lodged on the third floor of a house in the Rue des Marais in an apartment consisting of two rooms and a closet for two hundred and fifty francs. I went out to dinner in a boarding-house where there was an open table, and for this I paid forty francs a month. In the evening I did some copying. Ugly as I am, and very poor, I had to give up all ideas of marriage—"

As he heard this verdict pronounced on himself by poor Alain in a tone of angelic resignation, Godefroid gave a little start, which proved better than any speech could have done the similarity of their fate; and the good man, in reply to this eloquent gesture, seemed to pause for his hearer to speak.

"And no one ever loved you?" asked Godefroid.

"No one," he replied, "excepting Madame, who returns to all of us alike our love for her—a love I might almost call divine.—You must have seen it: we live in her life, as she lives in ours; we have but one soul among us; and though our enjoyments are not physical, they are none the less very intense, for we live only through the heart.—How can we help it, my dear boy? By the time women are capable of appreciating moral qualities they have done with externals, and are growing old.—I have suffered much, I can tell you!"

"Ah! that is the stage I am at—" said Godefroid.

"Under the Empire," the old man went on, bowing his head, "dividends were not very punctually paid; we had to be prepared for deferred payment. From 1802 to 1814 not a week passed that I did not ascribe my difficulties to Mongenod: 'But for Mongenod,' I used to think, 'I might have been married. But for him I should not be obliged to live in privation.'—But sometimes, too, I would say to myself, 'Perhaps the poor man is pursued by ill-luck out there!'

"In 1806, one day when I found my life a heavy burden to bear, I wrote him a long letter that I despatched via Holland. I had no answer; and for three years I waited, founding hopes on that reply which were constantly deceived. At last I resigned myself to my fate. To my five hundred francs of dividends, and twelve hundred francs of salary from the Mont-de-Piété, for it was raised, I added five hundred for my work as bookkeeper to a perfumer, Monsieur Birotteau. Thus I not only made both ends meet, but I saved eight hundred francs a year. By the beginning of 1814, I was able to invest nine thousand francs of savings in the funds, buying at forty; thus I had secured sixteen hundred francs a year for my old age. So then, with fifteen hundred francs a year from the Mont-de-Piété, six hundred as a bookkeeper, and sixteen hundred in dividends, I had an income of three thousand seven hundred francs. I took rooms in the Rue de Seine, and I lived in rather more comfort.

"My position brought me into contact with many of the very poor. For twelve years I have known, better than any one, what the misery of the world is; once or twice I have helped some poor creatures; and I felt the keenest pleasure when, out of ten that I had assisted, one or two families were rescued from their difficulties.

"It struck me that true beneficence did not consist in throwing money to the sufferers. Being charitable, in the common phrase, often appeared to me to be a sort of premium on crime. I set to work to study this question. I was by this time fifty years old, and my life was drawing to a close.

"'What good am I in the world?' I asked myself. 'To whom can I leave my money? When I shall have furnished my rooms handsomely, have secured a good cook, have made my life suitably comfortable, what am I to do with my time?'

"For eleven years of revolutions and fifteen years of poverty had wasted the happiest part of my life, had consumed it in labours that were fruitless, or devoted solely to the preservation of my person! At such an age no one can make an obscure and penurious youth the starting-point to reach a brilliant position; but every one may make himself useful. I understood, in short, that a certain supervision and much good advice would increase tenfold the value of money given, for the poor always need guidance; to enable them to profit by the work they do for others, it is not the intelligence of the speculator that is wanting.

"A few happy results that I achieved made me extremely proud. I discerned both an aim and an occupation, to say nothing of the exquisite pleasure to be derived from playing the part of Providence, even on the smallest scale."

"And you now play it on a large scale?" said Godefroid eagerly.

"Oh, you want to know too much!" said the old man. "Nay, nay.—Would you believe it," he went on after a pause, "the smallness of the means at my command constantly brought my thoughts back to Mongenod?

"'But for Mongenod I could have done so much more,' I used to reflect. 'If a dishonest man had not robbed me of fifteen hundred francs a year,' I often thought, 'I could have helped this or that family.'

"Thus excusing my inability by such an accusation, those to whom I gave nothing but words to comfort them joined me in cursing Mongenod. These maledictions were balm to my heart.

"One morning, in January 1816, my housekeeper announced—whom do you think?—Mongenod.—Monsieur Mongenod. And who should walk in but the pretty wife, now six-and-thirty, accompanied by three children; then came Mongenod, younger than when he left, for wealth and happiness shed a glory on those they favour. He had gone away lean, pale, yellow, and haggard; he had come back fat and well-liking, as flourishing as a prebendary, and well dressed. He threw himself into my arms, and finding himself coldly welcomed, his first words were:

"'Could I come any sooner, my friend? The seas have only been open since 1815, and it took me eighteen months to realise my property, close my accounts, and call in my assets. I have succeeded, my friend! When I received your letter in 1806, I set out in a Dutch vessel to bring you home a little fortune; but the union of Holland to the French Empire led to our being taken by the English, who transported me to the coast of Jamaica, whence by good luck I escaped.

"'On my return to New York I was a victim to bankruptcy; for Charlotte, during my absence, had not known how to be on her guard against swindlers. So I was compelled to begin again to accumulate a fortune.

"'However, here we are at last. From the way the children look at you, you may suppose that they have often heard of the benefactor of the family.'

"'Yes, indeed,' said pretty Madame Mongenod, 'we never passed a day without speaking of you. Your share has been allowed for in every transaction. We have longed for the happiness we enjoy at this moment of offering you your fortune, though we have never for a moment imagined that this "rector's tithe" can pay our debt of gratitude.'

"And as she spoke, Madame Mongenod offered me the beautiful casket you see there, which contained a hundred and fifty thousand-franc notes.

"'You have suffered much, my dear Alain, I know; but we could imagine all your sufferings, and we craked our brains to find means of sending you money; but without success,' Mongenod went on. 'You tell me you could not marry; but here is our eldest daughter. She has been brought up in the idea that she should be your wife, and she has five hundred thousand francs—'

"'God forbid that I should wreck her happiness!' cried I, as I beheld a girl as lovely as her mother had been at her age; and I drew her to me, and kissed her forehead.

"'Do not be afraid, my pretty child,' said I. 'A man of fifty and a girl of seventeen and so ugly an old fellow as I!—Never!'

"'Monsieur,' said she, 'my father's benefactor can never seem ugly in my eyes.'

"This speech, made with spontaneous candour, showed me that all Mongenod had told me was true. I offered him my hand, and we fell into each other's arms once more.

"'My friend,' said I, 'I have often abused you, cursed you—'

"'You had every right, Alain,' replied he, reddening. 'You were in poverty through my fault—'

"I took Mongenod's papers out of a box and restored them to him, after cancelling his note of hand.

"'Now you will all breakfast with me,' said I to the family party.

"'On condition of your dining with my wife as soon as we are settled,' said Mongenod, 'for we arrived only yesterday. We are going to buy a house, and I am about to open a bank in Paris for North American business to leave to that youngster,' he said, pointing to his eldest son, a lad of fifteen.

"We spent the afternoon together, and in the evening we all went to the theatre, for Mongenod and his party were dying to see a play. Next day I invested in the funds, and had then an income of about fifteen thousand francs in all. This released me from bookkeeping in the evening, and allowed me to give up my appointment, to the great satisfaction of all my subordinates.

"My friend died in 1827, after founding the banking house of Mongenod and Co., which made immense profits on the first loans issued at the time of the Restoration. His daughter, to whom he subsequently gave about a million of francs, married the Vicomte de Fontaine. The son whom you know is not yet married; he lives with his mother and his younger brother. We find them ready with all the money we may need.

"Frédéric—for his father, in America, had named him after me—Frédéric Mongenod, at seven-and-thirty, is one of the most skilful and respected bankers in Paris.

"Not very long since Madame Mongenod confessed to me that she had sold her hair for two crowns of six livres to be able to buy some bread. She gives twenty-four loads of wood every year, which I distribute among the poor, in return for the half-load I once sent her."

"Then this accounts for your connection with the house of Mongenod," said Godefroid. "And your fortune—"

The old man still looked at Godefroid with the same expression of mild irony.

"Pray go on," said Godefroid, seeing by Monsieur Alain's manner that he had more to say.

"This conclusion, my dear Godefroid, made the deepest impression on me. Though the man who had suffered so much, though my friend had forgiven me my injustice, I could not forgive myself."

"Oh!" said Godefroid.

"I determined to devote all my surplus income, about ten thousand francs a year, to acts of rational beneficence," Monsieur Alain calmly went on. "At about that time I met an Examining Judge of the department of the Seine named Popinot, whose death we mourned three years ago, and who for fifteen years practised the most enlightened charity in the Saint-Marcel quarter. He, in concert with the venerable vicar of Notre-Dame and with Madame, planned the work in which we are all engaged, and which, since 1823, has secretly effected some good results.

"This work has found a soul in Madame de la Chanterie; she is really the very spirit of the undertaking. The vicar has succeeded in making us more religious than we were at first, demonstrating the necessity for being virtuous ourselves if we desire to inspire virtue—for preaching, in fact, by example. And the further we progress in that path, the happier we are among ourselves. Thus it was my repentance for having misprized the heart of my boyhood's friend which led me to the idea of devoting to the poor, through myself, the fortune he brought home to me, which I accepted without demurring to the vast sum repaid to me for so small a loan; the application of it made it right."

This narrative, devoid of all emphasis, and told with touching simplicity of tone, gesture, and expression, would have been enough to make Godefroid resolve on joining in this noble and saintly work, if he had not already intended it.

"You know little of the world," said Godefroid, "if you had such scruples over a thing which would never have weighed on any other conscience."

"I know only the wretched," replied the good man. "I have no wish to know a world where men misjudge each other with so little compunction. Now it is nearly midnight, and I have to meditate on my chapter of the *Imitation*.—Good-night."

Godefroid took the kind old man's hand and pressed it with an impulse of genuine admiration.

"Can you tell me Madame de la Chanterie's history?" asked Godefroid.

"It would be impossible without her permission, for it is connected with one of the most terrible incidents of imperial politics. I first knew Madame through my friend Bordin; he knew all the secrets of that beautiful life; and it was he who led me, so to speak, to this house."

"At any rate, then," said Godefroid, "I thank you for having told me your life; it contains a lesson for me."

"Do you discern its moral?"

"Nay, tell it me," said Godefroid; "for I might see it differently to you—"

"Well, then," said the good man, "pleasure is but an accident in the life of the Christian; it is not his aim and end—and we learn this too late."

"What then happens when we are converted?" asked Godefroid.

"Look there!" said Alain, and he pointed to an inscription in letters of gold on a black ground, which the newcomer had not seen before, as this was the first time he had ever been into his companion's rooms. He turned round and read the words, "TRANSIRE BENEFACIENDO."

"That, my son, is the meaning we then find in life. That is our motto. If you become one of us, that constitutes your brevet. We read that text and take it as our counsel at every hour of the day, when we rise, when we go to bed, while we dress. Oh! if you could but know what infinite happiness is to be found in carrying out that device!"

"In what way?" said Godefroid, hoping for some explanations.

"In the first place, we are as rich as Baron de Nucingen.—But the *Imitation* prohibits our calling anything our own; we are but stewards; and if we feel a single impulse of pride, we are not worthy to be stewards. That would not be *transire benefaciendo*; it would be enjoyment in thought. If you say to yourself, with a certain dilation of the nostrils, 'I am playing the part of Providence'—as you might have thought this morning, if you had been in my place, giving new life to a whole family, you are a Sardanapalus at once—and wicked! Not one of our members ever thinks of himself when doing good. You must cast off all vanity, all pride, all self-consciousness; and it is difficult, I can tell you."

Godefroid bid Monsieur Alain good-night, and went to his own rooms, much moved by this story; but his curiosity was excited rather than satisfied, for the chief figure in the picture of this domestic scene was Madame de la Chanterie. This woman's history was to him so supremely interesting that he made the knowledge of it the first aim of his stay in the house. He understood that the purpose for which these five persons were associated was some great charitable endeavour; but he thought much less of that than of his heroine.

The neophyte spent some days in studying these choice spirits, amid whom he found himself, with greater attention than he had hitherto devoted to them; and he became the subject of a moral phenomenon which modern philanthropists have overlooked, from ignorance perhaps. The sphere in which he lived had a direct influence on Godefroid. The law which governs physical nature in respect to the influence of atmospheric conditions on the lives of the beings subject to them, also governs moral nature; whence it is to be inferred that the collecting in masses of the criminal class is one of the greatest social crimes, while absolute isolation is an experiment of which the success is very doubtful. Condemned felons ought, therefore, to be placed in religious institutions and surrounded with prodigies of goodness instead of being left among marvels of evil. The Church may be looked to for perfect devotion to this cause; for if She is ready to send missionaries to barbarous or savage nations, how gladly would She charge her religious Orders with the mission of rescuing and instructing the savages of civilised life! Every criminal is an atheist—often without knowing it.

Godefroid found his five companions endowed with the qualities they demanded of him; they were all free from pride or vanity, all truly humble and pious, devoid of the pretentiousness which constitutes devoutness in the invidious sense of the word. These virtues were contagious; he was filled with the desire to imitate these obscure heroes, and he ended by studying with ardour the book he had at first scorned. Within a fortnight he had reduced life to its simplest expression, to what it really is when regarded from the lofty point of view to which the religious spirit leads us. Finally, his curiosity, at first purely worldly and roused by many vulgar motives, became rarefied. He did not cease to be curious; it would have been difficult to lose all interest in the life of Madame de la Chanterie; but, without intending it, he showed a reserve which was fully appreciated by these men, in whom the Holy Spirit had developed wonderful depths of mind, as happens, indeed, with all who devote themselves to a religious life. The concentration of the moral powers, by whatever means or system, increases their scope tenfold.

"Our young friend is not yet a convert," said the good Abbé de Vèze; "but he wishes to be."

An unforeseen circumstance led to the revelation of Madame de la Chanterie's history, so that his intense interest in it was soon satisfied.

Paris was just then engrossed by the investigation of the case of the Barrière Saint-Jacques, one of those hideous trials which mark the history of our assizes. The trial derived its interest from the criminals themselves, whose daring and general superiority to ordinary culprits, with their cynical contempt for justice, really appalled the public. It was a noteworthy fact that no newspaper ever entered the Hôtel de la Chanterie, and Godefroid only heard of the rejection of the appeal to the Supreme Court from his master in bookkeeping; the trial had taken place long before he came to Madame de la Chanterie.

"Do you ever meet with such men as these atrocious scoundrels?" he asked his new friends. "Or, when you do, how do you deal with them?"

"In the first place," said Monsieur Nicolas, "there is no such thing as an atrocious scoundrel; there are mad creatures fit only for the asylum at Charenton; but with the exception of those rare pathological exceptions, what we find are simply men without religion, or who argue falsely, and the task of the charitable is to set souls upright and bring the erring into the right way."

"And to the apostle all things are possible," said the Abbé de Vèze; "he has God on his side."

"If you were sent to these two condemned men," said Godefroid, "you could do nothing with them."

"There would not be time," observed Monsieur Alain.

"As a rule," said Monsieur Nicolas, "the souls handed over to be dealt with by the Church are in utter impenitence, and the time is too short for miracles to be wrought. The men of whom you are speaking, if they had fallen into our hands, would have been men of mark; their energy is immense; but when once they have committed murder, it is impossible to do anything for them; human justice has taken possession of them—"

"Then you are averse to capital punishment?" said Godefroid.

Monsieur Nicolas hastily rose and left the room. "Never speak of capital punishment in the presence of Monsieur Nicolas. He once recognised in a criminal, whose execution it was his duty to superintend, a natural child of his own—"

"And who was innocent!" added Monsieur Joseph. At this moment Madame de la Chanterie, who had not been in the room, came in.

"Still, you must allow," Godefroid went on, addressing Monsieur Joseph, "that society cannot exist without capital punishment, and that these men, whose heads—"

Godefroid felt his mouth suddenly closed by a strong hand, and the Abbé de Vèze led away Madame de la Chanterie, pale and half dead.

"What have you done?" cried Monsieur Joseph. "Take him away, Alain," he said, removing the hand with which he had gagged Godefroid; and he followed the Abbé de Vèze into Madame's room.

"Come with me," said Alain to Godefroid. "You have compelled us to tell you the secrets of Madame's life."

In a few minutes the two friends were together in Monsieur Alain's room, as they had been when the old man had told Godefroid his own history.

"Well," said Godefroid, whose face sufficiently showed his despair at having been the cause of what might be called a catastrophe in this pious household.

"I am waiting till Manon shall have come to say how she is going on," replied the good man, as he heard the woman's step on the stairs.

"Monsieur, Madame is better. Monsieur l'Abbé managed to deceive her as to what had been said," and Manon shot a wrathful glance at Godefroid.

"Good Heavens!" exclaimed the unhappy young man, his eyes filling with tears.

"Come, sit down," said Monsieur Alain, seating himself. Then he paused to collect his thoughts.

"I do not know," said the kind old man, "that I have the talent necessary to give a worthy narrative of a life so cruelly tried. You must forgive me if you find the words of so poor a speaker inadequate to the magnitude of the events and catastrophes. You must remember that it is a very long time since I was at school, and that I date from a time when thoughts were held of more importance than effect—from a prosaic age, when we knew not how to speak of things except by their names."

Godefroid bowed with an expression of assent, in which his worthy old friend could discern his sincere admiration, and which plainly said, "I am listening."

"As you have just perceived, my young friend, it would be impossible for you to remain one of us without learning some of the particulars of that saintly woman's life. There are certain ideas, allusions, words, which are absolutely prohibited in this house, since they inevitably reopen wounds, of which the anguish might kill Madame if it were once or twice revived—"

"Good Heavens!" exclaimed Godefroid, "what have I done?"

"But for Monsieur Joseph, who happily interrupted you just as you were about to speak of the awful instrument of death, you would have annihilated the poor lady.—It is time that you should be told all; for you will be one of us, of that we are all convinced."

"Madame de la Chanterie," he went on after a short pause, "is descended from one of the first families of Lower Normandy. Her maiden name was Mademoiselle Barbe-Philiberte de Champignelles—of a younger branch of that house; and she was intended to take the veil unless a marriage could be arranged for her with the usual renunciations of property that were commonly required in poor families of high rank. A certain Sieur de la Chanterie, whose family had sunk into utter obscurity, though dating from the time of Philippe-Auguste's crusade, was anxious to recover the rank to which so ancient a name gave him a claim in the province of Normandy. But he had fallen quite from his high estate, for he had made money—some three hundred thousand francs—by supplying the commissariat for the army at the time of the war with Hanover. His son, trusting too much to this wealth, which provincial rumour magnified, was living in Paris in a way calculated to cause the father of a family some uneasiness.

"Mademoiselle de Champignelles' great merits became famous throughout the district of le Bessin; and the old man, whose little feof of la Chanterie lay between Caen and Saint-Lô, heard some expressions of regret that so accomplished a young lady, and one so capable of making a husband happy, should end her days in a convent. On his uttering a wish to seek her out, some hope was given him that he might obtain the hand of Mademoiselle Philiberte for his son if he were content to renounce any marriage portion. He went to Bayeux, contrived to have two or three meetings with the Champignelles family, and was fascinated by the young lady's noble qualities.

"At the age of sixteen, Mademoiselle de Champignelles gave promise of what she would become. She evinced well-founded piety, sound good sense, inflexible rectitude—one of those natures which will never veer in its affections even if they are the outcome of duty. The old nobleman, enriched by his somewhat illicit gains, discerned in this charming girl a wife who might keep his son in order by the authority of virtue and the ascendency of a character that was firm but not rigid; for, as you have seen, no one can be gentler than Madame de la Chanterie. Then, no one could be more confiding; even in the decline of life she has the candour of innocence; in her youth she would not believe in evil; such distrust as you may have seen in her she owes to her misfortunes. The old man pledged himself to the Champignelles to give them a discharge in full for the portion legitimately due to Mademoiselle Philiberte on the signing of the marriage-contract; in return, the Champignelles, who were connected with the greatest families, promised to have the feof of la Chanterie created a barony, and they kept their word. The bridegroom's aunt, Madame de Boisfrelon, the wife of the councillor to the Parlement who died in your rooms, promised to leave her fortune to her nephew.

"When all these arrangements were completed between the two families, the father sent for his son. This young man, at the time of his marriage, was five-and-twenty, and already a Master of Appeals; he had indulged in numerous follies with the young gentlemen of the time, living in their style; and the old army contractor had several times paid his debts to a considerable amount. The poor father, foreseeing further dissipation on the son's part, was only too glad to settle a part of his fortune on his daughter-in-law; but he was so cautious as to entail the estate of la Chanterie on the heirs male of the marriage—"

"A precaution," added Monsieur Alain in a parenthesis, "which the Revolution made useless."

"As handsome as an angel, and wonderfully skilled in all athletic exercises, the young Master of Appeals had immense powers of charming," he went on. "So Mademoiselle de Champignelles, as you may easily imagine, fell very much in love with her husband. The old man, made very happy by this promising beginning, and hoping that his son was a reformed character, sent the young couple to Paris. This was early in 1788. For nearly a year they were perfectly happy. Madame de la Chanterie was the object of all the little cares, the most delicate attentions that a devoted lover can lavish on the one and only woman he loves. Brief as it was, the honeymoon beamed brightly on the heart of the noble and unfortunate lady.

"As you know, in those days mothers all nursed their infants themselves. Madame de la Chanterie had a daughter. This time, when a wife ought to be the object of double devotion on her husband's part, was, on the contrary, the beginning of dreadful woes. The Master of Appeals was obliged to sell everything he could part with to pay old debts which he had not confessed, and more recent gambling debts. Then, suddenly, the National Assembly dissolved the Supreme Council and the Parlement, and abolished all the great law appointments that had been so dearly purchased. Thus the young couple, with the addition of their child, had no income to rely on but the revenues from the entailed estate, and from the portion settled on Madame de la Chanterie. Twenty months after their marriage this charming woman, at the age of seventeen and a half, found herself reduced to maintaining herself and the child at her breast by the work of her hands, in an obscure street where she hid herself. She then found herself absolutely deserted by her husband, who fell step by step into the society of the very lowest kind. Never did she blame her husband, never did she put him in the least in the wrong. She has told us that all through the worst time she prayed to God for her dear Henri.

"The rascal's name was Henri," remarked Monsieur Alain. "It is a name that must never be spoken here, any more than that of Henriette.—To proceed:

"Madame de la Chanterie, who never quitted her little room in the Rue de la Corderie-du-Temple unless to buy food or fetch her work, kept her head above water, thanks partly to an allowance of a hundred francs a month from her father-in-law, who was touched by so much virtue. However, the poor young wife, foreseeing that this support might fail her, had taken up the laborious work of a staymaker, and worked for a famous dressmaker. In fact, ere long the old contractor died, and his estate was consumed by his son under favour of the overthrow of the Monarchy.

"The erewhile Master of Appeals, now one of the most savage of all the presidents of the revolutionary tribunal, had become a terror in Normandy, and could indulge all his passions. Then, imprisoned in his turn on the fall of Robespierre, the hatred of the department condemned him to inevitable death. Madame de la Chanterie received a farewell letter announcing her husband's fate. She immediately placed her little girl in the care of a neighbour, and went off to the town where the wretch was in confinement, taking with her a few louis, which constituted her whole fortune. This money enabled her to get into the prison. She succeeded in helping her husband to escape, dressing him in clothes of her own, under circumstances very similar to those which not long after favoured Madame de la Valette. She was condemned to death, but the authorities were ashamed to carry out this act of revenge, and she was secretly released with the connivance of the Court over which her husband had formerly presided. She got back to Paris on foot without any money, sleeping at farmhouses, and often fed by charity."

"Good Heavens!" exclaimed Godefroid.

"Wait," said the old man, "that was nothing.—In the course of eight years the poor woman saw her husband three times. The first time the gentleman spent twenty-four hours in his wife's humble lodgings, and went away with all her money, after heaping on her every mark of affection, and leading her to believe in his complete reformation.— 'For I could not resist,' said she, 'a man for whom I prayed every day, and who filled my thoughts exclusively.'—The second time Monsieur de la Chanterie came in a dying state, and from some horrible disease! She nursed him, and saved his life; then she tried to reclaim him to decent feeling and a seemly life. After promising everything this angel begged of him, the revolutionary relapsed into hideous debaucheries, and in fact only escaped prosecution by the authorities by taking refuge in his wife's rooms, where he died unmolested.

"Still, all this was nothing!" said Alain, seeing dismay in Godefroid's face.

"No one in the world he had mixed with had known that the man was married. Two years after the miserable creature's death, she heard that there was a second Madame de la Chanterie, widowed and ruined like herself. The bigamous villain had found two such angels incapable of betraying him.—Towards 1803," the old man went on after a pause, "Monsieur de Boisfrelon, Madame de la Chanterie's uncle, having his name removed from the list of proscribed persons, came back to Paris and paid over to her two hundred thousand francs that the old Commissariat contractor had placed in his keeping, with instructions to hold it in trust for his niece. He persuaded the widow to return to Normandy, where she completed her daughter's education, and, by the advice of the old lawyer, purchased back one of the family estates under very favourable conditions."

"Ah!" sighed Godefroid.

"Oh! all this was nothing!" said Monsieur Alain. 'We have not yet come to the hurricane.—To proceed. In 1807, after four years of peace, Madame de la Chanterie saw her only daughter married to a gentleman whose piety, whose antecedents, and fortune seemed a guarantee from every point of view; a man who was reported to be the 'pet lamb' of the best society in the country-town where Madame and her daughter spent every winter. Remark: this society consisted of seven or eight families belonging to the highest French nobility—the d'Esgrignons, the Troisvilles, the Casterans, the Nouâtres, and the like.

"At the end of eighteen months this man deserted his wife and vanished in Paris, having changed his name. Madame de la Chanterie could never discover the cause of this separation till the lightning flash showed it in the midst of the storm. Her daughter, whom she had brought up with the greatest care and the purest religious feelings, preserved absolute silence on the subject.

"This lack of confidence was a great shock to Madame de la Chanterie. Many times already she had detected in her daughter certain indications of the father's adventurous spirit, strengthened by an almost manly determination of character. The husband had departed without let or hindrance, leaving his affairs in the utmost disorder. To this day Madame de la Chanterie is amazed at this catastrophe, which no human power could remedy. All the persons she privately consulted had assured her before the marriage that the young man's fortune was clear and unembarrassed, in land unencumbered by mortgages, when, at that very time, the estate had, for ten years, been loaded with debt far beyond its value. So everything was sold, and the poor young wife, reduced to her own little income, came back to live with her mother.

"Madame de la Chanterie subsequently learned that this man had been kept going by the most respectable persons in the district for their own benefit, for the wretched man owed them all more or less considerable sums of money. Indeed, ever since her arrival in the province, Madame de la Chanterie had been regarded as a prey.

"However, there were other reasons for this climax of disaster, which you will understand from a confidential communication addressed to the Emperor.

"This man had long since succeeded in winning the good graces of the leading Royalists of the Department by his devotion to the cause during the stormiest days of the Revolution. As one of Louis XVIII's most active emissaries, he had, since 1793, been mixed up in every conspiracy, always withdrawing at the right moment, and with so much dexterity as to give rise at last to suspicions of his honour. The King dismissed him from service, and he was excluded from all further scheming, so he retired to his estate, already deeply involved. All these antecedents, at that time scarcely known—for those who were initiated into the secrets of the Cabinet did not say much about so dangerous a colleague—made him an object almost of worship in a town devoted to the Bourbons, where the cruellest devices of the Chouans were regarded as honest warfare. The Esgrignons, the Casterans, the Chevalier de Valois, in short, the Aristocracy and the Church, received the Royalist with open arms, and took him to their bosom. This favour was supported by his creditors' earnest desire to be paid.

"This wretch, a match for the deceased la Chanterie, was able to keep up his part for three years; he affected the greatest piety, and subjugated his vices. During the first few months of his married life he had some little influence over his wife;

he did his utmost to corrupt her by his doctrines, if atheism may be called a doctrine, and by the flippant tone in which he spoke of the most sacred things.

"This backstairs diplomate had, on his return to the country, formed an intimacy with a young man, over head and ears in debt, like himself, but attractive, in so far that he had as much courage and honesty as the other had shown hypocrisy and cowardice. This guest at his house—whose charm and character could not fail to impress a young woman, to say nothing of his adventurous career—was a tool in the husband's hands which he used to support his infamous principles. The daughter never confessed to her mother the gulf into which circumstances had thrown her—for human prudence is no word for the caution exercised by Madame de la Chanterie when seeking a husband for her only child. And this last blow, in a life so devoted, so guileless, so religious as hers, tested as she had been by every kind of misfortune, filled Madame de la Chanterie with a distrust of herself which isolated her from her daughter; all the more so because her daughter, in compensation for her ill-fortune, insisted on perfect liberty, overruled her mother, and was sometimes very rough with her.

"Thus wounded in every feeling, cheated alike in her devotion and her love for her husband—to whom she had sacrificed her happiness, her fortune, and her life, without a murmur; cheated in the exclusively religious training she had given her daughter; cheated by the world, even in the matter of that daughter's marriage, and meeting with no justice from the heart in which she had implanted none but right feelings, she turned more resolutely to God, clinging to Him whose hand lay so heavy on her. She was almost a nun; she went to mass every morning, carried out monastic discipline, and saved in everything to be able to help the poor.

"Has any woman ever known a more saintly or more severely tried life than this noble creature, so mild to the unfortunate, so brave in danger, and always so perfect a Christian?" said the worthy man, appealing to Godefroid. "You know Madame, you know whether she is deficient in sense, judgment, and reflection. She has all these qualities in the highest degree. Well, and still all these misfortunes, which surely were enough to qualify any life as surpassing all others in adversity, were a trifle compared with what God had yet in store for this woman.—We will speak only of Madame de la Chanterie's daughter," said Monsieur Alain, going on with his narrative.

"At the age of eighteen, when she married, Mademoiselle de la Chanterie had an extremely delicate complexion, rather dark, with a brilliant colour, a slender form, and charming features. An elegantly formed brow was crowned by the most beautiful black hair, that matched well with bright and lively hazel eyes. A peculiar prettiness and a childlike countenance belied her real nature and masculine decisiveness. She had small hands and feet; in all her person there was something tiny and frail, which excluded any idea of strength and wilfulness. Never having lived away from her mother, her mind was absolutely innocent, and her piety remarkable.

"This young lady, like Madame de la Chanterie, was fanatically devoted to the Bourbons, and hated the Revolution; she regarded Napoleon's empire as a plague inflicted on France by Providence, as a punishment for the crimes of 1793. Such a conformity of opinion between the lady and her son-in-law was, as it always must be in such cases, a conclusive reason in favour of the marriage, in which all the aristocracy of the province took the greatest interest.

"This wretched man's friend had at the time of the rebellion in 1799 been the leader of a troop of Chouans. It would seem that the Baron—for Madame de la Chanterie's son-in-law was a Baron—had no object in throwing his wife and his friend together but that of extracting money from them. Though deeply in debt, and without any means of living, the young adventurer lived in very good style, and was able, no doubt, to help the promoter of royalist conspiracies.

"Here you will need a few words of explanation as to an association which made a great noise in its day," said Monsieur Alain, interrupting his narrative. "I mean that of the raiders known as the *Chauffeurs*. These brigands pervaded all the western provinces more or less; but their object was not so much pillage as a revival of the Royalist opposition. Advantage was taken of the very general resistance of the people to the law of conscription, which, as you know, was enforced with many abuses. Between Mortagne and Rennes, and even beyond, as far as the Loire, nocturnal raids were frequent, commonly to the injury of those who held national lands. These bands of destroyers were the terrors of the country. I am not exaggerating when I tell you that in some Departments the arm of Justice was practically paralysed. Those last thunders of civil war did not echo so far as you might suppose, accustomed as we now are to the startling publicity given by the press to the most trivial acts of political and private life. The Censor allowed nothing to appear in print that bore on polities, unless it were accomplished fact, and even that was distorted. If you will take the trouble to look through old files of the *Moniteur* and other newspapers, even those issued in the western provinces, you will find not a word concerning the four or five great trials which brought sixty or eighty of these rebels to the scaffold. *Brigands*, this was the name given under the Revolution to the Vendéans, the Chouans, and all who took up arms for the house of Bourbon; and it was still given in legal phraseology under the Empire to the Royalists who were victims to sporadic conspiracies. For to some vehement souls the Emperor and his government were 'the Enemy,' and everything seemed good that was adverse to him.—I am explaining the position, not justifying the opinions, and I will now go on with my story.

"So now," he said, after a pause, such as must occur in a long story, "you must understand that these Royalists were ruined by the war of 1793, though consumed by frantic passions; and if you can conceive of some exceptional natures consumed also by such necessities as those of Madame de la Chanterie's son-in-law and his friend the Chouan leader, you will see how it was that they determined to commit, for their private advantage, acts of robbery which their political opinions would justify, against the Imperial government for the advantage of the Cause.

"The young leader set to work to fan the ashes of the Chouan faction, to be ready to act at an opportune moment. There was, soon after, a terrible crisis in the Emperor's affairs when he was shut up in the island of Lobau, and it seemed that he must inevitably succumb to a simultaneous attack by England and by Austria. The victory of Wagram made the internal rebellion all but abortive. This attempt to revive the fires of civil war in Brittany, la Vendée, and part of Normandy, was unfortunately coincident with the Baron's money difficulties; he had flattered himself that he could contrive a separate expedition, of which the profits could be applied solely to redeem his property. But his wife and friend, with nobler feeling, refused to divert to private uses any sums that might be snatched at the sword's point from the State coffers; these were to be distributed to the rebel conscripts and Chouans, and to purchase weapons and ammunition to arm a general rising.

"At last, when after heated discussions the young Chouan, supported by the Baroness, positively refused to retain a hundred thousand francs in silver crowns which was to be seized from one of the Government Receivers' offices in the west to provide for the Royalist forces, the husband disappeared, to escape the execution on his person of several writs that were out against him. The creditors tried to extract payment from his wife, but the wretched man had dried up the spring of affection which prompts a woman to sacrifice herself for her husband.

"All this was kept from poor Madame de la Chanterie, but it was a trifle in comparison with the plot that lay behind this merely preliminary explanation.

"It is too late this evening," said the good man, looking at the clock, "and there is too much still to tell, to allow of my going on with the rest of the story. My old friend Bordin, who was made famous as a Royalist by his share in the great Simeuse trial, and who pleaded in the case of the *Chauffeurs* of Mortagne, gave me when I came to live here two documents which, as he died not long after, I still have in my possession. You will there find the facts set forth much more concisely than I could give them. The details are so complicated that I should lose myself in trying to state them, and it would take me more than two hours, while in these papers you will find them summarised. To-morrow morning I will tell you what remains to be told concerning Madame de la Chanterie, for when you have read these documents you will be sufficiently informed for me to conclude my tale in a few words."

He placed some papers, yellow with years, in Godefroid's hands; after bidding his neighbour good-night, the young man retired to his room, and before he went to sleep read the two documents here reproduced:

"Bill Of Indictment.

"Court of Criminal and Special Justice for the Department of the Orne.

"The Public Prosecutor to the Imperial Court of Justice at Caen, appointed to carry out his functions to the Special Criminal Court sitting by the Imperial decree of September 1809, in the town of Alençon, sets forth to the Court the following facts, as proved by the preliminary proceedings, to wit:

"That a conspiracy of brigands, hatched for a long time with extraordinary secrecy, and connected with a scheme for a general rising in the western departments, has vented itself in several attempts on the lives and property of citizens, and more especially in the attack with robbery, under arms, on a vehicle conveying, on the — of May, 18—, the Government moneys collected at Caen. This attack, recalling in its details the memories of the civil war now so happily at an end, showed deep-laid designs of a degree of villainy which cannot be excused by the vehemence of passion.

"From its inception to the end, the plot is extremely complicated, and the details numerous. The preliminary examinations lasted for more than a year, but the evidence forthcoming at every stage of the crime throws full light on the preparations made, on its execution, and results.

"The first idea of the plot was conceived by one Charles-Amédée-Louis-Joseph Rifoël, calling himself the Chevalier du Vissard, born at le Vissard, a hamlet of Saint-Mexme by Ernée, and formerly a leader of the rebels.

"This man, who was pardoned by His Majesty the Emperor at the time of the general peace and amnesty, and whose ingratitude to his sovereign has shown itself in fresh crimes, has already suffered the extreme penalty of the law as the punishment for his misdeeds; but it is necessary here to refer to some of his actions, as he had great influence over some of the accused now awaiting the verdict of justice, and he is concerned in every circumstance of the case.

"This dangerous agitator, who bore an alias, as is common with these rebels, and was known as *Pierrot*, used to wander about the western provinces enlisting partisans for a fresh rebellion; but his safest lurking-place was the château of Saint-Savin, the home of a woman named Lechantre and her daughter named Bryond, a house in the hamlet of Saint-Savin and in the district of Mortagne. This spot is famous in the most horrible annals of the rebellion of 1799. It was there that a courier was murdered, and his chaise plundered by a band of brigands under the command of a woman, helped by the notorious Marche-à-Terre. Hence brigandage may be said to be endemic in this neighbourhood.

"An intimacy for which we seek no name had existed for more than a year between the woman Bryond and the above-named Rifoël.

"It was close to this spot that, in the month of April 1808, an interview took place between Rifoël and one Boislaurier, a superior leader, known in the more serious risings in the west by the name of Auguste, and he it was who was the moving spirit of the rising now under the consideration of the Court.

"This obscure point, namely, the connection of these two leaders, is plainly proved by the evidence of numerous witnesses, and also stands as a demonstrated fact by the sentence of death carried out on Rifoël. From the time of that meeting, Boislaurier and Rifoël agreed to act in concert.

"They communicated to each other, and at first to no one else, their atrocious purpose, founded on his Royal and Imperial Majesty's absence, in command, at the time, of his forces in Spain; and then, or soon after, they must have plotted to capture the State moneys in transit, as the base for further operations.

"Some time later, one Dubut of Caen despatched a messenger to the château of Saint-Savin, namely, one Hiley, known as le Laboureur, long known as a robber of the diligences; he was charged with information as to trustworthy accomplices.

And it was thus, by Hiley's intervention, that the plot secured the co-operation from the first of one Herbomez, called Général-Hardi, a pardoned rebel of the same stamp as Rifoël, and, like him, a traitor to the amnesty.

"Herbomez and Hiley recruited in the neighbouring villages seven banditti, whose names must at once be set forth as follows:

"1. Jean Cibot, called Pille-Miche, one of the boldest brigands of a troop got together by Montauran in the year VII, and one of the actors in the robbery and murder of the Mortagne courier.

"2. Francois Lisieux, known as Grand-Fils, a rebel-conscript of the department of the Mayenne.

"3. Charles Grenier, or Fleur-de-Genet, a deserter from the 69th half-brigade.

"4. Gabriel Bruce, known as Gros-Jean, one of the fiercest Chouans of Fontaine's division.

"5. Jacques Horeau, called Stuart, ex-lieutenant of that brigade, one of Tinténiac's adherents, and well known by the share he took in the Quiberon expedition.

"6. Marie-Anne Cabot, called Lajeunesse, formerly huntsman to the Sieur Carol of Alençon.

"7. Louis Minard, a rebel conscript.

"These, when enrolled, were quartered in three different hamlets in the houses of Binet, Mélin, and Laravinière, inn or tavern-keepers, all devoted to Rifoël.

"The necessary weapons were at once provided by one Jean-François Léveillé, a notary, and the incorrigible abettor of the brigands, serving as a go-between for them with several leaders in hiding; and, in this town, by one Felix Courceuil, called the Confesseur, formerly surgeon to the rebel army of la Vendée; both these men are natives of Alençon. Eleven muskets were concealed in a house belonging to Bryond in a suburb of Alençon; but this was done without his knowledge, for he was at that time living in the country on his estate between Alençon and Mortagne.

"When Bryond left his wife to go her own way in the fatal road she had set out on, these muskets, cautiously removed from the house, were carried by the woman Bryond in her own carriage to the château of Saint-Savin.

"It was then that the Department of the Orne and adjacent districts were dismayed by acts of highway robbery that startled the authorities as much as the inhabitants of those districts which had so long enjoyed quiet; and these raids prove that the atrocious foes of the Government and the Empire had been kept informed of the secret coalition of 1809 by means of communications from abroad.

"Léveillé the notary, the woman Bryond, Dubut of Caen, Herbomez of Mayenne, Boislaurier of le Mans, and Rifoël were the ringleaders of the association, which was also joined by those criminals who have been already executed under the sentence passed on them with Rifoël, by those accused under this trial, and by several others who have escaped public vengeance by flight, or by the silence of their accomplices.

"It was Dubut who, as a resident near Caen, gave notice to Léveillé of the despatch of the money. Dubut made several journeys between Caen and Mortagne, and Léveillé also was often on the roads. It may here be noted that, at the time when the arms were moved, Léveillé, who came to visit Bruce, Grenier, and Cibot at Mélin's house, found them arranging the muskets in an inside shed, and helped them himself in doing so.

"A general meeting was arranged to take place at Mortagne at the *Écu de France* inn. All the accused were present in various disguises. It was on this occasion that Léveillé, the woman Bryond, Dubut, Herbomez, Boislaurier, and Hiley, the cleverest of the subordinate conspirators, of whom Cibot is the most daring, secured the co-operation of one Vauthier, called Vieux-Chêne, formerly a servant to the notorious Longuy, and now a stableman at the inn. Vauthier agreed to give the woman Bryond due notice of the passing of the chaise conveying the Government moneys, as it commonly stopped to bait at the inn.

"The opportunity ere long offered for assembling the brigand recruits who had been scattered about in various lodgings with great precaution, sometimes in one village, and sometimes in another, under the care of Courceuil and of Léveillé. The assembly was managed by the woman Bryond, who afforded the brigands a new hiding-place in the uninhabited parts of the château of Saint-Savin, at a few miles from Mortagne, where she had lived with her mother since her husband's departure. The brigands established themselves there with Hiley at their head, and spent several days there. The woman Bryond, with her waiting-maid Godard, took care to prepare with her own hands everything needed for lodging and feeding these guests. To this end she had trusses of hay brought in, and went to see the brigands in the shelter she had arranged for them, going to and fro with Léveillé. Provisions and victuals were procured under the orders and care of Courceuil, who took his orders from Rifoël and Boislaurier.

"The principal feat was decided on and the men fully armed; the brigands stole out of Saint-Savin every night; pending the transit of the Government chest, they carried out raids in the neighborhood, and the whole country was in terror under their repeated incursions. There can be no doubt that the robberies committed at La Sartinière, at Vonay, and at the château of Saint-Seny were the work of this band; their daring equalled their villainy, and they contrived to terrify their victims so effectually that no tales were told, so that justice could obtain no evidence.

"While levying contributions on all who held possession of the nationalised land, the brigands carefully reconnoitred the woods of Le Chesnay, which they had chosen to be the scene of their crime.

"Not far away is the village of Louvigny, where there is an inn kept by the brothers Chaussard, formerly gamekeepers on the property of Troisville, and this was to be the brigands' final rendezvous. The two brothers knew beforehand the part they were to play; Courceuil and Boislaurier had long before sounded them, and revived their hatred of the government of our august Emperor; and had told them that among the visitors who would drop in on them would be some men of their acquaintance—the formidable Hiley and the not less formidable Cibot.

"In fact, on the 6th the seven highwaymen, under the leadership of Hiley, arrived at the brother Chaussards' inn and spent two days there. On the 8th the chief led out his men, saying they were going three leagues away, and he desired the innkeepers to provide food, which was taken to a place where the roads met, a little way from the village. Hiley came home alone at night.

"Two riders—who were probably the woman Bryond and Rifoël, for it is said that she accompanied him in his expeditions, on horseback, and dressed as a man—arrived that evening and conversed with Hiley. On the following day Hiley wrote to Léveillé the notary; and one of the Chaussard brothers carried the letter and brought back the answer. Two hours later Bryond and Rifoël came on horseback to speak with Hiley.

"The upshot of all these interviews and coming and going was that a hatchet was indispensable to break open the cases. The notary went back with the woman Bryond to Saint-Savin, where they sought in vain for a hatchet.

"Thereupon he returned to the inn and met Hiley half-way, to whom he was to explain that no hatchet was to be found. Hiley made his way back and ordered supper at the inn for ten persons; he then brought in the seven brigands all armed. Hiley made them pile arms like soldiers. They all sat down and supped in haste, Hiley ordering a quantity of food to be packed for them to take away with them. Then he led the elder Chaussard aside and asked for a hatchet.

The innkeeper, much astonished, by his own account, refused to give him one. Courceuil and Boislaurier presently came in, and the three men spent the whole night pacing up and down the room and discussing their plan. Courceuil, nicknamed the Confessor, the most cunning of the band, took possession of a hatchet, and at about two in the morning they all went out by different doors.

"Every minute was now precious; the execution of the crime was fixed for that day. Hiley, Courceuil, and Boislaurier placed their men. Hiley, with Minard, Cabot, and Bruce, formed an ambush to the right of the wood of Le Chesnay. Boislaurier, Grenier, and Horeau occupied the centre. Courceuil, Herbomez, and Lisieux stood by the ravine under the fringe of the wood. All these positions are indicated on the subjoined plan to scale, drawn by the surveyor to the Government.

"The chaise, meanwhile, had started from Mortagne at about one in the morning, driven by one Rousseau, who was so far inculpated by circumstantial evidence as to make it seem desirable to arrest him. The vehicle, driving slowly, would reach the wood of Le Chesnay by about three. It was guarded by a single gendarme; the men were to breakfast at Donnery. There were three travellers, as it happened, besides the gendarme.

"The driver, who had been walking with them very slowly, on reaching the bridge of Le Chesnay, whipped the horses to a speed and energy that the others remarked upon, and turned into a cross-road known as the Senzey road. The chaise was soon lost to sight; the way it had gone was known to the gendarme and his companions only by the sound of the horses' bells; the men had to run to come up with it. Then they heard a shout: 'Stand, you rascals!' and four shots were fired.

"The gendarme, who was not hit, drew his sword and ran on in the direction he supposed the driver to have taken. He was stopped by four men, who all fired; his eagerness saved him, for he rushed past to desire one of the young travellers to run on and have the alarm bell tolled at Le Chesnay, but two of the brigands took steady aim, advancing towards him; he was forced to draw back a few steps; and just as he was about to turn the wood, he received a ball in the left armpit, which broke his arm; he fell, and found himself completely disabled.

"The shouting and shots had been heard at Donnery. The officer in command at this station hurried up with one of his gendarmes; a running fire led them away to the side of the wood furthest from the scene of the robbery. The single gendarme tried to intimidate the brigands by a hue and cry, and to delude them into the belief that a force was at hand.

"'Forward!' he cried. 'First platoon to the right! now we have them! Second platoon to the left!'

"The brigands on their side shouted, 'Draw! This way, comrades! Send up the men as fast as you can!'

"The noise of firing hindered the officer from hearing the cries of the wounded gendarme, and helping in the manoeuvre by which the other was keeping the robbers in check; but he could hear a clatter close at hand, arising from splitting the cases open. He advanced towards that side; four armed men took aim at him, and he called out, 'Surrender, villains!'

"They only replied, 'Stand, or you are a dead man!'

"He rushed forward; two muskets were fired, and he was hit, one ball going through his left leg into his horse's flank. The brave man, bleeding profusely, was forced to retire from the unequal struggle, shouting, but in vain, 'Help—come on—the brigands are at Le Chesnay.'

"The robbers, left masters of the field by superiority of numbers, pillaged the chaise which had been intentionally driven into a ravine. They blindfolded the driver, but this was only a feint. The chests were forced open, and bags of money strewed the ground. The horses were unharnessed and loaded with the coin. Three thousand francs' worth of copper money was scornfully left behind; three hundred thousand francs were carried off on four horses. They made for the village of Menneville adjacent to the town of Saint Savin.

"The horde and their booty stopped at a solitary house belonging to the Chaussard brothers, inhabited by their uncle, one Bourget, who had been in their confidence from the first. This old man, helped by his wife, received the brigands, warned them to be silent, unloaded the beasts, and then fetched up some wine. The wife remained on sentry by the château. The old man led the horses back to the wood and returned them to the driver; then he released the two young men who had been gagged as well as the accommodating driver. After refreshing themselves in great haste, the brigands went on their way. Courceuil, Hiley, and Boislaurier reviewed their party, and after bestowing on each a trifling recompense, sent off the men, each in a different direction.

"On reaching a spot called le Champ-Landry, these malefactors, obeying the prompting which so often leads such wretches into blunders and miscalculations, threw their muskets away into a field of standing corn. The fact that all three did so at the same time is a crowning proof of their collusion. Then, terrified by the boldness and success of their crime, they separated.

"The robbery having been committed, with the additional features of violence and attempt to murder, the chain of subsidiary events was already in preparation, and other actors were implicated in receiving and disposing of the stolen property. Rifoël, hidden in Paris, whence he pulled all the wires of the plot, sent an order to Léveillé to forward to him immediately fifty thousand francs. Courceuil, apt at the management of such felonies, had sent off Hiley to inform Léveillé of their success and of his arrival at Mortagne, where the notary at once joined them.

"Vauthier, to whose fidelity they believed they might trust, undertook to find the Chaussards' uncle; he went to the house, but was told by the old man that he must apply to the nephews, who had given over large sums to the woman Bryond. However, he bid Vauthier wait for him on the road, and he there gave him a bag containing twelve hundred francs, which Vauthier took to the woman Lechantre for her daughter.

"By Léveillé's advice Courceuil then went to Bourget, who sent him direct to his nephews. The elder Chaussard led Vauthier to the wood and showed him a tree beneath which a bag of a thousand francs was found buried. In short, Léveillé, Hiley, and Vauthier went to and fro several times, and each time obtained a small sum, trifling in comparison with the whole amount stolen.

"These moneys were handed over to the woman Lechantre at Mortagne; and, in obedience to a letter from her daughter, she carried them to Saint-Savin, whither the said Bryond had returned.

"It is not immediately necessary to inquire whether this woman Lechantre had any previous knowledge of the plot. For the present it need only be noted that she had left Mortagne to go to Saint-Savin the day before the crime was committed in order to fetch away her daughter; that the two women met half-way, and returned to Mortagne; that, on the following day, the notary, being informed of this by Hiley, went from Alençon to Mortagne, and straight to their house, where he persuaded them to transport the money, obtained with so much difficulty from the Chaussards and from Bourget, to a certain house in Alençon, presently to be mentioned as belonging to one Pannier, a merchant there. The woman Lechantre wrote to the man in charge at Saint-Savin to come to Mortagne and escort her and her daughter by cross-roads to Alençon. The money, amounting to twenty thousand francs in all, was packed into a vehicle at night, the girl Godard helping to dispose of it.

"The notary had planned the way they were to travel. They reached an inn kept by one of their allies, a man named Louis Chargegrain, in the hamlet of Littray. But in spite of the notary's precautions—he riding ahead of the chaise—some strangers were present and saw the portmanteaus and bags taken out which contained the coin.

"But just as Courceuil and Hiley, disguised as women, were consulting, in the market place at Alençon, with the afore-named Pannier—who since 1794 had been the rebels' treasurer, and who was devoted to Rifoël—as to the best means of transmitting the required sum to Rifoël, the terror occasioned by the arrests and inquiries already made was so great that the woman Lechantre, in her alarm, set off at night from the inn where they were, and fled with her daughter by country byways, leaving Léveillé behind, and took refuge in the hiding-places known to them in the château Saint-Savin. The same alarm came over the other criminals. Courceuil, Boislaurier, and his relation Dubut exchanged two thousand francs in silver for gold at a dealer's, and fled across Brittany to England.

"On arriving at Saint-Savin, the mother and daughter heard that Bourget was arrested with the driver and the runaway conscripts.

"The magistrates, the police, and the authorities acted with so much decision, that it was deemed necessary to protect the woman Bryond from their investigations, for all these felons were devotedly attached to her, and she had won them all. So she was removed from Saint-Savin, and hid at first at Alençon, where her adherents held council and succeeded in concealing her in Pannier's cellars.

"Hereupon fresh incidents occurred. After the arrest of Bourget and his wife, the Chaussards refused to give up any more money, saying they had been betrayed. This unexpected defection fell out at the very moment when all the conspirators were in the greatest need of supplies, if only as a means of escape. Rifoël was thirsting for money. Hiley, Cibot, and Léveillé now began to doubt the honesty of the two Chaussards. This led to a fresh complication which seems to demand the intervention of the law.

"Two gendarmes, commissioned to discover the woman Bryond, succeeded in getting into Pannier's house, where they were present at a council held by the criminals; but these men, false to the confidence placed in them, instead of arresting Bryond, were enslaved by her charms. These rascally soldiers—named Ratel and Mallet—showed the woman every form of interest and devotion, and offered to escort her to the Chaussards' inn and compel them to make restitution. The woman went off on horseback, dressed as a man, and accompanied by Ratel, Mallet, and the maid-servant Godard. She set out at night, and on reaching the inn she and one of the Chaussard brothers had a private but animated interview. She had a pistol, and was resolved to blow her accomplice's brains out in case of his refusal; in fact, he led her to the wood, and she brought back a heavy sack. In it she found copper coin and twelve-sou pieces to the value of fifteen hundred francs.

"It was then suggested that as many of the conspirators as could be got together should take the Chaussards by surprise, seize them, and put them to torture. Pannier, on hearing of this disappointment, flew into a rage and broke out in threats; and though the woman Bryond threatened him in return with Rifoël's vengeance, she was compelled to fly.

"All these facts were confessed by Ratel.

"Mallet, touched by her position, offered the woman Bryond a place of shelter; they all set off together and spent the night in the wood of Troisville. Then Mallet and Ratel, with Hiley and Cibot, went by night to the Chaussards' inn, but they found that the brothers had left the place, and that the remainder of the money had certainly been removed.

"This was the last attempt on the part of the conspirators to recover the stolen money.

"It is now important to define more accurately the part played by each of the criminals implicated in this affair.

"Dubut, Boislaurier, Gentil, Herbomez, Courceuil, and Hiley are all leaders, some in council, and some in action. Boislaurier, Dubut, and Courceuil, all three contumacious deserters, are habitual rebels, stirring up troubles, the implacable foes of Napoleon the Great, of his successes, his dynasty, and his government, of our new code of laws and of the Imperial constitution. Herbomez and Hiley, as their right-hand men, boldly carried out what the three others planned. The guilt of the seven instruments of the crime is beyond question—Cibot, Lisieux, Grenier, Bruce, Horeau, Cabot, and Minard. It is proved by the depositions of those who are now in the hands of justice: Lisieux died during the preliminary inquiry, and Bruce has evaded capture.

"The conduct of the chaise-driver Rousseau marks him as an accomplice. The slow progress on the highroad, the pace to which he flogged the horses on reaching the wood, his persistent statement that his head was muffled, whereas, by the evidence of the young fellow-travellers, the leader of the brigands had the handkerchief removed and ordered him to recognise the men,—all contribute to afford presumptive evidence of his collusion.

"As to the woman Bryond and Léveillé the notary, their complicity was constant and continuous from the first. They supplied funds and means for the crime; they knew of it and abetted it. Léveillé was constantly travelling to and fro. The woman Bryond invented plot upon plot; she risked everything—even her life—to secure the money. She lent her house, her carriage, and was concerned in the plot from the beginning, nor did she attempt to persuade the chief leader to desist from it when she might have exerted her evil influence to hinder it. She led the maid-servant Godard into its toils. Léveillé was so entirely mixed up in it, that it was he who tried to procure the hatchet needed by the robbers.

"The woman Bourget, Vauthier, the Chaussards, Pannier, the woman Lechantre, Mallet, and Ratel were all incriminated in various degrees, as also the innkeepers Mélin, Binet, Laravinière, and Chargegrain.

"Bourget died during the preliminary inquiry, after making a confession which leaves no doubt as to the part taken by Vauthier and the woman Bryond; and though he tried to mitigate the charge against his wife and his nephews the Chaussards, the reasons for his reticence are self-evident.

"But the Chaussards certainly knew that they were supplying provisions to highway robbers; they saw that the men were armed and were informed of all their scheme; they allowed them to take the hatchet needed for breaking open the chests, knowing the purpose for which it was required. Finally, they received wittingly the money obtained by the robbery, they hid it, and in fact made away with the greater part of it.

"Pannier, formerly treasurer to the rebel party, concealed the woman Bryond; he is one of the most dangerous participators in the plot of which he was informed from its origin. With regard to him we are in the dark as to some circumstances as yet unknown, but of which justice will take cognizance. He is Rifoël's immediate ally and in all the secrets of the ante-revolutionary party in the West; he greatly regretted the fact that Rifoël should have admitted the women into the plot or have trusted them at all. He forwarded money to Rifoël and received the stolen coin.

"As to the two gendarmes, Ratel and Mallet, their conduct deserves the utmost rigour of the law. They were traitors to their duty. One of them, foreseeing his fate, committed suicide after making some important revelations. The other, Mallet, denied nothing, and his confession removes all doubt.

"The woman Lechantre, in spite of her persistent denials, was informed of everything. The hypocrisy of this woman, who attempts to shelter her professed innocence under the practice of assumed devotion, is known by her antecedents to be prompt and intrepid in extremities. She asserts that she was deceived by her daughter, and believed that the money in question belonged to the man Bryond. The trick is too transparent. If Bryond had had any money, he would not have fled from the neighborhood to avoid witnessing his own ruin. Lechantre considered that there was no harm in the robbery when it was approved of by her ally Boislaurier. But how, then, does she account for Rifoël's presence at Saint-Savin, her daughter's expeditions and connection with the man, and the visit of the brigands who were waited on by the women Godard and Bryond? She says she sleeps heavily, and is in the habit of going to bed at seven o'clock, and did not know what answer to make when the examining Judge observed that then she must rise at daybreak and could not have failed to discern traces of the plot and of the presence of so many men, or to be uneasy about her daughter's nocturnal expeditions. To this she could only say that she was at her prayers.

"The woman is a model hypocrite. In fact, her absence on the day when the crime was committed, the care she took to remove her daughter to Mortagne, her journey with the money, and her precipitate flight when everything was discovered, the care with which she hid herself, and the circumstances of her arrest, all prove her complicity from an early stage of the affair. Her conduct was not that of a mother anxious to explain the danger to her daughter and to save her from it, but that of a terrified accomplice; and she was an accessory, not out of foolish affection, but from party spirit inspired by hatred, as is well known, for his Imperial Majesty's government. Maternal weakness indeed could not excuse her, and it must not be forgotten that consent, long premeditated, is an evident sign of her complicity.

"Not the crime alone, but its moving spirits, are now known. We see in it the monstrous combination of the delirium of faction with a thirst for rapine; murder prompted by party spirit, under which men take shelter, and justify themselves for the most disgraceful excesses. The orders of the leaders gave the signal for the robbery of State moneys to pay for subsequent violence; base and ferocious hirelings were found to do it for wretched pay, and fully prepared to murder; while the agitators to rebellion, not less guilty, helped in dividing and concealing the booty. What society can allow such attempts to go unpunished? The law has no adequate punishment.

"The Bench of this Criminal and Special Court, then, will be called upon to decide whether the afore-named Herbomez, Hiley, Cibot, Grenier, Horeau, Cabot, Minard, Mélin, Binet, Laravinière, Rousseau, the woman Bryond, Léveillé, the woman Bourget, Vauthier, the elder Chaussard, Pannier, the widow

Lechantre, and Mallet, all hereinbefore described and in presence of the Court, and the afore-named Boislaurier, Dubut, Courceuil, Bruce, Chaussard the younger, Chargegrain, and the girl Godard, being absent or having fled, are or are not guilty of the acts described in this bill of indictment.

"Given in to the Court at Caen the 1st of December, 180—

"(*Signed*) BARON BOURLAC."

This legal document, much shorter and more peremptory than such bills of indictment are in these days, so full of detail and so complete on every point, especially as to the previous career of the accused, excited Godefroid to the utmost. The bare, dry style of an official pen, setting forth, in red ink, as it were, the principal facts of the case, was enough to set his imagination working. Concise, reserved narrative is to some minds a problem in which they lose themselves in exploring the mysterious depths.

In the dead of night, stimulated by the silence, by the darkness, by the dreadful connection hinted at by Monsieur Main of this document with Madame de la Chanterie, Godefroid concentrated all his intelligence on the consideration of this terrible affair.

The name of Lechantre was evidently the first name of the la Chanterie family, whose aristocratic titular name had of course been curtailed under the Republic and the Empire.

His fancy painted the scenery where the drama was played out, and the figures of the accomplices rose before him. Imagination showed him, not indeed "the afore-named Rifoël," but the Chevalier du Vissard, a youth resembling Walter Scott's Fergus—in short, a French edition of the Jacobite. He worked out a romance on the passion of a young girl grossly betrayed by her husband's infamy—a tragedy then very fashionable—and in love with a young leader rebelling against the Emperor; rushing headlong, like Diana Vernon, into the toils of a conspiracy, fired with enthusiasm, and then, having started on the perilous descent, unable to check her wild career—Had she ended it on the scaffold?

The whole world seemed to rise before Godefroid. He was wandering through the groves of Normandy; he could see the Breton gentleman and Madame Bryond in the copse; he dwelt in the old château of Saint-Savin; he pictured the winning over of so many conspirators—the notary, the merchant, and the bold Chouan leaders. He could understand the almost unanimous adhesion of a district where the memory was still fresh of the famous Marche-à-Terre, of the Comtes de Bauvan and de Longuy, of the massacre at la Vivetière, and of the death of the Marquis de Montauran, of whose exploits he had heard from Madame de la Chanterie.

This vision, as it were, of men and things and places, was but brief. As he realised the fact that this story was that of the noble and pious old lady whose virtues affected him to the point of a complete metamorphosis, Godefroid, with a thrill of awe, took up the second document given to him by Monsieur Alain, which bore the title:

"AN APPEAL ON BEHALF OF MADAME HENRIETTE BRYOND DES TOURS-MINIÈRES, *née* LECHANTRE DE LA CHANTERIE."

"That settles it," thought Godefroid.

The paper ran as follows:

"We are condemned and guilty; but if ever the Sovereign had cause to exercise his prerogative of mercy, would it not be under the circumstances herein set forth?

"The culprit is a young woman, who says she is a mother, and is condemned to death.

"On the threshold of the prison, and in view of the scaffold, this woman will tell the truth. That statement will be in her favour, and to that she looks for pardon.

"The case, tried in the Criminal Court of Alençon, presents some obscure features, as do all cases where several accused persons have combined in a plot inspired by party feeling.

"His Imperial and Kingly Majesty's Privy Council are now fully informed as to the identity of a mysterious personage, known as *le Marchand*, whose presence in the department of the Orne was not disputed by the public authorities in the course of the trial, though the pleader for the Crown did not think it advisable to produce him in Court, and the defendants had no right to call him, nor, indeed, power to produce him.

"This man, as is well known to the Bench, to the local authorities, to the Paris police, and to the Imperial and Royal Council, is Bernard-Polydor Bryond de la Tour-Minières, who, since 1794, has been in correspondence with the Comte de Lille; he is known abroad as the Baron des Tours-Minières, and in the records of the Paris police as Contenson.

"He is a very exceptional man, whose youth and rank were stained by unremitting vice, such utter immorality and such criminal excesses, that so infamous a life would inevitably have ended on the scaffold but for the skill with which he played a double part under shelter of his two names. Still, as he is more and more the slave of his passions and insatiable necessities, he will at last fall below infamy, and find himself in the lowest depths in spite of indisputable gifts and an extraordinary mind.

"When the Comte de Lille's better judgment led to his forbidding Bryond to draw money from abroad, the man tried to get out of the blood-stained field on to which his necessities had led him. Was it that this career no longer paid him well enough? Or was it remorse or shame that led the man back to the district where his estates, loaded with debt when he went away, could have but little to yield even to his skill? This it is impossible to believe. It seems more probable that he had some mission to fulfil in those departments where some sparks were still lingering of the civil broils.

"When wandering through the provinces, where his perfidious adhesion to the schemes of the English and of the Comte de Lille gained him the confidence of certain families still attached to the party that the genius of our immortal Emperor has reduced to silence, he met one of the former leaders of the Rebellion—a man with whom he had had dealings as an envoy from abroad at the time of the Quiberon expedition, during the last rising in the year VII. He encouraged the hopes of this agitator, who has since paid the penalty of his treasonable plots on the scaffold. At that time, then, Bryond was able to learn all the secrets of the incorrigible faction who misprize the glory of His Majesty the Emperor Napoleon I., and the true interests of the country as represented by his sacred person.

"At the age of five-and-thirty, this man, who affected the deepest piety, who professed unbounded devotion to the interests of the Comte de Lille, and perfect adoration for the rebels of the West who perished in the struggle, who skilfully disguised the ravages of a youth of debauchery, and whose personal appearance was in his favour, came, under the protection of his creditors, who told no tales, and of the most extraordinary good-nature on the part of all the *ci-devants* of the district, to be introduced with all these claims on her regard to the woman Lechantre, who was supposed to have a very fine fortune. The scheme in view was to secure a marriage between Madame Lechantre's only daughter, Henriette, and this protégé of the Royalist party.

"Priests, ex-nobles, and creditors, all from different motives, conspired to promote the marriage between Bernard Bryond and Henriette Lechantre.

"The good judgment of the notary who took charge of Madame Lechantre's affairs, and his shrewd suspicions, led perhaps to the poor girl's undoing. For

Monsieur Chesnel, a notary at Alençon, settled the lands of Saint-Savin, the bride's sole estate, on her and her children, reserving a small charge on it and the right of residence to the mother for life.

"Bryond's creditors, who, judging from her methodical and economical style of living, had supposed that Madame Lechantre must have saved large sums, were disappointed in their hopes, and believing that she must be avaricious, they sued Bryond, and this led to a revelation of his impecuniosity and difficulties.

"Then the husband and wife quarrelled violently, and the young woman came to full knowledge of the dissipated habits, the atheistical opinions both in religion and in politics, nay, I may say, the utter infamy, of the man to whom fate had irrevocably bound her. Then Bryond, being obliged to let his wife into the secret of the atrocious plots against the Imperial Government, offered an asylum under his roof to Rifoël du Vissard.

"Rifoël's character, adventurous, brave, and lavish, had an extraordinary charm for all who came under his influence; of this there is abundant proof in the cases tried in no less than three special criminal courts.

"The irresistible influence, in fact the absolute power, he acquired over a young woman who found herself at the bottom of a gulf, is only too evident in the catastrophe of which the horror brings her as a suppliant to the foot of the throne. And His Imperial and Kingly Majesty's Council will have no difficulty in verifying the infamous collusion of Bryond, who, far from doing his duty as the guide and adviser of the girl intrusted to his care by the mother he had deceived, condoned and encouraged the intimacy between his wife Henriette and the rebel leader.

"This was the plan imagined by this detestable man, who makes it his glory that he respects nothing, and that he never considers any end but the gratification of his passions, while he regards every sentiment based on social or religious morality as a mere vulgar prejudice. And it may here be remarked that such scheming is habitual to a man who has been playing a double part ever since 1794, who for eight years has deceived the Comte de Lille and his adherents, probably deceiving at the same time the superior police of the Empire—for such men are always ready to serve the highest bidder.

"Bryond, then, was urging Rifoël to commit a crime; he it was who insisted on an armed attack and highway robbery of the State treasure in transit, and on heavy contributions to be extorted from the purchasers of the national land, by means of atrocious tortures which he invented, and which carried terror into five Departments. He demanded no less than three hundred thousand francs to pay off the mortgages on his property.

"In the event of any objection on the part of Rifoël or Madame Bryond, he intended to revenge himself for the contempt he had inspired in his wife's upright mind, by handing them both over to be dealt with by the law as soon as they should commit some capital crime.

"As soon as he perceived that party spirit was a stronger motive than self-interest in these two whom he had thus thrown together, he disappeared; he came to Paris, armed with ample information as to the state of affairs in the western departments.

"The Chaussard brothers and Vauthier were, it is well known, in constant correspondence with Bryond.

"As soon as the robbery on the chests from Caen was accomplished, Bryond, assuming the name of le Marchand, opened secret communications with the préfet and the magistrates. What was the consequence? No conspiracy of equal extent, and in which so many persons in such different grades of the social scale were involved, has ever been so immediately divulged to justice as this, of which the first attempt was the robbery of the treasure from Caen. Within six days of the crime, all the guilty parties had been watched and followed with a certainty that betrays perfect knowledge of the persons in question, and of their plans. The arrest, trial, and execution of Rifoël and his companions are a sufficient proof, and mentioned here only to demonstrate our knowledge of this fact, of which the Supreme Council knows every particular.

"If ever a condemned criminal might hope for the clemency of the Sovereign, may not Henriette Lechantre?

"Carried away by a passion and by rebellious principles imbibed with her mother's milk, she is, no doubt, unpardonable in the eye of the law; but in the sight of our most magnanimous Emperor, may not the most shameless betrayal on one hand, and the most vehement enthusiasm on the other, plead her cause?

"The greatest of Generals, the immortal genius who pardoned the Prince of Hatzfeld, and who, like God Himself, can divine the arguments suggested by a blind passion, may, perhaps, vouchsafe to consider the temptations invincible in the young, which may palliate her crime, great as it is.

"Twenty-two heads have already fallen under the sword of justice and the sentence of the three courts. One alone remains—that of a young woman of twenty, not yet of age. Will not the Emperor Napoleon the Great grant her time for repentance? Is not that a tribute to the grace of God?

"For Henriette Lechantre, wife of Bryond des Tour-Minières,

"BORDIN,

"Retained for the defence, Advocate in the Lower Court of the Department of the Seine."

This terrible tragedy haunted the little sleep Godefroid was able to get. He dreamed of decapitation, as the physician Guillotin perfected it with philanthropic intentions. Through the hot vapours of a nightmare he discerned a beautiful young woman, full of enthusiasm, undergoing the last preparations, drawn in a cart, and mounting the scaffold with a cry of "Vive le Roi!"

Godefroid was goaded by curiosity. He rose at daybreak, dressed, and paced his room, till at length he posted himself at the window, and mechanically stared at the sky, reconstructing the drama, as a modern romancer might, in several volumes. And always against the murky background of Chouans, of country folks, of provincial gentlemen, of rebel leaders, police agents, lawyers and spies, he saw the radiant figures of the mother and daughter; of the daughter deceiving her mother, the victim of a wretch, and of her mad passion for one of those daring adventurers who were afterwards regarded as heroes—a man who, to Godefroid's imagination, had points of resemblance to Georges Cadoudal and Charette, and the giants of the struggle between the Republic and the Monarchy.

As soon as Godefroid heard old Alain stirring, he went to his room; but on looking in through the half-opened door, he shut it again, and withdrew. The old man, kneeling on his prie-Dieu, was saying his morning prayers. The sight of that white head bent in an attitude of humble piety recalled Godefroid to a sense of duty, and he prayed too, with fervency.

"I was expecting you," said the good man when, at the end of a quarter of an hour, Godefroid entered his room. "I anticipated your impatience, and rose earlier than usual."

"Madame Henriette?—" Godefroid began, with evident agitation.

"Was Madame's daughter," replied Alain, interrupting him. "Madame's name is Lechantre de la Chanterie. Under the Empire old titles were not recognised, nor the names added to the patronymic or first surname. Thus the Baronne des Tours-Minières was 'the woman Bryond'; the Marquis d'Esgrignon was called Carol—Citizen Carol, and afterwards the Sieur Carol; the Troisvilles were the Sieurs Guibelin."

"But what was the end? Did the Emperor pardon her?"

"No, alas!" said Alain. "The unhappy little woman perished on the scaffold at the age of twenty-one.—After reading Bordin's petition, the Emperor spoke to the Supreme Judge much to this effect:

"'Why make an example of a spy? A secret agent ceases to be a man, and ought to have none of a man's feelings; he is but a wheel in the machine. Bryond did his duty. If our instruments of that kind were not what they are—steel bars, intelligent only in behalf of the Government they serve—government would be impossible. The sentences of Special Criminal Courts must be carried out, or my magistrates would lose all confidence in themselves and in me. And besides, the men who fought for these people are executed, and they were less guilty than their leaders. The women of the western provinces must be taught not to meddle in conspiracies. It is because the victim of the sentence is a woman that the law must take its course. No excuse is available as against the interests of authority.'

"This was the substance of what the Supreme Judge was so obliging as to repeat to Bordin after his interview with the Emperor. To re-establish tranquillity in the west, which was full of refractory conscripts, Napoleon thought it needful to produce a real 'terror.' The Supreme Judge, in fact, advised the lawyer to trouble himself no further about his clients."

"And the lady?" said Godefroid.

"Madame de la Chanterie was condemned to twenty-two years' imprisonment," replied Alain. "She had already been transferred to Bicêtre, near Rouen, to undergo her sentence, and nothing could be thought of till her Henriette was safe; for after these dreadful scenes, she was so wrapped up in her daughter that, but for Bordin's promise to petition for the mitigation of the sentence of death, it was thought that Madame would not have survived her condemnation. So they deceived the poor mother. She saw her daughter after the execution of the men who had been sentenced to death, but did not know that the respite was granted in consequence of a false declaration that her daughter was expecting her confinement."

"Ah, now I understand everything!" cried Godefroid.

"No, my dear boy. There are some things which cannot he guessed.—For a long time after that, Madame believed that her daughter was alive."

"How was that?"

"When Madame des Tours-Minières heard through Bordin that her appeal was rejected, the brave little woman had enough strength of mind to write a score of letters dated for several months after her execution to make her mother believe that she was still alive, but gradually suffering more and more from an imaginary malady, till it ended in death. These letters were spread over a period of two years. Thus Madame de la Chanterie was prepared for her daughter's death, but for a natural death; she did not hear of her execution till 1814.

"For two years she was kept in the common prison with the most infamous creatures of her sex, wearing the prison dress; then, thanks to the efforts of the Champignelles and the Beauséants, after the second year she was placed in a private cell, where she lived like a cloistered nun."

"And the others?"

"The notary Léveillé, Herbomez, Hiley, Cibot, Grenier, Hureau, Cabot, Minard, and Mallet were condemned to death, and executed the same day; Pannier, with Chaussard and Vauthier, was sentenced to twenty years' penal servitude; they were branded and sent to the hulks; but the Emperor pardoned Chaussard and Vauthier. Mélin, Laravinière, and Binet had five years' imprisonment. The woman Bourget was imprisoned for twenty-two years. Chargegrain and Rousseau were acquitted. Those who had got away were all sentenced to death, with the exception of the maid-servant Godard, who, as you have guessed, is none other than our good Manon."

"Manon!" exclaimed Godefroid in amazement.

"Oh, you do not yet know Manon," replied the worthy man. "That devoted soul, condemned to twenty-two years' imprisonment, had given herself up to justice that she might be with Madame de la Chanterie in prison. Our beloved vicar is the priest from Mortagne who gave the last sacrament to Madame des Tours-Minières, who had the fortitude to escort her to the scaffold, and to whom she gave her last farewell kiss. The same brave and exalted priest had attended the Chevalier du Vissard. So our dear Abbé de Vèze learned all the secrets of the conspirators."

"I see now when his hair turned white," said Godefroid.

"Alas!" said Alain.—"He received from Amédée du Vissard a miniature of Madame des Tours-Minières, the only likeness of her that exists; and the Abbé has been a sacred personage to Madame de la Chanterie ever since the day when she was restored triumphant to social life."

"How was that?" asked Godefroid in surprise.

"Well, on the restoration of Louis XVIII in 1814, Boislaurier, who was the younger brother of Monsieur de Boisfrelon, was still under the King's orders to organise a rising in the West—first in 1809, and afterwards in 1812. Their name is Dubut; the Dubut of Caen was related to them. There were three brothers: Dubut de Boisfranc, President of the Court of Subsidies; Dubut de Boisfrelon, Councillor at Law; and Dubut-Boislaurier, a Captain of Dragoons. Their father had given each the name of one of his three several estates to give them a title and status (*savonnette à la vilain*, as it was called), for their grandfather was a linen merchant. Dubut of Caen, who succeeded in escaping, was one of the branch who had stuck to trade; but he hoped, by devoting himself to the Royal cause, to be allowed to succeed to Monsieur de Boisfranc's title. And in fact Louis XVIII gratified the wish of his faithful adherent, who, in 1815, was made Grand Provost, and subsequently became a Public Prosecutor under the name of Boisfranc; he was President of one of the Higher Courts when he died. The Marquis du Vissard, the unhappy Chevalier's elder brother, created peer of France, and loaded with honours by the King, was made Lieutenant of the Maison Rouge, and when that was abolished became Préfet. Monsieur d'Herbomez had a brother who was made a Count and Receiver-General. The unfortunate banker Pannier died on the bulks of a broken heart. Boislaurier died childless, a Lieutenant-General and Governor of one of the Royal residences.

"Madame de la Chanterie was presented to His Majesty by Monsieur de Champignelles, Monsieur de Beauséant, the Duc de Verneuil, and the Keeper of the Seals.—'You have suffered much for me, Madame la Baronne,' said the King; 'you have every claim on my favour and gratitude.'

"'Sir,' she replied, 'your Majesty has so much to do in comforting the sufferers, that I will not add the burden of an inconsolable sorrow. To live forgotten, to mourn for my daughter, and do some good—that is all I have to live for. If anything could mitigate my grief, it would be the graciousness of my Sovereign, and the happiness of seeing that Providence did not suffer so much devoted service to be wasted.'"

"And what did the King do?" asked Godefroid.

"He restored to Madame de la Chanterie two hundred thousand francs in money," said the good man, "for the estate of Saint-Savin had been sold to make good the loss to the treasury. The letters of pardon granted to Madame la Baronne and her woman express the Sovereign's regret for all they had endured in his service, while acknowledging that the zeal of his adherents had carried them too far in action; but the thing that will seem to you most horrible of all is, that throughout his reign Bryond was still the agent of his secret police."

"Oh, what things kings can do!" cried Godefroid. "And is the wretch still living?"

"No. The scoundrel, who at any rate concealed his name, calling himself Contenson, died at the end of 1829, or early in 1830. He fell from a roof into the street when in pursuit of a criminal.—Louis XVIII was of the same mind as Napoleon as regards police agents.

"Madame de la Chanterie, a perfect saint, prays for this monster's soul, and has two masses said for him every year.

"Though her defence was undertaken by one of the famous pleaders of the day, the father of one of our great orators, Madame de la Chanterie, who knew nothing of her daughter's risks till the moment when the money was brought in—and even then only because Boislaurier, who was related to her, told her the facts—could never establish her innocence. The Président du Ronceret, and Blondet, Vice-President of the Court at Alençon, vainly tried to clear the poor lady; the influence of the notorious Mergi, the Councillor to the Supreme Court under the Empire, who presided over these trials—a man fanatically devoted to the Church and Throne, who afterwards, as Public Prosecutor, brought many a Bonapartist head under the axe—was so great at this time over his two colleagues that he secured the condemnation of the unhappy Baronne de la Chanterie. Bourlac and Mergi argued the case with incredible virulence. The President always spoke of the Baronne des Tours-Minières as the woman Bryond, and of Madame as the woman Lechantre. The names of all the accused were reduced to the barest Republican forms, and curtailed of all titles.

"There were some extraordinary features of the trial, and I cannot recall them all; but I remember one stroke of audacity, which may show you what manner of men these Chouans were.—The crowd that pressed to hear the trials was beyond anything your fancy can conceive of; it filled the corridors, and the square outside was thronged as if on market days. One morning at the opening of the Court, before the arrival of the judges, Pille-Miche, the famous Chouan, sprang over the balustrade into the middle of the mob, made play with his elbows, mixed with the crowd, and fled among the terrified spectators, 'butting like a wild boar,' as Bordin told me. The gendarmes and the people rushed to stop him, and he was caught on the steps just as he had reached the market-place. After this daring attempt, they doubled the guard, and a detachment of men-at-arms was posted on the square, for it was feared that there might be among the crowd some Chouans ready to aid and abet the accused. Three persons were crushed to death in the crowd in consequence of this attempt.

"It was subsequently discovered that Contenson—for, like my old friend Bordin, I cannot bring myself to call him Baron des Tours or Bryond, which is a respectable old name—that wretch, it was discovered, had made away with sixty thousand francs of the stolen treasure. He gave ten thousand to the younger Chaussard, whom he enticed into the police and inoculated with all his low tastes and vices; but all his accomplices were unlucky. The Chaussard who escaped was pitched into the sea by Monsieur de Boislaurier, who understood from something said by Pannier that Chaussard had turned traitor. Contenson indeed had advised him to join the fugitives in order to spy upon them. Vauthier was killed in Paris, no doubt by one of the Chevalier du Vissard's obscure but devoted followers. The younger Chaussard too was finally murdered in one of the nocturnal raids conducted by the police; it seems probable that Contenson took this means of ridding himself of his demands or of his remorse by sending him to sermon, as the saying goes.

"Madame de la Chanterie invested her money in the funds, and purchased this house by the particular desire of her uncle, the old Councillor de Boisfrelon, who in fact gave her the money to buy it. This quiet neighborhood lies close to the Archbishop's residence, where our beloved Abbé has an appointment under the Cardinal. And this was Madame's chief reason for acceding to the old lawyer's wish when his income, after twenty-five years of revolutions, was reduced to six thousand francs a year. Besides, Madame wished to close a life of such terrible misfortunes as had overwhelmed her for six-and-twenty years in almost cloistered seclusion.

"You may now understand the dignity, the majesty, of this long-suffering woman—august indeed, as I may say—"

"Yes," said Godefroid, "the stamp of all she has endured has given her an indefinable air of grandeur and majesty."

"Each blow, each fresh pang, has but increased her patience and resignation," Alain went on. "And if you could know her as we do, if you knew how keen her feelings are, and how active is the spring of tenderness that wells up in her heart, you would be afraid to take count of the tears she must shed, and her fervent prayers that ascend to God. Only those who, like her, have known but a brief season of happiness can resist such shocks. Hers is a tender heart, a gentle soul clothed in a frame of steel, tempered by privation, toil, and austerity."

"Such a life as hers explains the life of hermits," said Godefroid.

"There are days when I wonder what can be the meaning of such an existence. Is it that God reserves these utmost, bitterest trials for those of His creatures who shall sit on His right hand on the day after their death?" said the good old man, quite unaware that he was artlessly expressing Swedenborg's doctrine concerning the angels.

"What!" exclaimed Godefroid, "Madame de la Chanterie was mixed up with—?"

"Madame was sublime in prison," Main said. "In the course of three years the story of the Vicar of Wakefield came true, for she reclaimed several women of profligate lives. And in the course of her imprisonment, as she took note of the conduct of those confined with her, she learned to feel that great pity for the misery of the people which weighs on her soul, and has made her the queen of Parisian charity. It was in the horrible Bicêtre at Rouen that she conceived of the plan which we devote ourselves to carry out. It was, as she declared, a dream of rapture, an angelic inspiration in the midst of hell; she had no thought of ever seeing it realised.

"But here, in 1819, when peace seemed to be descending on Paris, she came back to her dream. Madame la Duchesse d'Angoulême, the Dauphiness, the Duchesse de Berri, the Archbishop, and then the Chancellor and some pious persons contributed very liberally to the first necessary expenses. The fund was increased by what we could spare from our income, for each of us spends no more than is absolutely necessary."

Tears rose to Godefroid's eyes.

"We are the faithful priesthood of a Christian idea, and belong body and soul to this work, of which Madame de la Chanterie is the founder and the soul—that lady whom you hear us respectfully designate as Madame."

"Ah, and I too am wholly yours!" cried Godefroid, holding out his hands to the worthy man.

"Now, do you understand that there are subjects of conversation absolutely prohibited here, never even to be alluded to?" Alain went on. "Do you appreciate the obligation of reticence under which we all feel ourselves to a lady whom we reverence as a saint? Do you understand the charm exerted by a woman made sacred by her misfortunes, having learned so many things, knowing the inmost secret of every form of suffering—a woman who has derived a lesson from every grief, whose every virtue has the twofold sanction of the hardest tests and of constant practice, whose soul is spotless and above reproach; who has known motherhood only through its sorrows, and conjugal affection only through its bitterness; on whom life never smiled but for a few months—for whom Heaven no doubt keeps a palm in store as the reward of such resignation and gentleness amid sorrows? Is she not superior to Job in that she has never murmured?

"So you need never again be surprised to find her speech so impressive, her old age so fresh, her spirit so full of communion, her looks so persuasive; she has had powers extraordinary bestowed on her as a confidante of the sorrowing, for she has known every sorrow. In her presence smaller griefs are mute."

"She is the living embodiment of charity," cried Godefroid with enthusiasm. "May I become one of you?"

"You must pass the tests, and above all else, *Believe*!" said the old man with gentle excitement. "So long as you have not hold on faith, so long as you have not assimilated in your heart and brain the divine meaning of Saint Paul's epistle on Charity, you can take no part in our work."

PARIS, 1843-1845.

THE SEAMY SIDE OF HISTORY

SECOND EPISODE: INITIATED

WHAT is nobly good is contagious, as evil is. And by the time Madame de la Chanterie's boarder had dwelt for some months in this silent old house, after the story told him by Monsieur Alain, which filled him with the deepest respect for the half-monastic life he saw around him, he became conscious of the ease of mind that comes of a regular life, of quiet habits and harmonious tempers in those we live with. In four months Godefroid, never hearing an angry tone or the least dispute, owned to himself that since he had come to years of discretion he did not remember ever being so completely at peace—for he could not say happy. He looked on the world from afar, and judged it sanely. At last the desire he had cherished these three months past to take his part in the deeds of this mysterious association had become a passion; and without being a very profound philosopher, the reader may imagine what strength such a passion may assume in seclusion.

So one day—a day marked as solemn by the ascendency of the Spirit—Godefroid, after sounding his heart and measuring his powers, went up to his good friend Alain—whom Madame de la Chanterie always called her lamb—for of all the dwellers under that roof he had always seemed to Godefroid the most accessible and the least formidable. To him, then, he would apply, to obtain from the worthy man some information as to the sort of priesthood which these Brethren in God exercised in Paris. Many allusions to a period of probation suggested to him that he would be put to initiatory tests of some kind. His curiosity had not been fully satisfied by what the venerable old man had told him of the reasons why he had joined Madame de la Chanterie's association; he wanted to know more about this.

At half-past ten o'clock that evening Godefroid found himself for the third time in Monsieur Alain's rooms, just as the old man was preparing to read his chapter of *The Imitation*. This time the mild old man could not help smiling, and he said to the young man, before allowing him to speak:

"Why do you apply to me, my dear boy, instead of addressing yourself to Madame? I am the most ignorant, the least spiritual, the most imperfect member of the household.—For the last three days Madame and my friends have seen into your heart," he added, with a little knowing air.

"And what have they seen?" asked Godefroid.

"Oh," said the good man, with perfect simplicity, "they have seen a guileless desire to belong to our community. But the feeling is not yet a very ardent vocation. Nay," he replied to an impulsive gesture of Godefroid's, "you have more curiosity than fervour. In fact, you have not so completely freed yourself from your old ideas but that you imagine something adventurous, something romantic, as the phrase goes, in the incidents of our life—"

Godefroid could not help turning red.

"You fancy that there is some resemblance between our occupations and those of the Khalifs in the *Arabian Nights*, and you anticipate a kind of satisfaction in playing the part of the good genius in the idyllic beneficences of which you dream! Ah, ha! my son, your smile of confusion shows me that we were not mistaken. How could you expect to conceal your thoughts from us, who make it our business to detect the hidden impulses of the soul, the cunning of poverty, the calculations of the needy; who are honest spies, the police of a merciful Providence, old judges whose code of law knows only absolution, and physicians of every malady whose only prescription is a wise use of money? Still, my dear boy, we do not quarrel with the motives that bring us a neophyte if only he stays with us and becomes a brother of our Order. We shall judge you by your works. There are two kinds of curiosity—one for good, and one for evil. At this moment your curiosity is for good. If you are to become a labourer in our vineyard, the juice of the grapes will give you perpetual thirst for the divine fruit. The initiation looks easy, but is difficult, as in every natural science. In well-doing, as in poetry, nothing can be easier than to clutch at its semblance; but here, as on Parnassus, we are satisfied with nothing short of perfection. To become one of us, you must attain to great knowledge of life—and of such life. Good God! Of that Paris life which defies the scrutiny of the Chief of the Police and his men. It is our task to unmask the permanent conspiracy of evil, and detect it under forms so endlessly changing that they might be thought infinite. In Paris, Charity must be as omniscient as Sin, just as the police agent must be as cunning as a thief. We have to be at once frank and suspicious; our judgment must be as certain and as swift as our eye.

"As you see, dear boy, we are all old and worn out; but then we are so well satisfied with the results we have achieved, that we wish not to die without leaving successors, and we hold you all the more dear because you may, if you will, be our first disciple. For us there is no risk, we owe you to God! Yours is a sweet nature turned sour, and since you came to live here the evil leaven is weaker. Madame's heavenly nature has had its effect on you.

"We held council yesterday; and as you have given me your confidence, my good brothers decided on making me your instructor and guide.—Are you satisfied?"

"Oh, my kind Monsieur Alain, your eloquence has aroused—"

"It is not I that speak well, my dear boy, it is that great deeds are eloquent.—We are always sure of soaring high if we obey God and imitate Jesus Christ so far as lies in man aided by faith."

"This moment has decided my fate; I feel the ardour of the neophyte!" cried Godefroid. "I too would fain spend my life in well-doing—"

"That is the secret of dwelling in God," replied the good man. "Have you meditated on our motto, *Transire benefaciendo*? *Transire* means to pass beyond this life, leaving a long train of good actions behind you."

"I have understood it so, and I have written up the motto of the order in front of my bed."

"That is well.—And that action, so trivial in itself, is of great value in my eyes.—Well, my son, I have your first task ready for you, I will see you with your foot in the stirrup. We must part.—Yes, for I have to leave our retreat and take my place in the heart of a volcano. I am going as foreman in a large factory where all the workmen are infected with communistic doctrines—and dream of social destruction, of murdering the masters, never seeing that this would be to murder industry, manufacture, and commerce.

"I shall remain there—who knows—a year, perhaps, as cashier, keeping the books, and making my way into a hundred or more humble homes, among men who were misled by poverty, no doubt, before they were deluded by bad books. However, we shall see each other here every Sunday and holiday; as I shall live in the same quarter of the town we may meet at the Church of Saint-Jacques du Haut-Pas; I shall attend mass there every morning at half-past seven. If you should happen to meet me elsewhere, you must never recognise me, unless I rub my hands with an air of satisfaction. That is one of our signals.—Like the deaf-mutes, we have a language by signs, of which the necessity will soon be more than abundantly evident to you."

Godefroid's expression was intelligible to Monsieur Alain, for he smiled and went on:

"Now for your business. We do not practise either beneficence or philanthropy as they are known to you, under a variety of branches which are preyed upon by swindlers, just like any other form of trade. We exercise charity as it is defined by our great and sublime master Saint Paul; for it is our belief, my son, that such charity alone can heal the woes of Paris. Thus, in our eyes, sorrow, poverty, suffering, trouble, evil—from whatever cause they may proceed and in whatever class of society we find them—have equal claims upon us. Whatever their creed or their opinions, the unfortunate are, first and foremost, unfortunate; we do not try to persuade them to look to our Holy Mother the Church till we have rescued them from despair and starvation. And even then we try to convert them by example and kindness, for thus we believe that we have the help of God. All coercion is wrong.

"Of all the wretchedness in Paris, the most difficult to discover and the bitterest to endure is that of the respectable middle-class, the better class of citizens, when they fall into poverty, for they make it a point of honour to conceal it. Such disasters as these, my dear Godefroid, are the object of our particular care. Such persons, when we help them, show intelligence and good feeling; they return us with interest what we may lend to them; and in the course of time their repayments cover the losses we meet with through the disabled, or by swindlers, or those whom misfortune has stultified. Sometimes we get useful information from those we have helped; but the work has grown to such vast dimensions, and its details are so numerous, that it is beyond our powers. Now, for the last seven or eight months, we have a physician in our employment in each district of the city of Paris. Each of us has four *arrondissements* (or wards) under his eye; and we are prepared to pay to each three thousand francs a year to take charge of our poor. He is required to give up his time and care to them by preference, but we do not prevent his taking other patients. Would you believe that we have not in eight months been able to find twelve such men, twelve good men, in spite of the pecuniary aid offered by our friends and acquaintance? You see, we needed men of absolute secrecy, of pure life, of recognised abilities, and with a love of doing good. Well, in Paris there are perhaps ten thousand men fit for the work, and yet in a year's search the twelve elect have not been found."

"Our Lord found it hard to collect His apostles," said Godefroid, "and there were a traitor and a disbeliever among them after all!"

"At last, within the past fortnight, each *arrondissement* has been provided with a *visitor*," said the old man, smiling—"for so we call our physicians—and, indeed, within that fortnight there has been a vast increase of business. However, we have worked all the harder. I tell you this secret of our infant fraternity because you must make acquaintance with the physician of your district, all the more so because we depend on him for information. This gentleman's name is Berton—Doctor Berton—and he lives in the Rue de l'Enfer.

"Now for the facts. Doctor Berton is attending a lady whose disease seems in some way to defy science. That indeed does not concern us, but only the Faculty; our business is to find out the poverty of the sick woman's family, which the doctor believes to be frightful, and concealed with a determination and pride that baffle all our inquiries. Hitherto, my dear boy, this would have been my task; but now the work to which I am devoting myself makes an assistant necessary in my four districts, and you must be that assistant. The family lives in the Rue Notre-Dame des Champs, in a house looking out over the Boulevard du Mont-Parnasse. You will easily find a room to let there, and while lodging there for a time you must try to discover the truth. Be sordid as regards your own expenses, but do not trouble your head about the money you give. I will send you such sums as we consider necessary, taking all the circumstances of the case into consideration. But study the moral character of these unfortunate people. A good heart and noble feelings are the security for our loans. Stingy to ourselves and generous to suffering, we must still be careful and never rash, for we dip into the treasury of the poor.—Go to-morrow, and remember how much power lies in your hands. The Brethren will be on your side."

"Ah!" cried Godefroid, "you have given me so much pleasure in trusting me to do good and be worthy of some day being one of you, that I shall not sleep for joy."

"Stay, my boy, one last piece of advice. The prohibition to recognise me unless I make the sign concerns the other gentlemen and Madame, and even the servants of the house. Absolute incognito is indispensable to all our undertakings, and we are so constantly obliged to preserve it that we have made it a law without exceptions. We must be unknown, lost in Paris.

"Remember, too, my dear Godefroid, the very spirit of our Order, which requires us never to appear as benefactors, but to play the obscure part of intermediaries. We always represent ourselves as the agents of some saintly and beneficent personage—are we not toiling for God?—so that no gratitude may be considered due to ourselves, and that we may not be supposed to be rich. True, sincere humility, not the false humility of those who keep in the shade that others may throw a light on them, must inspire and govern all your thoughts.— You may rejoice when you succeed; but so long as you feel the least impulse of vanity, you will be unworthy to join the Brotherhood. We have known two perfect men. One, who was one of our founders, Judge Popinot; the other, who was known by his works, was a country doctor who has left his name written in a remote parish. He, my dear Godefroid, was one of the greatest men of our day; he raised a whole district from a savage state to one of prosperity, from irreligion to the Catholic faith, from barbarism to civilisation. The names of those two men are graven on our hearts, and we regard them as our examples. We should be happy indeed if we might one day have in Paris such influence as that country doctor had in his own district.

"But here the plague-spot is immeasurable, and, so far, quite beyond our powers. May God long preserve Madame, and send us many such helpers as you, and then perhaps we may found an Institution that will lead men to bless His holy religion.

"Well, farewell. Your initiation now begins.

"Bless me! I chatter like a Professor, and was forgetting the most important matter. Here is the address of the family I spoke of," he went on, handing a scrap of paper to Godefroid. "And I have added the number of Monsieur Berton's house in the Rue de l'Enfer.—Now, go and pray God to help you."

Godefroid took the good old man's hands and pressed them affectionately, bidding him good-night, and promising to forget none of his injunctions.

"All you have said," he added, "is stamped on my memory for life."

Alain smiled with no expression of doubt, and rose to go and kneel on his prie-Dieu. Godefroid went back to his own room, happy in being at last allowed to know the mysteries of this household, and to have an occupation which, in his present frame of mind, was really a pleasure.

At breakfast next morning there was no Monsieur Alain, but Godefroid made no remark on his absence. Nor was he questioned as to the mission given him by the old man; thus he received his first lesson in secrecy. After breakfast, however, he took Madame de la Chanterie aside, and told her that he should be absent for a few days.

"Very well, my child," replied Madame de la Chanterie. "And try to do your sponsor credit, for Monsieur Alain has answered for you to his brethren."

Godefroid took leave of the other three men, who embraced him affectionately, seeming thus to give him their blessing on his outset in his laborious career.

Association—one of the greatest social forces which was the making of Europe in the Middle Ages—is based on feelings which have ceased, since 1792, to exist in France, where the individual is now supreme over the State. Association requires, in the first place, a kind of devotedness which is not understood in this country; a simplicity of faith which is contrary to the national spirit; and finally, a discipline against which everything rebels, and which nothing but the Catholic faith can exact. As soon as an Association is formed in France, each member of it, on returning home from a meeting where the finest sentiments have been expressed, makes a bed for himself of the collective devotion of this combination of forces, and tries to milk for his own benefit the cow belonging to all, till the poor thing, inadequate to meet so many individual demands, dies of attenuation.

None can tell how many generous emotions have been nipped, how many fervid germs have perished, how much resource has been crushed and lost to the country by the shameful frauds of the French secret Societies, of the patriotic fund for the Champs d'Asile (emigration to America), and other political swindles, which ought to have produced great and noble dramas, and turned out mere farces of the lower police courts.

It was the same with industrial as with political associations. Self-interest took the place of public spirit. The Corporations and Hanseatic Guilds of the Middle Ages, to which we shall some day return, are as yet out of the question; the only Societies that still exist are religious institutions, and at this moment they are being very roughly attacked, for the natural tendency of the sick is to rebel against the remedies and often to rend the physician. France knows not what self-denial means. Hence no Association can hold together but by the aid of religious sentiment, the only power that can quell the rebellion of the intellect, the calculations of ambition, and greed of every kind. Those who are in search of worlds fail to understand that Association has worlds in its gift.

Godefroid, as he made his way through the streets, felt himself a different man. Any one who could have read his mind would have wondered at the curious phenomenon of the communication of the spirit of union. He was no longer one man, but a being multiplied tenfold, feeling himself the representative of five persons whose united powers were at the back of all he did, and who walked with him on his way. With this strength in his heart, he was conscious of a fullness of life, a lofty power that uplifted him. It was, as he afterwards owned, one of the happiest moments of his life, for he rejoiced in a new sense—that of an omnipotence more absolute than that of despots. Moral force, like thought, knows no limits.

"This is living for others," said he to himself, "acting with others as if we were but one man, and acting alone as if we were all together! This is having Charity for a leader, the fairest and most living of all the ideals that have been created of the Catholic virtues.—Yes, this is living!—Come, I must subdue this childish exultation which Father Alain would laugh to scorn.—Still, is it not strange that it is by dint of trying to annul my Self that I have found the power so long wished for? The world of misfortune is to be my inheritance."

He crossed the precincts of Notre-Dame to the Avenue de l'Observatoire in such high spirits that he did not heed the length of the walk.

Having reached the Rue Notre-Dame des Champs, at the end of the Rue de l'Ouest, he was surprised to find such pools of mud in so handsome a quarter of the town, for neither of those streets was as yet paved. The foot-passenger had to walk on planks laid close to the walls of the marshy gardens, or creep by the houses on narrow side-paths, which were soon swamped by the stagnant waters that turned them into gutters.

After much seeking, he discovered the house described to him, and got to it, not without some difficulty. It was evidently an old manufactory which had been abandoned. The building was narrow, and the front was a long wall pierced with windows quite devoid of any ornament; but there were none of these square openings on the ground floor—only a wretched back-door.

Godefroid supposed that the owner had contrived a number of rooms in this structure to his own profit, for over the door there was a board scrawled by hand to this effect: *Several rooms to let*. Godefroid rang, but no one came; and as he stood waiting, a passer-by pointed out to him that there was another entrance to the house from the boulevard, where he would find somebody to speak to.

Godefroid acted on the information, and from the boulevard he saw the front of the house screened by the trees of a small garden-plot. This garden, very ill-kept, sloped to the house, for there is such a difference of level between the boulevard and the Rue Notre-Dame des Champs as to make the garden a sort of ditch. Godefroid went down the path, and at the bottom of it saw an old woman whose dilapidated garb was in perfect harmony with the dwelling.

"Was it you who rang in the Rue Notre-Dame?" she asked.

"Yes, madame.—Is it your business to show the rooms?"

On a reply in the affirmative from this portress, whose age it was difficult to determine, Godefroid inquired whether the house was tenanted by quiet folk;

his occupations required peace and silence; he was a bachelor, and wished to arrange with the doorkeeper to cook and clean for him.

On this hint the woman became gracious, and said:

"Monsieur could not have done better than to hit on this house; for excepting the days when there are doings at the *Chaumière*, the boulevard is as deserted as the Pontine Marshes—"

"Do you know the Pontine Marshes?" asked Godefroid.

"No, sir; but there is an old gentleman upstairs whose daughter is always in a dying state, and he says so.—I only repeat it. That poor old man will be truly glad to think that you want peace and quiet, for a lodger who stormed around would be the death of his daughter.—And we have two writers of some kind on the second floor, but they come in for the day at midnight, and then at night they go out at eight in the morning. Authors, they say they are, but I do not know where or when they work."

As she spoke, the portress led Godefroid up one of those horrible stairs built of wood and brick, in such an unholy alliance that it is impossible to say whether the wood is parting from the bricks or the bricks are disgusted at being set in the wood; while both materials seem to fortify their disunion by masses of dust in summer and of mud in winter. The walls, of cracked plaster, bore more inscriptions than the Academy of Belles-lettres ever invented.

The woman stopped on the first floor.

"Now, here, sir, are two very good rooms, opening into each other, and on to Monsieur Bernard's landing. He is the old gentleman I mentioned—and quite the gentleman. He has the ribbon of the Legion of Honour, but he has had great troubles, it would seem, for he never wears it.—When first they came they had a servant to wait on them, a man from the country, and they sent him away close on three years ago. The lady's young gentleman—her son—does everything now; he manages it all—"

Godefroid looked shocked.

"Oh!" said the woman, "don't be uneasy, they will say nothing to you; they never speak to anybody. The gentleman has been here ever since the revolution of July; he came in 1831.—They are some high provincial family, I believe, ruined by the change of government; and proud! and as mute as fishes.—For four years, sir, they have never let me do the least thing for them, for fear of having to pay.—A five-franc piece on New Year's day, that's every sou I get out of them.—Give me your authors! I get ten francs a month, only to tell everybody who comes to ask for them that they left at the end of last quarter."

All this babble led Godefroid to hope for an ally in this woman, who explained to him, as she praised the airiness of the two rooms and adjoining dressing-closets, that she was not the portress, but the landlord's deputy and housekeeper, managing everything for him to a great extent.

"And you may trust me, monsieur, I promise you! Madame Vauthier—that's me—would rather have nothing at all than take a sou of anybody else's."

Madame Vauthier soon came to terms with Godefroid, who wished to take the rooms by the month and ready furnished. These wretched lodgings, rented by students or authors "down on their luck," were let furnished or unfurnished, as might be required. The spacious lofts over the whole house were full of furniture. But Monsieur Bernard himself had furnished the rooms he was in.

In getting Madame Vauthier to talk, Godefroid discovered that her ambition was set up in a *pension bourgeoise*; but in the course of five years she had failed to meet with a single boarder among her lodgers. She inhabited the ground floor, on the side towards the boulevard; thus she was herself the doorkeeper, with the help of a big dog, a sturdy girl, and a boy who cleaned the boots, ran errands, and did the rooms, two creatures as poor as herself, in harmony with the squalor of the house and its inhabitants, and the desolate, neglected appearance of the garden in front.

They were both foundlings, to whom the widow Vauthier gave no wages but their food—and such food! The boy, of whom Godefroid caught a glimpse, wore a ragged blouse, list slippers instead of shoes, and sabots to go out in. With a shock of hair, as touzled as a sparrow taking a bath, and blackened hands, as soon as he had done the work of the house, he went off to measure wood logs in a woodyard hard by, and when his day was over—at half-past four for wood-sawyers—he returned for his occupations. He fetched water for the household from the fountain by the Observatory, and the widow supplied it to the lodgers, as well as the faggots which he chopped and tied.

Népomucène—this was the name of the widow Vauthier's slave—handed over his earnings to his mistress. In summertime the unhappy waif served as waiter in the wineshops by the barrière on Sundays and Mondays. Then the woman gave him decent clothes.

As for the girl, she cooked under the widow's orders, and helped her in. her trade work at other times, for the woman plied a trade; she made list slippers for peddlers to sell.

All these details were known to Godefroid within an hour, for Madame Vauthier took him all over the house, showing him how it had been altered. A silkworm establishment had been carried on there till 1828, not so much for the production of silk as that of the eggs—the seed, as it is called. Eleven acres of mulberry-trees at Mont-Rouge, and three acres in the Rue de l'Ouest, since built over, had supplied food for this nursery for silkworms' eggs.

Madame Vauthier was telling Godefroid that Monsieur Barbet, who had lent the capital to an Italian named Fresconi to carry on this business, had been obliged to sell those three acres to recover the money secured by a mortgage on the land and buildings, and was pointing out the plot of ground, lying on the other side of the Rue Notre-Dame des Champs, when a tall and meagre old man, with perfectly white hair, came in sight at the end of the street where it crosses the Rue de l'Ouest.

"In the very nick of time!" cried Madame Vauthier. "Look, that is your neighbour, Monsieur Bernard.—Monsieur Bernard," cried she, as soon as the old man was within hearing, "you will not be alone now; this gentleman here has just taken the rooms opposite yours—"

Monsieur Bernard looked up at Godefroid with an apprehensive eye that was easy to read; it was as though he had said, "Then the misfortune I have so long feared has come upon me!"

"What, monsieur," said he, "you propose to reside here?"

"Yes, monsieur," said Godefroid civilly. "This is no home for those who are lucky in the world, and it is the cheapest lodging I have seen in this part of the town. Madame Vauthier does not expect to harbour millionaires.—Good-day, then, Madame Vauthier; arrange things so that I may come in at six o'clock this evening. I shall return punctually."

And Godefroid went off towards the Rue de l'Ouest, walking slowly, for the anxiety he had read in the old man's face led him to suppose that he wanted to dispute the matter with him. And, in fact, after some little hesitation, Monsieur Bernard turned on his heel and walked quickly enough to come up with Godefroid.

"That old wretch! he wants to hinder him from coming back," said Madame Vauthier to herself. "Twice already he has played me that trick.—Patience! His rent is due in five days, and if he does not pay it down on the nail, out he goes! Monsieur Barbet is a tiger of a sort that does not need much lashing, and—I should like to know what he is saying to him—Félicité! Félicité! you lazy hussy, will you make haste?" cried the widow in a formidable croak, for she had assumed an affable piping tone in speaking to Godefroid.

The girl, a sturdy, red-haired slut, came running out.

"Just keep a sharp eye on everything for a few seconds, do you hear? I shall be back in five minutes."

And the widow Vauthier, formerly cook to the bookseller's shop kept by Barbet, one of the hardest money-lenders on short terms in the neighbourhood, stole out at the heels of her two lodgers, so as to watch them from a distance and rejoin Godefroid as soon as he and Monsieur Bernard should part company.

Monsieur Bernard was walking slowly, like a man in two minds, or a debtor seeking for excuses to give to a creditor who has left him to take proceedings.

Godefroid, in front of this unknown neighbour, turned round to look at him under pretence of looking about him. And it was not till they had reached the broad walk in the Luxembourg Gardens that Monsieur Bernard came up with Godefroid and addressed him.

"I beg your pardon a thousand times, monsieur," said he, bowing to Godefroid, who returned the bow, "for stopping you, when I have not the honour of knowing you; but is it your firm intention to live in the horrible house where I am lodging?"

"Indeed, monsieur—"

"I know," said the old man, interrupting Godefroid with a commanding air, "that you have a right to ask me what concern of mine it is to meddle in your affairs, to question you.—Listen, monsieur; you are young, and I am very old; I am older than my years, and they are sixty-six—I might be taken for eighty!—Age and misfortune justify many things, since the law exempts septuagenarians from various public duties; still, I do not dwell on the privileges bestowed by white hairs; it is you whom I am concerned for. Do you know that the part of the town in which you think of living is a desert by eight in the evening, and full of dangers, of which being robbed is the least? Have you noticed the wide plots where there are no houses, the waste ground and market gardens?—You will, perhaps, retort that I live there; but I, monsieur, am never out of doors after six in the evening. Or you will say that two young men are lodgers on the second floor, above the rooms you propose to take; but, monsieur, those two unhappy writers are the victims of writs out against them; they are pursued by their creditors; they are in hiding, and go out all day to come in at midnight; and as they always keep together and carry arms, they have no fear of being robbed.—I myself obtained permission from the chief of the police for them each to carry a weapon."

"Indeed, monsieur," said Godefroid, "I have no fear of robbers, for the same reasons as leave these gentlemen invulnerable, and so great a contempt for life, that if I should be murdered by mistake, I should bless the assassin."

"And yet you do not look so very wretched," said the old man, who was studying Godefroid.

"I have barely enough to live on, to give me bread, and I chose that part of town for the sake of the quiet that reigns there.—But may I ask, monsieur, what object you can have in keeping me out of the house?"

The old man hesitated; he saw Madame Vauthier in pursuit. Godefroid, who was examining him attentively, was surprised at the excessive emaciation to which grief, and perhaps hunger, or perhaps hard work, had reduced him; there were traces of all these causes of weakness on the face where the withered skin looked dried on to the bones, as if it had been exposed to the African sun. The forehead, which was high and threatening, rose in a dome above a pair of steel-blue eyes, cold, hard, shrewd, and piercing as those of a savage, and set in deep, dark, and very wrinkled circles, like a bruise round each. A large, long, thin nose, and the upward curve of the chin, gave the old man a marked likeness to the familiar features of Don Quixote; but this was a sinister Don Quixote, a man of no delusions, a terrible Don Quixote.

The old man, in spite of his look of severity, betrayed nevertheless the timidity and weakness that poverty gives to the unfortunate. And these two feelings seemed to have graven lines of ruin on a face so strongly framed that the destroying pickaxe of misery had rough hewn it. The mouth was expressive and grave. Don Quixote was crossed with the Président de Montesquieu.

The man's dress was of black cloth throughout, but utterly threadbare; the coat, old-fashioned in cut, and the trousers showed many badly-executed patches. The buttons had been recently renewed. The coat was fastened to the chin, showing no linen, and a rusty-black stock covered the absence of a collar. These black clothes, worn for many years, reeked of poverty. But the mysterious old man's air of dignity, his gait, the mind that dwelt behind that brow and lighted up those eyes, seemed irreconcilable with poverty. An observer would have found it hard to class this Parisian.

Monsieur Bernard was so absent-minded that he might have been taken for a professor of the college-quarter, a learned man lost in jealous and overbearing meditation; and Godefroid was filled with excessive interest and a degree of curiosity to which his beneficent mission added a spur.

"Monsieur," said the old man presently, "if I were assured that all you seek is silence and privacy, I would say, 'Come and live near me.' Take the rooms," he went on in a louder voice, so that the widow might hear him, as she passed them, listening to what they were saying. "I am a father, monsieur, I have no one belonging to me in the world but my daughter and her son to help me to endure the miseries of life; but my daughter needs silence and perfect quiet.—Every one who has hitherto come to take the rooms you wish to lodge in has yielded to the reasoning and the entreaties of a heart-broken father; they did not care in which street they settled of so desolate a part of the town, where cheap lodgings are plenty and boarding-houses at very low rates. But you, I see, are very much bent on it, and I can only beg you, monsieur, not to deceive me; for if you should, I can but leave and settle beyond the barrier.—And, in the first place, a removal might cost my daughter her life," he said in a broken voice, "and then, who knows whether the doctors who come to attend her—for the love of God—would come outside the gates?—"

If the man could have shed tears, they would have run down his cheeks as he spoke these last words; but there were tears in his voice, to use a phrase that has become commonplace, and he covered his brow with a hand that was mere bone and sinew.

"What, then, is the matter with madame, your daughter?" asked Godefroid in a voice of ingratiating sympathy.

"A terrible disease to which the doctors give a variety of names—or rather, which has no name.—All my fortune went—"

But he checked himself, and said, with one of those movements peculiar to the unfortunate:

"The little money I had—for in 1830, dismissed from a high position, I found myself without an income—in short, everything I had was soon eaten up by my daughter, who had already ruined her mother and her husband's family. At the present time the pension I draw hardly suffices to pay for necessities in the state in which my poor saintly daughter now is.—She has exhausted all my power to weep.

"I have endured every torment, monsieur; I must be of granite still to live—or rather, God preserves the father that his child may still have a nurse or a providence, for her mother died of exhaustion.

"Ay, young man, you have come at a moment when this old tree that has never bent is feeling the axe of suffering, sharpened by poverty, cutting at its heart. And I, who have never complained to anybody, will tell you about this long illness to keep you from coming to the house—or, if you insist, to show you how necessary it is that our quiet should not be disturbed.

"At this moment, monsieur, day and night, my daughter barks like a dog!"

"She is mad, then?" said Godefroid.

"She is in her right mind, and a perfect saint," replied Monsieur Bernard. "You will think I am mad when I have told you all. My only daughter is the child of a mother who enjoyed excellent health. I never in my life loved but one woman—she was my wife. I chose her myself, and married for love the daughter of one of the bravest colonels in the Imperial guard, a Pole formerly on the Emperor's staff, the gallant General Tarlovski. In the place I held strict morality was indispensable; but my heart is not adapted to accommodate my fancies—I loved my wife faithfully, and she deserved it. And I am as constant as a father as I was as a husband; I can say no more.

"My daughter never left her mother's care; no girl ever led a chaster or more Christian life than my dear child. She was more than pretty—lovely; and her husband, a young man of whose character I was certain, for he was the son of an old friend, a President of the Supreme Court, I am sure was in no way contributory to his wife's malady."

Monsieur Bernard and Godefroid involuntarily stood still a moment looking at each other.

"Marriage, as you know, often changes a woman's constitution," the old man went on. "My daughter's first child was safely brought into the world, a son—my grandson, who lives with us, and who is the only descendant of either of the united families. The second time my daughter was expecting an infant, she had such singular symptoms that the physicians, all puzzled, could only ascribe them to the singular conditions which sometimes occur in such cases, and which are recorded in the memoirs of medical science. The infant was born dead, literally strangled by internal convulsions. Thus began the illness—temporary conditions had nothing to do with it.—Perhaps you are a medical student?" Godefroid replied with a nod, which might be either negative or affirmative.

"After this disastrous child-bearing," Monsieur Bernard went on—"a scene that made so terrible an impression on my son-in-law that it laid the foundations of the decline of which he died—my daughter, at the end of two or three months, complained of general debility, more particularly affecting her feet, which felt, as she described it, as if they were made of cotton. This weakness became paralysis, but what a strange form of paralysis! You may bend my daughter's feet under her, twist them round, and she feels nothing. The limbs are there, but they seem to have no blood, no flesh, no bones. This condition, which is unlike any recognised disease, has attacked her arms and hands; it was supposed to be connected with her spine. Doctors and remedies have only made her worse; my poor child cannot move without dislocating her hips, shoulders, or wrists. We have had for a long time an excellent surgeon, almost in the house, who makes it his care, with the help of a doctor—or doctors, for several have seen her out of curiosity—to replace the joints—would you believe me, monsieur?—as often as three or four times a day.

"Ah! I was forgetting to tell you—for this illness has so many forms—that during the early weak stage, before paralysis supervened, my daughter was liable to the most extraordinary attacks of catalepsy. You know what catalepsy is. She would lie with her eyes open and staring, sometimes in the attitude in which the fit seized her. She has had the most incredible forms of this affection, even attacks of tetanus.

"This phase of the disease suggested to me the application of mesmerism as a cure when I saw her so strangely paralysed. Then, monsieur, my daughter became miraculously *clairvoyante*, her mind was subject to every marvel of somnambulism, as her body is to every form of disease."

Godefroid was indeed wondering whether the old man were quite sane.

"For my part," he went on, heedless of the expression of Godefroid's eyes, "I, brought up on Voltaire, Diderot, and Helvétius, am a son of the eighteenth century, of the Revolution; and I laughed to scorn all the records handed down from antiquity and middle ages of persons possessed—yes, and yet possession is the only explanation of the state my child is in. Even in her mesmeric sleep she has never been able to reveal the cause of her sufferings; she could not see it; and the methods of treatment suggested by her under those conditions, though carefully followed, have had no good result. For instance, she said she must be wrapped in a freshly-killed pig; then she was to have points of highly magnetised red-hot iron applied to her legs; to have metal sealing-wax on her spine.—And what a wreck she became; her teeth fell out; she became deaf, and then dumb; and suddenly, after six months of perfect deafness and silence, she recovered hearing and speech. She occasionally recovers the use of her hands as unexpectedly as she loses it, but for seven years she has never known the use of her feet.

"She has sometimes had well-defined and characteristic attacks of hydrophobia. Not only may the sight or sound of water, of a glass or a cup, rouse her to frenzy, but she barks like a dog, a melancholy bark, or howls as dogs do at the sound of an organ.

"She has several times seemed to be dying, and has received the last sacraments, and then come back to life again to suffer with full understanding and clearness of mind, for her faculties of heart and brain remain unimpaired.

Though she is alive, she has caused the death of her husband and her mother, who could not stand such repeated trials. Alas!— Nor is this all. Every function of nature is perverted; only a medical man could give you a complete account of the strange condition of every organ.

"In this state did I bring her to Paris from the country in 1829; for the famous physicians to whom I described the case—Desplein, Bianchon, and Haudry—believed I was trying to impose upon them. At that time magnetism was stoutly denied by the schools. Without throwing any doubt on the provincial doctors' good faith or mine, they thought there was some inaccuracy, or, if you like, some exaggeration, such as is common enough in families or in the sufferers themselves. But they have been obliged to change their views; to these phenomena, indeed, it is due that nervous diseases have of late years been made the subject of investigation, for this strange case is now classed as nervous. The last consultation held by these gentlemen led them to give up all medicine; they decided that nature must be studied, but left to itself; and since then I have had but one doctor—the doctor who attends the poor of this district. In fact, all that can be done is done to alleviate her sufferings, since their causes remain unknown."

The old man paused, as if this terrible confession were too much for him.

"For five years now my daughter has lived through alternations of amendment and relapse; but no new symptoms have appeared. She suffers more or less from the various forms of nervous attack which I have briefly described to you; but the paralysis of the legs and organic disturbances are constant. Our narrow means—increasingly narrow—compelled us to move from the rooms I took in 1829 in the Rue du Roule; and as my daughter cannot bear being moved, and I nearly lost her twice, first in coming to Paris, and then in moving her from the Beaujon side, I took the lodging in which we now are, foreseeing the disasters which ere long overtook us; for, after thirty years' service, I was kept waiting for my pension till 1833. I have drawn it only for six months, and the new government has crowned its severities by granting me only the minimum."

Godefroid expressed such surprise as seemed to demand entire confidence, and so the old man understood it, for he went on at once, not without a reproachful glance towards heaven.

"I am one of the thousand victims to political reaction. I carefully hide a name that is obnoxious to revenge; and if the lessons of experience ever avail from one generation to the next, remember, young man, never to lend yourself to the severity of any *side* in politics. Not that I repent of having done my duty, my conscience is at peace; but the powers of to-day have ceased to have that sense of common responsibility which binds governments together, however dissimilar; when zeal meets with a reward, it is the result of transient fear. The instrument, having served its purpose, is, sooner or later, completely forgotten. In me you see one of the staunchest supporters of the throne under the elder branch of the Bourbons, as I was, too, of the Imperial rule, and I am a beggar! As I am too proud to ask charity, no one will ever guess that I am suffering intolerable ills.

"Five days since, monsieur, the district medical officer who attends my daughter, or who watches the case, told me that he had no hope of curing a disease of which the symptoms vary every fortnight. His view is that neurotic patients are the despair of the Faculty because the causes lie in a system that defies investigation. He advises me to call in a certain Jewish doctor, who is spoken of as a quack; but at the same time he remarked that he was a foreigner, a Polish refugee, and that physicians are extremely jealous of certain extraordinary cures that have been much talked of; some people regard him as very learned and skilful.

"But he is exacting and suspicious; he selects his patients, and will not waste time; and then he is—a communist. His name is Halpersohn. My grandson has called on him twice, but in vain; for he has not yet been to the house, and I understand why."

"Why?" asked Godefroid.

"Oh, my grandson, who is sixteen, is worse clothed even than I am; and, will you believe me, monsieur, I dare not show myself to this doctor; my dress is too ill-suited to what is expected in a man of my age, and of some dignity too. If he should see the grandfather so destitute as I am when the grandson has shown himself in the same sorry plight, would he devote due care to my daughter? He would treat her as paupers are always treated.—And you must remember, monsieur, that I love my daughter for the grief she has caused me, as of old I loved her for the care she lavished upon me. She has become a perfect angel. Alas! She is now no more than a soul—a soul that beams on her son and on me; her body is no more, for she has triumphed over pain.

"Imagine what a spectacle for a father! My daughter's world is her bedroom. She must have flowers which she loves; she reads a great deal; and when she has the use of her hands, she works like a fairy. She knows nothing of the misery in which we live. Our life is such a strange one, that we can admit no one to our rooms.—Do you understand me, monsieur? Do you see that a neighbour is intolerable? I should have to ask so much of him that I should be under the greatest obligations—and I could never discharge them. In the first place, I have no time for anything: I am educating my grandson, and I work so hard, monsieur—so hard, that I never sleep for more than three or four hours at night."

"Monsieur," said Godefroid, interrupting the old man, to whom he had listened attentively while watching him with grieved attention, "I will be your neighbour, and I will help you—"

The old gentleman drew himself up with pride, indeed, with impatience, for he did not believe in any good thing in man.

"I will help you," repeated Godefroid, taking the old man's hands and pressing them warmly, "in such ways as I can.—Listen to me. What do you intend to make of your grandson?"

"He is soon to begin studying the law; I mean him to be an advocate."

"Then your grandson will cost you six hundred francs a year, and you—"

The old man said nothing.

"I have nothing," said Godefroid after a pause, "but I have influence; I will get at the Jewish doctor; and if your daughter is curable, she shall be cured. We will find means to repay this Halpersohn."

"Oh, if my daughter were cured, I would make the sacrifice that can be made but once; I would give up what I am saving for a rainy day."

"You may keep that too."

"Ah! what a thing it is to be young!" said the old man, shaking his head. "Good-bye, monsieur, or rather au revoir. The library is open, and as I have sold all my books, I have to go there every day for my work.

"I am grateful for the kind feeling you have shown; but we must see whether you can show me such consideration as I am obliged to require of a neighbour. That is all I ask of you—"

"Yes, monsieur, pray accept me as your neighbour; for Barbet, as you know, is not the man to put up long with empty rooms, and you might meet with a worse companion in misery than I.—I do not ask you to believe in me, only to allow me to be of use to you."

"And what interest can you have in serving me?" cried the old man, as he was about to go down the steps of the Cloister of the Carthusians, through which there was at that time a passage from the broad walk of the Luxembourg to the Rue d'Enfer.

"Have you never, in the course of your career, obliged anybody?"

The old man looked at Godefroid with knit brows, his eyes vague with reminiscence, like a man searching through the record of his life for an action for which he might deserve such rare gratitude; then he coldly turned away, after bowing with evident suspicion.

"Come! for a first meeting he was not particularly distant," said the disciple to himself.

Godefroid went at once to the Rue d'Enfer, the address given him by Monsieur Alain, and found Doctor Berton at home—a stern, cold man, who surprised him greatly by assuring him that the details given by Monsieur Bernard of his daughter's illness were absolutely correct; he then went in search of Doctor Halpersohn.

The Polish physician, since so famous, at that time lived at Chaillot in a little house in the Rue Marbeuf, of which he occupied the first floor. General Roman Zarnovicki lived on the ground floor, and the servants of the two refugees occupied the attics of the little hotel, only one storey high. Godefroid did not see the doctor; he had been sent for to some distance in the country by a rich patient. But Godefroid was almost glad not to have met him, for in his haste he had neglected to provide himself with money, and was obliged to return to the Hotel de la Chanterie to fetch some from his room.

These walks, and the time it took to dine in a restaurant in the Rue de l'Odéon, kept him busy till the hour when he was to take possession of his lodgings on the Boulevard Mont- Parnasse.

Nothing could be more wretched than the furniture provided by Madame Vauthier for the two rooms. It seemed as though the woman was in the habit of letting rooms not to be inhabited. The bed, the chairs, the tables, the drawers, the desk, the curtains, had all evidently been purchased at sales under compulsion of the law, where the money-lender had kept them on account, no cash value being obtainable—a not infrequent case.

Madame Vauthier, her arms akimbo, expected thanks, and she took Godefroid's smile for one of surprise.

"Oh yes, I have given you the best of everything, my dear Monsieur Godefroid," said she with an air of triumph. "Look what handsome silk curtains, and a mahogany bedstead that is not at all worm-eaten. It belonged to the Prince de Wissembourg, and was bought out of his mansion. When he left the Rue Louis-le-Grand, in 1809, I was scullery-maid in his kitchen, and from there I went to live with my landlord—"

Godefroid checked this confidential flow by paying his month's lodging in advance, and at the same time gave Madame Vauthier six francs, also in advance, for doing his rooms. At this moment he heard a bark; and if he had not been forewarned, he might have thought that his neighbour kept a dog in his lodgings.

"Does that dog bark at night?" he asked.

"Oh, be easy, sir, and have patience; there will not be above a week of it. Monsieur Bernard will not be able to pay his rent, and he will be turned out.—Still, they are queer folks, I must say! I never saw their dog.—For months that dog—for months, did I say?—for six months at a time you will never hear that dog, and you might think they didn't keep one. The creature never comes out of madame's room. There is a lady who is very bad; she has never been out of her bed since they carried her in. Old Monsieur Bernard works very hard, and his son too, who is a day pupil at the Collège Louis-le-Grand, where he is in the top class for philosophy, and he is but sixteen. A bright chap that! but that little beggar works like a good 'un.

"You will hear them presently moving the flower pots in the lady's room—for they eat nothing but dry bread, the old man and his grandson, but they buy flowers and nice things for her. She must be very bad, poor thing, never to have stirred out since she came; and if you take Monsieur Berton's word—he is the doctor who comes to see her—she never will go out but feet foremost."

"And what is this Monsieur Bernard?"

"A very learned man, so they say; for he writes and goes to work in the public libraries, and the master lends him money on account of what he writes."

"The master—who?"

"The landlord, Monsieur Barbet, the old bookseller; he has been in business this sixteen years. He is a man from Normandy, who once sold salad in the streets, and who started as a dealer in old books on the quay, in 1818; then he set up a little shop, and now he is very rich.—He is a sort of old Jew who runs six-and-thirty businesses at once, for he was a kind of partner with the Italian who built this great barn to keep silkworms in—"

"And so the house is a place of refuge for authors in trouble?" said Godefroid.

"Are you so unlucky as to be one?" asked the widow Vauthier.

"I am only a beginner," said Godefroid.

"Oh, my good gentleman, for all the ill I wish you, never get any further! A newspaper man, now—I won't say—"

Godefroid could not help laughing, and he bid the woman good-night—a cook unconsciously representing the whole middle class.

As he went to bed in the wretched room, floored with bricks that had not even been coloured, and hung with paper at seven sous the piece, Godefroid not only regretted his little lodging in the Rue Chanoinesse, but more especially the society of Madame de la Chanterie. There was a great void in his soul. He had already acquired certain habits of mind, and he could not remember ever having felt such keen regrets for anything in his previous life. This comparison, brief as it was, made a great impression on his mind; he understood that no life he could lead could compare with that he was about to embrace, and his determination to follow in the steps of good Father Alain was thenceforth unchangeable. If he had not the vocation, he had the will.

Next morning, Godefroid, whose new way of life accustomed him to rising very early, saw, out of his window, a youth of about seventeen, wearing a blouse, and coming in evidently from a public fountain, carrying in each hand a pitcher full of water. The lad's face, not knowing that any one could see him, betrayed his thoughts; and never had Godefroid seen one more guileless and more sad. The charm of youth was depressed by misery, study, and great physical fatigue. Monsieur Bernard's grandson was remarkable for an excessively white skin, in strong contrast to very dark-brown hair. He made three expeditions; and the third time he saw a load of wood being delivered which Godefroid had ordered the night before; for the winter, though late, of 1838 was beginning to be felt, and there had been a light fall of snow in the night.

Népomucène, who had just begun his day's work by fetching this wood, on which Madame Vauthier had already levied heavy toll, stood talking to the youth while waiting till the sawyer had cut up the logs for him to take indoors. It was very evident that the sight of this wood, and of the ominous grey sky, had reminded the lad of the desirability of laying in some fuel. And then suddenly, as if reproaching himself for waste of time, he took up the pitchers and hurried into the house. It was indeed half-past seven; and as he heard the quarters strike by the clock at the Convent of the Visitation, he reflected that he had to be at the Collège Louis-le-Grand by half-past eight.

At the moment when the young man went in, Godefroid opened his door to Madame Vauthier, who was bringing up some live charcoal to her new lodger; so it happened that he witnessed a scene that took place on the landing. A gardener living in the neighbourhood, after ringing several times at Monsieur Bernard's door without arousing anybody, for the bell was muffled in paper, had a rough dispute with the youth, insisting on the money due for the hire of plants which he had supplied. As the creditor raised his voice, Monsieur Bernard came out.

"Auguste," said he to his grandson, "get dressed. It is time to be off."

He himself took the pitchers and carried them into the ante-room of his apartment, where Godefroid could see stands filled with flowers; then he closed the door and came outside to talk to the nurseryman. Godefroid's door was ajar, for Népomucène was passing in and out and piling up the logs in the second room. The gardener had become silent when Monsieur Bernard appeared, wrapped in a purple silk dressing-gown, buttoned to the chin, and looking really imposing.

"You might ask for the money we owe you without shouting," said the gentleman.

"Be just, my dear sir," replied the gardener. "You were to pay me week by week, and now, for three months—ten weeks—I have had no money, and you owe me a hundred and twenty francs. We are accustomed to hire out our plants to rich people, who give us our money as soon as we ask for it, and I have called here five times. We have our rent to pay and our workmen, and I am no richer than you are. My wife, who used to supply you with milk and eggs, will not call this morning neither; you owe her thirty francs, and she would rather not come at all than come to nag, for she has a good heart, has my wife! If I listened to her, trade would never pay.—And that is why I came, you understand, for that is not my way of looking at things, you see—"

Just then out came Auguste, dressed in a miserable green cloth coat, and trousers of the same, a black cravat, and shabby boots. These clothes, though brushed with care, revealed the very last extremity of poverty, for they were too short and too tight, so that they looked as if the least movement on the lad's part would split them. The whitened seams, the dog's-eared corners, the worn-out button-holes, in spite of mending, betrayed to the least practised eye the stigmata of poverty. This garb contrasted painfully with the youthfulness of the wearer, who went off eating a piece of stale bread, in which his fine strong teeth left their mark. This was his breakfast, eaten as he made his way from the Boulevard du Mont-Parnasse to the Rue Saint-Jacques, with his books and papers under his arm, and on his head a cap far too small for his powerful head and his mass of fine dark hair.

As he passed his grandfather they exchanged rapid glances of deep dejection; for he saw that the old man was in almost irremediable difficulties, of which the consequences might be terrible. To make way for the student of philosophy, the gardener retreated as far as Godefroid's door; and at the moment when he reached the door, Népomucène, with a load of wood, came up to the landing, driving the creditor quite to the window.

"Monsieur Bernard," exclaimed the widow, "Do you suppose that Monsieur Godefroid took these rooms for you to hold meetings in?"

"I beg pardon, madame," replied the nurseryman, "the landing was crowded—"

"I did not mean it for you, Monsieur Cartier," said the woman.

"Stay here!" cried Godefroid, addressing the nurseryman.—"And you, my dear sir," he added, turning to Monsieur Bernard, whom this insolent remark left unmoved, "if it suits you to settle matters with your gardener in my room, pray come in."

The old gentleman, stupefied with trouble, gave Godefroid a stony look, which conveyed a thousand thanks.

"As for you, my dear Madame Vauthier, do not be so rough to monsieur, who, in the first place, is an old man, and to whom you also owe your thanks for having me as your lodger."

"Indeed!" exclaimed the woman.

"Besides, if poor folks do not help each other, who is to help them?—Leave us, Madame Vauthier; I can blow up my own fire. See to having my wood stowed in your cellar; I have no doubt you will take good care of it."

Madame Vauthier vanished; for Godefroid, by placing his fuel in her charge, had afforded pasture to her greed.

"Come in," said Godefroid, signing to the gardener, and setting two chairs for the debtor and creditor. The old man talked standing; the tradesman took a seat.

"Come, my good man," Godefroid went on, "the rich do not always pay so punctually as you say they do, and you should not dun a worthy gentleman for a few louis. Monsieur draws his pension every six months, and he cannot give you a draft in anticipation for so small a sum; but I will advance the money if you insist on it."

"Monsieur Bernard drew his pension about three weeks since, and he did not pay me. I should be very sorry to annoy him—"

"What, and you have been supplying him with flowers for—"

"Yes, monsieur, for six years, and he has always paid until now."

Monsieur Bernard, who was listening to all that might be going on in his own lodgings, and paying no heed to this discussion, heard screams through the partition, and hurried away in alarm, without saying a word.

"Come, come, my good man, bring some fine flowers, your best flowers, this very morning, to Monsieur Bernard, and let your wife send in some fresh eggs and milk; I will pay you myself this evening."

Cartier looked somewhat askance at Godefroid.

"Well, I suppose you know more about it than Madame Vauthier; she sent me word that I had better look sharp if I meant to be paid," said he. "Neither she nor I, sir, can account for it when people who live on bread, who pick up odds and ends of vegetables, and bits of carrot and potatoes, and turnip outside the eating-house doors—yes, sir, I have seen the boy filling a little basket,—well, when those people spend near on a hundred francs a month on flowers. The old man, they say, has but three thousand francs a year for his pension—"

"At any rate," said Godefroid, "if they ruin themselves in flowers, it is not for you to complain."

"Certainly not, sir, so long as I am paid."

"Bring me your bill."

"Very good, sir," said the gardener, with rather more respect. "You hope to see the lady they hide so carefully, no doubt?"

"Come, come, my good fellow, you forget yourself," said Godefroid stiffly. "Go home and pick out your best flowers to replace those you are taking away. If you can supply me with rich milk and new-laid eggs, you may have my custom. I will go this morning and look at your place."

"It is one of the best in Paris, and I exhibit at the Luxembourg shows. I have three acres of garden on the boulevard, just behind that of the *Grande-Chaumière*."

"Very good, Monsieur Cartier. You are richer than I am, I can see. So have some consideration for us; for who knows but that one day we may need each other."

The nurseryman departed, much puzzled as to what Godefroid could be.

"And time was when I was just like that!" said Godefroid to himself as he blew the fire. "What a perfect specimen of the commonplace citizen; a gossip, full of curiosity, possessed by the idea of equality, but jealous of other dealers; furious at not knowing why a poor invalid stays in her room and is never seen; secretive as to his profits, but vain enough to let out the secret if he could crow over his neighbour. Such a man ought to be lieutenant at least of his crew. How easily and how often in every age does the scene of Monsieur Dimanche recur! Another minute, and Cartier would have been my sworn ally!"

The old man's return interrupted this soliloquy, which shows how greatly Godefroid's ideas had changed during the past four months.

"I beg your pardon," said Monsieur Bernard, in a husky voice, "I see you have sent off the nurseryman quite satisfied, for he bowed politely. In fact, my young friend, Providence seems to have sent you here for our express benefit at the very moment when all seemed at an end! Alas! The man's chatter must have told you many things.—It is quite true that I drew my half-year's pension a fortnight since; but I had other and more pressing debts, and I was obliged to keep back the money for the rent or be turned out of doors. You, to whom I have confided the secret of my daughter's state—who have heard her—"

He looked anxiously at Godefroid, who nodded affirmation.

'Well, you can judge if that would not be her death-blow. For I should have to place her in a hospital.—My grandson and I have been dreading this day, not that Cartier was our chief fear; it is the cold—"

"My dear Monsieur Bernard, I have plenty of wood; take some!" cried Godefroid.

"But how can I ever repay such kindness?" said the old man.

"By accepting it without ceremony," answered Godefroid cordially, "and by giving me your entire confidence."

"But what claims have I on such generosity?" asked Monsieur Bernard with revived suspicions. "My pride and my grandson's is broken!" he exclaimed. "For we have already fallen so far as to argue with our two or three creditors. The very poor can have no creditors. Only those can owe money who keep up a certain external display which we have utterly lost.—But I have not yet lost my common sense, my reason," he added, as if speaking to himself.

"Monsieur," said Godefroid gravely, "the story you told me yesterday would draw tears from an usurer—"

"No, no! for Barbet the publisher, our landlord, speculates on my poverty, and sets his old servant, the woman Vauthier, to spy it out."

"How can he speculate on it?" asked Godefroid.

"I will tell you at another time," replied the old man. "My daughter may be feeling cold, and since you are so kind, and since I am in a situation to accept charity, even if it were from my worst enemy—"

"I will carry the wood," said Godefroid, who went across the landing with half a score of logs, which he laid down in his neighbour's outer room.

Monsieur Bernard had taken an equal number, and when he beheld this little stock of fuel, he could not conceal the simple, almost idiotic, smile by which men rescued from mortal and apparently inevitable danger express their joy, for there still is fear even in their belief.

"Accept all I can give you, my dear Monsieur Bernard, without hesitation, and when we have saved your daughter, and you are happy once more, I will explain everything. Till then leave everything to me.—I went to call on the Jewish doctor, but unfortunately Halpersohn is absent; he will not be back for two days."

Just then a voice which sounded to Godefroid, and which really was, sweet and youthful, called out, "Papa, papa!" in an expressive tone.

While talking to the old man, Godefroid had already remarked, through the crack of the door opposite to that on the landing, lines of neat white paint, showing that the sick woman's room must be very different from the others that composed the lodging. His curiosity was now raised to the highest pitch; the errand of mercy was to him no more than a means; its end was to see the invalid. He would not believe that any one who spoke in such a voice could be horrible to behold.

"You are taking too much trouble, papa," said the voice. "Why do not you have more servants—at your age—Dear me!"

"But you know, dear Vanda, that I will not allow any one to wait on you but myself or your boy."

These two sentences, which Godefroid overheard, though with some difficulty, for a curtain dulled the sound, made him understand the case. The sick woman, surrounded by every luxury, knew nothing of the real state in which her father and son lived. Monsieur Bernard's silk wrapper, the flowers, and his conversation with Cartier had already roused Godefroid's suspicions, and he stood riveted, almost confounded, by this marvel of paternal devotion. The contrast between the invalid's room as he imagined it and what he saw was in fact amazing. The reader may judge:

Through the door of a third room which stood open, Godefroid saw two narrow beds of painted wood like those of the vilest lodging-houses, with a straw mattress and a thin upper mattress; on each there was but one blanket. A small iron stove such as porters use to cook on, with a few lumps of dried fuel by the side of it, was enough to show the destitution of the owner, without other details in keeping with this wretched stove.

Godefroid by one step forward could see the pots and pans of the wretched household—glazed earthenware jars, in which a few potatoes were soaking in dirty water. Two tables of blackened wood, covered with papers and books, stood in front of a window looking out on the Rue Notre-Dame des Champs, and showed how the father and son occupied themselves in the evening. On each table there was a candlestick of wrought iron of the poorest description, and in them candles of the cheapest kind, eight to the pound. On a third table, which served as a dresser, there were two shining sets of silver-gilt forks and spoons, some plates, a basin and cup in Sèvres china, and a knife with a gilt handle lying in a case, all evidently for the invalid's use.

The stove was alight; the water in the kettle was steaming gently. A wardrobe of painted deal contained no doubt the lady's linen and possessions, for he saw on her father's bed the clothes he had worn the day before, spread by way of a covering.

Some other rags laid in the same way on his grandson's bed led him to conclude that this was all their wardrobe; and under the bed he saw their shoes.

The floor, swept but seldom no doubt, was like that of a schoolroom. A large loaf that had been cut was visible on a shelf over the table. In short, it was poverty in the last stage of squalor, poverty reduced to a system, with the decent order of a determination to endure it; driven poverty that has to do everything at home, that insists on doing it, but that finds it impossible, and so puts every poor possession to a wrong use. A strong and sickening smell pervaded the room, which evidently was but rarely cleaned.

The ante-room where Godefroid stood was at any rate decent, and he guessed that it commonly served to hide the horrors of the room inhabited by the old man and the youth. This room, hung with a Scotch plaid paper, had four walnut-wood chairs and a small table, and was graced with portraits—a coloured print of Horace Vernet's picture of the Emperor; those of Louis XVIII and Charles X; and one of Prince Poniatowski, a friend no doubt of Monsieur Bernard's father-in-law. There were cotton window-curtains bound with red and finished with fringe.

Godefroid, keeping an eye on Népomucène, and hearing him come up with a load of wood, signed to him to stack it noiselessly in Monsieur Bernard's ante-room; and, with a delicate feeling that showed he was making good progress, he shut the bedroom door that Madame Vauthier's boy might not see the old man's squalor.

The ante-room was partly filled up by three flower-stands full of splendid plants, two oval and one round, all three of rosewood, and elegantly finished; and Népomucène, as he placed the logs on the floor, could not help saying:

"Isn't that lovely?—It must cost a pretty penny!"

"Jean, do not make too much noise—" Monsieur Bernard called out.

"There, you hear him?" said Népomucène to Godefroid, "the poor old boy is certainly cracked!"

"And what will you be at his age?"

"Oh, I know sure enough!" said Népomucène; "I shall be in a sugar-basin."

"In a sugar-basin?"

"Yes, my bones will have been made into charcoal. I have seen the sugar-boilers' carts often enough at Mont Souris come to fetch bone-black for their works, and they told me they used it in making sugar." And with this philosophical reply, he went off for another basketful of wood.

Godefroid quietly closed Monsieur Bernard's door, leaving him alone with his daughter.

Madame Vauthier had meanwhile prepared her new lodger's breakfast, and came with Félicité to serve it. Godefroid, lost in meditation, was staring at the fire on the hearth. He was absorbed in reflecting on this poverty that included so many different forms of misery, though he perceived that it had its pleasures too; the ineffable joys and triumphs of fatherly and of filial devotion. They were like pearls sewn on sackcloth.

"What romance—even the most famous—can compare with such reality?" thought he. "How noble is the life that mingles with such lives as these, enabling the soul to discern their cause and effect; to assuage suffering and encourage what is good; to become one with misfortune and learn the secrets of such a home as this; to be an actor in ever-new dramas such as delight us in the works of the most famous authors!—I had no idea that goodness could be more interesting than vice."

"Is everything to your mind, sir?" asked Madame Vauthier, who, helped by Félicité, had placed the table close to Godefroid. He then saw an excellent cup of coffee with milk, a smoking hot omelette, fresh butter, and little red radishes.

"Where did you find those radishes?" asked Godefroid.

"Monsieur Cartier gave them to me," said she. "I thought you might like them, sir.

"And what do you expect me to pay for a breakfast like this every day?" said Godefroid.

"Well, monsieur, to be quite fair—it would be hard to supply it under thirty sous."

"Say thirty sous," said Godefroid. "But how is it that close by this, at Madame Machillot's, they only ask me forty-five francs a month for dinner, which is just thirty sous a day?"

"Oh, but what a difference, sir, between getting a dinner for fifteen people and going to buy everything that is needed for one breakfast: a roll, you see, eggs, butter,—lighting the fire—and then sugar, milk coffee.—Why, they will ask you sixteen sous for nothing but a cup of coffee with milk in the Place de l'Odéon, and you have to give a sou or two to the waiter!—Here you have no trouble at all; you breakfast at home, in your slippers.

"Well, then it is settled," said Godefroid.

"And even then, but for Madame Cartier, from whom I get the milk and eggs and parsley, I could not do it at all.—You must go and see their place, sir. Oh, it is really a fine sight. They employ five gardeners' apprentices, and Népomucène goes to help with the watering all the summer; they pay me to let him go. And you make a lot of money out of strawberries and melons.—You are very much interested in Monsieur Bernard, it would seem?" asked the widow in her sweetest tones. "For really to answer for their debts in that way!—But perhaps you don't know how much they owe.—There is the lady that keeps the circulating library on the Place Saint-Michel; she calls every three or four days for thirty francs, and she wants it badly too. Heaven above! that poor woman in bed does read and read. And at two sous a volume, thirty francs in two months—"

"Is a hundred volumes a month," said Godefroid.

"There goes the old fellow to fetch madame's cream and roll," the woman went on. "It is for her tea; for she lives on nothing but tea, that lady; she has it twice a day, and then twice a week she wants sweets.—She is dainty, I can tell you! The old boy buys her cakes and tarts at the pastry-cook's in the Rue de Buci. Oh, when it is for her, he sticks at nothing. He says she is his daughter!—Where's the man who would do all he does, and at his age, for his daughter? He is killing himself—himself and his Auguste—and all for her.—If you are like me, sir—I would give twenty francs to see her. Monsieur Berton says she is shocking, an object to make a show of.—They did well to come to this part of the town where nobody ever comes.—And you think of dining at Madame Machillot's, sir?"

"Yes, I thought of making an arrangement with her."

"Well, sir, it is not to interfere with any plan of yours; but, take 'em as you find 'em, you will find a better eating-place in the Rue de Tournon; you need not bind yourself for a month, and you will have a better table—"

"Where in the Rue de Tournon?"

"At the successors of old Madame Girard. That is where the gentlemen upstairs dine, and they are satisfied—they could not be better pleased."

"Very well, Madame Vauthier, I will take your advice and dine there."

"And, my dear sir," the woman went on, emboldened by the easy-going air which Godefroid had intentionally assumed, "do you mean to say, seriously, that you are such a flat as to think of paying Monsieur Bernard's debts?—I should be really very sorry; for you must remember, my good Monsieur Godefroid, that he is very near on seventy, and after him where are you? There's an end to his pension. What will there be to repay you? Young men are so rash. Do you know that he owes above a thousand crowns?"

"But to whom?" asked Godefroid.

"Oh, that is no concern of mine," said Madame Vauthier mysteriously. "He owes the money, and that's enough; and between you and me, he is having a hard time of it; he cannot get credit for a sou in all the neighbourhood for that very reason."

"A thousand crowns!" said Godefroid. "Be sure of one thing; if I had a thousand crowns, I should be no lodger of yours. But I, you see, cannot bear to see others suffering; and for a few hundred francs that it may cost me, I will make sure that my neighbour, a man with white hair, has bread and firing. Why, a man often loses as much at cards.—But three thousand francs—why, what do you think? Good Heavens!"

Madame Vauthier, quite taken in by Godefroid's affected candour, allowed a gleam of satisfaction to light up her face, and this confirmed her lodger's suspicions. Godefroid was convinced that the old woman was implicated in some plot against the hapless Monsieur Bernard.

"It is a strange thing, monsieur, what fancies come into one's head. You will say that I am very inquisitive; but yesterday, when I saw you talking to Monsieur Bernard, it struck me that you must be a publisher's clerk—for this is their part of the town. I had a lodger, a foreman printer, whose works are in the Rue de Vaugirard, and he was named the same name as you—"

"And what concern is it of yours what my business is?" said Godefroid.

"Lor'! whether you tell me or whether you don't, I shall know just the same," said the widow. "Look at Monsieur Bernard, for instance; well, for eighteen months I could never find out what he was; but in the nineteenth month I discovered that he had been a judge or a magistrate, or something of the kind, in the law, and that now he is writing a book about it. What does he get by it? That's what I say. And if he had told me, I should have held my tongue; so there!"

"I am not at present a publisher's agent, but I may be, perhaps, before long."

"There, I knew it!" exclaimed the woman eagerly, and turning from the bed she was making as an excuse to stay chattering to her lodger. "You have come to cut the ground from under—Well, well, 'a nod's as good as a wink'—"

"Hold hard!" cried Godefroid, standing between Madame Vauthier and the door. "Now, tell me, what are you paid to meddle in this?"

"Heyday!" cried the old woman, with a keen look at Godefroid. "You are pretty sharp after all!"

She shut and locked the outer door; then she came back and sat down by the fire.

"On my word and honour, as sure as my name is Vauthier, I took you for a student till I saw you giving your logs to old Father Bernard. My word, but you're a sharp one! By the Piper! you can play a part well! I thought you were a perfect flat. Now, will you promise me a thousand francs? For as sure as the day above us, old Barbet and Monsieur Métivier have promised me five hundred if I keep my eyes open."

"What? Not they! Two hundred at the very outside, my good woman, and only promised at that—and you cannot summons them for payment!—Look here; if you will put me in a position to get the job they are trying to manage with Monsieur Bernard, I will give you four hundred!—Come, now, what are they up to?"

"Well, they have paid him fifteen hundred francs on account for his work, and made him sign a bill for a thousand crowns. They doled it out to him a hundred francs at a time, contriving to keep him as poor as poor.—They set the duns upon him; they sent Cartier, you may wager."

At this, Godefroid, by a look of cynical perspicacity that he shot at the woman, made it clear to her that he quite understood the game she was playing for her landlord's benefit. Her speech threw a light on two sides of the question, for it also explained the rather strange scene between the gardener and himself.

"Oh yes!" she went on, "they have him fast; for where is he ever to find a thousand crowns! They intend to offer him five hundred francs when the work is in their hands complete, and five hundred francs per volume as they are brought out for sale. The business is all in the name of a bookseller these gentlemen have set up in business on the Quai des Augustins—"

"Oh yes—that little—what's-his-name?"

"Yes, that's your man.—Morand, formerly Monsieur Barbet's agent.—There is a heap of money to be got out of it, it would seem."

"There will be a heap of money to put into it," said Godefroid, with an expressive grimace.

There was a gentle knock at the door, and Godefroid, very glad of the interruption, rose to open it.

"All this is between you and me, Mother Vauthier," said Godefroid, seeing Monsieur Bernard.

"Monsieur Bernard," cried she, "I have a letter for you."

The old man went down a few steps.

"No, no, I have no letter for you, Monsieur Bernard; I only wished to warn you against that young fellow there. He is a publisher."

"Oh, that accounts for everything," said the old man to himself. And he came back to his neighbour's room with a quite altered countenance.

The calmly cold expression on Monsieur Bernard's face when he reappeared was in such marked contrast to the frank and friendly manner his gratitude had lent him, that Godefroid was struck by so sudden a change.

"Monsieur, forgive me for disturbing your solitude, but you have since yesterday loaded me with favours, and a benefactor confers rights on those whom he obliges."

Godefroid bowed.

"I, who for five years have suffered once a fortnight the torments of the Redeemer; I, who for six-and-thirty years was the representative of Society and the Government, who was then the arm of public vengeance, and who, as you may suppose, have no illusions left—nothing, nothing but sufferings,—well, monsieur, your careful attention in closing the door of the dog-kennel in which my grandson and I sleep—that trifling act was to me the cup of water of which Bossuet speaks. I found in my heart, my worn-out heart, which is as dry of tears as my withered body is of sweat, the last drop of that elixir which in youth leads us to see the best side of every human action, and I came to offer you my hand, which I never give to any one but my daughter; I came to bring you the heavenly rose of belief, even now, in goodness."

"Monsieur Bernard," said Godefroid, remembering good old Alain's injunctions, "I did nothing with a view to winning your gratitude.—You are under a mistake."

"That is frank and above board," said the old lawyer. 'Well, that is what I like. I was about to reproach you. Forgive me; I esteem you.—So you are a publisher, and you want to get my book in preference to Messieurs Barbet, Métivier, and Morand?—That explains all. You are prepared to deal with me as they were; only you do it with a good grace."

"Old Vauthier has just told you, I suppose, that I am a publisher's agent?"

"Yes," said he.

"Well, Monsieur Bernard, before I can say what we are prepared to *pay* more than those gentlemen *offer*, I must understand on what terms you stand with them."

"Very true," said the old man, who seemed delighted to find himself the object of a competition by which he could not fail to benefit. "Do you know what the work is?"

"No; I only know that there is something to be made by it."

"It is only half-past nine; my daughter has had her breakfast, my grandson Auguste will not come in till a quarter to eleven. Cartier will not be here with the flowers for an hour—we have time to talk, monsieur—monsieur who?"

"Godefroid."

"Monsieur Godefroid.—The book in question was planned by me in 1825, at a time when the Ministry, struck by the constant reduction of personal estate, drafted the Law of Entail and Seniority which was thrown out. I had observed many defects in our codes and in the fundamental principle of French law. The codes have been the subject of many important works; but all those treatises are essentially on jurisprudence; no one has been so bold as to study the results of the Revolution—or of Napoleon's rule, if you prefer it—as a whole, analysing the spirit of these laws and the working of their application. That is, in general terms, the purpose of my book. I have called it the *Spirit of the Modern Laws*. It covers organic law as well as the codes—all the codes, for we have five! My book, too, is in five volumes, and a sixth volume of authorities, quotations, and references. I have still three months' work before me.

"The owner of this house, a retired publisher, scented a speculation. I, in the first instance, thought only of benefiting my country. This Barbet has got the better of me.—You will wonder how a publisher could entrap an old lawyer; but you, monsieur, know my history, and this man is a money-lender. He has the sharp eye and the knowledge of the world that such men must have. His advances have just kept pace with my necessity; he has always come in at the very moment when despair has made me a defenceless prey."

"Not at all, my dear sir," said Godefroid. "He has simply kept Madame Vauthier as a spy.—But the terms, tell me honestly."

"They advanced me fifteen hundred francs, represented at the present rates by three bills for a thousand francs each, and these three thousand francs are secured to them by a lien on the property of my book, which I cannot dispose of elsewhere till I have paid off the bills; the bills have been protested; judgement has been pronounced.—Here monsieur, you see the complications of poverty.

"At the most moderate estimate, the first edition of this vast work, the result of ten years' labour and thirty-six years' experience, will be well worth ten thousand francs.—Well, just five days since, Morand offered me a thousand crowns and my note of hand paid off for all rights.—As I could never find three thousand two hundred and forty francs, unless you intervene between us, I must yield.

"They would not take my word of honour; for further security they insisted on bills of exchange which have been protested, and I shall be imprisoned for debt. If I pay up, these money-lenders will have doubled their loan; if I deal with them, they will make a fortune, for one of them was a paper-maker, and God only knows how low they can keep the price of materials. And then, with my name on it, they know that they are certain of a sale of ten thousand copies."

"Why, monsieur—you, a retired Judge—!"

"What can I say? I have not a friend, no one remembers me!—And yet I saved many heads even if I sentenced many to fall!—And then there is my daughter, my daughter whose nurse and companion I am, for I work only at night.—Ah! young man, none but the wretched should be set to judge the wretched. I see now that of yore I was too severe."

"I do not ask you your name, monsieur. I have not a thousand crowns at my disposal, especially if I pay Halpersohn and your little bills; but I can save you if you will pledge your word not to dispose of your book without due notice to me; it is impossible to embark in so important a matter without consulting professional experts. The persons I work for are powerful, and I can promise you success if you can promise me perfect secrecy, even from your children—and keep your word."

"The only success I care for is my poor Vanda's recovery; for, I assure you, the sight of such sufferings extinguishes every other feeling in a father's heart; the loss of fame is nothing to the man who sees a grave yawning at his feet—"

"I will call on you this evening. Halpersohn may come home at any moment, and I go every day to see if he has returned.—I will spend to-day in your service."

"Oh, if you could bring about my daughter's recovery, monsieur—, monsieur, I would make you a present of my book!"

"But," said Godefroid, "I am not a publisher."

The old man started with surprise.

"I could not help letting old Vauthier think so for the sake of ascertaining what snares had been laid for you."

"But who are you, then?"

"Godefroid," was the reply; "and as you have allowed me to supply you with the means of living better," added the young man, smiling, "you may call me Godefroid de Bouillon."

The old lawyer was too much touched to laugh at the jest. He held out his hand to Godefroid and grasped the young man's warmly.

"You wish to remain unknown?" said Monsieur Bernard, looking at Godefroid with melancholy, mixed with some uneasiness.

"If you will allow me."

'Well, do as you think proper.—And come in this evening; you will see my daughter, if her state allows."

This was evidently the greatest concession the poor father could make; and seeing Godefroid's grateful look, the old man had the pleasure of feeling that he was understood.

An hour later Cartier came back with some beautiful flowers, replanted the stands with his own hands in fresh moss, and Godefroid paid the bill, as he did the subscription to the lending library, for which the account was sent in soon after. Books and flowers were the staff of life to this poor sick—or rather, tormented woman, who could live on so little food.

As he thought of this family in the toils of disaster, like that of Laocoon—a sublime allegory of many lives!—Godefroid, making his way leisurely on foot to the Rue Marbeuf, felt in his heart that he was curious rather than benevolent. The idea of the sick woman, surrounded with luxuries in the midst of abject squalor, made him forget the horrible details of the strange nervous malady, which is happily an extraordinary exception, though abundantly proved by various historians. One of our gossiping chronicle writers, Tallemant des Réaux, mentions an instance. We like to think of women as elegant even in their worst sufferings, and Godefroid promised himself some pleasure in penetrating into the room which only the physician, the father, and the son had entered for six years past. However, he ended by reproaching himself for his curiosity. The neophyte even understood that his feeling, however natural, would die out by degrees as he carried out his merciful errands, by dint of seeing new homes and new sorrows. Such messengers, in fact, attain to a heavenly benignity which nothing can shock or amaze, just as in love we attain to a sublime quiescence of feeling in the conviction of its strength and duration, by a constant habit of submission and sweetness.

Godefroid was told that Halpersohn had come home during the night, but had been obliged to go out in his carriage the first thing in the morning to see the patients who were waiting for him. The woman at the gate told Godefroid to come back next morning before nine.

Remembering Monsieur Alain's advice as to parsimony in his personal expenses, Godefroid dined for twenty-five sous in the Rue de Tournon, and was rewarded for his self-denial by finding himself among compositors and proof-readers. He heard a discussion about the cost of production, and, joining in, picked up the information that an octavo volume of forty sheets, of which a thousand copies were printed, would not cost more than thirty sous per copy under favourable circumstances. He determined on going to inquire the price commonly asked for such volumes on sale at the law publishers, so as to be in a position to dispute the point with the publishers who had got a hold on Monsieur Bernard, if he should happen to meet them.

At about seven in the evening he came back to the Boulevard Mont-Parnasse along the Rue de Vaugirard, the Rue Madame, and the Rue de l'Ouest, and he saw how deserted that part of the town is, for he met nobody. It is true that the cold was severe, snow fell in large flakes, and the carts made no noise on the stones.

"Ah, here you are, monsieur!" said Madame Vauthier when she saw him. "If I had known you would come in so early, I would have lighted your fire."

"It is unnecessary," replied Godefroid, as the woman followed him; "I am going to spend the evening with Monsieur Bernard."

"Ah! very good. You are cousins, I suppose, that you are hand and glove with him by the second day. I thought perhaps you would have liked to finish what we were saying—"

"Oh, about the four hundred francs?" said Godefroid in an undertone. "Look here, Mother Vauthier, you would have had them this evening if you had said nothing to Monsieur Bernard. You want to hunt with the hounds and run with the hare, and you will get neither; for, so far as I am concerned, you have spoiled my game—my chances are altogether ruined—"

"Don't you believe that, my good sir. To-morrow, when you are at breakfast.—"

"Oh, to-morrow I must be off at daybreak like your authors."

Godefroid's past experience and life as a dandy and journalist had been so far of use to him as to lead him to guess that if he did not take this line, Barbet's spy would warn the publisher that there was something in the wind, and he would then take such steps as would ere long endanger Monsieur Bernard's liberty; whereas, by leaving the three usurious negotiators to believe that their schemes were not in peril, they would keep quiet.

But Godefroid was not yet a match for Parisian humanity when it assumes the guise of a Madame Vauthier. This woman meant to have Godefroid's money and her landlord's too. She flew off to Monsieur Barbet, while Godefroid changed his dress to call on Monsieur Bernard's daughter.

Eight o'clock was striking at the Convent of the Visitation, whose clock regulated the life of the whole neighbourhood, when Godefroid, full of curiosity, knocked at his friend's door. Auguste opened it; as it was Saturday, the lad spent his evening at home; Godefroid saw that he wore a jacket of black velvet, black trousers that were quite decent, and a blue silk tie; but his surprise at seeing the youth so unlike his usual self ceased when he entered the invalid's room. He at once understood the necessity for the father and the boy to be presentably dressed.

The walls of the room, hung with yellow silk, panelled with bright green cord, made the room look extremely cheerful; the cold tiled floor was covered by a flowered carpet on a white ground. The two windows, with their handsome curtains lined with white silk, were like bowers, the flower-stands were so full of beauty, and blinds hindered them from being seen from outside in a quarter where such lavishness was rare. The woodwork, painted white, and varnished, was touched up with gold lines. A heavy curtain, embroidered in tent stitch, with grotesque foliage on a yellow ground, hung over the door and deadened every sound from outside. This splendid curtain had been worked by the invalid, who embroidered like a fairy when she had the use of her hands.

Opposite the door, at the further end of the room, the chimney-shelf, covered with green velvet, had a set of very costly ornaments, the only relic of the wealth of the two families. There was a very curious clock; an elephant supporting a porcelain tower filled with beautiful flowers; two candelabra in the same style, and some valuable Oriental pieces. The fender, the dogs, and fire-irons were all of the finest workmanship.

The largest of the three flower stands stood in the middle of the room, and above it hung a porcelain chandelier of floral design.

The bed on which the judge's daughter lay was one of those fine examples of carved wood, painted white and gold, that were made in the time of Louis XV. By the invalid's pillow was a pretty inlaid table, on which were the various objects necessary for a life spent in bed; a bracket light for two candles was fixed to the wall, and could be turned backwards and forwards by a touch. In front of her was a bed-table, wonderfully contrived for her convenience. The bed was covered with a magnificent counterpane, and draped with curtains looped back in festoons; it was loaded with books and a work-basket, and among these various objects Godefroid would hardly have discovered the sick woman but for the tapers in the two candle-branches.

There seemed to be nothing of her but a very white face, darkly marked round the eyes by much suffering; her eyes shone like fire; and her principal ornament was her splendid black hair, of which the heavy curls, set out in bunches of numerous ringlets, showed that the care and arrangement of her hair occupied part of the invalid's day; a movable mirror at the foot of the bed confirmed the idea.

No kind of modern elegance was lacking, and a few trifling toys for poor Vanda's amusement showed that her father's affection verged on mania.

The old man rose from a very handsome easy-chair of Louis XV style, white and gold, and covered with needlework, and went forward a few steps to welcome Godefroid, who certainly would not have recognised him; for his cold, stern face had assumed the gay expression peculiar to old men who have preserved their dignity of manner and the superficial frivolity of courtiers. His purple wadded dressing-gown was in harmony with the luxury about him, and he took snuff out of a gold box set with diamonds.

"Here, my dear," said Monsieur Bernard to his daughter, "is our neighbour of whom I spoke to you." And he signed to his grandson to bring forward one of two armchairs, in the same style as his own, which were standing on each side of the fire.

"Monsieur's name is Godefroid, and he is most kind in standing on no ceremony—"

Vanda moved her head in acknowledgment of Godefroid's low bow; and by the movement of her throat as it bent and unbent, he discovered that all this woman's vitality was seated in her head. Her emaciated arms and lifeless hands lay on the fine white sheet like objects quite apart from the body, and that seemed to fill no space in the bed. The things needed for her use were on a set of shelves behind the bed, and screened by a silk curtain.

"You, my dear sir, are the first person, excepting only the doctors—who have ceased to be men to me—whom I have set eyes on for six years; so you can have no idea of the interest I have felt in you ever since my father told me you were coming to call on us. It was passionate, unconquerable curiosity, like that of our mother Eve. My father, who is so good to me; my son, of whom I am so fond, are undoubtedly enough to fill up the vacuum of a soul now almost bereft of body; but that soul is still a woman's after all! I recognised that in the childish joy I felt in the idea of your visit.—You will do us the pleasure of taking a cup of tea with us, I hope?"

"Yes, Monsieur Godefroid has promised us the pleasure of his company for the evening," said the old man, with the air of a millionaire doing the honours of his house.

Auguste, seated in a low, worsted-work chair by a small table of inlaid wood, finished with brass mouldings, was reading by the light of the wax-candles on the chimney-shelf.

"Auguste, my dear, tell Jean to bring tea in an hour's time."

She spoke with some pointed meaning, and Auguste replied by a nod.

"Will you believe, monsieur, that for the past six years no one has waited on me but my father and my boy, and I could not endure anybody else. If I were to lose them, I should die of it.—My father will not even allow Jean, a poor old Normandy peasant who has lived with us for thirty years—will not even let him come into the room."

"I should think not, indeed!" said the old man readily. "Monsieur Godefroid has seen him; he saws and brings in the wood, he cooks and runs errands, and wears a dirty apron; he would have made hay of all these pretty things, which are so necessary to my poor child, to whom this elegance is second nature."

"Indeed, madame, your father is quite right—"

"But why?" she urged. "If Jean had damaged my room, my father would have renewed it."

"Of course, my child; but what would have prevented me is the fact that you cannot leave it; and you have no idea what Paris workmen are. It would take them more than three months to restore your room! Only think of the dust that would come out of your carpet if it were taken up. Let Jean do your room! Do not think of such a thing. By taking the extreme care which only your father and your boy can take, we have spared you sweeping and dust; if Jean came in to help, everything would be done for in a month."

"It is not so much out of economy as for the sake of your health," said Godefroid. "Monsieur your father is quite right."

"Oh, I am not complaining," said Vanda in a saucy tone. Her voice had the quality of a concert; soul, action, and life were all concentrated in her eyes and her voice; for Vanda, by careful practice, for which time had certainly not been lacking, had succeeded in overcoming the difficulties arising from her loss of teeth.

"I am still happy, monsieur, in spite of the dreadful malady that tortures me; for wealth is certainly a great help in enduring my sufferings. If we had been in poverty, I should have died eighteen years ago, and I am still alive. I have many enjoyments, and they are all the keener because I live on, triumphing over death.—You will think me a great chatterbox," she added, with a smile.

"Madame," said Godefroid, "I could beg you to talk for ever, for I never heard a voice to compare with yours—it is music! Rubini is not more delightful—"

"Do not mention Rubini or the opera," said the old man sadly. "However rich we may be, it is impossible to give my daughter, who was a great musician, a pleasure to which she was devoted."

"I apologise," said Godefroid.

"You will fall into our ways," said the old man.

"This is your training," said the invalid, smiling. "When we have warned you several times by crying, 'Look out!' you will know all the blind man's buff of our conversation!"

Godefroid exchanged a swift glance with Monsieur Bernard, who, seeing tears in his new friend's eyes, put his finger to his lip as a warning not to betray the heroic devotion he and the boy had shown for the past seven years.

This devoted and unflagging imposture, proved by the invalid's entire deception, produced on Godefroid at this moment the effect of looking at a precipitous rock whence two chamois-hunters were on the point of falling.

The splendid gold and diamond snuff-box with which the old man trifled, leaning over the foot of his daughter's bed, was like the touch of genius which in a great actor wrings from us a cry of admiration. Godefroid looked at the snuff-box, wondering why it had not been sold or pawned, but he postponed the idea till he could discuss it with the old man.

"This evening, Monsieur Godefroid, my daughter was so greatly excited by the promise of your visit, that the various strange symptoms of her malady which, for nearly a fortnight past, have driven us to despair, suddenly disappeared. You may imagine my gratitude!"

"And mine!" cried Vanda, in an insinuating voice, with a graceful inclination of her head. "You are a deputation from the outer world.—Since I was twenty I have not known what a drawing-room is like, or a party, or a ball; and I love dancing, I am crazy about the play, and above all about music. Well, I imagine everything in my mind. I read a great deal, and my father tells me all about the gay world—" As he listened, Godefroid felt prompted to kneel at the feet of this poor old man.

"When he goes to the opera—and he often goes—he describes the dresses to me, and all the singers. Oh! I should like to be well again; in the first place, for my father's sake, for he lives for me alone, as I live for him and through him, and then for my son's—I should like him to know another mother. Oh! monsieur, what perfect men are my dear old father and my admirable son—Then I could wish for health also, that I might hear Lablache, Rubini, Tamburini, Grisi, the *Puritani* too!—But—"

"Come, my dear, compose yourself. If we talk about music, it is fatal!" said the old father, with a smile.

And that smile, which made him look younger, evidently constantly deceived the sick woman.

'Well, I will be good," said Vanda, with a saucy pout. "But let me have a harmonium."

This instrument had lately been invented; it could, by a little contrivance, be placed by the invalid's bed, and would only need the pressure of the foot to give out an organ-like tone. This instrument, in its most improved form, was as effective as a piano; but at that time it cost three hundred francs. Vanda, who read newspapers and reviews, had heard of such an instrument, and had been longing for one for two months past.

"Yes, madame, and I can procure you one," replied Godefroid at an appealing glance from the old man. "A friend of mine who is setting out for Algiers has a very fine one, which I will borrow of him; for before buying one, you had better try it. It is quite possible that the sound, which is strongly vibrating, may be too much for you."

"Can I have it to-morrow?" she asked, with the eagerness of a Creole.

"To-morrow!" objected Monsieur Bernard. "That is very soon; besides, to-morrow will be Sunday."

"To be sure," said she, looking at Godefroid, who felt as though he saw a soul fluttering, as he admired the ubiquity ofVanda's eyes.

Until now he had never understood what the power of the voice and eyes might be when the entire vitality was concentrated in them. Her glance was more than a glance; it was a flame, or rather a blaze of divine light, a communicative ray of life and intelligence, thought made visible. The voice, with its endless intonations, supplied the place of movement, gesture, and turns of the head. And her changing colour, varying like that of the fabled chameleon, made the illusion—or, if you will, the delusion—complete. That weary head, buried in a cambric pillow frilled with lace, was a complete woman.

Never in his life had Godefroid seen so noble a spectacle, and he could hardly endure his emotions. Another grand feature, where everything was strange in a situation so full of romance and of horror, was that the soul alone seemed to be living in the spectators. This atmosphere, where all was sentiment, had a celestial influence. They were as unconscious of their bodies as the woman in bed; everything was pure spirit. By dint of gazing at these frail remains of a pretty woman, Godefroid forgot the elegant luxury of the room, and felt himself in heaven. It was not till half-an-hour after that he noticed a what-not covered with curiosities, over which hung a noble portrait that Vanda desired him to look at, as it was by Géricault.

"Géricault," said she, "was a native of Rouen, and his family being under some obligations to my father, who was President of the Supreme Court there, he showed his gratitude by painting that masterpiece, in which you see me at the age of sixteen."

"You have there a very fine picture," said Godefroid, "and one that is quite unknown to those who have studied the rare works of that great genius."

"To me it is no longer an object of anything but affectionate regard," said she, "since I live only by my feelings; and I have a beautiful life," she went on, looking at her father with her whole soul in her eyes. "Oh, monsieur, if you could but know what my father is! Who would believe that the austere and dignified Judge to whom the Emperor owed so much that he gave him that snuff-box, and whom Charles X rewarded by the gift of that Sèvres tray"—and she looked at a side-table—"that the staunch upholder of law and authority, the learned political writer, has in a heart of rock all the tenderness of a mother?—Oh, papa, papa! Come, kiss me—I insist on it—if you love me."

The old man rose, leaned over the bed, and set a kiss on his daughter's high poetic brow, for her sickly fancies were not invariably furies of affection. Then he walked up and down the room, but without a sound, for he wore slippers—the work of his daughter's hands.

"And what is your occupation?" she asked Godefroid after a pause.

"Madame, I am employed by certain pious persons to take help to the unfortunate."

"A beautiful mission!" said she. "Do you know that the idea of devoting myself to such work has often occurred to me? But what ideas have not occurred to me?" said she, with a little shake of her head. "Pain is a torch that throws light on life, and if I ever recover my health—"

"You shall enjoy yourself, my child," the old man put in.

"Certainly I long to enjoy life," said she, "but should I be able for it?—My son, I hope, will be a lawyer, worthy of his two grandfathers, and he must leave me. What is to be done?—If God restores me to life, I will dedicate it to Him.—Oh, not till I have given you both as much of it as you desire!" she exclaimed, looking at her father and her boy. "There are times, my dear father, when Monsieur de Maistre's ideas work in my brain, and I fancy I am expatiating some sin."

"That is what comes of reading so much!" cried the old man, visibly grieved.

"There was that brave Polish General, my great-grandfather; he meddled very innocently in the concerns of Poland—"

"Now we have come back to Poland!" exclaimed Bernard.

"How can I help it, papa? My sufferings are intolerable, they make me hate life, and disgust me with myself. Well, what have I done to deserve them? Such an illness is not mere disordered health; it is a complete wreck of the whole constitution, and—"

"Sing the national air your poor mother used to sing; it will please Monsieur Godefroid, I have spoken to him of your voice," said her father, evidently anxious to divert his daughter's mind from the ideas she was following out.

Vanda began to sing in a low, soft voice a hymn in the Polish tongue, which left Godefroid bewildered with admiration and sadness. This melody, a good deal like the long-drawn melancholy tunes of Brittany, is one of those poetic airs that linger in the mind long after being heard. As he listened to Vanda, Godefroid at first looked at her; but he could not bear the ecstatic eyes of this remnant of a woman now half-crazed, and he gazed at some tassels that hung on each side of the top of the bed.

"Ah, ha!" said Vanda, laughing at Godefroid's evident curiosity, "you are wondering what those are for?"

"Vanda, Vanda, be calm, my child! See, here comes the tea.—This, monsieur, is a very expensive contrivance," he said to Godefroid. "My daughter cannot raise herself, nor can she remain in bed without its being made and the sheets changed. Those cords work over pulleys, and by slipping a sheet of leather under her and attaching it to rings at the corners to those ropes, we can lift her without fatiguing her or ourselves."

"Yes, I am carried up—up!" said Vanda deliriously.

Auguste happily came in with a teapot, which he set on a little table, where he also placed the Sèvres tray, covered with sandwiches and cakes. Then he brought in the cream and butter. This diverted the sick woman's mind; she had been on the verge of an attack.

"Here, Vanda, is Nathan's last novel. If you should lie awake to-night, you will have something to read."

"*La Perle de Dol*! That will be a love-story no doubt.— Auguste, what do you think? I am to have a harmonium!"

Auguste raised his head quickly, and looked strangely at his grandfather.

"You see how fond he is of his mother!" Vanda went on.—"Come and kiss me, dear rogue.—No, it is not your grandfather that you must thank, but Monsieur Godefroid; our kind neighbour promises to borrow one for me to-morrow morning.—What is it like, monsieur?"

Godefroid, at a nod from the old man, gave a long description of the harmonium while enjoying the tea Auguste had made, which was of superior quality and delicious flavour.

At about half-past ten the visitor withdrew, quite overpowered by the frantic struggle maintained by the father and son, while admiring their heroism and the patience that enabled them, day after day, to play two equally exhausting parts.

"Now," said Monsieur Bernard, accompanying him to his own door, "now you know the life I lead! At every hour I have to endure the alarms of a robber, on the alert for everything. One word, one look might kill my daughter. One toy removed from those she is accustomed to see about her would reveal everything to her, for mind sees through walls."

"Monsieur," said Godefroid, "on Monday Halpersohn will pronounce his opinion on your daughter, for he is at home again. I doubt whether science can restore her frame."

"Oh, I do not count upon it," said the old man with a sigh. "If they will only make her life endurable.—I trusted to your tact, monsieur, and I want to thank you, for you understood.—Ah! the attack has come on!" cried he, hearing a scream. "She has done too much—"

He pressed Godefroid's hand and hurried away.

At eight next morning Godefroid knocked at the famous doctor's door. He was shown up by the servant to a room on the first floor of the house, which he had had time to examine while the porter found the man-servant.

Happily, Godefroid's punctuality had saved him the vexation of waiting, as he had hoped it might. He was evidently the first-comer. He was led through a very plain ante-room into a large study, where he found an old man in a dressing-gown, smoking a long pipe. The dressing-gown, of black moreen, was shiny with wear, and dated from the time of the Polish dispersion.

"What can I do to serve you?" said the Jew, "for you are not ill."

And he fixed Godefroid with a look that had all the sharp inquisitiveness of the Polish Jew, eyes which seem to have ears.

To Godefroid's great surprise, Halpersohn was a man of fifty-six, with short bow-legs and a broad, powerful frame. There was an Oriental stamp about the man, and his face must in youth have been singularly handsome; the remains showed a marked Jewish nose, as long and as curved as a Damascus scimitar. His forehead was truly Polish, broad and lofty, wrinkled all over like crumpled paper, and recalling that of a Saint-Joseph by some old Italian master. His eyes were sea-green, set like a parrot's in puckered gray lids, and expressive of cunning and avarice in the highest degree. His mouth, thin and straight, like a cut in his face, lent this sinister countenance a crowning touch of suspiciousness.

The pale, lean features—for Helpersohn was extraordinarily thin—were crowned by ill-kept grey hair, and graced by a very thick, long beard, black streaked with white, that hid half his face, so that only the forehead and eyes, the cheek-bones, nose, and lips were visible.

This man, a friend of the agitator Lelewel, wore a black velvet cap that came down in a point on his forehead and showed off its mellow hue, worthy of Rembrandt's brush.

The doctor, who subsequently became equally famous for his talents and his avarice, startled Godefroid by his question, and the young man asked himself, "Can he take me for a thief?"

The reply to the question was evident on the doctor's table and chimney-piece. Godefroid had fancied himself the first-comer—he was the last. His patients had laid very handsome sums on the table and shelf, for Godefroid saw piles of twenty and forty-franc pieces and two thousand-franc notes. Was all this the fruit of a single morning? He greatly doubted it, and he suspected an ingenious trick. The infallible but money-loving doctor perhaps tried thus to encourage his patients' liberality, and to make his rich clients believe that be was given banknotes as if they were curl-papers.

Moïse Halpersohn was no doubt largely paid, for he cured his patients, and cured them of those very complaints which the profession gave up in despair.

It is very little known in Western Europe that the Slav nations possess a store of medical secrets. They have a number of sovereign remedies derived from their intercourse with the Chinese, the Persians, the Cossacks, the Turks, and the Tartars. Some peasant women, regarded as witches, have been known to cure hydrophobia completely in Poland with the juice of certain plants. There is among those nations a great mass of uncodified information as to the effects of certain plants and the powdered bark of trees, which is handed down from family to family, and miraculous cures are effected there.

Halpersohn, who for five or six years was regarded as a charlatan, with his powders and mixtures, had the innate instinct of a great healer. Not only was he learned, he had observed with great care, and had travelled all over Germany, Russia, Persia, and Turkey, where he had picked up much traditional lore; and as he was learned in chemistry, he became a living encyclopedia of the secrets preserved by "the good women," as they were called, the midwives and "wise women" of every country whither he had followed his father, a wandering trader.

It must not be supposed that the scene in *Richard in Palestine*, in which Saladin cures the King of England, is pure fiction. Halpersohn has a little silk bag, which he soaks in water till it is faintly coloured, and certain fevers yield to this infusion taken by the patient. The virtues residing in plants are infinitely various, according to him, and the most terrible maladies admit of cure. He, however, like his brother physicians, pauses sometimes before the incomprehensible. Halpersohn admires the invention of homoeopathy, less for its medical system than for its therapeutics; he was at that time in correspondence with Hedenius of Dresden, Chelius of Heidelberg, and the other famous Germans, but keeping his own hand dark though it was full of discoveries. He would have no pupils.

The setting of this figure, which might have stepped out of a picture by Rembrandt, was quite in harmony with it. The study, hung with green flock paper, was poorly furnished with a green divan. The carpet, also of moss green, showed the thread. A large armchair covered with black leather, for the patients, stood near the window, which was hung with green curtains. The doctor's seat was a study-chair with arms, in the Roman style, of mahogany with a green leather seat. Besides the chimney-piece and the long table at which he wrote, there was in the middle of the wall opposite the fireplace a common iron chest supporting a clock of Vienna granite, on which stood a bronze group of Love sporting with Death, the gift of a famous German sculptor whom Halpersohn had, no doubt, cured. A tazza between two candlesticks was all the ornament of the chimney-shelf. Two bracket shelves, one at each end of the divan, served to place trays on, and Godefroid noted that there were silver bowls on them, water-bottles, and table-napkins.

This simplicity, verging on bareness, struck Godefroid, who took everything in at a glance, and he recovered his presence of mind.

"I am perfectly well, monsieur. I have not come to consult you myself, but on behalf of a lady whom you ought long since to have seen—a lady living on the Boulevard du Mont-Parnasse."

"Oh yes, that lady has sent her son to me several times. Well, monsieur, tell her to come to see me?"

"Tell her to come!" cried Godefroid indignantly. "Why, monsieur, she cannot be lifted from her bed to a sofa; she has to be raised by straps."

"You are not a doctor?" asked the Jew, with a singular grimace which made his face look even more wicked.

"If Baron de Nucingen sent to tell you that he was ill and to ask you to visit him, would you reply, 'Tell him to come to me'?"

"I should go to him," said the Jew drily, as he spat into a Dutch spittoon made of mahogany and filled with sand.

"You would go to him," Godefroid said mildly, "because the Baron has two millions a year, and—"

"Nothing else has to do with the matter. I should go."

"Very well, monsieur, you may come and see the lady on the Boulevard du Mont-Parnasse for the same reason. Though I have not such a fortune as the Baron de Nucingen, I am here to tell you that you can name your own price for the cure, or, if you fail, for your care of her. I am prepared to pay you in advance. But how is it, monsieur, that you, a Polish exile, a communist, I believe, will make no sacrifice for the sake of Poland! For this lady is the granddaughter of General Tarlovski, Prince Poniatowski's friend—"

"Monsieur, you came to ask me to prescribe for this lady, and not to give me your advice. In Poland I am a Pole; in Paris a Parisian. Every one does good in his own way, and you may believe me when I tell you that the greed attributed to me has its good reasons. The money I accumulate has its uses; it is sacred. I sell health; rich persons can pay for it, and I make them buy it. The poor have their physicians.—If I had no aim in view, I should not practise medicine. I live soberly, and I spend my time in rushing from one to another; I am by nature lazy, and I used to be a gambler. You may draw your own conclusions, young man!—You are not old enough to judge the aged!"

Godefroid kept silence.

"You live with the granddaughter of the foolhardy soldier who had no courage but for fighting, and who betrayed his country to Catherine II?"

"Yes, monsieur."

"Then be at home on Monday at three o'clock," said he, laying down his pipe and taking up his notebook, in which he wrote a few words. "When I call, you will please to pay me two hundred francs; then, if I undertake to cure her, you will give me a thousand crowns.—I have been told," he went on, "that the lady is shrunken as if she had fallen in the fire."

"It is a case, monsieur, if you will believe the first physicians of Paris, of nervous disease, with symptoms so strange that no one can imagine them who has not seen them."

"Ah, yes, now I remember the details given me by that little fellow.—Till to-morrow, monsieur."

Godefroid left with a bow to this singular and extraordinary man. There was nothing about him to show or suggest a medical man, not even in that bare consulting-room, where the only article of furniture that was at all remarkable was the ponderous chest, made by Huret or Fichet.

Godefroid reached the Passage Vivienne in time to purchase a splendid harmonium before the shop was shut, and he despatched it forthwith to Monsieur Bernard, whose address he gave.

Then he went to the Rue Chanoinesse, passing along the Quai des Augustins, where he hoped still to find a bookseller's shop open; he was, in fact, so fortunate, and had a long conversation on the cost of law-books, with the clerk in charge.

He found Madame de la Chanterie and her friend just come in from high mass, and he answered her first inquiring glance with a significant shake.

"And our dear Father Alain is not with you?" said he.

"He will not be here this Sunday," replied Madame de la Chanterie. "You will not find him here till this day week, unless you go to the place where you know you can meet him."

"Madame," said Godefroid, in an undertone, "you know I am less afraid of him than of these gentlemen, and I intended to confess to him."

"And I?"

"Oh, you—I will tell you everything, for I have many things to say to you. As a beginning, I have come upon the most extraordinary case of destitution, the strangest union of poverty and luxury, and figures of a sublimity which outdoes the inventions of our most admired romancers."

"Nature, and especially moral nature, is always as far above art as God is above His creatures. But come," said Madame de la Chanterie, "and tell me all about your expedition into the unknown lands where you made your first venture."

Monsieur Nicolas and Monsieur Joseph—for the Abbé de Vèze had remained for a few minutes at Notre-Dame—left Madame de la Chanterie alone with Godefroid; and he, fresh from the emotions he had gone through the day before, related every detail with the intensity, the gesticulation, and the eagerness that come of the first impression produced by such a scene and its accessories of men and things. He had a success too; for Madame de la Chanterie, calm and gentle as she was, and accustomed to look into gulfs of suffering, shed tears.

"You did right," said she, "to send the harmonium."

"I wish I could have done much more," replied Godefroid, "since this is the first family through whom I have known the pleasures of charity; I want to secure to the noble old man the chief part of the profits on his great work. I do not know whether you have enough confidence in me to enable me to undertake such a business. From the information I have gained, it would cost about nine thousand francs to bring out an edition of fifteen hundred copies, and their lowest selling value would be twenty-four thousand francs. As we must, in the first instance, pay off the three thousand and odd francs that have been advanced on the manuscript, we should have to risk twelve thousand francs.

"Oh, madame! if you could but imagine how bitterly, as I made my way hither from the Quai des Augustins, I rued having so foolishly wasted my little fortune. The Genius of Charity appeared to me, as it were, and filled me with the ardour of a neophyte; I desire to renounce the world, to live the life of these gentlemen, and to be worthy of you. Many a time during the past two days have I blessed the chance that brought me to your house. I will obey you in every particular till you judge me worthy to join the brotherhood."

"Well," said Madame de la Chanterie very seriously, after a few minutes of reflection, "listen to me, I have important things to say to you. You have been fascinated, my dear boy, by the poetry of misfortune. Yes, misfortune often has a poetry of its own; for, to me, poetry is a certain exaltation of feeling, and suffering is feeling. We live so much through suffering!"

"Yes, madame, I was captured by the demon of curiosity. How could I help it! I have not yet acquired the habit of seeing into the heart of these unfortunate lives, and I cannot set out with the calm resolution of your three pious soldiers of the Lord. But I may tell you, it was not till I had quelled this incitement that I devoted myself to your work."

"Listen, my very dear son," said Madame de la Chanterie, saying the words with a saintly sweetness which deeply touched Godefroid, "we have forbidden ourselves absolutely—and this is no exaggeration, for we do not allow ourselves even to think of what is forbidden—we have forbidden ourselves ever to embark in a speculation. To print a book for sale, and looking for a return, is business, and any transaction of that kind would involve us in the difficulties of trade. To be sure, it looks in this case very feasible, and even necessary. Do you suppose that it is the first instance of the kind that has come before us? Twenty times, a hundred times, we have seen how a family, a concern, could be saved. But, then, what should we have become in undertaking matters of this kind? We should be simply a trading firm. To be a sleeping partner with the unfortunate is not work; it is only helping misfortune to work. In a few days you may meet with even harder cases than this; will you do the same thing? You would be overwhelmed.

"Remember, for one thing, that the house of Mongenod, for a year past, has ceased to keep our accounts. Quite half of your time will be taken up by keeping our books. There are, at this time, nearly two thousand persons in our debt in Paris; and of those who may repay us, at any rate, it is necessary that we should check the amounts they owe us. We never sue—we wait. We calculate that half of the money given out is lost. The other half sometimes returns doubled.

"Now, suppose this lawyer were to die, the twelve thousand francs would be badly invested! But if his daughter recovers, if his grandson does well, if he one day gets another appointment—then, if he has any sense of honour, he will remember the debt, and return the funds of the poor with interest. Do you know that more than one family, raised from poverty and started by us on the road to fortune by considerable loans without interest, has saved for the poor and returned us sums of double and sometimes treble the amount?

"This is our only form of speculation.

"In the first place, as to this case which interests you, and ought to interest you, consider that the sale of the lawyer's book depends on its merits; have you read it? Then, even if the work is excellent, how many excellent books have remained two or three years without achieving the success they deserved. How many a wreath is laid on a tomb! And, as I know, publishers have ways of driving bargains and taking their charges, which make the business one of the most risky and the most difficult to disentangle of all in Paris. Monsieur Nicolas can tell you about these difficulties, inherent in the nature of book-making. So, you see, we are prudent; we have ample experience of every kind of misery, as of every branch of trade, for we have long been studying Paris. The Mongenods give us much help; they are a light to our path, and through them we know that the Bank of France is always suspicious of the book-trade, though it is a noble trade—but it is badly conducted.

"As to the four thousand francs needed to save this noble family from the horrors of indigence, I will give you the money; for the poor boy and his grandfather must be fed and decently dressed.—There are sorrows, miseries, wounds, which we bind up at once without inquiring who it is that we are helping; religion, honour, character, are not inquired into; but as soon as it is a case of lending the money belonging to the poor to assist the unfortunate under the more active form of industry or trade, then we require some guarantee, and are as rigid as the money-lenders. So, for all beyond this immediate relief, be satisfied with finding the most honest publisher for the old man's book. This is a matter for Monsieur Nicolas. He is acquainted with lawyers and professors and authors of works in jurisprudence; next Saturday he will, no doubt, be prepared with some good advice for you.

"Be easy; the difficulty will be got over if possible. At the same time, it might be well if Monsieur Nicolas could read the magistrate's book; if you can persuade him to lend it."

Godefroid was amazed at this woman's sound sense, for he had believed her to be animated solely by the spirit of charity. He knelt on one knee and kissed one of her beautiful hands, saying:

"Then you are Reason too!"

"In our work we have to be everything," said she, with the peculiar cheerfulness of a true saint.

There was a brief silence, broken by Godefroid, who exclaimed;

"Two thousand debtors, did you say, madame? Two thousand accounts! It is tremendous!"

"Two thousand accounts, which may lead, as I have told you, to our being repaid from the delicate honour of the borrowers. But there are three thousand more—families who will never make us any return but in thanks. Thus, as I have told you, we feel that it is necessary to keep books; and if your secrecy is above suspicion, you will be our financial oracle. We ought to keep a day-book, a ledger, a book of current expenses, and a cash-book. Of course, we have receipts, notes of hand, but it takes a great deal of time to look for them—Here come the gentlemen."

Godefroid, at first serious and thoughtful, took little part in the conversation; he was bewildered by the revelation Madame de la Chanterie had just imparted to him in a way which showed that she meant it to be the reward of his zeal.

"Two thousand families indebted to us!" said he to himself. "Why, if they all cost as much as Monsieur Bernard will cost us, we must have millions sown broadcast in Paris!"

This reflection was one of the last promptings of the worldly spirit which was fast dying out in Godefroid. As he thought the matter over, he understood that the united fortunes of Madame de la Chanterie, of Messieurs Alain, Nicolas, Joseph, and Judge Popinot, with the gifts collected by the Abbé de Vèze, and the loans from the Mongenods, must have produced a considerable capital; also, that in twelve or fifteen years this capital, with the interest paid on it by those who had shown their gratitude, must have increased like a snowball, since the charitable holders took nothing from it. By degrees he began to see clearly how the immense affair was managed, and his wish to co-operate was increased.

At nine o'clock he was about to return on foot to the Boulevard du Mont-Parnasse; but Madame de la Chanterie, distrustful of so lonely a neighbourhood, insisted on his taking a cab. As he got out of the vehicle, though the shutters were so closely fastened that not a gleam of light was visible, Godefroid heard the sounds of the instrument; and Auguste, who, no doubt, was watching for Godefroid's return, half opened the door on the landing, and said:

"Mamma would very much like to see you, and my grandfather begs you will take a cup of tea."

Godefroid went in and found the invalid transfigured by the pleasure of the music; her face beamed and her eyes sparkled like diamonds.

"I ought to have waited for you, to let you hear the first chords; but I flew at this little organ as a hungry man rushes on a banquet. But you have a soul to understand me, and I know I am forgiven."

Vanda made a sign to her son, who placed himself where he could press the pedal that supplied the interior of the instrument with wind; and, with her eyes raised to heaven like Saint Cecilia, the invalid, whose hands had for a time recovered their strength and agility, performed some variations on the prayer in *Mosè* which her son had bought for her. She had composed them in a few hours. Godefroid discerned in her a talent identical with that of Chopin. It was a soul manifesting itself by divine sounds in which sweet melancholy predominated.

Monsieur Bernard greeted Godefroid with a look expressing a sentiment long since in abeyance. If the tears had not been for ever dried up in the old man scorched by so many fierce sorrows, his eyes would at this moment have been wet.

The old lawyer was fingering his snuff-box and gazing at his daughter with unutterable rapture.

"To-morrow, madame," said Godefroid, when the music had ceased, "your fate will be sealed, for I have good news for you. The famous Halpersohn will come at three o'clock.—And he has promised," he added in Monsieur Bernard's ear, "to tell me the truth."

The old man rose, and taking Godefroid by the hand, led hi into a corner of the room near the fireplace. He was trembling.

"What a night lies before me! It is the final sentence!" said he in a whisper. "My daughter will be cured or condemned!"

"Take courage," said Godefroid, "and after tea come to my rooms."

"Cease playing, my child," said Monsieur Bernard; "you will bring on an attack. Such an expenditure of strength will be followed by a reaction."

He made Auguste remove the instrument, and brought his daughter her cup of tea with the coaxing ways of a nurse who wants to anticipate the impatience of a baby.

"And what is this doctor like?" asked she, already diverted by the prospect of seeing a stranger.

Vanda, like all prisoners, was consumed by curiosity. When the physical symptoms of her complaint gave her some respite, they seemed to develop in her mind, and then she had the strangest whims and violent caprices. She wanted to see Rossini, and cried because her father, who could, she imagined, do everything, assured her he could not bring him.

Godefroid gave her a minute description of the Jewish physician and his consulting-room, for she knew nothing of the steps taken by her father. Monsieur Bernard had enjoined silence on his grandson as to his visits to Halpersohn; he had so much feared to excite hopes which might not be realised. Vanda seemed to hang on the words that fell from Godefroid's lips; she was spellbound and almost crazy, so ardent did her desire become to see the strange Pole.

"Poland has produced many singular and mysterious figures," said the old lawyer. "Just now, for instance, besides this doctor there is Hoëné Vronski the mathematician and seer, Mickievicz the poet, the inspired Tovianski, and Chopin with his superhuman talent. Great national agitations always produce these crippled giants."

"Oh, my dear papa, what a man you are! If you were to write down all that we hear you say simply to entertain me, you would make a fortune! For, would you believe me, monsieur, my kind old father invents tales for me when I have no more novels to read, and so sends me to sleep. His voice lulls me, and he often soothes my pain with his cleverness. Who will ever repay him?—Auguste, my dear boy, you ought to kiss your grandfather's footprints for me."

The youth looked at his mother with his fine eyes full of tears; and that look, overflowing with long repressed compassion, was a poem in itself. Godefroid rose, took Auguste's hand, and pressed it warmly.

"God has given you two angels for your companions, madame!" he exclaimed.

"Indeed I know it. And I blame myself for so often provoking them. Come, dear Auguste, and kiss your mother. He is a son, monsieur, of whom any mother would be proud. He is as good as gold, candid—a soul without sin; but a rather too impassioned creature, like his mamma. God has nailed me to my bed to preserve me perhaps from the follies women commit—when they have too much heart!" she ended with a smile.

Godefroid smiled in reply and bowed good-night.

'Good-night, monsieur; and be sure to thank your friend, for he has made a poor cripple very happy."

"Monsieur," said Godefroid when he was in his rooms, alone with Monsieur Bernard, who had followed him, "I think I may promise you that you shall not be robbed by those three sharpers. I can get the required sum, but you must place the papers proving the loan in my hands. If I am to do anything more, you should allow me to have your book—not to read myself, for I am not learned enough to judge of it, but to be read by an old lawyer I know, a man of unimpeachable integrity, who will undertake, according to the character of the work, to find a respectable firm with whom you may deal on equitable terms.—On this, however, I do not insist.

"Meanwhile, here are five hundred francs," he went on, offering a note to the astonished lawyer, "to supply your more pressing wants. I ask for no receipt; you will be indebted on no evidence but that of your conscience, and your conscience may lie silent till you have to some extent recovered yourself.—I will settle with Halpersohn."

"But who are you?" asked the old man, sinking on to a chair.

"I," replied Godefroid, "am nobody; but I serve certain powerful persons to whom your necessities are now made known, and who take an interest in you.—Ask no more."

"And what motive can these persons have—?"

"Religion, monsieur," replied Godefroid.

"Is it possible?—Religion!"

"Yes, the Catholic, Apostolic, Roman religion."

"Then you are of the Order of Jesus?"

"No, monsieur," said Godefroid. "Be perfectly easy. No one has any design on you beyond that of helping you and restoring your family to comfort."

"Can philanthropy then wear any guise but that of vanity?"

"Nay, monsieur, do not insult holy Catholic Charity, the virtue described by Saint Paul!" cried Godefroid eagerly.

At this reply Monsieur Bernard began to stride up and down the room.

"I accept!" he suddenly said. "And I have but one way of showing my gratitude—that is, by intrusting you with my work. The notes and quotations are unnecessary to a lawyer; and I have, as I told you, two months' work before me yet in copying them out.—To-morrow then," and he shook hands with Godefroid.

"Can I have effected a conversion?" thought Godefroid, struck by the new expression he saw on the old man's face as he had last spoken.

Next day, at three o'clock, a hackney coach stopped at the door, and out stepped Halpersohn, buried in a vast bearskin coat. The cold had increased in the course of the night, and the thermometer stood at ten degrees below freezing.

The Jewish doctor narrowly though furtively examined the room in which his visitor of yesterday received him, and Godefroid detected a gleam of suspicion sparkling in his eye like the point of a dagger. This swift flash of doubt gave Godefroid an internal chill; he began to think that this man would be merciless in his money dealings; and it is so natural to think of genius as allied to goodness, that this gave him an impulse of disgust.

"Monsieur," said he, "I perceive that the plainness of my lodgings arouses your uneasiness; so you will not be surprised at my manner of proceeding. Here are your two hundred francs, and here, you see, are three notes for a thousand francs each"—and he drew out the notes which Madame de la Chanterie had given him to redeem Monsieur Bernard's manuscript. "If you have any further doubts as to my solvency, I may refer you, as a guarantee for the carrying out of my pledge, to Messrs. Mongenod the bankers, Rue de la Victoire."

"I know them," said Halpersohn, slipping the ten gold pieces into his pocket.

"And he will go there!" thought Godefroid.

"And where does the sick lady live?" asked the doctor, rising, as a man who knows the value of time.

"Come this way, monsieur," said Godefroid, going first to show him the way.

The Jew cast a shrewd and scrutinising glance on the rooms he went through, for he had the eye of a spy; and he was able to see the misery of poverty through the door into Monsieur Bernard's bedroom, for, unluckily, Monsieur Bernard had just been putting on the dress in which he always showed himself to his daughter, and in his haste to admit his visitors he left the door of his kennel ajar.

He bowed with dignity to Halpersohn, and softly opened his daughter's bedroom door.

"Vanda, my dear, here is the doctor," he said.

He stood aside to let Halpersohn pass, still wrapped in his furs.

The Jew was surprised at the splendour of this room, which in this part of the town seemed anomalous; but his astonishment was of no long duration, for he had often seen in the houses of German and Polish Jews a similar discrepancy between the display of extreme penury and concealed wealth. While walking from the door to the bed he never took his eyes off the sufferer; and when he stood by her side, he said to her in Polish:

"Are you a Pole?"

"I am not; my mother was."

"Whom did your grandfather, General Tarlovski, marry?"

"A Pole."

"Of what province?"

"A Sobolevska of Pinsk."

"Good.—And this gentleman is your father?"

"Yes, monsieur."

"Monsieur," said Halpersohn, "is your wife—"

"She is dead," replied Monsieur Bernard.

"Was she excessively fair?" said Halpersohn, with some impatience at the interruption.

"Here is a portrait of her," replied Monsieur Bernard, taking down a handsome frame containing several good miniatures.

Halpersohn was feeling the invalid's head and hair, while he looked at the portrait of Vanda Tarlovska *née* Comtesse Sobolevska.

"Tell me the symptoms of the patient's illness." And he seated himself in the armchair, gazing steadily at Vanda during twenty minutes, while the father and daughter spoke by turns.

"And how old is the lady?"

"Eight-and-thirty."

"Very good!" he said as he rose. "Well, I undertake to cure her. I cannot promise to give her the use of her legs, but she can be cured. Only, she must be placed in a private hospital in my part of the town."

"But, monsieur, my daughter cannot be moved—"

"I will answer for her life," said Halpersohn sententiously. "But I answer for her only on those conditions.—Do you know she will exchange her present symptoms for another horrible form of disease, which will last for a year perhaps, or six months at the very least?—You can come to see her, as you are her father."

"And it is certain?" asked Monsieur Bernard.

"Certain," repeated the Jew. "Your daughter has a vicious humour, a national disorder, in her blood, and it must be brought out. When you bring her, carry her to the Rue Basse-Saint-Pierre at Chaillot—Dr. Halpersohn's private hospital."

"But how?"

"On a stretcher, as the sick people are always carried to a hospital."

"But it will kill her to be moved."

"No."

And Halpersohn, as he spoke this curt *No*, was at the door, where Godefroid met him on the landing.

The Jew, who was suffocating with heat, said in his ear:

"The charge will be fifteen francs a day, besides the thousand crowns; three months paid in advance."

"Very good, monsieur.—And," asked Godefroid, standing on the step of the cab into which the doctor had hurried, "you answer for the cure?"

"Positively," said the Pole. "Are you in love with the lady?"

"No," said Godefroid.

"You must not repeat what I am about to tell you, for I am saying it only to prove to you that I am sure of the cure; but if you say anything about it, you will be the death of the woman—"

Godefroid replied only by a gesture.

"For seventeen years she has been suffering from the disease known as *Plica Polonica*, which can produce all these torments; I have seen the most dreadful cases. Now I am the only man living who knows how to bring out the *Plica* in such a form as to be curable, for not every one gets over it. You see, monsieur, that I am really very liberal. If this were some great lady—a Baronne de Nucingen or any other wife or daughter of some modern Croesus—I should get a hundred—two hundred thousand francs for this cure—whatever I might like to ask!—However, that is a minor misfortune."

"And moving her?"

"Oh, she will seem to be dying, but she will not die of it! She may live a hundred years when once she is cured.—Now, Jacques, quick—Rue Monsieur, and make haste!" said he to the driver.

He left Godefroid standing in the street, where he gazed in bewilderment after the retreating cab.

"Who on earth is that queer-looking man dressed in bearskin?" asked Madame Vauthier, whom nothing could escape. "Is it true, as the hackney coachman said, that he is the most famous doctor in Paris?"

"And what can that matter to you, Mother Vauthier?"

"Oh, not at all," said she with a sour face.

"You made a great mistake in not siding with me," said Godefroid, as he slowly went into the house. "You would have done better than by sticking to Monsieur Barbet and Monsieur Métivier; you will get nothing out of them."

"And am I on their side?" retorted she with a shrug. "Monsieur Barbet is my landlord, that is all."

It took two days to persuade Monsieur Bernard to part from his daughter and carry her to Chaillot. Godefroid and the old lawyer walked all the way, one on each side of the stretcher, screened in with striped blue-and-white tickings, on which the precious patient lay, almost tied down to the mattress, so greatly did her father fear the convulsions of a nervous attack. However, having set out at three o'clock, the procession reached the private hospital at five, when it was dusk. Godefroid paid the four hundred and fifty francs demanded for the three months' board, and took a receipt for it; then, when he went down to pay the two porters, Monsieur Bernard joined him and took from under the mattress a very voluminous sealed packet, which he handed to Godefroid.

"One of these men will fetch you a cab," said he, "for you cannot carry those four volumes very far. This is my book; place it in my censor's hands; I will leave it with him for a week. I shall remain at least a week in this neighbourhood, for I cannot abandon my daughter to her fate. I know my grandson; he can mind the house, especially with you to help him; and I commend him to your care. If I were myself what once I was, I would ask you my critic's name; for if he was once a magistrate, there were few whom I did not know—"

"It is no mystery," said Godefroid, interrupting Monsieur Bernard. "Since you show such entire confidence in me, I may tell you that the reader is the President Lecamus de Tresnes."

"Oh, of the Supreme Court in Paris. Take it—by all means. He is one of the noblest men of our time. He and the late Judge Popinot, the judge of the Lower Court, were lawyers worthy of the best days of the old Parlements. All my fears, if I had any, must vanish.—And where does he live? I should like to go and thank him when he has taken so much trouble."

"You will find him in the Rue Chanoinesse, under the name of Monsieur Nicolas. I am just going there.—But your agreement with those rascals?"

"Auguste will give it you," said the old man, going back into the hospital.

A cab was found on the Quai de Billy and brought by one of the men; Godefroid got in and stimulated the driver by the promise of drink money if he drove quickly to the Rue Chanoinesse, where he intended to dine.

Half an hour after Vanda's removal, three men, dressed in black, were let in by Madame Vauthier at the door in the Rue Notre-Dame des Champs, where they had been waiting, no doubt, till the coast should be clear. They went upstairs under the guidance of the Judas in petticoats, and gently knocked at Monsieur Bernard's door. As it happened to be a Thursday, the young collegian was at home. He opened the door, and three men slipped like shadows into the outer room.

"What do you want, gentlemen?" asked the youth. "This is Monsieur Bernard's—that is to say, Monsieur le Baron—?"

"But what do you want here?"

"Oh, you know that pretty well, young man, for your grandfather has just gone off with a closed litter, I am told.—Well, that does not surprise us; he shows his wisdom. I am a bailiff, and I have come to seize everything here. On Monday last you were summoned to pay three thousand francs and the expenses to Monsieur Métivier, under penalty of imprisonment; and as a man who has grown onions knows the smell of chives, the debtor has taken the key of the fields rather than wait for that of the lock-up. However, if we cannot secure him, we can get a wing or a leg of his gorgeous furniture—for we know all about it, young man, and we are going to make an official report."

"Here are some stamped papers that your grandpapa would never take," said the widow Vauthier, shoving three writs into Auguste's hand.

"Stay here, ma'am; we will put you in possession. The law gives you forty sous a day; it is not to be sneezed at."

"Ah, ha! Then I shall see what there is in the grand bedroom!" cried Madame Vauthier.

"You shall not go into my mother's room!" cried the lad in a fury, as he flung himself between the door and the three men in black.

On a sign from their leader, the two men and a lawyer's clerk who came in seized Auguste.

"No resistance, young man; you are not master here. We shall draw up a charge, and you will spend the night in the lock-up."

At this dreadful threat, Auguste melted into tears.

"Oh, what a mercy," cried he, "that mamma is gone! This would have killed her!"

The men and the bailiff now held a sort of council with the widow Vauthier. Auguste understood, though they talked in a low voice, that what they chiefly wanted was to seize his grandfather's manuscripts, so he opened the bedroom door.

"Walk in then, gentlemen," said he, "but spoil nothing. You will be paid to-morrow morning." Then, still in tears, he went into his own squalid room, snatched up all his grandfather's notes, and stuffed them into the stove, where he knew that there was not a spark of fire.

The thing was done so promptly, that the bailiff, though he was keen and cunning, and worthy of his employers Barbet and Métivier, found the boy in tears on a chair when he rushed into the room, having concluded that the manuscripts would not be in the ante-room. Though books and manuscripts may not legally be seized for debt, the lien signed by the old lawyer in this case justified the proceeding. Still, it would have been easy to find means of delaying the distraint, as Monsieur Bernard would certainly have known. Hence the necessity for acting with cunning.

The widow Vauthier had been an invaluable ally to her landlord by failing to serve his notices on her lodger; her plan was to throw them on him when entering at the heels of the officers of justice; or, if necessary, to declare to Monsieur Bernard that she had supposed them to be intended for the two writers who had been absent for two days.

The inventory of the goods took above an hour to make out, for the bailiff would omit nothing, and regarded the value as sufficient to pay off the debts.

As soon as the officers were gone, the poor youth took the writs and hurried away to find his grandfather at Halpersohn's hospital; for, as the bailiff assured him that Madame Vauthier was responsible for everything under heavy penal ties, he could leave the place without fear.

The idea of his grandfather being taken to prison for debt drove the poor boy absolutely mad—mad in the way in which the young are mad; that is to say, a victim to the dangerous and fatal excitement in which every energy of youth is in a ferment and may lead to the worst as to the most heroic actions.

When poor Auguste reached the Rue Basse-Saint-Pierre the doorkeeper told him that he did not know what had become of the father of the patient brought in at five o'clock, but that by Monsieur Halpersohn's orders no one—not even her father—was to be allowed to see the lady for a week, or it might endanger her life.

This reply put a climax to Auguste's desperation. He went back again to the Boulevard du Mont-Parnasse, revolving the most extravagant schemes as he went. He got home by about half-past eight, almost starving, so exhausted by hunger and grief, that he accepted when Madame Vauthier invited him to share her supper, consisting of a stew of mutton and potatoes. The poor boy dropped half dead into a chair in the dreadful woman's room.

Encouraged by the old woman's coaxing and insinuating words, he answered a few cunningly arranged questions about Godefroid, and gave her to understand that it was he who would pay off his grandfather's debts on the morrow, and that to him they owed the improvement that had taken place in their prospects during the past week. The widow listened to all this with an affectation of doubt, plying Auguste with a few glasses of wine.

At ten o'clock the wheels of a cab were heard to stop in front of the house, and the woman exclaimed:

"Oh, there is Monsieur Godefroid!"

Auguste took the key of his rooms and went upstairs to see the kind friend of the family; but he found Godefroid so entirely unlike himself, that he hesitated to speak till the thought of his grandfather's danger spurred the generous youth.

This is what had happened in the Rue Chanoinesse, and had caused Godefroid's stern expression of countenance.

The neophyte, arriving in good time, had found Madame de la Chanterie and her adherents in the drawing-room, and he had taken Monsieur Nicolas aside to deliver to him the *Spirit of the Modern Laws*. Monsieur Nicolas at once carried the sealed parcel to his room, and came down to dinner. Then, after chatting during the first part of the evening, he went up again, intending to begin reading the work.

Godefroid was greatly surprised when, a few minutes after, Manon came from the old judge to beg him to go up to speak with him. Following Manon, he was led to Monsieur Nicolas' room; but he could pay no attention to its details, so greatly was he startled by the evident distress of a man usually so placid and firm.

"Did you know," said Monsieur Nicolas, quite the Judge again, "the name of the author of this work?"

"Monsieur Bernard," said Godefroid. "I know him only by that name. I did not open the parcel—"

"True," said Monsieur Nicolas. "I broke the seals myself.—And you made no inquiry as to his previous history?"

"No. I know that he married for love the daughter of General Tarlovski, that his daughter is named Vanda after her mother, and his grandson Auguste. And the portrait I saw of Monsieur Bernard is, I believe, in the dress of a Presiding Judge—a red gown."

"Look here!" said Monsieur Nicolas, and held out the title of the work in Auguste's handwriting, and in the following form:

THE SPIRIT
OF THE MODERN LAWS
BY
M. BERNARD-JEAN-BAPTISTE MACLOUD
BARON BOURLAC
Formerly Attorney-General to the High Court of Justice at Rouen
Commander of the Legion of Honour.

"Oh! The man who condemned Madame, her daughter, and the Chevalier du Vissard!" said Godefroid in a choked voice.

His knees gave way, and the neophyte dropped on to a chair.

"What a beginning!" he murmured.

"This, my dear Godefroid, is a business that comes home to us all. You have done your part; we must deal with it now! I beg you to do nothing further of any kind; go and fetch whatever you left in your rooms; and not a word!—In fact, absolute silence. Tell Baron Bourlac to apply to me.

Between this and then, we shall have decided how it will be best to act in such circumstances."

Godefroid went downstairs, called a hackney cab, and hurried back to the Boulevard du Mont-Parnasse, filled with horror as he thought of the examination and trials at Caen, of the hideous drama that ended on the scaffold, and of Madame de la Chanterie's sojourn in Bicêtre. He understood the neglect into which this lawyer, almost a second Fouquier-Tinville, had fallen in his old age, and the reasons why he so carefully concealed his name.

"I hope Monsieur Nicolas will take some terrible revenge for poor Madame de la Chanterie!"

He had just thought out this not very Christian wish, when he saw Auguste.

"What do you want of me?" asked Godefroid.

"My dear sir, a misfortune has befallen us which is turning my brain! Some scoundrels have been here to take possession of everything belonging to my mother, and they are hunting for my grandfather to put him into prison. But it is not by reason of these disasters that I turn to you for help," said the lad with Roman pride; "it is to beg you to do me such a service as you would do to a condemned criminal—"

"Speak," said Godefroid.

"They wanted to get hold of my grandfather's manuscripts; and as I believe he placed the work in your hands, I want to beg you to take the notes, for the woman will not allow me to remove a thing.—Put them with the volumes, and then—"

"Very well," said Godefroid, "make haste and fetch them." While the lad went off, to return immediately, Godefroid reflected that the poor boy was guilty of no crime, that he must not break his heart by telling him about his grandfather, or the desertion which was the punishment in his sad old age of the passions of his political career; he took the packet not unkindly.

"What is your mother's name?" he asked.

"My mother, monsieur, is the Baronne de Mergi. My father was the son of the Presiding Judge of the Supreme Court at Rouen."

"Ah!" said Godefroid, "so your grandfather married his daughter to the son of the famous Judge Mergi?"

"Yes, monsieur."

"Leave me, my little friend," said Godefroid.

He went out on to the landing with the young Baron de Mergi, and called Madame Vauthier.

"Mother Vauthier," said he, "you can relet my rooms; I am never coming back again."

And he went down to the cab.

"Have you intrusted anything to that gentleman?" asked the widow of Auguste.

"Yes," said the lad.

"You're a pretty fool. He is one of your enemies' agents. He has been at the bottom of it all, you may be sure. It is proof enough that the trick has turned out all right that he never means to come back. He told me I could let his rooms."

Auguste flew out, and down the boulevard, running after the cab, and at last succeeded in stopping it by his shouts and cries.

"What is it?" asked Godefroid.

"My grandfather's manuscripts?"

"Tell him to apply for them to Monsieur Nicolas."

The lad took this reply as the cruel jest of a thief who has no shame left; he sat down in the snow as he saw the cab set off again at a brisk trot.

He rose in a fever of fierce energy and went home to bed, worn out with rushing about Paris, and quite heart-broken.

Next morning, Auguste de Mergi awoke to find himself alone in the rooms where yesterday his mother and his grandfather had been with him, and he went through all the miseries of his position, of which he fully understood the extent. The utter desertion of the place, hitherto so amply filled, where every minute had brought with it a duty and an occupation, was so painful to him, that he went down to ask the widow Vauthier whether his grandfather had come in during the night or early morning; for he himself had slept very late, and he supposed that if the Baron Bourlac had come home the woman would have warned him against his pursuers. She replied, with a sneer, that he must know full well where to look for his grandfather; for if he had not come in, it was evident that he had taken up his abode in the "Château de Clichy." This impudent irony from the woman who, the day before, had cajoled him so effectually, again drove the poor boy to frenzy, and he flew to the private hospital in the Rue Basse-Saint-Pierre in despair, as he thought of his grandfather in prison.

Baron Bourlac had hung about all night in front of the hospital which he was forbidden to enter, or close to the house of Doctor Halpersohn, whom he naturally wished to call to account for this conduct. The doctor did not get home till two in the morning. The old man, who, at half-past one, had been at the doctor's door, had just gone off to walk in the Champs-Elysées, and when he returned at half-past two the gatekeeper told him that Monsieur Halpersohn was now in bed and asleep, and was on no account to be disturbed.

Here, alone, at half-past two in the morning, the unhappy father, in utter despair, paced the quay, and under the trees, loaded with frost, of the sidewalks of the Cours-la-Reine, waiting for the day.

At nine o'clock he presented himself at the doctor's, and asked him why he thus kept his daughter under lock and key.

"Monsieur," said Halpersohn, "I yesterday made myself answerable for your daughter's recovery; and at this moment I am responsible for her life, and you must understand that in such a case I must have sovereign authority. I may tell you that your daughter yesterday took a remedy which will give her the *Plica*, that till the disease is brought out the lady must remain invisible. I will not allow myself to lose my patient or you to lose your daughter by exposing her to any excitement, any error of treatment; if you really insist on seeing her, I shall demand a consultation of three medical men to protect myself against any responsibility, as the patient might die."

The old man, exhausted with fatigue, had dropped on to a chair; he quickly rose, however, saying:

"Forgive me, monsieur; I have spent the night in mortal anguish, for you cannot imagine how much I love my daughter, whom I have nursed for fifteen years between life and death, and this week of waiting is torture to me!"

The Baron left Halpersohn's study, tottering like a drunken man, the doctor giving him his arm to the top of the stairs.

About an hour later, he saw Auguste de Mergi walk into his room. On questioning the lodge-keeper of the private hospital, the poor lad had just heard that the father of the lady admitted the day before had called again in the evening, had asked for her, and had spoken of going early in the day to Doctor Halpersohn, who, no doubt, would know something about him. At the moment when Auguste de Mergi appeared in the doctor's room, Halpersohn was breakfasting off a cup of chocolate and a glass of water, all on a small round table; he did not disturb himself for the youth, but went on soaking his strip of bread in the chocolate; for he ate nothing but a roll, cut into four with an accuracy that argued some skill as an operator. Halpersohn had, in fact, practised surgery in the course of his travels.

"Well, young man," said he as Vanda's son came in, "you too have come to require me to account for your mother?"

"Yes, monsieur," said Auguste.

The young fellow had come forward as far as the large table, and his eye was immediately caught by several bank notes lying among the little piles of gold pieces. In the position in which the unhappy boy found himself, the temptation was stronger than his principles, well grounded as they were. He saw before him the means of rescuing his grandfather, and saving the fruits of twenty years' labour imperiled by avaricious speculators. He fell. The fascination was as swift as thought, and justified itself by an idea of self-immolation that smiled on the boy. He said to himself:

"I shall be done for, but I shall save my mother and my grandfather."

Under this stress of antagonism between his reason and the impulse to crime, he acquired, as madmen do, a strange and fleeting dexterity, and instead of asking after his grandfather, he listened and agreed to all the doctor was saying.

Halpersohn, like all acute observers, had understood the whole past history of the father, the daughter, and her son.

He had scented or guessed the facts which Madame de Mergi's conversation had confirmed, and he felt in consequence a sort of benevolence towards his new clients;—as to respect or admiration, he was incapable of them.

"Well, my dear boy," said he familiarly, "I am keeping your mother to restore her to you young, handsome, and in good health. Hers is one of those rare diseases which doctors find very interesting; and besides, she is, through her mother, a fellow-countrywoman of mine. You and your grandfather must be brave enough to live without seeing her for a fortnight, and madame—?"

"La Baronne de Mergi."

"If she is a Baroness, you are Baron—?" asked Halpersohn.

At this moment the theft was effected. While the doctor was looking at his bread, heavy with chocolate, Auguste snatched up four folded notes, and had slipped them into his trousers pocket, affecting to keep his hand there out of sheer embarrassment.

"Yes, monsieur, I am a Baron. So too is my grandfather; he was public prosecutor at the time of the Restoration."

"You blush, young man. You need not blush because you are a Baron and poor—it is a very common case."

"And who told you, monsieur, that we are poor?"

"Well, your grandfather told me that he had spent the night in the Champs-Élysées; and though I know no palace where there is so fine a vault overhead as that which was glittering at two o'clock this morning, it was cold, I can tell you, in the palace where your grandfather was taking his airing. A man does not go to the Hôtel *de la belle-Étoile* by preference."

"Has my grandfather been here?" cried Auguste, seizing the opportunity to beat a retreat. "Thank you, monsieur. I will come again, with your permission, for news of my mother."

As soon as he got out, the young Baron went off to the bailiff's office, taking a hackney cab to get there the sooner. The man gave up the agreement, and the bill of costs duly receipted, and then desired the young man to take one of the clerks with him to release the person in charge from her functions.

"And as Messrs. Barbet and Métivier live in your part of the town," added he, "my boy will take them the money and desire them to restore you the deed of lien on the property."

Auguste, who understood nothing of these phrases and formalities, submitted. He received seven hundred francs in silver, the change out of his four thousand franc notes, and went off in the clerk's company. He got into the cab in a state of indescribable bewilderment, for the end being achieved, remorse was making itself felt; he saw himself disgraced and cursed by his grandfather, whose austerity was well known to him; and he believed that his mother would die of grief if she heard of his guilt. All nature had changed before his eyes. He was lost; he no longer saw the snow, the houses looked like ghosts.

No sooner was he at home than the young Baron decided on his course of action, and it was certainly that of an honest man. He went into his mother's room and took the diamond snuff-box given to his grandfather by the Emperor to send it with the seven hundred francs to Doctor Halpersohn with the following letter, which required several rough copies:

"MONSIEUR,—The fruits of twenty years' labour—my grandfather's work—were about to be absorbed by some money-lenders, who threatened him with imprisonment. Three thousand three hundred francs were enough to save him; and seeing so much gold on your table, I could not resist the idea of seeing my parent free by thus making good to him the earnings of his long toil. I borrowed from you, without your leave, four thousand francs; but as only three thousand three hundred francs were needed, I send you the remaining seven hundred, and with them a snuff-box set with diamonds, given by the Emperor to my grandfather; this will, I hope, indemnify you.

"If you should not after this believe that I, who shall all my life regard you as my benefactor, am a man of honour, if you will at any rate preserve silence as to an action so unjustifiable in any other circumstances, you will have saved my grandfather as you will save my mother, and I shall be for life your devoted slave.

"AUGUSTE DE MERGI."

At about half-past two, Auguste, who had walked to the Champs-Élysées, sent a messenger on to deliver at Doctor Halpersohn's door a sealed box containing ten louis, a five-hundred-franc note, and the snuff-box; then he slowly went home across the Pont d'Iéna by the Invalides and the Boulevards, trusting to Doctor Halpersohn's generosity.

The physician, who had at once discovered the theft, had meanwhile changed his views as to his clients. He supposed that the old man had come to rob him, and, not having succeeded, had sent this boy. He put no credence in the rank and titles they had assumed, and went off at once to the public prosecutor's office to state his case, and desire that immediate steps should be taken for the prosecution.

The prudence of the law rarely allows of such rapid proceedings as the complaining parties would wish; but, at about three in the afternoon, a police officer, followed by some detectives, who affected to be lounging on the boulevard, was catechising Madame Vauthier as to her lodgers, and the widow quite unconsciously was confirming the constable's suspicions.

Népomucène, scenting the policeman, thought that it was the old man they wanted; and as he was very fond of Monsieur Auguste, he hurried out to meet Monsieur Bernard, whom he intercepted in the Avenue de l'Observatoire.

"Make your escape, monsieur," cried he. "They have come to take you. The bailiffs were in yesterday and laid hands on everything. Mother Vauthier, who has hidden some stamped papers of yours, said you would be in Clichy by last night or this morning. There, do you see those sneaks?"

The old judge recognised the men as bailiffs, and he understood everything.

"And Monsieur Godefroid?" he asked.

"Gone, never to come back. Mother Vauthier says he was a spy for your enemies."

Monsieur Bourlac determined that he would go at once to Barbet, and in a quarter of an hour he was there; the old bookseller lived in the Rue Sainte-Catherine-d'Enfer.

"Oh, you have come yourself to fetch your agreement," said the publisher, bowing to his victim. "Here it is," and, to the Baron's great amazement, he handed him the document, which the old lawyer took, saying:

"I do not understand—"

"Then it was not you who paid up?" said Barbet.

"Are you paid?"

"Your grandson carried the money to the bailiff this morning."

"And is it true that you took possession of my goods yesterday?"

"Have you not been home for two days?" said Barbet. "Still, a retired public prosecutor must know what it is to be threatened with imprisonment for debt!"

On this the Baron bowed coldly to Barbet, and returned home, supposing that the authorities had in fact come in search of the authors living on the first floor. He walked slowly, absorbed in vague apprehensions, for Népomucène's warning seemed to him more and more inexplicable. Could Godefroid have betrayed him? He mechanically turned down the Rue Notre-Dame des Champs, and went in by the back door, which happened to be open, running against Népomucène.

"Oh, monsieur, make haste, come on; they are taking Monsieur Auguste to prison; they caught him on the boulevard; it was him they were hunting—they have been questioning him—"

The old man, with a spring like a tiger's, rushed through the house and garden and out on to the boulevard, as swift as an arrow, and was just in time to see his grandson get into a hackney coach between three men.

"Auguste," he cried, "what is the meaning of this?" The youth burst into tears, and turned faint.

"Monsieur," said he to the police officer, whose scarf struck his eye, "I am Baron Bourlac, formerly a public prosecutor; for pity's sake, explain the matter."

"Monsieur, if you are Baron Bourlac, you will understand it in two words. I have just questioned this young man, and he has unfortunately confessed—"

"What?"

"A theft of four thousand francs from Doctor Halpersohn."

"Auguste! Is it possible?"

"Grandpapa, I have sent him your diamond snuff-box as a guarantee. I wanted to save you from the disgrace of imprisonment."

"Wretched boy, what have you done?" cried the Baron. "The diamonds are false; I sold the real stones three years ago."

The police officer and his clerk looked at each other with strange meaning. This glance, full of suggestions, was seen by the Baron, and fell like a thunderbolt.

"Monsieur," said he to the officer, "be quite easy; I will go and see the public prosecutor; you can testify to the delusion in which I have kept my daughter and my grandson. You must do your duty, but in the name of humanity, send my grandson to a cell by himself.—I will go to prison.—Where are you taking him?"

"Are you Baron Bourlac?" said the constable.

"Oh! Monsieur—"

"Because the public prosecutor, the examining judge, and I myself could not believe that such men as you and your grandson could be guilty; like the doctor, we concluded that some swindlers had borrowed your names."

He took the Baron aside and said:

"Were you at Doctor Halpersohn's house this morning?"

"Yes, monsieur."

"And your grandson too, about half-an-hour later?"

"I know nothing about that; I have this instant come in, and I have not seen my grandson since yesterday."

"The writs he showed me and the warrant for arrest explain everything," said the police agent. "I know his motive for the crime. I ought indeed to arrest you, monsieur, as abetting your grandson, for your replies confirm the facts alleged by the complainant; but the notices served on you, and which I return to you," he added, holding out a packet of stamped papers which he had in his hand, "certainly prove you to be Baron Bourlac. At the same time, you must be prepared to be called up before Monsieur Marest, the examining judge in this case. I believe I am right in relaxing the usual rule in consideration of your past dignity.

"As to your grandson, I will speak of him to the public prosecutor as soon as I go in, and we will show every possible consideration for the grandson of a retired judge, and the victim of a youthful error. Still, there is the indictment, the accused has confessed; I have sent in my report, and have a warrant for his imprisonment; I cannot help myself. As to the place of detention, your grandson will be taken to the Conciergerie."

"Thank you, monsieur," said the miserable Bourlac. He fell senseless on the snow, and tumbled into one of the rainwater cisterns, which at that time divided the trees on the boulevard.

The police officer called for help, and Népomucène hurried out with Madame Vauthier. The old man was carried indoors, and the woman begged the police constable, as he went by the Rue d'Enfer, to send Doctor Berton as quickly as possible.

"What is the matter with my grandfather?" asked poor Auguste.

"He is crazed, sir. That is what comes of thieving!"

Auguste made a rush as though to crack his skull; but the two men held him back.

"Come, come, young man. Take it quietly," said the officer. "Be calm. You have done wrong, but it is not irremediable."

"But pray, monsieur, tell the woman that my grandfather has probably not touched food for these twenty-four hours."

"Oh, poor creatures!" said the officer to himself.

He stopped the coach, which had started, and said a word in his clerk's ear; the man ran off to speak to old Vauthier, and then returned at once.

Monsieur Berton was of opinion that Monsieur Bernard—for he knew him by no other name—was suffering from an attack of high fever; but when Madame Vauthier had told him of all the events that had led up to it in the way in which a housekeeper tells a story, the doctor thought it necessary to report the whole business next day to Monsieur Alain at the Church of Saint-Jacques du Haut-Pas, and Monsieur Alain sent a pencil note by messenger to Monsieur Nicolas, Rue Chanoinesse.

Godefroid, on reaching home the night before, had given the notes on the book to Monsieur Nicolas, who spent the greater part of the night in reading the first volume of Baron Bourlac's work.

On the following day Madame de la Chanterie told Godefroid that if his determination still held good, he might begin on his work at once.

Godefroid, initiated by her into the financial secrets of the Society, worked for seven or eight hours a day, and for several months, under the supervision of Frédéric Mongenod, who came every Sunday to look through the work, and who praised him for the way in which it was done.

"You are a valuable acquisition for the saints among whom you live," said the banker when all the accounts were clearly set forth and balanced. "Two or three hours a day will now be enough to keep the accounts in order, and during the rest of your time you can help them, if you still feel the vocation as you did six months since."

This was in the month of July 1838. During the time that had elapsed since the affair of the Boulevard du Mont-Parnasse, Godefroid, eager to prove himself worthy of his companions, had never asked a single question as to Baron Bourlac; for, as he had not heard a word, nor found anything in the account-books that bore on the matter, he suspected that the silence that was preserved with regard to the two men who had been so ruthless to Madame de la Chanterie, was intended as a test to which he was being put, or perhaps as proof that the noble lady's friends had avenged her.

But, two months later, in the course of a walk one day, he went as far as the Boulevard du Mont-Parnasse, managed to meet Madame Vauthier, and asked her for some news of the Bernard family.

"Who can tell, my dear Monsieur Godefroid, what has become of those people. Two days after your expedition—for it was you, you cunning dog, who blabbed to my landlord—somebody came who took that old swaggerer off my hands. Then, in four-and-twenty hours, everything was cleared out—not a stick left, nor a word said—perfect strangers to me, and they told me nothing. I believe he packed himself off to Algiers with his precious grandson; for Népomucène, who was very devoted to that young thief—he is no better than he should be himself—did not find him in the Conciergerie, and he alone knows where they are, and the scamp has gone off and left me. You bring up these wretched foundlings, and this is the reward you get; they leave you high and dry. I have not been able to find any one to take his place, and as the neighbourhood is very crowded, and the house is full, I am worked to death."

And Godefroid would never have known anything more of Baron Bourlac but for the conclusion of the adventure, which came about through one of the chance meetings which occur in Paris.

In the month of September, Godefroid was walking down the Champs-Élysées, when, as he passed the end of the Rue Marbeuf, he remembered Doctor Halpersohn.

"I ought to call on him," thought he, "and ask if he cured Bourlac's daughter. What a voice, what a gift she had! She wanted to dedicate herself to God!"

As he got to the Rond-Point, Godefroid crossed the road hurriedly to avoid the carriages that came quickly down the grand avenue, and he ran up against a youth who had a young-looking woman on his arm.

"Take care!" cried the young man. "Are you blind?"

'Why, it is you!" cried Godefroid, recognising Auguste de Mergi.

Auguste was so well dressed, so handsome, so smart, so proud of the lady he was escorting, that, but for the memories that rushed on his mind, Godefroid would hardly have recognised them.

"Why, it is dear Monsieur Godefroid!" exclaimed the lady. On hearing the delightful tones of Vanda's enchanting voice, and seeing her walking, Godefroid stood riveted to the spot.

"Cured!" he exclaimed.

"Ten days ago he allowed me to walk," she replied.

"Halpersohn?"

"Yes," said she. "And why have you never come to see us?—But, indeed, you were wise. My hair was not cut off till about a week ago. This that you see is but a wig; but the doctor assures me it will grow again!—But we have so much to say to each other. Will you not come to dine with us?—Oh, that harmonium!—Oh, monsieur!" and she put her handkerchief to her eyes. "I will treasure it all my life! My son will preserve it as a relic.—My father has sought for you all through Paris, and he is anxiously in search, too, of his unknown benefactors. He will die of grief if you cannot help him to find them. He suffers from the darkest melancholy, and I cannot always succeed in rousing him from it."

Fascinated alike by the voice of this charming woman recalled from the grave, and by that of irresistible curiosity, Godefroid gave his arm to the hand held out by the Baronne de Mergi, who let her son go on in front with an errand, which the lad had understood from his mother's nod.

"I shall not take you far; we are living in the Allée d'Antin in a pretty little house *à l'Anglaise*; we have it all to ourselves, each of us occupies a floor. Oh, we are very comfortable! And my father believes that you have had a great deal to do with the good fortune that is poured upon us—"

"I?"

"Did you not know that a place has been created for him in consequence of a report from the Minister for Public Instruction, a Chair of Legislature, like one at the Sorbonne? My father will give his first course of lectures in the month of November next. The great work on which he was engaged will be published in a month or so; the house of Cavalier is bringing it out on half-profits with my father, and has paid him thirty thousand francs on account of his share; so he is buying the house we live in. The Minister of Justice allows me a pension of twelve hundred francs as the daughter of a retired magistrate; my father has his pension of a thousand crowns, and he had five thousand francs with his professorship. We are so economical that we shall be almost rich.

"My Auguste will begin studying the law a few months hence; meanwhile, he has employment in the public prosecutor's office, and gets twelve hundred francs.—Oh, Monsieur Godefroid, never mention that miserable business of my poor Auguste's. For my part, I bless him every day for the deed which his grandfather has not yet forgiven. His mother blesses him, Halpersohn is devoted to him, but the old public prosecutor is implacable!"

"What business?" asked Godefroid.

"Ah! that is just like your generosity!" cried Vanda. "You have a noble heart. Your mother must be proud of you!—"

"On my word, I know nothing of the matter you allude to," said Godefroid

"Really, you did not hear?" And she frankly told the story of Auguste's borrowing from the doctor, admiring her son for the action.

"But if I am to say nothing about this before the Baron," said Godefroid, "tell me how your son got out of the scrape."

"Well," said Vanda, "as I told you, my son is in the public prosecutor's office, and has met with the greatest kindness. He was not kept more than eight-and-forty hours in the Conciergerie, where he was lodged with the governor. The worthy doctor, who did not get Auguste's beautiful, sublime letter till the evening, withdrew the charge; and by the intervention of a former presiding judge of the Supreme Court—a man my father had never even seen—the public prosecutor had the police agent's report and the warrant for arrest both destroyed. In fact, not a trace of the affair survives but in my heart, in my son's conscience, and in his grandfather's mind—who, since that day, speaks to my boy in the coldest terms, and treats him as a stranger.

"Only yesterday, Halpersohn was interceding for him; but my father, who will not listen to me, much as he loves me, replied: 'You are the person robbed, you can and ought to forgive. But I am answerable for the thief—and when I sat on the Bench, I never pronounced a pardon!'—'You will kill your daughter,' said Halpersohn—I heard them. My father kept silence."

"But who is it that has helped you?"

"A gentleman who is, we believe, employed to distribute the benefactions of the Queen."

"What is he like?" asked Godefroid.

"He is a grave, thin man, sad-looking—something like my father. It was he who had my father conveyed to the house where we now are, when he was in a high fever. And, just fancy, as soon as my father was well, I was removed from the private hospital and brought there, where I found my old bedroom just as though I had never left it.—Halpersohn, whom the tall gentleman had quite bewitched—how I know not—then told me all about my father's sufferings, and how he had sold the diamonds off his snuff-box! My father and my boy often without bread, and making believe to be rich in my presence!—Oh, Monsieur Godefroid, those two men are martyrs! What can I say to my father? I can only repay him and my son by suffering for them, like them."

"And had the tall gentleman something of a military air?"

"Oh, you know him!" cried Vanda, as they reached the door of the house.

She seized Godefroid's hand with the grip of a woman in hysterics, and dragging him into a drawing-room of which the door stood open, she exclained—"Father, Monsieur Godefroid knows your benefactor."

Baron Bourlac, whom Godefroid found dressed in a style suitable to a retired judge of his high rank, held out his hand to Godefroid, and said:

"I thought as much."

Godefroid shook his head in negation of any knowledge of the details of this noble revenge; but the Baron did not give him time to speak.

"Monsieur," he went on, "only Providence can be more powerful, only Love can be more thoughtful, only Motherhood can be more clear-sighted, than your friends who are allied with those great divinities.—I bless the chance that has led to our meeting again, for Monsieur Joseph has vanished completely; and as he has succeeded in avoiding every snare I could lay to ascertain his real name and residence, I should have died in grief.—But here, read his letter.—And you know him?"

Godefroid read as follows:

> "Monsieur le Baron Bourlac, the money we have laid out for you by the orders of a charitable lady amounts to a sum of fifteen thousand francs. Take note of this, that it may be repaid either by you or by your descendants when your family is sufficiently prosperous to allow of it, for it belongs to the poor. When such repayment is possible, deposit the money you owe with the Brothers Mongenod, bankers. God forgive you your sins!"

The letter was mysteriously signed with five crosses.

Godefroid returned it.—"The five crosses, sure enough!" said he to himself.

"Now, since you know all," said the old man, "you who were this mysterious lady's messenger—tell me her name."

"Her name!" cried Godefroid; "her name! Unhappy man, never ask it! never try to find it out.—Oh, madame," said he, taking Madame de Mergi's hand in his own, which shook, "if you value your father's sanity, keep him in his ignorance; never let him make any attempt—"

The father, the daughter, and Auguste stood frozen with amazement.

"Well, then, the woman who has preserved your daughter for you," said Godefroid, looking at the old lawyer, "who has restored her to you, young, lovely, fresh, and living—who has snatched her from the grave—who has rescued your grandson from disgrace—who has secured to you a happy and respected old age—who has saved you all three—" he paused, "is a woman whom you sent innocent to the hulks for twenty years," he went on, addressing Monsieur Bourlac, "on whom, from your judgment-seat, you poured every insult, whose saintliness you mocked at, and from whom you snatched a lovely daughter to send her to the most horrible death, for she was guillotined!"

Godefroid, seeing Vanda drop senseless on to a chair, rushed out of the room, and from thence into the Allée d'Antin, where he took to his heels.

"If you would earn my forgiveness," said Baron Bourlac to his grandson, "follow that man and find out where he lives."

Auguste was off like a dart.

By half-past eight next morning, Baron Bourlac was knocking at the old yellow gate of the Hotel de la Chanterie, Rue Chanoinesse. He asked for Madame de la Chanterie, and the porter pointed to the stone steps. Happily they were all going to breakfast, and Godefroid recognised the Baron in the courtyard through one of the loopholes that lighted the stairs. He had but just time to fly down and into the drawing-room where they were all assembled, crying out—"Baron Bourlac."

On hearing this name, Madame de la Chanterie, supported by the Abbé de Vèze, disappeared into her room.

"You shall not come in, you imp of Satan!" cried Manon, who recognised the lawyer, and placed herself in front of the drawing-room door. "Do you want to kill my mistress?"

"Come, Manon, let the gentleman pass," said Monsieur Alain.

Manon dropped on to a chair as if her knees had both given way at once.

"Gentlemen," said the Baron in a voice of deep emotion, as he recognised Godefroid and Monsieur Joseph, and bowed to the two strangers, "Beneficence confers a claim on those benefited by it!"

"You owe nothing to us," said the worthy Alain; "you owe everything to God."

"You are saints, and you have the serenity of saints," replied the old lawyer.

"You will hear me, I beg.—I have learned that the superhuman blessings that have been heaped on me for eighteen months past are the work of a person whom I deeply injured in the course of my duty; it was fifteen years before I was assured of her innocence; this, gentlemen, is the single remorse I have known as due to the exercise of my powers.—Listen! I have not much longer to live, but I shall lose that short term of life, necessary still to my children whom Madame de la Chanterie has saved, if I cannot win her forgiveness. Gentlemen, I will remain kneeling on the square of Notre-Dame till she has spoken one word!—I will wait for her there!—I will kiss the print of her feet; I will find tears to soften her heart—I who have been dried up like a straw by seeing my daughter's sufferings—"

The door of Madame de la Chanterie's room was opened, the Abbé de Vèze came through like a shade, and said to Monsieur Joseph:

"That voice is killing Madame."

"What! she is there! She has passed there!" cried Bourlac. He fell on his knees, kissed the floor, and melted into tears, crying in a heartrending tone:

"In the name of Jesus who died on the Cross, forgive! forgive! For my child has suffered a thousand deaths!"

The old man collapsed so entirely that the spectators believed he was dead.

At this moment Madame de la Chanterie appeared like a spectre in the doorway, leaning, half-fainting, against the side-post.

"In the name of Louis XVI and Marie Antoinette, whom I see on the scaffold, of Madame Elizabeth, of my daughter, and of yours—in the name of Jesus, I forgive you."

As he heard the words, the old man looked up and said:

"Thus are the angels avenged."

Monsieur Joseph and Monsieur Nicolas helped him to his feet, and led him out to the courtyard; Godefroid went to call a coach; and when they heard the rattle of wheels, Monsieur Nicolas said as he helped the old man into it:

"Come no more, monsieur, or you will kill the mother too. The power of God is infinite, but human nature has its limits."

That day Godefroid joined the Order of the Brethren of Consolation.

VIERZCHOVNIA, UKRAINE, *December* 1847.

A PRINCE OF BOHEMIA

To Henri Heine.

I inscribe this to you, my dear Heine, to you that represent in Paris the ideas and poetry of Germany, in Germany the lively and witty criticism of France; for you better than any other will know whatsoever this Study may contain of criticism and of jest, of love and truth.

DE BALZAC.

"MY dear friend," said Mme. de la Baudraye, drawing a pile of manuscript from beneath her sofa cushion, "will you pardon me in our present straits for making a short story of something which you told me a few weeks ago?"

"Anything is fair in these times. Have you not seen writers serving up their own hearts to the public, or very often their mistress' hearts when invention fails? We are coming to this, dear; we shall go in quest of adventures, not so much for the pleasure of them as for the sake of having the story to tell afterwards."

"After all, you and the Marquise de Rochefide have paid the rent, and I do not think, from the way things are going here, that I ever pay yours."

"Who knows? Perhaps the same good luck that befell Mme. de Rochefide may come to you."

"Do you call it good luck to go back to one's husband?"

"No; only great luck. Come, I am listening."

And Mme. de la Baudraye read as follows:

"Scene—a splendid salon in the Rue de Chartres-du-Roule. One of the most famous writers of the day discovered sitting on a settee beside a very illustrious Marquise, with whom he is on such terms

> of intimacy, as a man has a right to claim when a woman singles him out and keeps him at her side as a complacent *souffre-douleur* rather than a makeshift."

"Well," says she, "have you found those letters of which you spoke yesterday? You said that you could not tell me all about *him* without them?"

"Yes, I have them."

"It is your turn to speak; I am listening like a child when his mother begins the tale of *Le Grand Serpentin Vert*."

"I count the young man in question in that group of our acquaintances which we are wont to style our friends. He comes of a good family; he is a man of infinite parts and ill-luck, full of excellent dispositions and most charming conversation; young as he is, he has seen much, and while awaiting better things, he dwells in Bohemia. Bohemianism, which by rights should be called the doctrine of the Boulevard des Italiens, finds its recruits among young men between twenty and thirty, all of them men of genius in their way, little known, it is true, as yet, but sure of recognition one day, and when that day comes, of great distinction. They are distinguished as it is at carnival time, when their exuberant wit, repressed for the rest of the year, finds a vent in more or less ingenious buffoonery.

"What times we live in! What an irrational central power which allows such tremendous energies to run to waste! There are diplomatists in Bohemia quite capable of overturning Russia's designs, if they but felt the power of France at their backs. There are writers, administrators, soldiers, and artists in Bohemia; every faculty, every kind of brain is represented there. Bohemia is a microcosm. If the Czar would buy Bohemia for a score of millions and set its population down in Odessa—always supposing that they consented to leave the asphalt of the boulevards—Odessa would be Paris with the year. In Bohemia, you find the flower doomed to wither and come to nothing; the flower of the wonderful young manhood of France, so sought after by Napoleon and Louis XIV, so neglected for the last thirty years by the modern Gerontocracy that is blighting everything else—that splendid young manhood of whom a witness so little prejudiced as Professor Tissot wrote, 'On all sides the Emperor employed a younger generation in every way worthy of him; in his councils, in the general administration, in negotiations bristling with difficulties or full of danger, in the government of conquered countries; and in all places Youth responded to his demands upon it. Young men were for Napoleon the *missi hominici* of Charlemagne.'

"The word Bohemia tells you everything. Bohemia has nothing and lives upon what it has. Hope is its religion; faith (in oneself) its creed; and charity is supposed to be its budget. All these young men are greater than their misfortune; they are under the feet of Fortune, yet more than equal to Fate. Always ready to mount and ride an *if*, witty as a *feuilleton*, blithe as only those can be that are deep in debt and drink deep to match, and finally—for here I come to my point—hot lovers, and what lovers! Picture to yourself Lovelace, and Henri Quatre, and the Regent, and Werther, and Saint-Preux, and René, and the Maréchal de Richelieu—think of all these in a single man, and you will have some idea of their way of love. What lovers! Eclectic of all things in love, they will serve up a passion to a woman's order; their hearts are like a bill of fare in a restaurant. Perhaps they have never read Stendhal's *De l'Amour*, but unconsciously they put it in practice. They have by heart their chapters—Love-Taste, Love-Passion, Love-Caprice, Love-Crystallised, and more than all, Love-Transient. All is good in their eyes. They invented the burlesque axiom, 'In the sight of man, all women are equal.' The actual text is more vigorously worded, but as in my opinion the spirit is false, I do not stand nice upon the letter.

"My friend, madame, is named Gabriel Jean Anne Victor Benjamin George Ferdinand Charles Edward Rusticoli, Comte de la Palférine. The Rusticolis came to France with Catherine dei Medici, having been ousted about that time from their infinitesimal Tuscan sovereignty. They are distantly related to the house of Este, and connected by marriage with the Guises. On the Day of Saint-Bartholomew they slew a goodly number of Protestants, and Charles IX bestowed the hand of the heiress of the Comte de la Palférine upon the Rusticoli of that time. The Comté, however, being a part of the confiscated lands of the Duke of Savoy, was repurchased by Henri IV when that great king so far blundered as to restore the fief; and in exchange, the Rusticoli—who had borne arms long before the Medici bore them, to-wit, *argent* a cross flory *azure* (the cross flower-de-luced by letters patent granted by Charles IX), and a count's coronet, with two peasants for supporters with the motto IN HOC SIGNO VINCIMUS—the Rusticoli, I repeat, retained their title, and received a couple of offices under the crown with the government of a province.

"From the time of the Valois till the reign of Richelieu, as it may be called, the Rusticoli played a most illustrious part; under Louis XIV their glory waned somewhat, under Louis XV it went out altogether. My friend's grandfather wasted all that was left to the once brilliant house with Mlle. Laguerre, whom he first discovered, and brought into fashion before Bouret's time.

Charles Edward's own father was an officer without any fortune in 1789. The Revolution came to his assistance; he had the sense to drop his title, and became plain Rusticoli. Among other deeds, M. Rusticoli married a wife during the war in Italy, a Capponi, a goddaughter of the Countess of Albany (hence La Palférine's final names). Rusticoli was one of the best colonels in the army. The Emperor made him a commander of the Legion of Honour and a count. His spine was slightly curved, and his son was wont to say of him laughingly that he was *un comte refait (contrefait).*

"General Count Rusticoli, for he became a brigadier-general at Ratisbon and a general of the division on the field of Wagram, died at Vienna almost immediately after his promotion, or his name and ability would sooner or later have brought him the marshal's bâton. Under the Restoration he would certainly have repaired the fortunes of a great and noble family so brilliant even as far back as 1100, centuries before they took the French title—for the Rusticoli had given a pope to the church and twice revolutionised the kingdom of Naples—so illustrious again under the Valois; so dexterous in the days of the Fronde, that obstinate Frondeurs though they were, they still existed through the reign of Louis XIV. Mazarin favoured them; there was the Tuscan strain in them still, and he recognised it.

"To-day, when Charles Edward de la Palférine's name is mentioned, not three persons in a hundred know the history of his house. But the Bourbons have actually left a Foix-Grailly to live by his easel.

"Ah! if you but knew how brilliantly Charles Edward accepts his obscure position! how he scoffs at the bourgeois of 1830! What Attic salt in his wit! He would be the king of Bohemia, if Bohemia would endure a king. His *verve* is in exhaustible. To him we owe a map of the country and the names of the seven castles which Nodier could not discover."

"The one thing wanting in one of the cleverest skits of our time," said the Marquise.

"You can form your own opinion of La Palférine from a few characteristic touches," continued Nathan. "He once came upon a friend of his, a fellow-Bohemian, involved in a dispute on the boulevard with a bourgeois who chose to consider himself affronted. To the modern powers that be, Bohemia is insolent in the extreme. There was talk of calling one another out.

"'One moment,' interposed La Palférine, as much Lauzun for the occasion as Lauzun himself could have been. 'One moment. Monsieur was born, I suppose?'

"'What, sir?'

"'Yes, are you born? What is your name?'

"'Godin."

"'Godin, eh!' exclaimed La Palférine's friend.

"'One moment, my dear fellow,' interrupted La Palférine. 'There are the Trigaudins. Are you one of them?'

"Astonishment.

"'No? Then you are one of the new dukes of Gaëta, I suppose, of imperial creation? No? Oh, well, how can you expect my friend to cross swords with you when he will be secretary of an embassy and ambassador *some day,* and you will owe him respect? *Godin!* the thing is non-existent! You are a nonentity, Godin. My friend cannot be expected to beat the air! When one is somebody, one cannot fight with a nobody! Come, my dear fellow—good-day.'

"'My respects to madame,' added the friend.

"Another day La Palférine was walking with a friend who flung his cigar end in the face of a passer-by. The recipient had the bad taste to resent this.

"'You have stood your antagonist's fire,' said the young Count, 'the witnesses declare that honour is satisfied.'

"La Palférine owed his tailor a thousand francs, and the man instead of going himself sent his assistant to ask for the money. The assistant found the unfortunate debtor up six pairs of stairs at the back of a yard at the further end of the Faubourg du Roule. The room was unfurnished save for a bed (such a bed!), a table, and such a table! La Palférine heard the preposterous demand—'A demand which I should qualify as illegal,' he said when he told us the story, 'made, as it was, at seven o'clock in the morning.'

"'Go,' he answered, with the gesture and attitude of a Mirabeau, 'tell your master in what condition you find me.'

"The assistant apologised and withdrew. La Palférine, seeing the young man on the landing, rose in the attire celebrated in verse in *Britannicus* to add, 'Remark the stairs! Pay particular attention to the stairs; do not forget to tell him about the stairs!'

"In every position into which chance has thrown La Palférine, he has never failed to rise to the occasion. All that he does is witty and never in bad taste; always and in everything he displays the genius of Rivarol, the polished subtlety of the old French noble. It was he who told that delicious anecdote of a friend of Laffitte the banker. A national fund had been started to give back to Laffitte the mansion in which the Revolution of 1830 was brewed, and this friend appeared at the offices of the fund with, 'Here are five francs, give me a hundred sous change!'—A caricature was made of it.—It was once La Palférine's misfortune, in judicial style, to make a young girl a mother. The girl, not a very simple innocent, confessed all to her mother, a respectable matron, who hurried forthwith to La Palférine and asked what he meant to do.

"'Why, madame,' said he, 'I am neither a surgeon nor a midwife.'

"She collapsed, but three or four years later she returned to the charge, still persisting in her inquiry, 'What did La Palférine mean to do?'

"'Well, madame,' returned he, 'when the child is seven years old, an age at which a boy ought to pass out of women's hands'—an indication of entire agreement on the mother's part—'if the child is really mine'—another gesture of assent—'if there is a striking likeness, if he bids fair to be a gentleman, if I can recognise in him my turn of mind, and more particularly the Rusticoli air; then, oh—ah!'—a new movement from the matron— 'on my word and honour, I will make him a cornet of—sugar-plums!'

"All this, if you will permit me to make use of the phraseology employed by M. Sainte-Beuve for his biographies of obscurities—this, I repeat, is the playful and sprightly yet already somewhat decadent side of a strong race. It smacks rather of the Parc-aux-Cerfs than of the Hôtel de Rambouillet. It is a race of the strong rather than of the sweet; I incline to lay a little debauchery to its charge, and more than I should wish in brilliant and generous natures; it is gallantry after the fashion of the Maréchal de Richelieu, high spirits and frolic carried rather too far; perhaps we may see in it the *outrances* of another age, the Eighteenth Century pushed to extremes; it harks back to the Musketeers; it is an exploit stolen from Champcenetz; nay, such light-hearted inconstancy takes us back to the festooned and ornate period of the old court of the Valois. In an age as moral as the present, we are bound to regard audacity of this kind sternly; still, at the same time that 'cornet of sugar-plums' may serve to warn young girls of the perils of lingering where fancies, more charming than chastened, come thickly from the first; on the rosy flowery unguarded slopes, where trespasses ripen into errors full of equivocal effervescence, into too palpitating issues. The anecdote puts La Palférine's genius before you in all its vivacity and completeness. He realises Pascal's *entre-deux*, he comprehends the whole scale between tenderness and pitilessness, and, like Epaminondas, he is equally great in extremes. And not merely so, his epigram stamps the epoch; the *accoucheur* is a modern innovation. All the refinements of modern civilisation are summed up in the phrase. It is monumental."

"Look here, my dear Nathan, what farrago of nonsense is this?" asked the Marquise in bewilderment.

"Madame la Marquise," returned Nathan, "you do not know the value of these 'precious' phrases; I am talking Sainte-Beuve, the new kind of French.—I resume. Walking one day arm in arm with a friend along the boulevard, he was accosted by a ferocious creditor, who inquired:

"'Are you thinking of me, sir?'

"'Not the least in the world,' answered the Count.

"Remark the difficulty of the position. Talleyrand, in similar circumstances, had already replied, 'You are very inquisitive, my dear fellow!' To imitate the inimitable great man was out of the question.—La Palférine, generous as Buckingham, could not bear to be caught empty-handed. One day when he had nothing to give a little Savoyard chimney-sweeper, he dipped a hand into a barrel of grapes in a grocer's doorway and filled the child's cap from it. The little one ate away at his grapes; the grocer began by laughing, and ended by holding out his hand.

"'Oh, fie! monsieur,' said La Palférine, 'your left hand ought not to know what my right hand doth.'

"With his adventurous courage, he never refuses any odds, but there is wit in his bravado. In the Passage de l'Opéra he chanced to meet a man who had spoken slightingly of him, elbowed him as he passed, and then turned and jostled him a second time.

"'You are very clumsy!'

"'On the contrary; I did it on purpose.'

"The young man pulled out his card. La Palférine dropped it. 'It has been carried too long in the pocket. Be good enough to give me another.'

"On the ground he received a thrust; blood was drawn; his antagonist wished to stop.

"'You are wounded, monsieur!'

"'I disallow the *botte,*' said La Palférine, as coolly as if he had been in the fencing-saloon; then as he riposted (sending the point home this time), he added, 'There is the right thrust, monsieur!'

"His antagonist kept his bed for six months.

"This, stiff following on M. Sainte-Beuve's tracks, recalls the *raffinés*, the fine-edged raillery of the best days of the monarchy. In this speech you discern an untrammelled but drifting life; a gaiety of imagination that deserts us when our first youth is past. The prime of the blossom is over, but there remains the dry compact seed with the germs of life in it, ready against the coming winter. Do you not see that these things are symptoms of something unsatisfied, of an unrest impossible to analyse, still less to describe, yet not incomprehensible; a something ready to break out if occasion calls into flying upleaping flame? It is the *accidia* of the cloister; a trace of sourness, of ferment engendered by the enforced stagnation of youthful energies, a vague, obscure melancholy."

"That will do," said the Marquise; "you are giving me a mental shower bath."

"It is the early afternoon languor. If a man has nothing to do, he will sooner get into mischief than do nothing at all; this invariably happens in France. Youth at the present day has two sides to it; the studious or unappreciated, and the ardent or *passionné*."

"That will do!" repeated Mme. de Rochefide, with an authoritative gesture. "You are setting my nerves on edge."

"To finish my portrait of La Palférine, I hasten to make the plunge into the gallant regions of his character, or you will not understand the peculiar genius of an admirable representative of a certain section of mischievous youth—youth strong enough, be it said, to laugh at the position in which it is put by those in power; shrewd enough to do no work, since work profiteth nothing, yet so full of life that it fastens upon pleasure—the one thing that cannot be taken away. And meanwhile a bourgeois, mercantile, and bigoted policy continues to cut off all the sluices through which so much aptitude and ability would find an outlet. Poets and men of science are not wanted.

"To give you an idea of the stupidity of the new court, I will tell you of something which happened to La Palférine. There is a sort of relieving officer on the civil list. This functionary one day discovered that La Palférine was in dire distress, drew up a report, no doubt, and brought the descendant of the Rusticolis fifty francs by way of alms. La Palférine received the visitor with perfect courtesy, and talked of various persons at court.

"'Is it true,' he asked, 'that Mlle. d'Orléans contributes such and such a sum to this benevolent scheme started by her nephew? If so, it is very gracious of her.'

"Now La Palférine had a servant, a little Savoyard, aged ten, who waited on him without wages. La Palférine called him Father Anchises, and used to say, 'I have never seen such a mixture of besotted foolishness with great intelligence; he would go through fire and water for me; he understands everything—and yet he cannot grasp the fact that I can do nothing for him.'

"Anchises was despatched to a livery stable with instructions to hire a handsome brougham with a man in livery behind it. By the time the carriage arrived below, La Palférine had skilfully piloted the conversation to the subject of the functions of his visitor, whom he has since called 'the unmitigated misery man,' and learned the nature of his duties and his stipend.

"'Do they allow you a carriage to go about the town in this way?'

"'Oh! no.'

"At that La Palférine and a friend who happened to be with him went downstairs with the poor soul, and insisted on putting him into the carriage. It was raining in torrents. La Palférine had thought of everything. He offered to drive the official to the next house on his list; and when the almoner came down again, he found the carriage waiting for him at the door. The man in livery handed him a note written in pencil:

> "'The carriage has been engaged for three days. Count Rusticoli de la Palférine is too happy to associate himself with Court charities by lending wings to Royal beneficence.'

"La Palférine now calls the civil list the uncivil list.

"He was once passionately loved by a lady of somewhat light conduct. Antonia lived in the Rue du Helder; she had seen and been seen to some extent, but at the time of her acquaintance with La Palférine she had not yet 'an establishment.' Antonia was not wanting in the insolence of old days, now degenerating into rudeness among women of her class. After a fortnight of unmixed bliss, she was compelled, in the interest of her civil list, to return to a less exclusive system; and La Palférine, discovering a certain lack of sincerity in her dealings with him, sent Madame Antonia a note which made her famous.

> "'MADAME,—Your conduct causes me much surprise and no less distress. Not content with rending my heart with your disdain, you have been so little thoughtful as to retain a toothbrush, which my means will not permit me to replace, my estates being mortgaged beyond their value.
>
> "'Adieu, too fair and too ungrateful friend! May we meet again in a better world.
>
> "'CHARLES EDWARD.'

"Assuredly (to avail ourselves yet further of Sainte-Beuve's Babylonish dialect), this far outpasses the raillery of Sterne's *Sentimental Journey*; it might be Scarron without his grossness. Nay, I do not know but that Molière in his lighter mood would not have said of it, as of Cyrano de Bergerac's best—'This is mine.' Richelieu himself was not more complete when he wrote to the princess waiting for him in the Palais Royal—'Stay there, my queen, to charm the scullion lads.' At the same time, Charles Edward's humour is less biting. I am not sure that this kind of wit was known among the Greeks and Romans. Plato, possibly, upon a closer inspection approaches it, but from the austere and musical side—"

"No more of that jargon," the Marquise broke in, "in print it may be endurable; but to have it grating upon my ears is a punishment which I do not in the least deserve."

"He first met Claudine on this wise," continued Nathan. "It was one of the unfilled days, when Youth is a burden to itself; days when youth, reduced by the overweening presumption of Age to a condition of potential energy and dejection, emerges therefrom (like Blondet under the Restoration), either to get into mischief or to set about some colossal piece of buffoonery, half excused by the very audacity of its conception. La Palférine was sauntering, cane in hand, up and down the pavement between the Rue de Grammont and the Rue de Richelieu, when in the distance he descried a woman too elegantly dressed, covered, as he phrased it, with a great deal of portable property, too expensive and too carelessly worn for its owner to be other than a princess of the Court or of the stage, it was not easy at first to say which. But after July 1830, in his opinion, there is no mistaking the indications—the princess can only be a princess of the stage.

"The Count came up and walked by her side as if she had given him an assignation. He followed her with a courteous persistence, a persistence in good taste, giving the lady from time to time, and always at the right moment, an authoritative glance, which compelled her to submit to his escort. Anybody but La Palférine would have been frozen by his reception, and disconcerted by the lady's first efforts to rid herself of her cavalier, by her chilly air, her curt speeches; but no gravity, with all the will in the world, could hold out long against La Palférine's jesting replies. The fair stranger went into her milliner's shop. Charles Edward followed, took a seat, and gave his opinions and advice like a man that meant to pay. This coolness disturbed the lady. She went out.

"On the stairs she spoke to her persecutor.

"'Monsieur, I am about to call upon one of my husband's relatives, an elderly lady, Mme. de Bonfalot—'

"'Ah! Mme. de Bonfalot, charmed, I am sure. I am going there.'

"The pair accordingly went. Charles Edward came in with the lady, every one believed that she had brought him with her. He took part in the conversation, was lavish of his polished and brilliant wit. The visit lengthened out. That was not what he wanted.

"'Madame,' he said, addressing the fair stranger, 'do not forget that your husband is waiting for us, and only allowed us a quarter of an hour.'

"Taken aback by such boldness (which, as you know, is never displeasing to you women), led captive by the conqueror's glance, by the astute yet candid air which Charles Edward can assume when he chooses, the lady rose, took the arm of her self-constituted escort, and went downstairs, but on the threshold she stopped to speak to him.

"'Monsieur, I like a joke—'

"'And so do I.'

"She laughed.

"'But this may turn to earnest,' he added; 'it only rests with you. I am the Comte de la Palférine, and I am delighted that it is in my power to lay my heart and my fortune at your feet.'

"La Palférine was at that time twenty-two years old. (This happened in 1834.) Luckily for him, he was fashionably dressed. I can paint his portrait for you in a few words.

He was the living image of Louis XIII, with the same white forehead and gracious outline of the temples, the same olive skin (that Italian olive tint which turns white where the light falls on it), the brown hair worn rather long, the black 'royale,' the grave and melancholy expression, for La Palférine's character and exterior were amazingly at variance.

"At the sound of the name, and the sight of its owner, something like a quiver thrilled through Claudine. La Palférine saw the vibration, and shot a glance at her out of the dark depths of almond-shaped eyes with purpled lids, and those faint lines about them which tell of pleasures as costly as painful fatigue. With those eyes upon her, she said— 'Your address?'

"'What want of address!'

"'Oh, pshaw!' she said, smiling. 'A bird on the bough?'

"'Good-bye, madame, you are such a woman as I seek, but my fortune is far from equalling my desire—'

"He bowed, and there and then left her. Two days later, by one of the strange chances that can only happen in Paris, he had betaken himself to a money-lending wardrobe dealer to sell such of his clothing as he could spare. He was just receiving the price with an uneasy air, after long chaffering, when the stranger lady passed and recognised him.

"'Once for all,' cried he to the bewildered wardrobe dealer, 'I tell you I am not going to take your trumpet!'

"He pointed to a huge, much-dinted musical instrument, hanging up outside against a background of uniforms, civil and military. Then, proudly and impetuously, he followed the lady.

"From that great day of the trumpet these two understood one another to admiration. Charles Edward's ideas on the subject of love are as sound as possible. According to him, a man cannot love twice, there is but one love in his lifetime, but that love is a deep and shoreless sea. It may break in upon him at any time, as the grace of God found St. Paul; and a man may live sixty years and never know love. Perhaps, to quote Heine's superb phrase, it is 'the secret malady of the heart'—a sense of the Infinite that there is within us, together with the revelation of the ideal Beauty in its visible form. This love, in short, comprehends both the creature and creation. But so long as there is no question of this great poetical conception, the loves that cannot last can only be taken lightly, as if they were in a manner snatches of song compared with Love the epic.

"To Charles Edward the adventure brought neither the thunderbolt signal of love's coming, nor yet that gradual revelation of an inward fairness which draws two natures by degrees more and more strongly each to each. For there are but two ways of love—love at first sight, doubtless akin to the Highland 'second-sight,' and that slow fusion of two natures which realises Plato's 'man-woman.' But if Charles Edward did not love, he was loved to distraction. Claudine found love made complete, body and soul; in her, in short, La Palférine awakened the one passion of her life; while for him Claudine was only a most charming mistress. The Devil himself, a most potent magician certainly, with all hell at his back, could never have changed the natures of these two unequal fires. I dare affirm that Claudine not unfrequently bored Charles Edward.

"'Stale fish and the woman you do not love are only fit to fling out of the window after three days,' he used to say.

"In Bohemia there is little secrecy observed over these affairs. La Palférine used to talk a good deal of Claudine; but, at the same time, none of us saw her, nor so much as knew her name. For us Claudine was almost a mythical personage. All of us acted in the same way, reconciling the requirements of our common life with the rules of good taste. Claudine, Hortense, the Baroness, the Bourgeoise, the Empress, the Spaniard, the Lioness,—these were cryptic titles which permitted us to pour out our joys, our cares, vexations, and hopes, and to communicate our discoveries. Further, none of us went. It has been known, in Bohemia, that chance discovered the identity of the fair unknown; and at once, as by tacit convention, not one of us spoke of her again. This fact may show how far youth possesses a sense of true delicacy. How admirably certain natures of a finer clay know the limit line where jest must end, and all that host of things French covered by the slang word *blague*, a word which will shortly be cast out of the language (let us hope), and yet it is the only one which conveys an idea of the spirit of Bohemia.

"So we often used to joke about Claudine and the Count—'*Toujours Claudine?*' sung to the air of *Toujours Gessler.*—'What are you making of Claudine?'—'How is Claudine?'

"'I wish you all such a mistress, for all the harm I wish you,' La Palférine began one day. 'No greyhound, no basset-dog, no poodle can match her in gentleness, submissiveness, and complete tenderness. There are times when I reproach myself, when I take myself to task for my hard heart. Claudine obeys with saintly sweetness. She comes to me, I tell her to go, she goes, she does not even cry till she is out in the courtyard. I refuse to see her for a whole week at a time. I tell her to come at such an hour on Tuesday; and be it midnight or six o'clock in the morning, ten o'clock, five o'clock, breakfast time, dinner time, bed time, any particularly inconvenient hour in the day—she will come, punctual to the minute, beautiful, beautifully dressed, and enchanting. And she is a married woman, with all the complications and duties of a household. The fibs that she must invent, the reasons she must find for conforming to my whims would tax the ingenuity of some of us! . . . Claudine never wearies; you can always count upon her. It is not love, I tell her, it is infatuation. She writes to me every day; I do not read her letters; she found that out, but still she writes. See here; there are two hundred letters in this casket. She begs me to wipe my razors on one of her letters every day, and I punctually do so. She thinks, and rightly, that the sight of her handwriting will put me in mind of her.'

"La Palférine was dressing as he told us this. I took up the letter which he was about to put to this use, read it, and kept it, as he did not ask to have it back. Here it is. I looked for it, and found it as I promised.

"*Monday (Midnight)*.

"'Well, my dear, are you satisfied with me? I did not even ask for your hand, yet you might easily have given it to me, and I longed so much to hold it to my heart, to my lips. No, I did not ask, I am so afraid of displeasing you. Do you know one thing? Though I am cruelly sure that anything I do is a matter of perfect indifference to you, I am none the less extremely timid in my conduct: the woman that belongs to you, whatever her title to call herself yours, must not incur so much as the shadow of blame. In so far as love comes from the angels in heaven, from whom there are no secrets hid, my love is as pure as the purest; wherever I am I feel that I am in your presence, and I try to do you honour.

"'All that you said about my manner of dress impressed me very much; I began to understand how far above others are those that come of a noble race. There was still some thing of the opera girl in my gowns, in my way of dressing my hair. In a moment I saw the distance between me and good taste. Next time you shall receive a duchess, you shall not know me again! Ah! how good you have been to your Claudine! How many and many a time I have thanked you for telling me those things! What interest lay in those few words! You had taken thought for that thing belonging to you called Claudine? *This* imbecile would never have opened my eyes; he thinks that everything I do is right; and besides, he is much too humdrum, too matter-of-fact to have any feeling for the beautiful.

"'Tuesday is very slow of coming for my impatient mind! On Tuesday I shall be with you for several hours. Ah! when it comes I will try to think that the hours are months, that it will be so always. I am living in hope of that morning now, as I shall live upon the memory of it afterwards. Hope is memory that craves; and recollection, memory sated. What a beautiful life within life thought makes for us in this way!

"'Sometimes I dream of inventing new ways of tenderness all my own, a secret which no other woman shall guess. A cold sweat breaks out over me at the thought that something may happen to prevent this meeting. Oh, I would break with him for good, if need was, but nothing here could possibly interfere; it would be from your side. Perhaps you may decide to go out, perhaps to go to see some other woman. Oh! spare me this Tuesday for pity's sake. If you take it from me, Charles, you do not know what *he* will suffer; I should drive him wild. But even if you do not want me, if you are going out, let me come, all the same, to be with you while you dress; only to see you, I ask no more than that; only to show you that I love you without a thought of self.

"'Since you gave me leave to love you, for you gave me leave, since I am yours; since that day I loved and love you with the whole strength of my soul; and I shall love you for ever, for once having loved *you*, no one could, no one ought to love another. And, you see, when those eyes that ask nothing but to see you are upon you, you will feel that in your Claudine there is a something divine, called into existence by you.

"'Alas! with you I can never play the coquette. I am like a mother with her child; I endure anything from you; I, that was once so imperious and proud. I have made dukes and princes fetch and carry for me; aides-de-camp, worth more than all the court of Charles X put together, have done my errands, yet I am treating you as my spoilt child. But where is the use of coquetry? It would be pure waste. And yet, monsieur, for want of coquetry I shall never inspire love in you. I know it; I feel it; yet I do as before, feeling a power that I cannot withstand, thinking that this utter self-surrender will win me the sentiment innate in all men (so he tells me) for the thing that belongs to them.

"Wednesday.

"'Ah! how darkly sadness entered my heart yesterday when I found that I must give up the joy of seeing you. One single thought held me back from the arms of Death!—It was thy will! To stay away was to do thy will, to obey an order from thee. Oh! Charles, I was so pretty; I looked a lovelier woman for you than that beautiful German princess whom you gave me for an example, whom I have studied at the Opéra. And yet—you might have thought that I had overstepped the limits of my nature. You have left me no confidence in myself; perhaps I am plain after all. Oh! I loathe myself, I dream of my radiant Charles Edward, and my brain turns. I shall go mad, I know I shall. Do not laugh, do not talk to me of the fickleness of women. If we are inconstant, *you* are strangely capricious. You take away the hours of love that made a poor creature's happiness for ten whole days; the hours on which she drew to be charming and kind to all that came to see her! After all, you were the source of my kindness to *him*; you do not know what pain you give him. I wonder what I must do to keep you, or simply to keep the right to be yours sometimes. . . . When I think that you never would come here to me! . . . With what delicious emotion I would wait upon you!—There are other women more favoured than I. There are women to whom you say, "I love you." To me you have never said more than "You are a good girl." Certain speeches of yours, though you do not know it, gnaw at my heart. Clever men sometimes ask me what I am thinking. . . . I am thinking of my self-abasement—the prostration of the poorest outcast in the presence of the Saviour.'

"There are still three more pages, you see. La Palférine allowed me to take the letter, with the traces of tears that still seemed hot upon it! Here was proof of the truth of his story. Marcas, a shy man enough with women, was in ecstasies over a second which he read in his corner before lighting his pipe with it.

"'Why, any woman in love will write that sort of thing!' cried La Palférine. 'Love gives all women intelligence and style, which proves that here in France style proceeds from the matter and not from the words. See now how well this is thought out, how clear-headed sentiment is'—and with that he reads us another letter, far superior to the artificial and laboured productions which we novelists write.

"One day poor Claudine heard that La Palférine was in a critical position; it was a question of meeting a bill of exchange. An unlucky idea occurred to her; she put a tolerably large sum in gold into an exquisitely embroidered purse and went to him.

"'Who has taught you to be so bold as to meddle with my household affairs?' La Palférine cried angrily. 'Mend my socks and work slippers for me, if it amuses you. So!— you will play the duchess, and you turn the story of Danaë against the aristocracy.'

"He emptied the purse into his hand as he spoke, and made as though he would fling the money in her face. Claudine, in her terror, did not guess that he was joking; she shrank back, stumbled over a chair, and fell with her head against the corner of the marble chimney-piece. She thought she should have died. When she could speak, poor woman, as she lay on the bed, all that she said was, 'I deserved it, Charles!'

"For a moment La Palférine was in despair; his anguish revived Claudine. She rejoiced in the mishap; she took advantage of her suffering to compel La Palférine to take the money and release him from an awkward position. Then followed a variation on La Fontaine's fable, in which a man blesses the thieves that brought him a sudden impulse of tenderness from his wife. And while we are upon this subject, another saying will paint the man for you.

"Claudine went home again, made up some kind of tale as best she could to account for her bruised forehead, and fell dangerously ill. An abscess formed in the head. The doctor—Bianchon, I believe—yes, it was Bianchon—wanted to cut off her hair. The Duchesse de Berri's hair is not more beautiful than Claudine's; she would not hear of it, she told Bianchon in confidence that she could not allow it to be cut without leave from the Comte de Palférine. Bianchon went to Charles Edward. Charles Edward heard him with much seriousness. The doctor had explained the case at length, and showed that it was absolutely necessary to sacrifice the hair to insure the success of the operation.

"'Cut off Claudine's hair!' cried he in peremptory tones. 'No. I would sooner lose her.'"

"Even now, after a lapse of four years, Bianchon still quotes that speech; we have laughed over it for half an hour together. Claudine, informed of the verdict, saw in it a proof of affection; she felt sure that she was loved. In the face of her weeping family, with her husband on his knees, she was inexorable. She kept her hair. The strength that came with the belief that she was loved came to her aid, the operation succeeded perfectly. There are stirrings of the inner life which throw all the calculations of surgery into disorder and baffle the laws of medical science.

"Claudine wrote a delicious letter to La Palférine, a letter in which the orthography was doubtful and the punctuation all to seek, to tell him of the happy result of the operation, and to add that Love was wiser than all the sciences.

"'Now,' said La Palférine one day, 'what am I to do to get rid of Claudine?'

"'Why, she is not at all troublesome; she leaves you master of your actions,' objected we.

"'That is true,' returned La Palférine, 'but I do not choose that anything shall slip into my life without my consent.'

"From that day he set himself to torment Claudine. It seemed that he held the bourgeoise, the nobody, in utter horror; nothing would satisfy him but a woman with a title. Claudine, it was true, had made progress; she had learned to dress as well as the best-dressed women of the Faubourg Saint-Germain; she had freed her bearing of unhallowed traces; she walked with a chastened, inimitable grace; but this was not enough. This praise of her enabled Claudine to swallow down the rest.

"But one day La Palférine said, 'If you wish to be the mistress of one La Palférine, poor, penniless, and without prospects as he is, you ought at least to represent him worthily. You should have a carriage and livened servants and a title. Give me all the gratifications of vanity that will never be mine in my own person. The woman whom I honour with my regard ought never to go on foot; if she is bespattered with mud, I suffer. That is how I am made. If she is mine, she must be admired of all Paris. All Paris shall envy me my good fortune. If some little whipper-snapper seeing a brilliant countess pass in her brilliant carriage shall say to himself, "Who can call such a divinity his?" and grow thoughtful—why, it will double my pleasure.'

"La Palférine owned to us that he flung this programme at Claudine's head simply to rid himself of her. As a result he was stupefied with astonishment for the first and probably the only time in his life.

"'Dear,' she said, and there was a ring in her voice that betrayed the great agitation which shook her whole being, 'it is well. All this shall be done, or I will die.'

"She let fall a few happy tears on his hand as she kissed it.

"'You have told me what I must do to be your mistress still,' she added; 'I am glad.'

"'And then' (La Palférine told us) 'she went out with a little coquettish gesture like a woman that has had her way. As she stood in my garret doorway, tall and proud, she seemed to reach the stature of an antique sibyl.'

"All this should sufficiently explain the manners and customs of the Bohemia in which the young *condottiere* is one of the most brilliant figures," Nathan continued after a pause. "Now it so happened that I discovered Claudine's identity, and could understand the appalling truth of one line which you perhaps overlooked in that letter of hers. It was on this wise."

The Marquise, too thoughtful now for laughter, bade Nathan "Go on," in a tone that told him plainly how deeply she had been impressed by these strange things, and even more plainly how much she was interested in La Palférine.

"In 1829, one of the most influential, steady, and clever of dramatic writers was du Bruel. His real name is unknown to the public, on the play-bills he is de Cursy. Under the Restoration he had a place in the Civil Service; and being really attached to the elder branch, he sent in his resignation bravely in 1830, and ever since has written twice as many plays to fill the deficit in his budget made by his noble conduct. At that time du Bruel was forty years old; you know the story of his life. Like many of his brethren, he bore a stage dancer an affection hard to explain, but well known in the whole world of letters. The woman, as you know, was Tullia, one of the *premiers sujets* of the Académie Royale de Musique. Tullia is merely a pseudonym like du Bruel's name of de Cursy.

"For the ten years between 1817 and 1827 Tullia was in her glory on the heights of the stage of the Opéra. With more beauty than education, a mediocre dancer with rather more sense than most of her class, she took no part in the virtuous reforms which ruined the corps de ballet; she continued the Guimard dynasty. She owed her ascendency, moreover, to various well-known protectors, to the Duc de Rhétoré (the Duc de Chaulieu's eldest son), to the influence of a famous Superintendent of Fine Arts, and sundry diplomatists and rich foreigners. During her apogee she had a neat little house in the Rue Chauchat, and lived as Opéra nymphs used to live in the old days. Du Bruel was smitten with her about the time when the Duke's fancy came to an end in 1823. Being a mere subordinate in the Civil Service, du Bruel tolerated the Superintendent of Fine Arts, believing that he himself was really preferred. After six years this connection was almost a marriage. Tullia has always been very careful to say nothing of her family; we have a vague idea that she comes from Nanterre. One of her uncles, formerly a simple bricklayer or carpenter, is now, it is said, a very rich contractor, thanks to her influence and generous loans. This fact leaked out through du Bruel. He happened to say that Tullia would inherit a fine fortune sooner or later. The contractor was a bachelor; he had a weakness for the niece to whom he is indebted.

"'He is not clever enough to be ungrateful,' said she.

"In 1829 Tullia retired from the stage of her own accord. At the age of thirty she saw that she was growing somewhat stouter, and she had tried pantomime without success. Her whole art consisted in the trick of raising her skirts, after Noblet's manner, in a pirouette which inflated them balloon-fashion and exhibited the smallest possible quantity of clothing to the pit. The aged Vestris had told her at the very beginning that this *temps,* well executed by a fine woman, is worth all the art imaginable. It is the chest-note C of dancing. For which reason, he said, the very greatest dancers—Camargo, Guimard, and Taglioni, all of them thin, brown, and plain—could only redeem their physical defects by their genius. Tullia, still in the height of her glory, retired before younger and cleverer dancers; she did wisely. She was an aristocrat; she had scarcely stooped below the noblesse in her *liaisons*; she declined to dip her ankles in the troubled waters of July. Insolent and beautiful as she was, Claudine possessed handsome souvenirs, but very little ready money; still, her jewels were magnificent, and she had as fine furniture as any one in Paris.

"On quitting the stage when she, forgotten to-day, was yet in the height of her fame, one thought possessed her—she meant du Bruel to marry her; and at the time of this story, you must understand that the marriage had taken place, but was kept a secret. How do women of her class contrive to make a man marry them after seven or eight years of intimacy? What springs do they touch? What machinery do they set in motion? But, however comical such domestic dramas may be, we are not now concerned with them. Du Bruel was secretly married; the thing was done.

"Cursy before his marriage was supposed to be a jolly companion; now and again he stayed out all night, and to some extent led the life of a Bohemian; he would unbend at a supper-party. He went out to all appearance to a rehearsal at the Opéra-Comique, and found himself in some unaccountable way at Dieppe, or Baden, or Saint-Germain; he gave dinners, led the Titanic thriftless life of artists, journalists, and writers; levied his tribute on all the greenrooms of Paris; and, in short, was one of us. Finot, Lousteau, du Tillet, Desroches, Bixiou, Blondet, Couture, and des Lupeaulx tolerated him in spite of his pedantic manner and ponderous official attitude. But once married, Tullia made a slave of du Bruel. There was no help for it. He was in love with Tullia, poor devil.

"'Tullia' (so he said) 'had left the stage to be his alone, to be a good and charming wife.' And somehow Tullia managed to induce the most Puritanical members of du Bruel's family to accept her. From the very first, before any one suspected her motives, she assiduously visited old Mme. de Bonfalot, who bored her horribly; she made handsome presents to mean old Mme. de Chissé, du Bruel's great-aunt; she spent a summer with the latter lady, and never missed a single mass. She even went to confession, received absolution, and took the sacrament; but this, you must remember was in the country, and under the aunt's eyes.

"'I shall have real aunts now, do you understand?' she said to us when she came back in the winter.

"She was so delighted with her respectability, so glad to renounce her independence, that she found means to compass her end. She flattered the old people. She went on foot every day to sit for a couple of hours with Mme. du Bruel the elder while that lady was ill—a Maintenon's stratagem which amazed du Bruel. And he admired his wife without criticism; he was so fast in the toils already that he did not feel his bonds.

"Claudine succeeded in making him understand that only under the elastic system of a bourgeois government, only at the bourgeois court of the Citizen-King, could a Tullia, now metamorphosed into a Mme. du Bruel, be accepted in the society which her good sense prevented her from attempting to enter. Mme. de Bonfalot, Mme. de Chissé, and Mme. du Bruel received her; she was satisfied. She took up the position of a well-conducted, simple, and virtuous woman, and never acted out of character. In three years' time she was introduced to the friends of these ladies.

"'And still I cannot persuade myself that young Mme. du Bruel used to display her ankles, and the rest, to all Paris, with the light of a hundred gas-jets pouring upon her,' Mme. Anselme Popinot remarked naïvely.

"From this point of view, July 1830 inaugurated an era not unlike the time of the Empire, when a waiting-woman was received at Court in the person of Mme. Garat, a chief-justice's 'lady.' Tullia had completely broken, as you may guess, with all her old associates; of her former acquaintances, she only recognised those who could not compromise her. At the time of her marriage she had taken a very charming little hôtel between a court and a garden, lavishing money on it with wild extravagance and putting the best part of her furniture and du Bruel's into it. Everything that she thought common or ordinary was sold. To find anything comparable to her sparkling splendour, you could only look back to the days when a Sophie Arnould, a Guimard, or a Duthé, in all her glory, squandered the fortunes of princes.

"How far did this sumptuous existence affect du Bruel? It is a delicate question to ask, and a still more delicate one to answer. A single incident will suffice to give you an idea of Tullia's crotchets. Her bed-spread of Brussels lace was worth ten thousand francs. A famous actress had another like it. As soon as Claudine heard this, she allowed her cat, a splendid Angora, to sleep on the bed. That trait gives you the woman. Du Bruel dared not say a word; he was ordered to spread abroad that challenge in luxury, so that it might reach the other. Tullia was very fond of this gift from the Duc de Rhétoré; but one day, five years after her marriage, she played with her cat to such purpose that the coverlet—furbelows, flounces, and all—was torn to shreds, and replaced by a sensible quilt, a quilt that was a quilt, and not a symptom of the peculiar form of insanity which drives these women to make up by an insensate luxury for the childish days when they lived on raw apples, to quote the expression of a journalist. The day when the bed-spread was torn to tatters marked a new epoch in her married life.

"Cursy was remarkable for his ferocious industry. Nobody suspects the source to which Paris owes the patch-and-powder eighteenth century vaudevilles that flooded the stage. Those thousand-and-one vaudevilles, which raised such an outcry among the *feuilletonistes,* were written at Mme. du Bruel's express desire. She insisted that her husband should purchase the hôtel on which she had spent so much, where she had housed five hundred thousand francs' worth of furniture. Wherefore Tullia never enters into explanations; she understands the sovereign woman's reason to admiration.

"'People made a good deal of fun of Cursy,' said she; 'but, as a matter of fact, he found this house in the eighteenth century rouge-box, powder, puffs, and spangles. He would never have thought of it but for me,' she added, burying herself in her cushions in her fireside corner.

"She delivered herself thus on her return from a first night. Du Bruel's piece had succeeded, and she foresaw an avalanche of criticisms. Tullia had her At Homes. Every Monday she gave a tea-party; her society was as select as might be, and she neglected nothing that could make her house pleasant. There was bouillotte in one room, conversation in another, and sometimes a concert (always short) in the large drawing-room. None but the most eminent artists performed in her house. Tullia had so much good sense, that she attained to the most exquisite tact, and herein, in all probability, lay the secret of her ascendency over du Bruel; at any rate, he loved her with the love which use and wont at length makes indispensable to life. Every day adds another thread to the strong, irresistible, intangible web, which enmeshes the most delicate fancies, takes captive every most transient mood, and binding them together, holds a man captive hand and foot, heart and head.

"Tullia knew Cursy well; she knew every weak point in his armour, knew also how to heal his wounds.

"A passion of this kind is inscrutable for any observer, even for a man who prides himself, as I do, on a certain expertness. It is everywhere unfathomable; the dark depths in it are darker than in any other mystery; the colors confused even in the highest lights.

"Cursy was an old playwright, jaded by the life of the theatrical world. He liked comfort; he liked a luxurious, affluent, easy existence; he enjoyed being a king in his own house; he liked to be host to a party of men of letters in a hotel resplendent with royal luxury, with carefully chosen works of art shining in the setting. Tullia allowed du Bruel to enthrone himself amid the tribe; there were plenty of journalists whom it was easy enough to catch and ensnare; and, thanks to her evening parties and a well-timed loan here and there, Cursy was not attacked too seriously—his plays succeeded. For these reasons he would not have separated from Tullia for an empire. If she had been unfaithful, he would probably have passed it over, on condition that none of his accustomed joys should be retrenched; yet, strange to say, Tullia caused him no twinges on this account. No fancy was laid to her charge; if there had been any, she certainly had been very careful of appearances.

"'My dear fellow,' du Bruel would say, laying down the law to us on the boulevard, 'there is nothing like one of these women who have sown their wild oats and got over their passions. Such women as Claudine have lived their bachelor life; they have been over head and ears in pleasure, and make the most adorable wives that could be wished; they have nothing to learn, they are formed, they are not in the least prudish; they are well broken in, and indulgent.

So I strongly recommend everybody to take the "remains of a racer." I am the most fortunate man on earth.'

"Du Bruel said this to me himself with Bixiou there to hear it.

"'My dear fellow,' said the caricaturist, 'perhaps he is right to be in the wrong.'

"About a week afterwards, du Bruel asked us to dine with him one Tuesday. That morning I went to see him on a piece of theatrical business, a case submitted to us for arbitration by the commission of dramatic authors. We were obliged to go out again; but before we started he went to Claudine's room, knocked, as he always does, and asked for leave to enter.

"'We live in grand style,' said he, smiling; 'we are free. Each is independent.'

"We were admitted. Du Bruel spoke to Claudine. 'I have asked a few people to dinner to-day—"

"'Just like you!' cried she. 'You ask people without speaking to me; I count for nothing here.—Now' (taking me as arbitrator by a glance) 'I ask you yourself. When a man has been so foolish as to live with a woman of my sort; for, after all, I was an opera dancer—yes, I ought always to remember that, if other people are to forget it—well, under those circumstances, a clever man seeking to raise his wife in public opinion would do his best to impose her upon the world as a remarkable woman, to justify the step he had taken by acknowledging that in some ways she was something more than ordinary women. The best way of compelling respect from others is to pay respect to her at home, and to leave her absolute mistress of the house. Well, and yet it is enough to waken one's vanity to see how frightened he is of seeming to listen to me. I must be in the right ten times over if he concedes a single point.'

"(Emphatic negative gestures from du Bruel at every other word.)

"'Oh, yes, yes,' she continued quickly, in answer to this mute dissent. 'I know all about it, du Bruel, my dear, I that have been like a queen in my house all my life till I married you. My wishes were guessed, fulfilled, and more than fulfilled. After all, I am thirty-five, and at five-and-thirty a woman cannot expect to be loved. Ah, if I were a girl of sixteen, if I had not lost something that is dearly bought at the Opéra, what attention you would pay me, M. du Bruel! I feel the most supreme contempt for men who boast that they can love and grow careless and neglectful in little things as time grows on. You are short and insignificant, you see, du Bruel; you love to torment a woman; it is your only way of showing your strength. A Napoleon is ready to be swayed by the woman he loves; he loses nothing by it; but as for such as you, you believe that you are nothing apparently, you do not wish to be ruled.—Five and-thirty, my dear boy,' she continued, turning to me, 'that is the clue to the riddle.—"No," does he say again?—You know quite well that I am thirty-seven. I am very sorry, but just ask your friends to dine at the *Rocher de Cancale*. I *could* have them here, but I will not; they shall not come. And then perhaps my poor little monologue may engrave that salutary maxim, "Each is master at home," upon your memory. That is our charter,' she added, laughing, with a return of the opera girl's giddiness and caprice.

"'Well, well, my dear little puss; there, there, never mind. We can manage to get on together,' said du Bruel, and he kissed her hands, and we came away. But he was very wroth.

"The whole way from the Rue de la Victoire to the boulevard a perfect torrent of venomous words poured from his mouth like a waterfall in flood; but as the shocking language which he need on the occasion was quite unfit to print, the report is necessarily inadequate.

"'My dear fellow, I will leave that vile, shameless opera dancer, a worn-out jade that has been set spinning like a top to every operatic air; a foul hussy, an organ-grinder's monkey! Oh, my dear boy, you have taken up with an actress; may the notion of marrying your mistress never get a hold on you. It is a torment omitted from the hell of Dante, you see. Look here! I will beat her; I will give her a thrashing; I will give it to her! Poison of my life, she sent me off like a running footman.'

"By this time we had reached the boulevard, and he had worked himself up to such a pitch of fury that the words stuck in his throat.

"'I will kick the stuffing out of her!'

"'And why?'

"'My dear fellow, you will never know the thousand-and-one fancies that slut takes into her head. When I want to stay at home, she, forsooth, must go out; when I want to go out, she wants me to stop at home; and she spouts out arguments and accusations and reasoning and talks and talks till she drives you crazy. Right means any whim that they happen to take into their heads, and wrong means our notion. Overwhelm them with something that cuts their arguments to pieces—they hold their tongues and look at you as if you were a dead dog. My happiness indeed! I lead the life of a yard-dog; I am a perfect slave. The little happiness that I have with her costs me dear. Confound it all. I will leave her everything and take myself off to a garret. Yes, a garret and liberty. I have not dared to have my own way once in these five years.'

"But instead of going to his guests, Cursy strode up and down the boulevard between the Rue de Richelieu and the Rue du Mont Blanc, indulging in the most fearful imprecations, his unbounded language was most comical to hear. His paroxysm of fury in the street contrasted oddly with his peaceable demeanour in the house. Exercise assisted him to work off his nervous agitation and inward tempest. About two o'clock, on a sudden frantic impulse, he exclaimed:

"'These damned females never know what they want. I will wager my head now that if I go home and tell her that I have sent to ask my friends to dine with me at the *Rocher de Cancale,* she will not be satisfied though she made the arrangement herself.—But she will have gone off somewhere or other. I wonder whether there is something at the bottom of all this, an assignation with some goat? No. In the bottom of her heart she loves me!'"

The Marquise could not help smiling.

"Ah, madame," said Nathan, looking keenly at her, "only women and prophets know how to turn faith to account. Du Bruel would have me go home with him," he continued, "and we went slowly back. It was three o'clock. Before he appeared, he heard a stir in the kitchen, saw preparations going forward, and glanced at me as he asked the cook the reason of this.

"'Madame ordered dinner,' said the Woman. 'Madame dressed and ordered a cab, and then she changed her mind and ordered it again for the theatre this evening.'

"'Good,' exclaimed du Bruel, 'what did I tell you?'

"We entered the house stealthily. No one was there. We went from room to room until we reached a little boudoir, and came upon Tullia in tears. She dried her eyes without affectation, and spoke to du Bruel.

"'Send a note to the *Rocher de Cancale*,' she said, 'and ask your guests to dine here.'

"She was dressed as only women of the theatre can dress, in a simply-made gown of some dainty material, neither too costly nor too common, graceful, and harmonious in outline and colouring; there was nothing conspicuous about her, nothing exaggerated—a word now dropping out of use, to be replaced by the word 'artistic,' used by fools as current coin. In short, Tullia looked like a gentlewoman. At thirty-seven she had reached the prime of a Frenchwoman's beauty. At this moment the celebrated oval of her face was divinely pale; she had laid her hat aside; I could see a faint down like the bloom of fruit softening the silken contours of a cheek itself so delicate. There was a pathetic charm about her face with its double cluster of fair hair; her brilliant grey eyes were veiled by a mist of tears; her nose, delicately carved as a Roman cameo, with its quivering nostrils; her little mouth, like a child's even now; her long queenly throat, with the veins standing out upon it; her chin, flushed for the moment by some secret despair; the pink tips of her ears, the hands that trembled under her gloves, everything about her told of violent feeling. The feverish twitching of her eyebrows betrayed her pain. She looked sublime.

"Her first words had crushed du Bruel. She looked at us both, with that penetrating, impenetrable cat-like glance which only actresses and great ladies can use. Then she held out her hand to her husband.

"'Poor dear, you had scarcely gone before I blamed myself a thousand times over. It seemed to me that I had been horribly ungrateful. I told myself that I had been unkind.—Was I very unkind?' she asked, turning to me.—'Why not receive your friends? Is it not your house? Do you want to know the reason of it all? Well, I was afraid that I was not loved; and indeed I was half-way between repentance and the shame of going back. I read the newspapers, and saw that there was a first night at the Variétés, and I thought you had meant to give the dinner to a collaborator. Left to myself, I gave way, I dressed to hurry out after you—poor pet.'

Du Bruel looked at me triumphantly, not a vestige of a recollection of his orations *contra Tullia* in his mind.

"'Well, dearest, I have not spoken to any one of them,' he said.

"'How well we understand each other!' quoth she.

"Even as she uttered those bewildering sweet words, I caught sight of something in her belt, the corner of a little note thrust sidewise into it; but I did not need that indication to tell me that Tullia's fantastic conduct was referable to occult causes. Woman, in my opinion, is the most logical of created beings, the child alone excepted. In both we behold a sublime phenomenon, the unvarying triumph of one dominant, all-excluding thought. The child's thought changes every moment; but while it possesses him, he acts upon it with such ardour that others give way before him, fascinated by the ingenuity, the persistence of a strong desire. Woman is less changeable, but to call her capricious is a stupid insult. Whenever she acts, she is always swayed by one dominant passion; and wonderful it is to see how she makes that passion the very centre of her world.

"Tullia was irresistible; she twisted du Bruel round her fingers, the sky grew blue again, the evening was glorious. And ingenious writer of plays as he is, he never so much as saw that his wife had buried a trouble out of sight.

"'Such is life, my dear fellow,' he said to me, 'ups and downs and contrasts.'

"'Especially life off the stage,' I put in.

"'That is just what I mean,' he continued. 'Why, but for these violent emotions, one would be bored to death! Ah! that has the gift of rousing me.'

'We went to the Variétés after dinner; but before we left the house I slipped into du Bruel's room, and on a shelf among a pile of waste papers found the copy of the *Petites Affiches*, in which, agreeably to the reformed law, notice of the purchase of the house was inserted. The words stared me in the face— 'At the request of Jean François du Bruel and Claudine Chaffaroux, his wife—' *Here* was the explanation of the whole matter. I offered my arm to Claudine, and allowed the guests to descend the stairs in front of us. When we were alone—'If I were La Palférine,' I said, 'I would not break an appointment.'

"Gravely she laid her finger on her lips. She leant on my arm as we went downstairs, and looked at me with almost something like happiness in her eyes because I knew La Palférine. Can you see the first idea that occurred to her? She thought of making a spy of me, but I turned her off with the light jesting talk of Bohemia.

"A month later after a first performance of one of du Bruel's plays, we met in the vestibule of the theatre. It was raining; I went to call a cab. We had been delayed for a few minutes, so that there were no cabs in sight. Claudine scolded du Bruel soundly; and as we rolled through the streets (for she set me down at Florine's), she continued the quarrel with a series of most mortifying remarks.

"'What is this about?' I inquired.

"'Oh, my dear fellow, she blames me for allowing you to run out for a cab, and thereupon proceeds to wish for a carriage.'

"'As a dancer,' said she, 'I have never been accustomed to use my feet except on the boards. If you have any spirit, you will turn out four more plays or so in a year; you will make up your mind that succeed they must, when you think of the end in view, and that your wife will not walk in the mud. It is a shame that I should have to ask for it. You ought to have guessed my continual discomfort during the five years since I married you.'

"'I am quite willing,' returned du Bruel. 'But we shall ruin ourselves.'

"'If you run into debt,' she said, 'my uncle's money will clear it off some day.'

"'You are quite capable of leaving me the debts and taking the property.'

"'Oh! is that the way you take it?' retorted she. 'I have nothing more to say to you; such a speech stops my mouth.'

"'Whereupon du Bruel poured out his soul in excuses and protestations of love. Not a word did she say. He took her hands, she allowed him to take them; they were like ice, like a dead woman's hands. Tullia, you can understand, was playing to admiration the part of corpse that women can play to show you that they refuse their consent to anything and everything; that for you they are suppressing soul, spirit, and life, and regard themselves as beasts of burden. Nothing so provokes a man with a heart as this strategy. Women can only use it with those who worship them.

"She turned to me. 'Do you suppose,' she said scornfully, 'that a Count would have uttered such an insult even if the thought had entered his mind? For my misfortune I have lived with dukes, ambassadors, and great lords, and I know their ways. How intolerable it makes bourgeois life! After all, a playwright is not a Rastignac nor a Rhétoré——'

"Du Bruel looked ghastly at this. Two days afterwards we met in the *foyer* at the Opéra, and took a few turns together. The conversation fell on Tullia.

"'Do not take my ravings on the boulevard too seriously,' said he; 'I have a violent temper.'

"For two winters I was a tolerably frequent visitor at du Bruel's house, and I followed Claudine's tactics closely. She had a splendid carriage. Du Bruel entered public life; she made him abjure his Royalist opinions. He rallied himself; he took his place again in the administration; the National Guard was discreetly canvassed, du Bruel was elected major, and behaved so valorously in a street riot, that he was decorated with the rosette of an officer of the Legion of Honour. He was appointed Master of Requests and head of a department. Uncle Chaffaroux died and left his niece forty thousand francs per annum, three-fourths of his fortune Du Bruel became a deputy; but beforehand, to save the necessity of re-election, he secured his nomination to the Council of State. He reprinted divers archæological treatises, a couple of political pamphlets, and a statistical work, by way of pretext for his appointment to one of the obliging academies of the Institut. At this moment he is a Commander of the Legion, and (after fishing in the troubled waters of political intrigue) has quite recently been made a peer of France and a count. As yet our friend does not venture to bear his honours; his wife merely puts 'La Comtesse du Bruel' on her cards. The sometime playwright has the Order of Leopold, the Order of Isabella, the Cross of Saint-Vladimir, second class, the Order of Civil Merit of Bavaria, the Papal Order of the Golden Spur,—all the lesser orders, in short, besides the Grand Cross.

"THERE, CHILD!" HE SAID, "I WILL DO SOMETHING FOR YOU;
I WILL PUT YOU—IN MY WILL"

"Three months ago Claudine drove to La Palférine's door in her splendid carriage with its armorial bearings. Du Bruel's grandfather was a farmer of taxes ennobled towards the end of Louis Quatorze's reign. Chérin composed his coat-of-arms for him, so the Count's coronet looks not amiss above a scutcheon innocent of Imperial absurdities. In this way, in the short space of three years, Claudine had carried out the programme laid down for her by the charming, light-hearted La Palférine.

"One day, just a month ago, she climbed the miserable staircase to her lover's lodging; climbed in her glory, dressed like a real countess of the Faubourg Saint-Germain, to our friend's garret. La Palférine, seeing her, said, 'You have made a peeress of yourself I know. But it is too late, Claudine; every one is talking just now about the Southern Cross, I should like to see it!'

"'I will get it for you.'

"La Palférine burst into a peal of Homeric laughter.

"'Most distinctly,' he returned, 'I do *not* wish to have a woman as ignorant as a carp for my mistress, a woman that springs like a flying fish from the green-room of the Opéra to Court, for I should like to see you at the Court of the Citizen King.'

"She turned to me.

"'What is the Southern Cross?' she asked, in a sad, downcast voice.

"I was struck with admiration for this indomitable love, outdoing the most ingenious marvels of fairy tales in real life—a love that would spring over a precipice to find a roe's egg, or to gather the singing flower. I explained that the Southern Cross was a nebulous constellation even brighter than the Milky Way, arranged in the form of a cross, and that it could only be seen in southern latitudes.

"'Very well, Charles, let us go,' said she.

"La Palférine, ferocious though he was, had tears in his eyes; but what a look there was in Claudine's face, what a note in her voice! I have seen nothing like the thing that followed, not even in the supreme touch of a great actor's art; nothing to compare with her movement when she saw the hard eyes softened in tears; Claudine sank upon her knees and kissed La Palférine's pitiless hand. He raised her with his grand manner, his 'Rusticoli air,' as he calls it— 'There, child!' he said, 'I will do something for you; I will put you—in my will.'

"Well," concluded Nathan, "I ask myself sometimes whether du Bruel is really deceived. Truly there is nothing more comic, nothing stranger than the sight of a careless young fellow ruling a married couple, his slightest whims received as law, the weightiest decisions revoked at a word from him. That dinner incident, as you can see, is repeated times without number, it interferes with important matters. Still, but for Claudine's caprices, du Bruel would be de Cursy still, one vaudevillist among five hundred; whereas he is in the House of Peers."

"You will change the names, I hope!" said Nathan, addressing Mme. de la Baudraye.

"I should think so! I have only set names to the masks for you. My dear Nathan," she added in the poet's ear, "I know another case in which the wife takes du Bruel's place."

"And the catastrophe?" queried Lousteau, returning just at the end of Mme. de la Baudraye's story.

"I do not believe in catastrophes. One has to invent such good ones to show that art is quite a match for chance; and nobody reads a book twice, my friend, except for the details."

"But there is a catastrophe," persisted Nathan.

"What is it?"

"The Marquise de Rochefide is infatuated with Charles Edward. My story excited her curiosity."

"Oh, unhappy woman!" cried Mme. de la Baudraye.

"Not so unhappy," said Nathan, "for Maxime de Trailles and La Palférine have brought about a rupture between the Marquis and Mme. Schontz, and they mean to make it up between Arthur and Béatrix."

1839—1845.

A MAN OF BUSINESS

To Monsieur le Baron James de Rothschild, Banker and Austrian Consul-General at Paris.

THE word *lorette* is a euphemism invented to describe the status of a personage, or a personage of a status, of which it is awkward to speak; the French Académie, in its modesty, having omitted to supply a definition out of regard for the age of its forty members. Whenever a new word comes to supply the place of an unwieldy circumlocution, its fortune is assured; the word *lorette* has passed into the language of every class of society, even where the lorette herself will never gain an entrance. It was only invented in 1840, and derived beyond a doubt from the agglomeration of such swallows' nests about the Church of Our Lady of Loretto. This information is for etymologists only. Those gentlemen would not be so often in a quandary if medieval writers had only taken such pains with details of contemporary manners as we take in these days of analysis and description.

Mlle. Turquet, or Malaga, for she is better known by her pseudonym,[1] was one of the earliest parishioners of that charming church. At the time to which this story belongs, that lighthearted and lively damsel gladdened the existence of a notary with a wife somewhat too bigoted, rigid, and frigid for domestic happiness.

Now, it so fell out that one Carnival evening Maître Cardot was entertaining guests at Mlle. Turquet's house—Desroches the attorney, Bixiou of the caricatures, Lousteau the journalist, Nathan, and others; it is quite unnecessary to give any further description of these personages, all bearers of illustrious names in the *Comédie Humaine*. Young La Palférine, in spite of his title of Count and his great descent, which, alas! means a great descent in fortune likewise, had honoured the notary's little establishment with his presence.

At dinner, in such a house, one does not expect to meet the patriarchal beef, the skinny fowl and salad of domestic and family life, nor is there any attempt at the hypocritical conversation of drawing-rooms furnished with highly respectable matrons. When, alas! will respectability be charming? When will the women in good society vouchsafe to show rather less of their shoulders and rather more wit or geniality? Marguerite Turquet, the Aspasia of the Cirque-Olympique, is one of those frank, very living personalities to whom all is forgiven, such unconscious sinners are they, such intelligent penitents; of such as Malaga one might ask, like Cardot—a witty man enough, albeit a notary—to be well "deceived." And yet you must not think that any enormities were committed. Desroches and Cardot were good fellows grown too grey in the profession not to feel at ease with Bixiou, Lousteau, Nathan, and young La Palférine. And they on their side had too often had recourse to their legal advisers, and knew them too well to try to "draw them out," in lorette language.

Conversation, perfumed with seven cigars, at first was as fantastic as a kid let loose, but finally it settled down upon the strategy of the constant war waged in Paris between creditors and debtors.

Now, if you will be so good as to recall the history and antecedents of the guests, you will know that in all Paris you could scarcely find a group of men with more experience in this matter; the professional men on one hand, and the artists on the other, were something in the position of magistrates and criminals hobnobbing together. A set of Bixiou's drawings to illustrate life in the debtors' prison, led the conversation to take this particular turn; and from debtors' prisons they went to debts.

It was midnight. They had broken up into little knots round the table and before the fire, and gave themselves up to the burlesque fun which is only possible or comprehensible in Paris and in that particular region which is bounded by the Faubourg Montmartre, the Rue Chaussée d'Antin, the upper end of the Rue de Navarin and the line of the boulevards.

In ten minutes' time they had come to an end of all the deep reflections, all the moralisings, small and great, all the bad puns made on a subject already exhausted by Rabelais three hundred and fifty years ago. It is not a little to their credit that the pyrotechnic display was cut short with a final squib from Malaga.

"It all goes to the shoemakers," she said. "I left a milliner because she failed twice with my hats. The vixen has been here twenty-seven times to ask for twenty francs. She did not know that we never have twenty francs. One has a thousand francs, or one sends to one's notary for five hundred; but twenty francs I have never had in my life. My cook and my maid may, perhaps, have so much between them; but for my own part, I have nothing but credit, and I should lose that if I took to borrowing small sums. If I were to ask for twenty francs, I should have nothing to distinguish me from my colleagues that walk the boulevard."

"Is the milliner paid?" asked La Palférine.

"Oh, come now, are you turning stupid?" said she, with a wink. "She came this morning for the twenty-seventh time, that is how I came to mention it."

"What did you do?" asked Desroches.

"I took pity upon her, and—ordered a little hat that I have just invented, a quite new shape. If Mlle. Amanda succeeds with it, she will say no more about the money, her fortune is made."

"In my opinion," put in Desroches, "the finest things that I have seen in a duel of this kind give those who know Paris a far better picture of the city than all the fancy portraits that they paint. Some of you think that you know a thing or two," he continued, glancing round at Nathan, Bixiou, La Palférine, and Lousteau, "but the king of the ground is a certain Count, now busy ranging himself. In his time, he was supposed to be the cleverest, adroitest, canniest, boldest, stoutest, most subtle and experienced of all the pirates, who, equipped with fine manners, yellow kid gloves, and cabs, have ever sailed or ever will sail upon the stormy sea of Paris. He fears neither God nor man. He applies in private life the principles that guide the English Cabinet. Up to the time of his marriage, his life was one continual war, like—Lousteau's, for instance. I was, and am still his solicitor."

"And the first letter of his name is Maxime de Trailles," said La Palférine.

"For that matter, he has paid every one, and injured no one," continued Desroches. "But as our friend Bixiou was saying just now, it is a violation of the liberty of the subject to be made to pay in March when you have no mind to pay till October. By virtue of this article of his particular code, Maxime regarded a creditor's scheme for making him pay at once as a swindler's trick. It was long since he had grasped the significance of the bill of exchange in all its bearings, direct and remote. A young man once, in my place, called a bill of exchange the 'asses' bridge' in his hearing. 'No,' said he, 'it is the Bridge of Sighs; it is the shortest way to an execution.' Indeed, his knowledge of commercial law was so complete, that a professional could not have taught him any thing. At that time he had nothing, as you know. His carriage and horses were jobbed; he lived in his valet's house; and, by the way, he will be a hero to his valet to the end of the chapter, even after the marriage that he proposes to make. He belonged to three clubs, and dined at one of them whenever he did not dine out. As a rule, he was to be found very seldom at his own address—"

"He once said to me," interrupted La Palférine, "'My one affectation is the pretence that I make of living in the Rue Pigalle.'"

"'Well," resumed Desroches, "he was one of the combatants; and now for the other. You have heard more or less talk of one Claparon?"

"Had hair like this!" cried Bixiou, ruffling his locks till they stood on end. Gifted with the same talent for mimicking absurdities which Chopin the pianist possesses to so high a degree, he proceeded forthwith to represent the character with startling truth.

"He rolls his head like this when he speaks; he was once a commercial traveller; he has been all sorts of things—"

"Well, he was born to travel, for at this minute, as I speak, he is on the sea on his way to America," said Desroches. "It is his only chance, for in all probability he will be condemned by default as a fraudulent bankrupt next session."

"Very much at sea!" exclaimed Malaga.

"For six or seven years this Claparon acted as man of straw, cat's-paw, and scapegoat to two friends of ours, du Tillet and Nucingen; but in 1829 his part was so well known that—"

"Our friends dropped him," put in Bixiou.

"They left him to his fate at last, and he wallowed in the mire," continued Desroches. "In 1833 he went into partnership with one Cérizet—"

'What! he that promoted a joint-stock company so nicely that the Sixth Chamber cut short his career with a couple of years in jail?" asked the lorette.

"The same. Under the Restoration, between 1823 and 1827, Cérizet's occupation consisted in first putting his name intrepidly to various paragraphs, on which the public prosecutor fastened with avidity, and subsequently marching off to prison. A man could make a name for himself with small expense in those days. The Liberal party called their provincial champion 'the courageous Cérizet,' and towards 1828 so much zeal received its reward in 'general interest.'

"'General interest' is a kind of civic crown bestowed on the deserving by the daily press. Cérizet tried to discount the 'general interest' taken in him. He came to Paris, and, with some help from capitalists in the Opposition, started as a broker, and conducted financial operations to some extent, the capital being found by a man in hiding, a skilful gambler who overreached himself, and in consequence, in July 1830, his capital foundered in the shipwreck of the Government."

"Oh! it was he whom we used to call the System," cried Bixiou.

"Say no harm of him, poor fellow," protested Malaga.

"D'Estourny was a good sort."

"You can imagine the part that a ruined man was sure to play in 1830 when his name in politics was 'the courageous Cérizet.' He was sent off into a very snug little sub-prefecture. Unluckily for him, it is one thing to be in opposition—any missile is good enough to throw, so long as the fight lasts; but quite another to be in office. Three months later, he was obliged to send in his resignation. Had he not taken it into his head to attempt to win popularity? Still, as he had done nothing as yet to imperil his title of 'courageous Cérizet,' the Government proposed by way of compensation that he should manage a newspaper; nominally an Opposition paper, but Ministerialist *in petto*. So the fall of this noble nature was really due to the Government. To Cérizet, as manager of the paper, it was rather too evident that he was as a bird perched on a rotten bough; and then it was that he promoted that nice little joint-stock company, and thereby secured a couple of years in prison; he was caught, while more ingenious swindlers succeeded in catching the public."

"We are acquainted with the more ingenious," said Bixiou; "let us say no ill of the poor fellow; he was nabbed; Couture allowed them to squeeze his cash-box; who would ever have thought it of him?"

"At all events, Cérizet was a low sort of fellow, a good deal damaged by low debauchery. Now for the duel I spoke about. Never did two tradesmen of the worst type, with the worst manners, the lowest pair of villains imaginable, go into partnership in a dirtier business. Their stock-in-trade consisted of the peculiar idiom of the man about town, the audacity of poverty, the cunning that comes of experience, and a special knowledge of Parisian capitalists, their origin, connections, acquaintances, and intrinsic value. This partnership of two 'dabblers' (let the Stock Exchange term pass, for it is the only word which describes them), this partnership of dabblers did not last very long. They fought like famished curs over every bit of garbage.

"The earlier speculations of the firm of Cérizet and Claparon were, however, well planned. The two scamps joined forces with Barbet, Chaboisseau, Samanon, and usurers of that stamp, and bought up hopelessly bad debts.

"Claparon's place of business at that time was a cramped entresol in the Rue Chabannais—five rooms at a rent of seven hundred francs at most. Each partner slept in a little closet, so carefully closed from prudence, that my head-clerk could never get inside. The furniture of the other three rooms—an antechamber, a waiting room, and a private office—would not have fetched three hundred francs altogether at a distress-warrant sale. You know enough of Paris to know the look of it; the stuffed horsehair-covered chairs, a table covered with a green cloth, a trumpery clock between a couple of candle sconces, growing tarnished under glass shades, the small gilt-framed mirror over the chimney-piece, and in the grate a charred stick or two of firewood which had lasted them for two winters, as my head-clerk put it. As for the office, you can guess what it was like—more letter-files than business letters, a set of common pigeonholes for either partner, a cylinder desk, empty as the cash-box, in the middle of the room, and a couple of armchairs on either side of a coal fire. The carpet on the floor was bought cheap at second-hand (like the bills and bad debts). In short, it was the mahogany furniture of furnished apartments which usually descends from one occupant of chambers to another during fifty years of service. Now you know the pair of antagonists.

"During the first three months of a Partnership dissolved four months later in a bout of fisticuffs, Cérizet and Claparon bought up two thousand francs' worth of bills bearing Maxime's signature (since Maxime is his name), and filled a couple of letter files to bursting with judgements, appeals, orders of the court, distress-warrant, application for stay of proceedings and all the rest of it; to put it briefly, they had bills for three thousand two hundred francs odd centimes, for which they had given five hundred francs; the transfer being made under private seal, with special power of attorney, to save the expense of registration. Now it so happened at this juncture, Maxime, being of ripe age, was seized with one of the fancies peculiar to the man of fifty—"

"Antonia!" exclaimed La Palférine. "That Antonia whose fortune I made by writing to ask for a toothbrush!"

"Her real name is Chocardelle," said Malaga, not over well pleased by the fine-sounding pseudonym.

"The same," continued Desroches.

"It was the only mistake Maxime ever made in his life. But what would you have, no vice is absolutely perfect?" put in Bixiou.

"Maxime had still to learn what sort of a life a man may be led into by a girl of eighteen when she is minded to take a header from her honest garret into a sumptuous carriage; it is a lesson that all statesmen should take to heart. At this time, de Marsay had just been employing his friend, our friend de Trailles, in the high comedy of politics. Maxime had looked high for his conquests; he had no experience of untitled women; and at fifty years he felt that he had a right to take a bite of a little so-called wild fruit, much as a sportsman will halt under a peasant's apple-tree. So the Count found a reading-room for Mlle. Chocardelle, a rather smart little place to be had cheap, as usual—"

"Pooh!" said Nathan. "She did not stay in it six months. She was too handsome to keep a reading-room."

"Perhaps you are the father of her child?" suggested the lorette.

Desroches resumed.

"Since the firm bought up Maxime's debts, Cérizet's likeness to a bailiff's officer grew more and more striking, and one morning after seven fruitless attempts he succeeded in penetrating into the Count's presence. Suzon, the old manservant, albeit he was by no means in his novitiate, at last mistook the visitor for a petitioner, come to propose a thousand crowns if Maxime would obtain a licence to sell postage stamps for a young lady. Suzon, without the slightest suspicion of the little scamp, a thoroughbred Paris street-boy into whom prudence had been rubbed by repeated personal experience of the police-courts, induced his master to receive him. Can you see the man of business, with an uneasy eye, a bald forehead, and scarcely any hair on his head, standing in his threadbare jacket and muddy boots—"

"What a picture of a Dun!" cried Lousteau.

"—standing before the Count, that image of flaunting Debt, in his blue flannel dressing-gown, slippers worked by some Marquise or other, trousers of white woollen stuff, and a dazzling shirt? There he stood, with a gorgeous cap on his black dyed hair, playing with the tassels at his waist—"

"'Tis a bit of genre for anybody who knows the pretty little morning room, hung with silk and full of valuable paintings, where Maxime breakfasts," said Nathan. "You tread on a Smyrna carpet, you admire the sideboards filled with curiosities and rarities fit to make a King of Saxony envious—"

"Now for the scene itself," said Desroches, and the deepest silence followed.

"'Monsieur le Comte,' began Cérizet, 'I have come from a M. Charles Claparon, who used to be a banker—'

"'Ah! poor devil, and what does he want with me?'

"'Well, he is at present your creditor for a matter of three thousand two hundred francs, seventy-five centimes, principal, interest, and costs—"

"'Coutelier's business?' put in Maxime, who knew his affairs as a pilot knows his coast.

"'Yes, Monsieur le Comte,' said Cérizet with a bow. 'I have come to ask your intentions.'

"'I shall only pay when the fancy takes me,' returned Maxime, and he rang for Suzon. 'It was very rash of Claparon to buy up bills of mine without speaking to me beforehand. I am sorry for him, for he did so very well for such a long time as a man of straw for friends of mine. I always said that a man must really be weak in his intellect to work for men that stuff themselves with millions, and to serve then so faithfully for such low wages. And now here he gives me another proof of his stupidity! Yes, men deserve what they get. It is your own doing whether you get a crown on your forehead or a bullet through your head; whether you are a millionaire or a porter, justice is always done you. I cannot help it, my dear fellow; I myself am not a king, I stick to my principles. I have no pity for those that put me to expense or do not know their business as creditors.—Suzon! my tea! Do you see this gentleman?' he continued when the man came in. 'Well, you have allowed yourself to be taken in, poor old boy. This gentleman is a creditor; you ought to have known him by his boots. No friend nor foe of mine, nor those that are neither and want something of me, come to see me on foot.—My dear M. Cérizet, do you understand? You will not wipe your boots on my carpet again' (looking as he spoke at the mud that whitened the enemy's soles). 'Convey my compliments and sympathy to Claparon, poor buffer, for I shall file this business under the letter Z.'

"All this with an easy good-humour fit to give a virtuous citizen the colic.

"'You are wrong, Monsieur le Comte,' retorted Cérizet, in a slightly peremptory tone. 'We will be paid in full, and that in a way which you may not like. That was why I came to you first in a friendly spirit, as is right and fit between gentlemen—'

"'Oh! so that is how you understand it?' began Maxime, enraged by this last piece of presumption. There was something of Talleyrand's wit in the insolent retort, if you have quite grasped the contrast between the two men and their costumes. Maxime scowled and looked full at the intruder; Cérizet not merely endured the glare of cold fury, but even returned it, with an icy, cat-like malignance and fixity of gaze.

"'Very good, sir, go out—'

"'Very well, good-day, Monsieur le Comte. We shall be quits before six months are out.'

"'If you can steal the amount of your bill, which is legally due I own, I shall be indebted to you, sir,' replied Maxime. 'You will have taught me a new precaution to take. I am very much your servant.'

"'Monsieur le Comte,' said Cérizet, 'it is I, on the, contrary, who am yours.'

"Here was an explicit, forcible, confident declaration on either side. A couple of tigers confabulating, with the prey before them, and a fight impending, would have been no finer and no shrewder than this pair; the insolent fine gentleman as great a blackguard as the other in his soiled and mud-stained clothes.

"Which will you lay your money on?" asked Desroches, looking round at an audience, surprised to find how deeply it was interested.

"A pretty story!" cried Malaga. "My dear boy, go on, I beg of you. This goes to one's heart."

"Nothing commonplace could happen between two fighting cocks of that calibre," added La Palférine.

"Pooh!" cried Malaga, "I will wager my cabinet-maker's invoice (the fellow is dunning me) that the little toad was too many for Maxime."

"I bet on Maxime," said Cardot. "Nobody ever caught him napping."

Desroches drank off a glass that Malaga handed to him. "Mlle. Chocardelle's reading-room," he continued, after a pause, "was in the Rue Coquenard, just a step or two from the Rue Pigalle where Maxime was living. The said Mlle. Chocardelle lived at the back on the garden side of the house, beyond a big, dark place where the books were kept. Antonia left her aunt to look after the business—"

"Had she an aunt even then?" exclaimed Malaga. "Hang it all, Maxime did things handsomely."

"Alas! it was a real aunt," said Desroches; "her name was—let me see—"

"Ida Bonamy," said Bixiou.

"So as Antonia's aunt took a good deal of the work off her hands, she went to bed late and lay late of a morning, never showing her face at the desk until the afternoon, some time between two and four. From the very first her appearance was enough to draw custom. Several elderly men in the quarter used to come, among them a retired coach-builder, one Croizeau. Beholding this miracle of female loveliness through the window-panes, he took it into his head to read the newspapers in the beauty's reading-room; and a sometime custom-house officer, named Denisart, with a ribbon in his button-hole, followed the example. Croizeau chose to look upon Denisart as a rival. '*Môsieur*,' he said afterwards, 'I did not know what to buy for you!'

"That speech should give you an idea of the man. The Sieur Croizeau happens to belong to a particular class of old man which should be known as 'Coquerels' since Henri Monnier's time; so well did Monnier render the piping voice, the little mannerisms, little queue, little sprinkling of powder, little movements of the head, prim little manner, and tripping gait in the part of Coquerel in *La Famille Improvisée.* This Croizeau used to hand over his halfpence with a flourish and a 'There, fair lady!'

"Mme. Ida Bonamy the aunt was not long in finding out through the servant that Croizeau, by popular report of the neighborhood of the Rue de Buffault, where he lived, was a man of exceeding stinginess, possessed of forty thousand francs per annum. A week after the instalment of the charming librarian he was delivered of a pun:

"'You lend me books (*livres*), but I give you plenty of francs in return,' said he.

"A few days later he put on a knowing little air, as much as to say, 'I know you are engaged, but my turn will come one day; I am a widower.'

"He always came arrayed in fine linen, a cornflower blue coat, a paduasoy waistcoat, black trousers, and black ribbon bows on the double soled shoes that creaked like an abbé's; he always held a fourteen franc silk hat in his hand.

"'I am old and I have no children,' he took occasion to confide to the young lady some few days after Cérizet's visit to Maxime. 'I hold my relations in horror. They are peasants born to work in the fields. Just imagine it, I came up from the country with six francs in my pocket, and made my fortune here. I am not proud. A pretty woman is my equal. Now would it not be nicer to be Mme. Croizeau for some years to come than to do a Count's pleasure for a twelvemonth? He will go off and leave you some time or other; and when that day comes, you will think of me . . . your servant, my pretty lady!'

"All this was simmering below the surface. The slightest approach at love-making was made quite on the sly. Not a soul suspected that the trim little old fogy was smitten with Antonia; and so prudent was the elderly lover, that no rival could have guessed anything from his behaviour in the reading-room. For a couple of months Croizeau watched the retired custom-house official; but before the third month was out he had good reason to believe that his suspicions were groundless. He exerted his ingenuity to scrape an acquaintance with Denisart, came up with him in the street, and at length seized his opportunity to remark, 'It is a fine day, sir!'

"Whereupon the retired official responded with, 'Austerlitz weather, sir. I was there myself—I was wounded indeed, I won my Cross on that glorious day.'

"And so from one thing to another the two drifted wrecks of the Empire struck up an acquaintance. Little Croizeau was attached to the Empire through his connection with Napoleon's sisters. He had been their coach-builder and had frequently dunned them for money; so he gave out that he 'had had relations with the Imperial family.' Maxime, duly informed by Antonia of the 'nice old man's' proposals (for so the aunt called Croizeau), wished to see him. Cérizet's declaration of war had so far taken effect that he of the yellow kid gloves was studying the position of every piece, however insignificant, upon the board; and it so happened that at the mention of that 'nice old man,' an ominous tinkling sounded in his ears. One evening, therefore, Maxime seated himself among the book-shelves in the dimly lighted back room, reconnoitred the seven or eight customers through the chink between the green curtains, and took the little coach-builder's measure. He gauged the man's infatuation, and was very well satisfied to find that the varnished doors of a tolerably sumptuous future were ready to turn at a word from Antonia so soon as his own fancy had passed off.

"'And that other one yonder?' asked he, pointing out the stout fine-looking elderly man with the Cross of the Legion of Honour. 'Who is he?'

"'A retired custom-house officer.'

"'The cut of his countenance is not reassuring,' said Maxime, beholding the Sieur Denisart.

"And indeed the old soldier held himself upright as a steeple. His head was remarkable for the amount of powder and pomatum bestowed upon it; he looked almost like a postilion at a fancy ball. Underneath that felted covering, moulded to the top of the wearer's cranium, appeared an elderly profile, half-official, half-soldierly, with a comical admixture of arrogance,—altogether something like caricatures of the *Constitutionnel.* The sometime official finding that age, and hair-powder, and the conformation of his spine made it impossible to read a word without spectacles, sat displaying a very creditable expanse of chest with all the pride of an old man with a mistress. Like old General Montcornet, that pillar of the Vaudeville, he wore earrings. Denisart was partial to blue; his roomy trousers and well-worn greatcoat were both of blue cloth.

"'How long is it since that old fogy came here?' inquired Maxime, thinking that he saw danger in the spectacles.

"'Oh, from the beginning,' returned Antonia, 'pretty nearly two months ago now.'

"'Good,' said Maxime to himself, 'Cérizet only came to me a month ago.—Just get him to talk,' he added in Antonia's ear; 'I want to hear his voice.'

"'Pshaw,' said she, 'that is not so easy. He never says a word to me.'

"'Then why does he come here?' demanded Maxime.

"'For a queer reason,' returned the fair Antonia. 'In the first place, although he is sixty-nine, he has a fancy; and because he is sixty-nine, he is as methodical as a clock face. Every day at five o'clock the old gentleman goes to dine with her in the Rue de la Victoire. (I am sorry for her.) Then at six o'clock, he comes here, reads steadily at the papers for four hours, and goes back at ten o'clock. Daddy Croizeau says that he knows M. Denisart's motives, and approves his conduct; and in his place, he would do the same. So I know exactly what to expect. If ever I am Mme. Croizeau, I shall have four hours to myself between six and ten o'clock.'

"Maxime looked through the directory, and found the following reassuring item:

"DENISART,[1] retired custom-house officer, Rue de la Victoire.

"His uneasiness vanished.

"Gradually the Sieur Denisart and the Sieur Croizeau began to exchange confidences. Nothing so binds two men together as a similarity of views in the matter of womankind. Daddy Croizeau went to dine with 'M. Denisart's fair lady,' as he called her. And here I must make a somewhat important observation.

"The reading-room had been paid for half in cash, half in bills signed by the said Mlle. Chocardelle. The *quart d'heure de Rabelais* arrived; the Count had no money. So the first bill of three thousand-franc bills was met by the amiable coach-builder; that old scoundrel Denisart having recommended him to secure himself with a mortgage on the reading-room.

"'For my own part,' said Denisart, 'I have seen pretty doings from pretty women. So, in all cases, even when I have lost my head, I am always on my guard with a woman. There is this creature, for instance; I am madly in love with her; but this is not her furniture; no, it belongs to me. The lease is taken out in my name.'

"You know Maxime! He thought the coach-builder uncommonly green. Croizeau might pay all three bills, and get nothing for a long while; for Maxime felt more infatuated with Antonia than ever."

"I can well believe it," said La Palférine. "She is the *bella Imperia* of our day."

"With her rough skin!" exclaimed Malaga; "so rough, that she ruins herself in bran baths!"

"Croizeau spoke with a coach-builder's admiration of the sumptuous furniture provided by the amorous Denisart as a setting for his fair one, describing it all in detail with diabolical complacency for Antonia's benefit," continued Desroches. "The ebony chests inlaid with mother-of-pearl and gold wire, the Brussels carpets, a mediæval bedstead worth three thousand francs, a Boule clock, candelabra in the four corners of the dining-room, silk curtains, on which Chinese patience had wrought pictures of birds, and hangings over the doors, worth more than the portress that opened them.

"'And that is what *you* ought to have, my pretty lady.— And that is what I should like to offer you,' he would conclude. 'I am quite aware that you scarcely care a bit about me; but, at my age, we cannot expect too much. Judge how much I love you; I have lent you a thousand francs. I must confess that, in all my born days, I have not lent anybody that much—'

"He held out his penny as he spoke, with the important air of a man that gives a learned demonstration.

"That evening at the Variétés, Antonia spoke to the Count.

"'A reading-room is very dull, all the same,' said she; 'I feel that I have no sort of taste for that kind of life, and I see no future in it. It is only fit for a widow that wishes to keep body and soul together, or for some hideously ugly thing that fancies she can catch a husband with a little finery.'

"'It was your own choice,' returned the Count. Just at that moment, in came Nucingen, of whom Maxime, king of lions (the 'yellow kid gloves' were the lions of that day) had won three thousand francs the evening before. Nucingen had come to pay his gaming debt.

"'Ein writ of attachment haf shoost peen served on me by der order of dot teufel Glabaron,' he said, seeing Maxime's astonishment.

"Oh, so that is how they are going to work, is it?' cried Maxime. 'They are not up to much, that pair—'

"'It makes not,' said the banker, 'bay dem, for dey may apply demselfs to oders pesides, und do you harm. I dake dees bretty voman to vitness dot I haf baid you dees morning, long pefore dat writ vas serfed.'"

"Queen of the boards," smiled La Palférine, looking at Malaga, "thou art about to lose thy bet."

"Once, a long time ago, in a similar case," resumed Desroches, "a too honest debtor took fright at the idea of a solemn declaration in a court of law, and declined to pay Maxime after notice was given. That time we made it hot for the creditor by piling on writs of attachment, so as to absorb the whole amount in costs—"

"Oh, what is that?" cried Malaga; "it all sounds like gibberish to me. As you thought the sturgeon so excellent at dinner, let me take out the value of the sauce in lessons in chicanery."

"Very well," said Desroches. "Suppose that a man owes you money, and your creditors serve a writ of attachment upon him; there is nothing to prevent all your other creditors from doing the same thing. And now what does the court do when all the creditors make application for orders to pay? *The court divides the whole sum attached, proportionately among them all.* That division, made under the eye of a magistrate, is what we call a *contribution*. If you owe ten thousand francs, and your creditors issue writs of attachment on a debt due to you of a thousand francs, each one of them gets so much per cent, 'so much in the pound,' in legal phrase; so much (that means) in proportion to the amounts severally claimed by the creditors. But—the creditors cannot touch the money without a special order from the clerk of the court. Do you guess what all this work drawn up by a judge and prepared by attorneys must mean? It means a quantity of stamped paper full of diffuse lines and blanks, the figures almost lost in vast spaces of completely empty ruled columns. The first proceeding is to deduct the costs. Now, as the costs are precisely the same whether the amount attached is one thousand or one million francs, it is not difficult to eat up three thousand francs (for instance) in costs, especially if you can manage to raise counter applications."

"And an attorney always manages to do it," said Cardot. "How many a time one of you has come to me with, 'What is there to be got out of the case?'"

"It is particularly easy to manage it if the debtor eggs you on to run up costs till they eat up the amount. And, as a rule, the Count's creditors took nothing by that move, and were out of pocket in law and personal expenses. To get money out of so experienced a debtor as the Count, a creditor should really be in a position uncommonly difficult to reach; it is a question of being creditor and debtor both, for then you are legally entitled to work the confusion of rights, in law language—"

"To the confusion of the debtor?" asked Malaga, lending an attentive ear to this discourse.

"No, the confusion of rights of debtor and creditor, and pay yourself through your own hands. So Claparon's innocence in merely issuing writs of attachment eased the Count's mind. As he came back from the Variétés with Antonia, he was so much the more taken with the idea of selling the reading-room to pay off the last two thousand francs of the purchase-money, because he did not care to have his name made public as a partner in such a concern. So he adopted Antonia's plan. Antonia wished to reach the higher ranks of her calling, with splendid rooms, a maid, and a carriage; in short, she wanted to rival our charming hostess, for instance—"

"She was not woman enough for that," cried the famous beauty of the Circus; "still, she ruined young d'Esgrignon very neatly."

"Ten days afterwards, little Croizeau, perched on his dignity, said almost exactly the same thing, for the fair Antonia's benefit," continued Desroches.

"'Child,' said he, 'your reading-room is a hole of a place. You will lose your complexion; the gas will ruin your eyesight. You ought to come out of it; and, look here, let us take advantage of an opportunity. I have found a young lady for you that asks no better than to buy your reading-room. She is a ruined woman with nothing before her but a plunge into the river; but she has four thousand francs in cash, and the best thing to do is to turn them to account, so as to feed and educate a couple of children.'

"'Very well. It is kind of you, Daddy Croizeau,' said Antonia.

"'Oh, I shall be much kinder before I have done. Just imagine it, poor M. Denisart has been worried into the jaundice! Yes, it has gone to the liver, as it usually does with susceptible old men. It is a pity he feels things so. I told him so myself; I said, "Be passionate, there is no harm in that, but as for taking things to heart—draw the line at that! It is the way to kill yourself." Really I would not have expected him to take on so about it; a man that has sense enough and experience enough to keep away as he does while he digests his dinner—'

"'But what is the matter?' inquired Mlle. Chocardelle.

"'That little baggage with whom I dined has cleared out and left him! . . . Yes. Gave him the slip without any warning but a letter, in which the spelling was all to seek.'

"'There, Daddy Croizeau, you see what comes of boring a woman—'

"'It is indeed a lesson, my pretty lady,' said the guileful Croizeau. 'Meanwhile, I have never seen a man in such a state. Our friend Denisart cannot tell his left hand from his right; he will not go back to look at the "scene of his happiness," as he calls it. He has so thoroughly lost his wits, that he proposes that I should buy all Hortense's furniture (Hortense was her name) for four thousand francs.'

"'A pretty name,' said Antonia.

"'Yes. Napoleon's stepdaughter was called Hortense. I built carriages for her, as you know.'

"'Very well, I will see,' said cunning Antonia; 'begin by sending this young woman to me.'

"Antonia hurried off to see the furniture, and came back fascinated. She brought Maxime under the spell of antiquarian enthusiasm. That very evening the Count agreed to the sale of the reading-room. The establishment, you see, nominally belonged to Mlle. Chocardelle. Maxime burst out laughing at the idea of little Croizeau's finding him a buyer. The firm of Maxime and Chocardelle was losing two thousand francs, it is true, but what was the loss compared with four glorious thousand-franc notes in hand? 'Four thousand francs of live coin!—there are moments in one's life when one would sign bills for eight thousand to get them,' as the Count said to me.

"Two days later the Count must see the furniture himself, and took the four thousand francs upon him. The sale had been arranged; thanks to little Croizeau's diligence, he pushed matters on; he had 'come round' the widow, as he expressed it. It was Maxime's intention to have all the furniture removed at once to a lodging in a new house in the Rue Tronchet, taken in the name of Mme. Ida Bonamy; he did not trouble himself much about the nice old man that was about to lose his thousand francs. But he had sent beforehand for several big furniture vans.

"Once again he was fascinated by the beautiful furniture which a wholesale dealer would have valued at six thousand francs. By the fireside sat the wretched owner, yellow with jaundice, his head tied up in a couple of printed handkerchiefs, and a cotton night-cap on the top of them; he was huddled up in wrappings like a chandelier, exhausted, unable to speak, and altogether so knocked to pieces that the Count was obliged to transact his business with the man-servant. When he had paid down the four thousand francs, and the servant had taken the money to his master for a receipt, Maxime turned to tell the man to call up the vans to the door; but even as he spoke, a voice like a rattle sounded in his ears.

"'It is not worth while, Monsieur le Comte. You and I are quits; I have six hundred and thirty francs fifteen centimes to give you!'

"To his utter consternation he saw Cérizet, emerged from his wrappings like a butterfly from the chrysalis, holding out the accursed bundle of documents.

"'When I was down on my luck, I learned to act on the stage,' added Cérizet. 'I am as good as Bouffé at old men.'

"'I have fallen among thieves!' shouted Maxime.

"'No, Monsieur le Comte, you are in Mlle. Hortense's house. She is a friend of old Lord Dudley's; he keeps her hidden away here; but she has the bad taste to like your humble servant.'

"'If ever I longed to kill a man,' so the Count told me afterwards, 'it was at that moment; but what could one do? Hortense showed her pretty face, one had to laugh. To keep my dignity, I flung her the six hundred francs. "There's for the girl," said I.'"

"That is Madame all over!" cried La Palférine.

"More especially as it was little Croizeau's money," added Cardot the profound.

"Maxime scored a triumph," continued Desroches, "for Hortense exclaimed, 'Oh! if I had only known that it was you!'

"A pretty 'confusion' indeed!" put in Malaga. "You have lost, milord," she added, turning to the notary.

And in this way the cabinetmaker, to whom Malaga owed a hundred crowns, was paid.

Paris, 1845.

1. See *La fausse Maitresse*.

GAUDISSART II

To Madame la Princesse Cristina de Belgiojoso, née Trivulzio.

TO know how to sell, to be able to sell, and to sell. People generally do not suspect how much of the stateliness of Paris is due to these three aspects of the same problem. The brilliant display of shops as rich as the salons of the noblesse before 1789; the splendours of cafés which eclipse, and easily eclipse, the Versailles of our day; the shop-window illusions, new every morning, nightly destroyed; the grace and elegance of the young men that come in contact with fair customers; the piquant faces and costumes of young damsels, who cannot fail to attract the masculine customer; and (and this especially of late) the length, the vast spaces, the Babylonish luxury of galleries where shopkeepers acquire a monopoly of the trade in various articles by bringing them all together,—all this is as nothing. Everything, so far, has been done to appeal to a single sense, and that the most exacting and jaded human faculty, a faculty developed ever since the days of the Roman Empire, until, in our own times, thanks to the efforts of the most fastidious civilisation the world has yet seen, its demands are grown limitless. That faculty resides in the "eyes of Paris."

Those eyes require illuminations costing a hundred thousand francs, and many-colored glass palaces a couple of miles long and sixty feet high; they must have a fairyland at some fourteen theatres every night, and a succession of panoramas and exhibitions of the triumphs of art; for them a whole world of suffering and pain, and a universe of joy, must revolve through the boulevards or stray through the streets of Paris; for them encyclopædias of carnival frippery and a score of illustrated books are brought out every year, to say nothing of caricatures by the hundred, and vignettes, lithographs, and prints by the thousand. To please those eyes, fifteen thousand francs' worth of gas must blaze every night; and, to conclude, for their delectation the great city yearly spends several millions of francs in opening up views and planting trees. And even yet this is as nothing—it is only the material side of the question; in truth, a mere trifle compared with the expenditure of brain power on the shifts, worthy of Molière, invented by some sixty thousand assistants and forty thousand damsels of the counter, who fasten upon the customer's purse, much as myriads of Seine whitebait fall upon a chance crust floating down the river.

Gaudissart in the mart is at least the equal of his illustrious namesake, now become the typical commercial traveller. Take him away from his shop and his line of business, he is like a collapsed balloon; only among his bales of merchandise do his faculties return, much as an actor is sublime only upon the boards. A French shopman is better educated than his fellows in other European countries; he can at need talk asphalt, Bal Mabille, polkas, literature, illustrated books, railways, politics, parliament, and revolution; transplant him! take away his stage, his yardstick, his artificial graces; he is foolish beyond belief; but on his own boards, on the tight-rope of the counter, as he displays a shawl with a speech at his tongue's end, and his eye on his customer, he puts the great Talleyrand into the shade; he has more wit than a Désaugiers, more wiles than Cleopatra; he is a match for a Monrose and a Molière to boot. Talleyrand in his own house would have outwitted Gaudissart, but in the shop the parts would have been reversed.

An incident will illustrate the paradox.

Two charming duchesses were chatting with the above-mentioned great diplomatist. The ladies wished for a bracelet; they were waiting for the arrival of a man from a great Parisian jeweller. A Gaudissart accordingly appeared with three bracelets of marvellous workmanship. The great ladies hesitated. Choice is a mental lightning flash; hesitate—there is no more to be said, you are at fault. Inspiration in matters of taste will not come twice. At last, after about ten minutes, the Prince was called in. He saw the two duchesses confronting doubt with its thousand facets, unable to decide between the transcendent merits of two of the trinkets, for the third had been set aside at once. Without leaving his book, without a glance at the bracelets, the Prince looked at the jeweller's assistant.

"Which would you choose for your sweetheart?" asked he.

The young man indicated one of the pair.

"In that case, take the other, you will make two women happy," said the subtlest of modern diplomatists, "and make your sweetheart happy too, in my name."

The two fair ladies smiled, and the young shopman took his departure, delighted with the Prince's present and the implied compliment to his taste.

A woman alights from her splendid carriage before one of the expensive shops where shawls are sold in the Rue Vivienne. She is not alone; women almost always go in pairs on these expeditions; always make the round of half a score of shops before they make up their minds, and laugh together in the intervals over the little comedies played for their benefit. Let us see which of the two acts most in character—the fair customer or the seller, and which has the best of it in such miniature vaudevilles?

If you attempt to describe a sale, the central fact of Parisian trade, you are in duty bound, if you attempt to give the gist of the matter, to produce a type, and for this purpose a shawl or a châtelaine costing some three thousand francs is a more exciting purchase than a length of lawn or dress that costs three hundred. But know, oh foreign visitors from the Old World and the New (if ever this study of the physiology of the Invoice should be by you perused), that this selfsame comedy is played in haberdashers' shops over a barège at two francs or a printed muslin at four francs the yard.

And you, princess, or simple citizen's wife, whichever you may be, how should you distrust that good-looking, very young man, with those frank, innocent eyes, and a cheek like a peach covered with down? He is dressed almost as well as your—cousin, let us say. His tones are as soft as the woollen stuffs which he spreads before you. There are three or four more of his like. One has dark eyes, a decided expression, and an imperial manner of saying, "This is what you wish"; another, that blue-eyed youth, diffident of manner and meek of speech, prompts the remark, "Poor boy! he was not born for business"; a third, with light auburn hair, and laughing tawny eyes, has all the lively humour, and activity, and gaiety of the South; while the fourth, he of the tawny red hair and fan-shaped beard, is rough as a communist, with his portentous cravat, his sternness, his dignity, and curt speech.

These varieties of shopmen, corresponding to the principal types of feminine customers, are arms, as it were, directed by the head, a stout personage with a full-blown countenance, a partially bald forehead, and a chest measure befitting a Ministerialist deputy. Occasionally this person wears the ribbon of the Legion of Honour in recognition of the manner in which he supports the dignity of the French draper's wand. From the comfortable curves of his figure you can see that he has a wife and family, a country house, and an account with the Bank of France. He descends like a *deus ex machinâ,* whenever a tangled problem demands a swift solution. The feminine purchasers are surrounded on all sides with urbanity, youth, pleasant manners, smiles, and jests; the most seeming-simple human products of civilisation are here, all sorted in shades to suit all tastes.

Just one word as to the natural effects of architecture, optical science, and house decoration; one short, decisive, terrible word, of history made on the spot. The work which contains this instructive page is sold at number 76 Rue de Richelieu, where above an elegant shop, all white and gold and crimson velvet, there is an entresol into which the light pours straight from the Rue de Ménars, as into a painter's studio—clean, clear, even daylight. What idler in the streets has not beheld the Persian, that Asiatic potentate, ruffling it above the door at the corner of the Rue de la Bourse and the Rue de Richelieu, with a message to deliver *urbi et orbi*, "Here I reign more tranquilly than at Lahore"? Perhaps but for this immortal analytical study, archaeologists might begin to puzzle their heads about him five hundred years hence, and set about writing quartos with plates (like M. Quatremère's work on Olympian Jove) to prove that Napoleon was something of a Sofi in the East before he became "Emperor of the French." Well, the wealthy shop laid siege to the poor little entresol; and after a bombardment with bank notes, entered and took possession. The Human Comedy gave way before the comedy of cashmeres. The Persian sacrificed a diamond or two from his crown to buy that so necessary daylight; for a ray of sunlight shows the play of the colours, brings out the charms of a shawl, and doubles its value; 'tis an irresistible light; literally, a golden ray. From this fact you may judge how far Paris shops are arranged with a view to effect.

But to return to the young assistants, to the beribboned man of forty whom the King of the French receives at his table, to the red-bearded head of the department with his autocrat's air. Week by week these emeritus Gaudissarts are brought in contact with whims past counting; they know every vibration of the cashmere chord in the heart of woman. No one, be she lady or lorette, a young mother of a family, a respectable tradesman's wife, a woman of easy virtue, a duchess or a brazen-fronted ballet-dancer, an innocent young girl or a too innocent foreigner, can appear in the shop, but she is watched from the moment when she first lays her fingers upon the door-handle. Her measure is taken at a glance by seven or eight men that stand, in the windows, at the counter, by the door, in a corner, in the middle of the shop, meditating, to all appearance, on the joys of a bacchanalian Sunday holiday. As you look at them, you ask yourself involuntarily, "What can they be thinking about?" Well, in the space of one second, a woman's purse, wishes, intentions, and whims are ransacked more thoroughly than a travelling carriage at a frontier in an hour and three-quarters. Nothing is lost on these intelligent rogues. As they stand, solemn as noble fathers on the stage, they take in all the details of a fair customer's dress; an invisible speck of mud on a little shoe, an antiquated hat-brim, soiled or ill-judged bonnet-strings, the fashion of the dress, the age of a pair of gloves. They can tell whether the gown was cut by the intelligent scissors of a Victorine IV.; they know a modish gewgaw or a trinket from Froment-Meurice. Nothing, in short, which can reveal a woman's quality, fortune, or character passes unremarked.

Tremble before them. Never was the Sanhedrim of Gaudissarts, with their chief at their head, known to make a mistake. And, moreover, they communicate their conclusions to one another with telegraphic speed, in a glance, a smile, the movement of a muscle, a twitch of the lip. If you watch them, you are reminded of the sudden outbreak of light along the Champs-Elysées at dusk; one gas-jet does not succeed another more swiftly than an idea flashes from one shopman's eyes to the next.

At once, if the lady is English, the dark, mysterious, portentous Gaudissart advances like a romantic character out of one of Byron's poems.

If she is a city madam, the oldest is put forward. He brings out a hundred shawls in fifteen minutes; he turns her head with colours and patterns; every shawl that he shows her is like a circle described by a kite wheeling round a hapless rabbit, till at the end of half an hour, when her head is swimming and she is utterly incapable of making a decision for herself, the good lady, meeting with a flattering response to all her ideas, refers the question to the assistant, who promptly leaves her on the horns of a dilemma between two equally irresistible shawls.

"This, madame, is very becoming—apple-green, the colour of the season; still, fashions change; while as for this other black-and-white shawl (an opportunity not to be missed), you will never see the end of it, and it will go with any dress."

This is the A B C of the trade.

"You would not believe how much eloquence is wanted in that beastly line," the head Gaudissart of this particular establishment remarked quite lately to two acquaintances (Duronceret and Bixiou) who had come trusting in his judgement to buy a shawl. "Look here; you are artists and discreet, I can tell you about the governor's tricks, and of all the men I ever saw, he is the cleverest. I do not mean as a manufacturer, there M. Fritot is first; but as a salesman. He discovered the 'Selim' shawl,' *an absolutely unsaleable* article, yet we never bring it out but we sell it. We keep always a shawl worth five or six hundred francs in a cedar-wood box, perfectly plain outside, but lined with satin. It is one of the shawls that Selim sent to the Emperor Napoleon. It is our Imperial Guard; it is brought to the front whenever the day is almost lost; *il se vend et ne meurt pas*—it sells its life dearly time after time."

As he spoke, an Englishwoman stepped from her jobbed carriage and appeared in all the glory of that phlegmatic humour peculiar to Britain and to all its products which make believe they are alive. The apparition put you in mind of the Commandant's statue in *Don Juan,* it walked along, jerkily by fits and starts, in an awkward fashion invented in London, and cultivated in every family with patriotic care.

"An Englishwoman!" he continued for Bixiou's ear. "An Englishwoman is our Waterloo. There are women who slip through our fingers like eels; we catch them on the staircase. There are lorettes who chaff us, we join in the laugh, we have a hold on them because we give credit. There are sphinx-like foreign ladies; we take a quantity of shawls to their houses, and arrive at an understanding by flattery; but an Englishwoman!—you might as well attack the bronze statue of Louis Quatorze! That sort of woman turns shopping into an occupation, an amusement. She quizzes us, forsooth!"

The romantic assistant came to the front.

"Does madame wish for real Indian shawls or French, something expensive or—"

"I will see." (*Je véraie.*)

"How much would madame propose—"

"I will see."

The shopman went in quest of shawls to spread upon the mantle-stand, giving his colleagues a significant glance. "What a bore!" he said plainly, with an almost imperceptible shrug of the shoulders.

"These are our best quality in Indian red, blue, and pale orange—all at ten thousand francs. Here are shawls at five thousand francs, and others at three."

The Englishwoman took up her eyeglass and looked round the room with gloomy indifference; then she submitted the three stands to the same scrutiny, and made no sign.

"Have you any more?" (*Havaivod'hôte?*) demanded she.

"Yes, madame. But perhaps madame has not quite decided to take a shawl?"

"Oh, quite decided" (*trei-deycidai*).

The young man went in search of cheaper wares. These he spread out solemnly as if they were things of price, saying by his manner, "Pay attention to all this magnificence!"

"These are much more expensive," said he. "They have never been worn; they have come by courier direct from the manufacturers at Lahore."

"Oh! I see," said she; "they are much more like the thing I want."

The shopman kept his countenance in spite of inward irritation, which communicated itself to Duronceret and Bixiou. The Englishwoman, cool as a cucumber, appeared to rejoice in her phlegmatic humour.

"What price?" she asked, indicating a sky-blue shawl covered with a pattern of birds nestling in pagodas.

"Seven thousand francs."

She took it up, wrapped it about her shoulders, looked in the glass, and handed it back again.

"No, I do not like it at all." (*Je n'ame pouinte.*)

A long quarter of an hour went by in trying on other shawls; to no purpose.

"This is all we have, madame," said the assistant, glancing at the master as he spoke.

"Madame is fastidious, like all persons of taste," said the head of the establishment, coming forward with that tradesman's suavity in which pomposity is agreeably blended with subservience. The Englishwoman took up her eyeglass and scanned the manufacturer from head to foot, unwilling to understand that the man before her was eligible for Parliament and dined at the Tuileries.

"I have only one shawl left," he continued, "but I never show it. It is not to everybody's taste; it is quite out of the common. I was thinking this morning of giving it to my wife. We have had it in stock since 1805; it belonged to the Empress Josephine."

"Let me see it, monsieur."

"Go for it," said the master, turning to a shopman. "It is at my house."

"I should be very much pleased to see it," said the English lady.

This was a triumph. The splenetic dame was apparently on the point of going. She made as though she saw nothing but the shawls; but all the while she furtively watched the shopmen and the two customers, sheltering her eyes behind the rims of her eyeglasses.

"It cost sixty thousand francs in Turkey, madame."

"Oh!" (*hâu!*)

"It is one of seven shawls which Selim sent, before his fall, to the Emperor Napoleon. The Empress Josephine, a Creole, as you know, my lady, and very capricious in her tastes, exchanged this one for another brought by the Turkish ambassador, and purchased by my predecessor; but I have never seen the money back. Our ladies in France are not rich enough; it is not as it is in England. The shawl is worth seven thousand francs; and taking interest and compound interest altogether, it makes up fourteen or fifteen thousand by now—"

"How does it make up?" asked the Englishwoman.

"Here it is, madame."

With precautions, which a custodian of the Dresden *Grüne Gewölbe* might have admired, he took out an infinitesimal key and opened a square cedar-wood box. The Englishwoman was much impressed with its shape and plainness. From that box, lined with black satin, he drew a shawl worth about fifteen hundred francs, a black pattern on a golden-yellow ground, of which the startling colour was only surpassed by the surprising efforts of the Indian imagination.

"Splendid," said the lady, in a mixture of French and English, "it is really handsome. Just my ideal" (*idéol*) "of a shawl; it is very magnificent." The rest was lost in a madonna's pose assumed for the purpose of displaying a pair of frigid eyes which she believed to be very fine.

"It was a great favourite with the Emperor Napoleon; he took—"

"A great favourite," repeated she with her English accent. Then she arranged the shawl about her shoulders and looked at herself in the glass. The proprietor took it to the light, gathered it up in his hands, smoothed it out, showed the gloss on it, played on it as Liszt plays on the pianoforte keys.

"It is very fine; beautiful, sweet!" said the lady, as composedly as possible.

Duronceret, Bixiou, and the shopmen exchanged amused glances. "The shawl is sold," they thought.

"Well, madame?" inquired the proprietor, as the Englishwoman appeared to be absorbed in meditations infinitely prolonged.

"Decidedly," said she; "I would rather have a carriage" (*une vôteure*).

All the assistants, listening with silent rapt attention, started as one man, as if an electric shock had gone through them.

"I have a very handsome one, madame," said the proprietor with unshaken composure; "it belonged to a Russian princess, the Princess Narzicof; she left it with me in payment for goods received. If madame would like to see it, she would be astonished. It is new; it has not been in use altogether for ten days; there is not its like in Paris."

The shopmen's amazement was suppressed by profound admiration.

"I am quite willing."

"If madame will keep the shawl," suggested the proprietor, "she can try the effect in the carriage." And he went for his hat and gloves.

"How will this end?" asked the head assistant, as he watched his employer offer an arm to the English lady and go down with her to the jobbed brougham.

By this time the thing had come to be as exciting as the last chapter of a novel for Duronceret and Bixiou, even without the additional interest attached to all contests, however trifling, between England and France.

Twenty minutes later the proprietor returned.

"Go to the Hôtel Lawson (here is the card, 'Mrs. Noswell'), and take an invoice that I will give you. There are six thousand francs to take."

"How did you do it?" asked Duronceret, bowing before the king of invoices.

"Oh, I saw what she was, an eccentric woman that loves to be conspicuous. As soon as she saw that every one stared at her, she said, 'Keep your carriage, monsieur, my mind is made up; I will take the shawl.' While M. Bigorneau (indicating the romantic-looking assistant) was serving, I watched her carefully; she kept one eye on you all the time to see what you thought of her; she was thinking more about you than of the shawls. Englishwomen are peculiar in their distaste (for one cannot call it taste); they do not know what they want; they make up their minds to be guided by circumstances at the time, and not by their own choice. I saw the kind of woman at once, tired of her husband, tired of her brats, regretfully virtuous, craving excitement, always posing as a weeping willow …"

These were his very words.

Which proves that in all other countries of the world a shopkeeper is a shopkeeper; while in France, and in Paris more particularly, he is a student from a Collège Royal, a well-read man with a taste for art, or angling, or the theatre, and consumed, it may be, with a desire to be M. Cunin-Gridaine's successor, or a colonel of the National Guard, or a member of the General Council of the Seine, or a referee in the Commercial Court.

"M. Adolphe," said the mistress of the establishment, addressing the slight fair-haired assistant, "go to the joiner and order another cedar-wood box."

"And now," remarked the shopman who had assisted Duronceret and Bixiou to choose a shawl for Mme. Schontz, "now we will go through our old stock to find another Selim shawl."

PARIS, *November* 1844.

SARRASINE

To Monsieur Charles Bernard du Grail.

I WAS buried in one of those profound reveries to which everybody, even a frivolous man, is subject in the midst of the most uproarious festivities. The clock on the Élysée-Bourbon had just struck midnight. Seated in a window recess and concealed behind the undulating folds of a curtain of watered silk, I was able to contemplate at my leisure the garden of the mansion at which I was passing the evening. The trees, being partly covered with snow, were outlined indistinctly against the greyish background formed by a cloudy sky, barely whitened by the moon. Seen through the medium of that strange atmosphere, they bore a vague resemblance to spectres carelessly enveloped in their shrouds, a gigantic image of the famous *Dance of Death*. Then, turning in the other direction, I could gaze admiringly upon the dance of the living! a magnificent salon, with walls of silver and gold, with gleaming chandeliers, and bright with the light of many candles. There the loveliest, the wealthiest women in Paris, bearers of the proudest titles, moved hither and thither, fluttered from room to room in swarms, stately and gorgeous, dazzling with diamonds; flowers on their heads and breasts, in their hair, scattered over their dresses or lying in garlands at their feet. Light quiverings of the body, voluptuous movements, made the laces and gauzes and silks swirl about their graceful figures. Sparkling glances here and there eclipsed the lights, and the blaze of the diamonds, and fanned the flame of hearts already burning too brightly. I detected also significant nods of the head for lovers and repellent attitudes for husbands. The exclamations of the card-players at every unexpected *coup*, the jingle of gold, mingled with the music and the murmur of conversation; and to put the finishing touch to the vertigo of that multitude, intoxicated by all the seductions the world can offer, a perfume-laden atmosphere and general exaltation acted upon their over-wrought imaginations. Thus, at my right was the depressing, silent image of death; at my left the decorous bacchanalia of life; on the one side nature, cold and gloomy, and in mourning garb; on the other side, man on pleasure bent. And, standing on the borderland of those two incongruous pictures, which, repeated thousands of times in divers ways, make Paris the most entertaining and most philosophical city in the world, I played a mental *macédoine*,[1] half jesting, half funereal. With my left foot I kept time to the music, and the other felt as if it were in a tomb. My leg was, in fact, frozen by one of those draughts which congeal one half of the body while the other suffers from the intense heat of the salons—a state of things not unusual at balls.

"Monsieur de Lanty has not owned this house very long, has he?"

"Oh, yes! It is nearly ten years since the Maréchal de Carigliano sold it to him."

"Ah!"

"These people must have an enormous fortune."

"They surely must."

'What a magnificent party! It is almost insolent in its splendour."

"Do you imagine they are as rich as Monsieur de Nucingen or Monsieur de Gondreville?"

"Why, don't you know?"

I leaned forward and recognised the two persons who were talking as members of that inquisitive genus which, in Paris, busies itself exclusively with the *Whys* and *Hows*. *Where does he come from? Who are they? What's the matter with him? What has she done?* They lowered their voices and walked away in order to talk more at their ease on some retired couch. Never was a more promising mine laid open to seekers after mysteries. No one knew from what country the Lanty family came, nor to what source—commerce, extortion, piracy, or inheritance—they owed a fortune estimated at several millions. All the members of the family spoke Italian, French, Spanish, English and German, with sufficient fluency to lead one to suppose that they had lived long among those different peoples. Were they gypsies? were they buccaneers?

"Suppose they're the devil himself," said divers young politicians, "they entertain mighty well."

"The Comte de Lanty may have plundered some *Casbah* for all I care; I would like to marry his daughter!" cried a philosopher.

Who would not have married Marianina, a girl of sixteen, whose beauty realized the fabulous conceptions of Oriental poets! Like the Sultan's daughter in the tale of the *Wonderful Lamp*, she should have remained always veiled. Her singing obscured the imperfect talents of the Malibrans, the Sontags, and the

Fodors, in whom some one dominant quality always mars the perfection of the whole; whereas Marianina combined in equal degree purity of tone, exquisite feeling, accuracy of time and intonation, science, soul, and delicacy. She was the type of that hidden poesy, the link which connects all the arts and which always eludes those who seek it. Modest, sweet, well-informed and clever, none could eclipse Marianina unless it were her mother.

Have you ever met one of those women whose startling beauty defies the assaults of time, and who seem at thirty-six more desirable than they could have been fifteen years earlier? Their faces are impassioned souls; they fairly sparkle; each feature gleams with intelligence; each possesses a brilliancy of its own, especially in the light. Their captivating eyes attract or repel, speak or are silent; their gait is artlessly seductive; their voices unfold the melodious treasures of the most coquettishly sweet and tender tones. Praise of their beauty, based upon comparisons, flatters the most sensitive self-esteem. A movement of their eyebrows, the slightest play of the eye, the curling of the lip, instils a sort of terror in those whose lives and happiness depend upon their favour. A maiden inexperienced in love and easily moved by words may allow herself to be seduced; but in dealing with women of this sort, a man must be able, like M. de Jaucourt, to refrain from crying out when, in hiding him in a closet, the lady's maid crushes two of his fingers in the crack of a door. To love one of these omnipotent sirens is to stake one's life, is it not? And that, perhaps, is why we love them so passionately! Such was the Comtesse de Lanty.

Filippo, Marianina's brother, inherited, as did his sister, the Countess' marvellous beauty. To tell the whole story in a word, that young man was a living image of Antinoüs, with somewhat slighter proportions. But how well such a slender and delicate figure accords with youth, when an olive complexion, heavy eyebrows, and the gleam of a velvety eye promise virile passions, noble ideas for the future! If Filippo remained in the hearts of young women as a type of manly beauty, he likewise remained in the memory of all mothers as the best match in France.

The beauty, the great wealth, the intellectual qualities, of these two children came entirely from their mother. The Comte de Lanty was a short, thin, ugly little man, as dismal as a Spaniard, as great a bore as a banker. He was looked upon, however, as a profound politician, perhaps because he rarely laughed, and was always quoting M. de Metternich or Wellington.

This mysterious family had all the attractiveness of a poem by Lord Byron, whose difficult passages were translated differently by each person in fashionable society; a poem that grew more obscure and more sublime from strophe to strophe. The reserve which Monsieur and Madame de Lanty maintained concerning their origin, their past lives, and their relations with the four quarters of the globe would not, of itself, have been for long a subject of wonderment in Paris. In no other country, perhaps, is Vespasian's maxim more thoroughly understood. Here gold pieces, even when stained with blood or mud, betray nothing, and represent everything. Provided that good society knows the amount of your fortune, you are classed among those figures which equal yours, and no one asks to see your credentials, because everybody knows how little they cost. In a city where social problems are solved by algebraic equations, adventurers have many chances in their favour. Even if this family were of gypsy extraction, it was so wealthy, so attractive, that fashionable society could well afford to overlook its little mysteries. But, unfortunately, the enigmatical history of the Lanty family offered a perpetual subject of curiosity, not unlike that aroused by the novels of Anne Radcliffe.

People of an observing turn, of the sort who are bent upon finding out where you buy your candelabra, or who ask you what rent you pay when they are pleased with your apartments, had noticed, from time to time, the appearance of an extraordinary personage at the fêtes, concerts, balls, and routs given by the countess. It was a man. The first time that he was seen in the house was at a concert, when he seemed to have been drawn to the salon by Marianina's enchanting voice.

"I have been cold for the last minute or two," said a lady near the door to her neighbour.

The stranger, who was standing near the speaker, moved away.

"This is very strange! now I am warm," she said, after his departure. "Perhaps you will call me mad, but I cannot help thinking that my neighbour, the gentleman in black who just walked away, was the cause of my feeling cold."

Ere long the exaggeration to which people in society are naturally inclined, produced a large and growing crop of the most amusing ideas, the most curious expressions, the most absurd fables concerning this mysterious individual. Without being precisely a vampire, a ghoul, a fictitious man, a sort of Faust or Robin des Bois, he partook of the nature of all these anthropomorphic conceptions, according to those persons who were addicted to the fantastic. Occasionally some German would take for realities these ingenious jests of Parisian evil-speaking. The stranger was simply *an old man*. Some young men, who were accustomed to decide the future of Europe every morning in a few fashionable phrases, chose to see in the stranger some great criminal, the possessor of enormous wealth. Novelists described the old man's life and gave some really interesting details of the atrocities committed by him while he was in the service of the Prince of Mysore. Bankers, men of a more positive nature, devised a specious fable.

"Bah!" they would say, shrugging their broad shoulders pityingly, "that little old fellow's a *Genoese head!*"

"If it is not an impertinent question, monsieur, would you have the kindness to tell me what you mean by a Genoese head?"

"I mean, monsieur, that he is a man upon whose life enormous sums depend, and whose good health is undoubtedly essential to the continuance of this family's income. I remember that I once heard a mesmerist, at Madame d'Espard's, undertake to prove by very specious historical deductions, that this old man, if put under the magnifying glass, would turn out to be the famous Balsamo, otherwise called Cagliostro. According to this modern alchemist, the Sicilian had escaped death, and amused himself making gold for his grandchildren. And the Bailli of Ferette declared that he recognised in this extraordinary personage the Comte de Saint-Germain."

Such nonsense as this, put forth with the assumption of superior cleverness, with the air of raillery, which in our day characterise a society devoid of faith, kept alive vague suspicions concerning the Lanty family. At last, by a strange combination of circumstances, the members of that family justified the conjectures of society by adopting a decidedly mysterious course of conduct with this old man, whose life was, in a certain sense, kept hidden from all investigations.

If he crossed the threshold of the apartment he was supposed to occupy in the Lanty mansion, his appearance always caused a great sensation in the family. One would have supposed that it was an event of the greatest importance. Only Filippo, Marianina, Madame de Lanty, and an old servant enjoyed the privilege of assisting the unknown to walk, to rise, to sit down. Each one of them kept a close watch on his slightest movements. It seemed as if he were some enchanted person upon whom the happiness, the life, or the fortune of all depended. Was it fear or affection? Society could discover no indication which enabled them to solve this problem. Concealed for months at a time in the depths of an unknown sanctuary, this familiar spirit suddenly emerged, furtively as it were, unexpectedly, and appeared in the salons like the fairies of old, who alighted from their winged dragons to disturb festivities to which they had not been invited. Only the most experienced observers could divine the anxiety, at such times, of the masters of the house, who were peculiarly skilful in concealing their feelings. But sometimes, while dancing a quadrille, the too ingenuous Marianina would cast a terrified glance at the old man, whom she watched closely from the circle of dancers. Or perhaps Filippo would leave his place and glide through the crowd to where he stood, and remain beside him, affectionate and watchful, as if the touch of man, or the faintest breath, would shatter that extraordinary creature. The countess would try to draw nearer to him without apparently intending to join him; then, assuming a manner and an expression in which servility and affection, submissiveness and tyranny, were equally noticeable, she would say two or three words, to which the old man almost always deferred; and he would disappear, led, or I might better say carried away, by her. If Madame de Lanty were not present, the Count would employ a thousand ruses to reach his side; but it always seemed as if he found difficulty in inducing him to listen, and he treated him like a spoiled child, whose mother gratifies his whims and at the same time suspects mutiny. Some prying persons having ventured to question the Comte de Lanty indiscreetly, that cold and reserved individual seemed not to understand their questions. And so, after many attempts, which the circumspection of all the members of the family rendered fruitless, no one sought to discover a secret so well guarded. Society spies, triflers, and politicians, weary of the strife, ended by ceasing to concern themselves about the mystery.

But at that moment, it may be, there were in those gorgeous salons philosophers who said to themselves, as they discussed an ice or a sherbet, or placed their empty punch glasses on a tray:

"I should not be surprised to learn that these people are knaves. That old fellow who keeps out of sight and appears only at the equinoxes or solstices, looks to me exactly like an assassin."

"Or a bankrupt."

"There's very little difference. To destroy a man's fortune is worse sometimes than to kill the man himself."

"I bet twenty louis, monsieur; there are forty due me."

"Faith, monsieur; there are only thirty left on the cloth."

"Just see what a mixed company there is here! One can't play cards in peace."

"Very true. But it's almost six months since we saw the Spirit. Do you think he's a living being?"

"Well, barely."

These last remarks were made in my neighbourhood by persons whom I did not know, and who passed out of hearing just as I was summarising in one last thought my reflections, in which black and white, life and death, were inextricably mingled. My wandering imagination, like my eyes, contemplated alternately the festivities, which had now reached the climax of their splendour, and the gloomy picture presented by the gardens. I have no idea how long I meditated upon those two faces of the human medal; but I was suddenly aroused by the stifled laughter of a young woman. I was stupefied at the picture presented to my eyes. By virtue of one of the strangest of nature's freaks, the thought half draped in black, which was tossing about in my brain, emerged from it and stood before me personified, living; it had come forth like Minerva from Jupiter's brain, tall and strong; it was at once a hundred years old and twenty-two; it was alive and dead. Escaped from his chamber, like a madman from his cell, the little old man had evidently crept behind a long line of people who were listening attentively to Marianina's voice as she finished the cavatina from *Tancred*. He seemed to have come up through the floor, impelled by some stage mechanism. He stood for a moment motionless and sombre, watching the festivities, a murmur of which had perhaps reached his ears. His almost somnambulistic preoccupation was so concentrated upon things that, although he was in the midst of many people, he saw nobody. He had taken his place unceremoniously beside one of the most fascinating women in Paris, a young and graceful dancer, with slender figure, a face as fresh as a child's, all pink and white, and so fragile, so transparent, that it seemed that a man's glance must pass through her as the sun's rays pass through flawless glass. They stood there before me, side by side, so close together, that the stranger rubbed against the gauze dress, and the wreaths of flowers, and the hair, slightly crimped, and the floating ends of the sash.

I had brought that young woman to Madame de Lanty's ball. As it was her first visit to that house, I forgave her her stifled laugh; but I hastily made an imperious sign which abashed her and inspired respect for her neighbour. She sat down beside me. The old man did not choose to leave the charming creature, to whom he clung capriciously with the silent and apparently causeless obstinacy to which very old persons are subject, and which makes them resemble children. In order to sit down beside the young lady he needed a folding-chair. His slightest movements were marked by the inert heaviness, the stupid hesitancy, which characterise the movements of a paralytic. He sat slowly down upon his chair with great caution, mumbling some unintelligible words. His cracked voice resembled the noise made by a stone falling into a well. The young woman nervously pressed my hand, as if she were trying to avoid a precipice, and shivered when that man at whom she happened to be looking, turned upon her two lifeless, sea-green eyes, which could be compared to nothing save tarnished mother-of-pearl.

"I am afraid," she said, putting her lips to my ear.

"You can speak," I replied; "he hears with great difficulty."

"You know him, then?"

"Yes."

Thereupon she summoned courage to scrutinise for a moment that creature for which no human language has a name, form without substance, a being without life, or life without action. She was under the spell of that timid curiosity which impels women to seek perilous excitement, to gaze at chained tigers and boa-constrictors, shuddering all the while because the barriers between them are so weak. Although the little old man's back was bent like a day-labourer's, it was easy to see that he must formerly have been of medium height. His excessive thinness, the slenderness of his limbs, proved that he had always been of slight build. He wore black silk breeches which hung about his fleshless thighs in folds, like a lowered veil. An anatomist would instinctively have recognised the symptoms of consumption in its advanced stages, at sight of the tiny legs which served to support that strange frame. You would have said that they were a pair of cross-bones on a gravestone. A feeling of profound horror seized the heart when a close scrutiny revealed the marks made by decrepitude upon that frail machine.

He wore a white waistcoat embroidered with gold, in the old style, and his linen was of dazzling whiteness. A shirt-frill of English lace, yellow with age, the magnificence of which a queen might have envied, formed a series of yellow ruffles on his breast; but upon him the lace seemed rather a worthless rag than an ornament. In the centre of the frill a diamond of inestimable value gleamed like a sun. That superannuated splendour, that display of treasure, of great intrinsic worth, but utterly without taste, served to bring out in still bolder relief the strange creature's face. The frame was worthy of the portrait. That dark face was full of angles and furrowed deep in every direction; the chin was furrowed; there were great hollows at the temples; the eyes were sunken in yellow orbits. The maxillary bones, which his indescribable gauntness caused to protrude, formed deep cavities in the centre of both cheeks. These protuberances, as the light fell upon them, caused curious effects of light and shadow which deprived that face of the last vestige of resemblance to the human countenance. And then, too, the lapse of years had drawn the fine, yellow skin so close to the bones that it described a multitude of wrinkles everywhere, either circular like the ripples in the water caused by a stone which a child throws in, or star-shaped like a pane of glass cracked by a blow; but everywhere very deep, and as close together as the leaves of a closed book. We often see more hideous old men; but what contributed more than aught else to give to the spectre that rose before us the aspect of an artificial creation was the red and white paint with which he glistened. The eyebrows shone in the light with a lustre which disclosed a very well executed bit of painting. Luckily for the eye, saddened by such a mass of ruins, his corpse-like skull was concealed beneath a light wig, with innumerable curls which indicated extraordinary pretensions to elegance. Indeed, the feminine coquettishness of this fantastic apparition was emphatically asserted by the gold ear-rings which hung at his ears, by the rings containing stones of marvellous beauty which sparkled on his fingers, like the brilliants in a river of gems around a woman's neck. Lastly, this species of Japanese idol had constantly upon his blue lips, a fixed, unchanging smile, the shadow of an implacable and sneering laugh, like that of a death's head. As silent and motionless as a statue, he exhaled the musk-like odour of the old dresses which a duchess' heirs exhume from her wardrobe during the inventory. If the old man turned his eyes toward the company, it seemed that the movements of those globes, no longer capable of reflecting a gleam, were accomplished by an almost imperceptible effort; and, when the eyes stopped, he who was watching them was not certain finally that they had moved at all. As I saw, beside that human ruin, a young woman whose bare neck and arms and breast were white as snow; whose figure was well-rounded and beautiful in its youthful grace; whose hair, charmingly arranged above an alabaster forehead, inspired love; whose eyes did not receive but gave forth light, who was sweet and fresh, and whose fluffy curls, whose fragrant breath, seemed too heavy, too harsh, too overpowering for that shadow, for that man of dust—ah! the thought that came into my mind was of death and life, an imaginary arabesque, a half-hideous chimera, divinely feminine from the waist up.

"And yet such marriages are often made in society!" I said to myself.

"He smells of the cemetery!" cried the terrified young woman, grasping my arm as if to make sure of my protection, and moving about in a restless, excited way, which convinced me that she was very much frightened. "It's a horrible vision," she continued; "I cannot stay here any longer. If I look at him again I shall believe that Death himself has come in search of me. But is he alive?"

She placed her hand on the phenomenon, with the boldness which women derive from the violence of their wishes, but a cold sweat burst from her pores, for, the instant she touched the old man, she heard a cry like the noise made by a rattle. That shrill voice, if indeed it were a voice, escaped from a throat almost entirely dry. It was at once succeeded by a convulsive little cough like a child's, of a peculiar resonance. At that sound, Marianina, Filippo, and Madame de Lanty looked toward us, and their glances were like lightning flashes. The young woman wished that she were at the bottom of the Seine. She took my arm and pulled me away toward a boudoir. Everybody, men and women, made room for us to pass. Having reached the further end of the suite of reception-rooms, we entered a small semi-circular cabinet. My companion threw herself on a divan, breathing fast with terror, not knowing where she was.

"You are mad, madame," I said to her.

"But," she rejoined, after a moment's silence, during which I gazed at her in admiration, "is it my fault? Why does Madame de Lanty allow ghosts to wander round her house?"

"Nonsense," I replied; "you are doing just what fools do. You mistake a little old man for a spectre."

"Hush," she retorted, with the imposing, yet mocking, air which all women are so well able to assume when they are determined to put themselves in the right. "Oh! what a sweet boudoir!" she cried, looking about her. "Blue satin hangings always produce an admirable effect. How cool it is! Ah! the lovely picture!" she added, rising and standing in front of a magnificently framed painting.

We stood for a moment gazing at that marvel of art, which seemed the work of some supernatural brush. The picture represented Adonis stretched out on a lion's skin. The lamp, in an alabaster vase, hanging in the centre of the boudoir, cast upon the canvas a soft light which enabled us to grasp all the beauties of the picture.

"Does such a perfect creature exist?" she asked me, after examining attentively, and not without a sweet smile of satisfaction, the exquisite grace of the outlines, the attitude, the colour, the hair, in fact everything.

"He is too beautiful for a man," she added, after such a scrutiny as she would have bestowed upon a rival.

Ah! how sharply I felt at that moment those pangs of jealousy in which a poet had tried in vain to make me believe! the jealousy of engravings, of pictures, of statues, wherein artists exaggerate human beauty, as a result of the doctrine which leads them to idealise everything.

"It is a portrait," I replied. "It is a product of Vien's genius. But that great painter never saw the original, and your admiration will be modified somewhat perhaps, when I tell you that this study was made from a statue of a woman."

"But who is it?"

I hesitated.

"I insist upon knowing," she added earnestly.

"I believe," I said, "that this *Adonis* represents a—a relative of Madame de Lanty."

I had the chagrin of seeing that she was lost in contemplation of that figure. She sat down in silence, and I seated myself beside her and took her hand without her noticing it. Forgotten for a portrait! At that moment we heard in the silence a woman's footstep and the faint rustling of a dress. We saw the youthful Marianina enter the boudoir, even more resplendent by reason of her expression of innocence than by reason of her grace and her fresh costume; she was walking slowly and leading with motherly care, with a daughter's solicitude, the spectre in human attire, who had driven us from the music-room; as she led him, she watched with some anxiety the slow movement of his feeble feet. They walked painfully across the boudoir to a door hidden in the hangings. Marianina knocked softly. Instantly a tall, thin man, a sort of familiar spirit, appeared as if by magic. Before intrusting the old man to this mysterious guardian, the lovely child, with deep veneration, kissed the ambulatory corpse, and her chaste caress was not without a touch of that graceful playfulness, the secret of which only a few privileged women possess.

"*Addio, addio!*" she said, with the sweetest inflection of her young voice.

She added to the last syllable a wonderfully executed trill, in a very low tone, as if to depict the overflowing affection of her heart by a poetic expression. The old man, suddenly arrested by some memory, remained on the threshold of that secret retreat. In the profound silence we heard the sigh that came forth from his breast; he removed the most beautiful of the rings with which his skeleton fingers were laden, and placed it in Marianina's bosom. The young madcap laughed, plucked out the ring, slipped it on one of her fingers over her glove, and ran hastily back toward the salon, where the orchestra were, at that moment, beginning the prelude of a contra-dance.

She spied us.

"Ah! were you here?" she said, blushing.

After a searching glance at us as if to question us, she ran away to her partner with the careless petulance of her years.

"What does this mean?" queried my young partner. "Is he her husband? I believe I am dreaming. Where am I?"

"You!" I retorted, "you, madame, who are easily excited, and who, understanding so well the most imperceptible emotions, are able to cultivate in a man's heart the most delicate of sentiments, without crushing it, without shattering it at the very outset, you who have compassion for the tortures of the heart, and who, with the wit of the Parisian, combine a passionate temperament worthy of Spain or Italy—"

She realised that my words were heavily charged with bitter irony; and, thereupon, without seeming to notice it, she interrupted me to say:

"Oh! you describe me to suit your own taste. A strange kind of tyranny! You wish me not to be *myself!*"

"Oh! I wish nothing," I cried, alarmed by the severity of her manner. "At all events, it is true, is it not, that you like to hear stories of the fierce passions kindled in our hearts by the enchanting women of the South?"

"Yes. And then?"

"Why, I will come to your house about nine o'clock to-morrow evening, and elucidate this mystery for you."

"No," she replied, with a pout; "I wish it done now."

"You have not yet given me the right to obey you when you say, 'I wish it.'"

"At this moment," she said, with an exhibition of coquetry of the sort that drives men to despair, "I have a most violent desire to know this secret. To-morrow it may be that I will not listen to you."

She smiled and we parted, she still as proud and as cruel, I as ridiculous, as ever. She had the audacity to waltz with a young aide-de-camp, and I was by turns angry, sulky, admiring, loving, and jealous.

"Until to-morrow," she said to me, as she left the ball about two o'clock in the morning.

"I won't go," I thought. "I give you up. You are a thousand times more capricious, more fanciful, than—my imagination."

The next evening we were seated in front of a bright fire in a dainty little salon, she on a couch, I on cushions almost at her feet, looking up into her face. The street was silent. The lamp shed a soft light. It was one of those evenings which delight the soul, one of those moments which are never forgotten, one of those hours passed in peace and longing, whose charm is always in later years a source of regret, even when we are happier. What can efface the deep imprint of the first solicitations of love?

"Go on," she said. "I am listening."

"But I dare not begin. There are passages in the story which are dangerous to the narrator. If I become excited, you will make me hold my peace."

"Speak."

"I obey.

"Ernest-Jean Sarrasine was the only son of a prosecuting attorney of Franche-Comté," I began, after a pause. "His father had, by faithful work, amassed a fortune which yielded an income of six to eight thousand francs, then considered a colossal fortune for an attorney in the provinces. Old Maître Sarrasine, having but one child, determined to give him a thorough education; he hoped to make a magistrate of him, and to live long enough to see, in his old age, the grandson of Mathieu Sarrasine, a ploughman in the Saint-Dié country, seated on the lilies, and dozing through the sessions for the greater glory of the Parliament; but Heaven had not that joy in store for the attorney. Young Sarrasine, intrusted to the care of the Jesuits at an early age, gave indications of an extraordinarily unruly disposition. His was the childhood of a man of talent. He would not study except as his inclination led him, often rebelled, and sometimes remained for whole hours at a time buried in tangled meditations, engaged now in watching his comrades at play, now in forming mental pictures of Homer's heroes. And, when he did choose to amuse himself, he displayed extraordinary ardour in his games. Whenever there was a contest of any sort between a comrade and himself, it rarely ended without bloodshed. If he were the weaker, he would use his teeth. Active and passive by turns, either lacking in aptitude, or too intelligent, his abnormal temperament caused him to distrust his masters as much as his schoolmates. Instead of learning the elements of the Greek language, he drew a picture of the reverend father who was interpreting a passage of Thucydides, sketched the teacher of mathematics, the prefect, the assistants, the man who administered punishment, and smeared all the walls with shapeless figures. Instead of singing the praises of the Lord in the chapel, he amused himself, during the services, by notching a bench; or, when he had stolen a piece of wood, he would carve the figure of some saint. If he had no wood or stone or pencil, he worked out his ideas with bread. Whether he copied the figures in the pictures which adorned the choir, or improvised, he always left at his seat rough sketches whose obscene character drove the young fathers to despair; and the evil-tongued alleged that the Jesuits smiled at them. At last, if we are to believe college traditions, he was expelled because, while awaiting his turn to go to the confessional one Good Friday, he carved a figure of the Christ from a stick of wood. The impiety evidenced by that figure was too flagrant not to draw down chastisement on the artist. He had actually had the hardihood to place that decidedly cynical image on the top of the tabernacle!

"Sarrasine came to Paris to seek a refuge against the threats of a father's malediction. Having one of those strong wills which know no obstacles, he obeyed the behests of his genius and entered Bouchardon's studio. He worked all day and went about at night begging for subsistence Bouchardon, marvelling at the young artist's intelligence and rapid progress, soon divined his pupil's destitute condition; he assisted him, became attached to him, and treated him like his own child. Then, when Sarrasine's genius stood revealed in one of those works wherein future talent contends with the effervescence of youth, the generous Bouchardon tried to restore him to the old attorney's good graces. The paternal wrath subsided in face of the famous sculptor's authority. All Besançon congratulated itself on having brought forth a future great man. In the first outburst of delight due to his flattered vanity, the miserly attorney supplied his son with the means to appear to advantage in society. The long and laborious study demanded by the sculptor's profession subdued for a long time Sarrasine's impetuous temperament and unruly genius. Bouchardon, foreseeing how violently the passions would some day rage in that youthful heart, as highly tempered perhaps as Michelangelo's, smothered its vehemence with constant toil. He succeeded in restraining within reasonable bounds Sarrasine's extraordinary impetuosity, by forbidding him to work, by proposing diversions when he saw that he was carried away by the violence of some idea, or by placing important work in his hands when he saw that he was on the point of plunging into dissipation. But with that passionate nature, gentleness was always the most powerful of all weapons, and the master did not acquire great influence over his pupil until he had aroused his gratitude by fatherly kindness.

"At the age of twenty-two Sarrasine was forcibly removed from the salutary influence which Bouchardon exercised over his morals and his habits. He paid the penalty of his genius by winning the prize for sculpture founded by the Marquis de Marigny, Madame de Pompadour's brother, who did so much for art. Diderot praised Bouchardon's pupil's statue as a masterpiece. Not without profound sorrow did the king's sculptor witness the departure for Italy of a young man whose profound ignorance of the things of life he had, as a matter of principle, refrained from enlightening. Sarrasine was Bouchardon's guest for six years. Fanatically devoted to his art, as Canova was at a later day, he rose at dawn and went to the studio, there to remain until night, and lived with his muse alone. If he went to the Comédie-Française, he was dragged thither by his master. He was so bored at Madame Geoffrin's, and in the fashionable society to which Bouchardon tried to introduce him, that he preferred to remain alone, and held aloof from the pleasures of that licentious age. He had no other mistresses than sculpture and Clotilde, one of the celebrities of the Opéra. Even that intrigue was of brief duration. Sarrasine was decidedly ugly, always badly dressed, and naturally so independent, so irregular in his private life, that the illustrious nymph, dreading some catastrophe, soon remitted the sculptor to love of the arts. Sophie Arnould made some witty remark on the subject. She was surprised, I think, that her colleague was able to triumph over statues.

"Sarrasine started for Italy in 1758. On the journey his ardent imagination took fire beneath a sky of copper and at sight of the marvellous monuments with which the fatherland of the arts is strewn. He admired the statues, the frescoes, the pictures; and, fired with a spirit of emulation, he went on to Rome, burning to inscribe his name between the names of Michelangelo and Bouchardon. At first, therefore, he divided his time between his studio work and examination of the works of art which abound in Rome. He had already passed a fortnight in the ecstatic state into which all youthful imaginations fall at sight of the queen of ruins, when he happened one evening to enter the Argentina theatre, in front of which there was an enormous crowd. He inquired the reasons for the presence of so great a throng, and every one answered by two names:

"'Zambinella! Jomelli!"

"He entered and took a seat in the pit, crowded between two unconscionably stout *abbati*; but luckily he was quite near the stage. The curtain rose. For the first time in his life he heard the music whose charms Monsieur Jean-Jacques Rousseau had extolled so eloquently at one of Baron d'Holbach's evening parties. The young sculptor's senses were lubricated, so to speak, by Jomelli's harmonious strains. The languorous peculiarities of those skilfully blended Italian voices plunged him in an ecstasy of delight. He sat there, mute and motionless, not even conscious of the crowding of the two priests. His soul poured out through his ears and his eyes. He seemed to be listening with every one of his pores. Suddenly a whirlwind of applause greeted the appearance of the prima donna. She came forward coquettishly to the footlights and courtesied to the audience with infinite grace. The brilliant light, the enthusiasm of a vast multitude, the illusion of the stage, the glamour of a costume which was most attractive for the time, all conspired in that woman's favour. Sarrasine cried aloud with pleasure. He saw before him at that moment the ideal beauty whose perfections he had hitherto sought here and there in nature, taking from one model, often of humble rank, the rounded outline of a shapely leg; from another the contour of the breast; from another her white shoulders; stealing the neck of that young girl, the hands of this woman, and the polished knees of yonder child, but never able to find beneath the cold skies of Paris the rich and satisfying creations of ancient Greece. La Zambinella displayed in her single person, intensely alive and delicate beyond words, all those exquisite proportions of the female form which he had so ardently longed to behold, and of which a sculptor is the most severe and at the same time the most passionate judge. She had an expressive mouth, eyes instinct with love, flesh of dazzling whiteness. And add to these details, which would have filled a painter's soul with rapture, all the marvellous charms of the Venuses worshiped and copied by the chisel of the Greeks. The artist did not tire of admiring the inimitable grace with which the arms were attached to the body, the wonderful roundness of the throat, the graceful curves described by the eyebrows and the nose, and the perfect oval of the face, the purity of its clean-cut lines, and the effect of the thick, drooping lashes which bordered the large and voluptuous eyelids. She was more than a woman; she was a masterpiece! In that unhoped-for creation there was love enough to enrapture all mankind, and beauties calculated to satisfy the most exacting critic.

"Sarrasine devoured with his eyes what seemed to him Pygmalion's statue descended from its pedestal. When La Zambinella sang, he was beside himself. He was cold; then suddenly he felt a fire burning in the secret depths of his being, in what, for lack of a better word, we call the heart. He did not applaud, he said nothing; he felt a mad impulse, a sort of frenzy of the sort that seizes us only at the age when there is a something indefinably terrible and infernal in our desires. Sarrasine longed to rush upon the stage and seize that woman. His strength, increased a hundredfold by a moral depression impossible to describe,—for such phenomena take place in a sphere inaccessible to human observation,—insisted upon manifesting itself with deplorable violence. Looking at him, you would have said that he was a cold, dull man. Renown, science, future, life, prizes, all vanished.

"'To win her love or die!' Such was the sentence Sarrasine pronounced upon himself.

"He was so completely intoxicated that he no longer saw theatre, audience, or actors, no longer heard the music. Nay, more, there was no space between him and La Zambinella; he possessed her; his eyes, fixed steadfastly upon her, took possession of her. An almost diabolical power enabled him to feel the breath of that voice, to inhale the fragrant powder with which her hair was covered, to see the slightest inequalities of her face, to count the blue veins which threaded their way beneath the satiny skin. And that fresh, brisk voice of silvery *timbre*, flexible as a thread to which the faintest breath of air gives form, which it rolls and unrolls, tangles and blows away, that voice attacked his heart so fiercely that he more than once uttered an involuntary exclamation, extorted by the convulsive ecstasy too rarely evoked by human passions. He was soon obliged to leave the theatre. His trembling legs almost refused to bear him. He was prostrated, weak, like a nervous man who has given way to a terrible burst of anger. He had had such exquisite pleasure, or perhaps had suffered so, that his life had flowed away like water from an overturned vessel. He felt a void within him, a sense of goneness like the utter lack of strength which discourages a convalescent just recovering from a serious sickness. Overwhelmed by inexplicable melancholy, he sat down on the steps of a church. There, with his back resting against a pillar, he lost himself in a fit of meditation as confused as a dream. Passion had dealt him a crushing blow. On his return to his apartments he was seized by one of those paroxysms of activity which reveal to us the presence of new principles in our existence. A prey to that first fever of love which resembles pain as much as pleasure, he sought to defeat his impatience and his frenzy by sketching La Zambinella from memory. It was a sort of material meditation. Upon one leaf La Zambinella appeared in that pose, apparently calm and cold, affected by Raphael, Georgione, and all the great painters. On another, she was coyly turning her head as she finished a roulade, and seemed to be listening to herself. Sarrasine drew his mistress in all poses: he drew her unveiled, seated, standing, reclining, chaste, and amorous—interpreting, thanks to the delirious activity of his pencil, all the fanciful ideas which beset our imagination when our thoughts are completely engrossed by a mistress. But his frantic thoughts outran his pencil. He met La Zambinella, spoke to her, entreated her, exhausted a thousand years of life and happiness with her, placing her in all imaginable situations, trying the future with her, so to speak. The next day he sent his servant to hire a box near the stage for the whole season. Then, like all young men of powerful feelings, he exaggerated the difficulties of his undertaking, and gave his passion, for its first pasturage, the joy of being able to admire his mistress without obstacle. The golden age of love, during which we enjoy our own sentiments, and in which we are almost as happy by ourselves, was not likely to last long with Sarrasine. However, events surprised him when he was still under the spell of that springtime hallucination, as naïve as it was voluptuous. In a week he lived a whole lifetime, occupied through the day in moulding the clay with which he succeeded in copying La Zambinella, not withstanding the veils, the skirts, the waists, and the bows of ribbon which concealed her from him. In the evening, installed at an early hour in his box, alone, reclining on a sofa, he made for himself, like a Turk drunk with opium, a happiness as fruitful, as lavish, as he wished. First of all, he familiarised himself gradually with the too intense emotions which his mistress' singing caused him; then he taught his eyes to look at her, and was finally able to contemplate her at his leisure without fearing an explosion of concealed frenzy, like that which had seized him the first day. His passion became more profound as it became more tranquil. But the unsociable sculptor would not allow his solitude, peopled as it was with images, adorned with the fanciful creations of hope, and full of happiness, to be disturbed by his comrades. His love was so intense and so ingenuous, that he had to undergo the innocent scruples with which we are assailed when we love for the first time. As he began to realise that he would soon be required to bestir himself, to intrigue, to ask where La Zambinella lived, to ascertain whether she had a mother, an uncle, a guardian, a family,—in a word, as he reflected upon the methods of seeing her, of speaking to her, he felt that his heart was so swollen with such ambitious ideas, that he postponed those cares until the following day, as happy in his physical sufferings as in his intellectual pleasures."

"But," said Madame de Rochefide, interrupting me, "I see nothing of Marianina or her little old man in all this."

'You see nothing but him!" I cried, as vexed as an author for whom some one has spoiled the effect of a *coup de théâtre.*

"For some days," I resumed after a pause, "Sarrasine had been so faithful in attendance in his box, and his glances expressed such passionate love, that his passion for La Zambinella's voice would have been town-talk in Paris, if the episode had happened here; but in Italy, madame, every one goes to the theatre for his own enjoyment, with all his own passions, with a heartfelt interest which precludes all thought of espionage with opera-glasses. However, the sculptor's frantic admiration could not long escape the notice of the performers, male and female. One evening the Frenchman noticed that they were laughing at him in the wings. It is hard to say what violent measures he might have resorted to, had not La Zambinella come on the stage. She cast at Sarrasine one of those eloquent glances which often say more than women intend. That glance was a complete revelation in itself. Sarrasine was beloved!

"'If it is a mere caprice,' he thought, already accusing his mistress of too great ardour, 'she does not know the sort of domination to which she is about to become subject. Her caprice will last, I trust, as long as my life.'

"At that moment, three light taps on the door of his box attracted the artist's attention. He opened the door. An old woman entered with an air of mystery.

"'Young man,' she said, 'if you wish to be happy, be prudent. Wrap yourself in a cloak, pull a broad-brimmed hat over your eyes, and be on the Rue du Corso, in front of the Hôtel d'Espagne, about ten o'clock to-night."

"'I will be there,' he replied, putting two louis in the duenna's wrinkled hand.

"He rushed from his box, after a sign of intelligence to La Zambinella, who lowered her voluptuous eyelids modestly, like a woman overjoyed to be understood at last. Then he hurried home, in order to borrow from his wardrobe all the charms it could loan him. As he left the theatre, a stranger grasped his arm.

"'Beware, Signor Frenchman,' he said in his ear. 'This is a matter of life and death. Cardinal Cicognara is her protector, and he is no trifler.'

"If a demon had placed the deep pit of hell between Sarrasine and La Zambinella, he would have crossed it with one stride at that moment. Like the horses of the immortal gods described by Homer, the sculptor's love had traversed vast spaces in a twinkling.

"'If death awaited me on leaving the house, I would go the more quickly,' he replied.

"'*Poverino*!' cried the stranger, as he disappeared.

"To talk of danger to a man in love is to sell him pleasure. Sarrasine's valet had never seen his master so painstaking in the matter of dress. His finest sword, a gift from Bouchardon, the bow-knot Clotilde gave him, his coat with gold braid, his waistcoat of cloth of silver, his gold snuff-box, his valuable watch, everything was taken from its place, and he arrayed himself like a maiden about to appear before her first lover. At the appointed hour, drunk with love and boiling over with hope, Sarrasine, his nose buried in his cloak, hurried to the rendezvous appointed by the old woman. She was waiting.

"'You are very late,' she said. 'Come.'

"She led the Frenchman through several narrow streets and stopped in front of a palace of attractive appearance. She knocked; the door opened. She led Sarrasine through a labyrinth of stairways, galleries, and apartments which were lighted only by uncertain gleams of moonlight, and soon reached a door through the cracks of which stole a bright light, and from which came the joyous sound of several voices. Sarrasine was suddenly blinded when, at a word from the old woman, he was admitted to that mysterious apartment and found himself in a salon as brilliantly lighted as it was sumptuously furnished; in the centre stood a bountifully supplied table, laden with inviolable bottles, with laughing decanters whose red facets sparkled merrily. He recognised the singers from the theatre, male and female, mingled with charming women, all ready to begin an artists' spree and waiting only for him. Sarrasine restrained a feeling of displeasure and put a good face on the matter. He had hoped for a dimly lighted chamber, his mistress leaning over a brazier, a jealous rival within two steps, death and love, confidences exchanged in low tones, heart to heart, hazardous kisses, and faces so near together that La Zambinella's hair would have touched caressingly his desire-laden brow, burning with happiness.

"'*Vive la folie!*' he cried. '*Signori e belle donne*, you will allow me to postpone my revenge and bear witness to my gratitude for the welcome you offer a poor sculptor.'

"After receiving congratulations not lacking in warmth from most of those present, whom he knew by sight, he tried to approach the couch on which La Zambinella was nonchalantly reclining. Ah! how his heart beat when he spied a tiny foot in one of those slippers which—if you will allow me to say so, madame—formerly imparted to a woman's feet such a coquettish, voluptuous look that I cannot conceive how men could resist them. Tightly fitting white stockings with green clocks, short skirts, and the pointed, high-heeled slippers of Louis XV's time contributed somewhat, I fancy, to the demoralisation of Europe and the clergy."

"Somewhat!" exclaimed the marchioness. "Have you read nothing, pray?"

"La Zambinella," I continued, smiling, "had boldly crossed her legs, and as she prattled swung the upper one, a duchess' attitude very well suited to her capricious type of beauty, overflowing with a certain attractive suppleness. She had laid aside her stage costume, and wore a waist which outlined a slender figure, displayed to the best advantage by a *panier* and a satin dress embroidered with blue flowers. Her breast, whose treasures were concealed by a coquettish arrangement of lace, was of a gleaming white. Her hair was dressed almost like Madame du Barry's; her face, although overshadowed by a large cap, seemed only the daintier therefore, and the powder was very becoming to her. To see her thus was to adore her. She smiled graciously at the sculptor. Sarrasine, disgusted beyond measure at finding himself unable to speak to her without witnesses, courteously seated himself beside her, and discoursed of music, extolling her prodigious talent; but his voice trembled with love and fear and hope.

"'What do you fear?' queried Vitagliani, the most celebrated singer in the troupe. 'Go on, you have no rival here to fear.'

"After he had said this the tenor smiled silently. The lips of all the guests repeated that smile, in which there was a lurking expression of malice likely to escape a lover. The publicity of his love was like a sudden dagger-thrust in Sarrasine's heart. Although possessed of a certain strength of character, and although nothing that might happen could subdue the violence of his passion, it had not before occurred to him that La Zambinella was almost a courtesan, and that he could not hope to enjoy at one and the same time the pure delights which make a maiden's love so sweet, and the passionate transports with which one must purchase the perilous favours of an actress. He reflected and resigned himself to his fate. The supper was served. Sarrasine and La Zambinella seated themselves side by side without ceremony. During the first half of the feast the artists exercised some restraint, and the sculptor was able to converse with the singer. He found that she was very bright and quick-witted; but she was amazingly ignorant and seemed weak and superstitious. The delicacy of her organs was reproduced in her understanding. When Vitagliani opened the first bottle of champagne, Sarrasine read in his neighbour's eyes a shrinking dread of the report caused by the release of the gas. The involuntary shudder of that thoroughly feminine temperament was interpreted by the amorous artist as indicating extreme delicacy of feeling. This weakness delighted the Frenchman. There is so much of the element of protection in a man's love!

"'You may make use of my power as a shield!'

"Is not that sentence written at the root of all declarations of love? Sarrasine, who was too passionately in love to make fine speeches to the fair Italian, was, like all lovers, grave, jovial, meditative, by turns. Although he seemed to listen to the guests, he did not hear a word that they said, he was so wrapped up in the pleasure of sitting by her side, of touching her hand, of waiting on her. He was swimming in a sea of concealed joy. Despite the eloquence of divers glances they exchanged, he was amazed at La Zambinella's continued reserve toward him. She had begun, it is true, by touching his foot with hers and stimulating his passion with the mischievous pleasure of a woman who is free and in love; but she had suddenly enveloped herself in maidenly modesty, after she had heard Sarrasine relate an incident which illustrated the extreme violence of his temper. When the supper became a debauch, the guests began to sing, inspired by the Peralta and the Pedro-Ximenes. There were fascinating duets, Calabrian ballads, Spanish *sequidillas*, and Neapolitan *canzonettes*. Drunkenness was in all eyes, in the music, in the hearts and voices of the guests. There was a sudden overflow of bewitching vivacity, of cordial unconstraint, of Italian good nature, of which no words can convey an idea to those who know only the evening parties of Paris, the routs of London, or the clubs of Vienna. Jests and words of love flew from side to side like bullets in a battle, amid laughter, impieties, invocations to the Blessed Virgin or the *Bambino.* One man lay on a sofa and fell asleep. A young woman listened to a declaration, unconscious that she was spilling Xeres wine on the tablecloth. Amid all this confusion La Zambinella, as if terror-stricken, seemed lost in thought. She refused to drink, but ate perhaps a little too much; but gluttony is attractive in women, it is said. Sarrasine, admiring his mistress' modesty, indulged in serious reflections concerning the future.

"'She desires to be married, I presume,' he said to himself.

"Thereupon he abandoned himself to blissful anticipations of marriage with her. It seemed to him that his whole life would be too short to exhaust the living spring of happiness which he found in the depths of his heart. Vitagliani, who sat on his other side, filled his glass so often that, about three in the morning, Sarrasine, while not absolutely drunk, was powerless to resist his delirious passion. In a moment of frenzy he seized the woman and carried her to a sort of boudoir which opened from the salon, and toward which he had more than once turned his eyes. The Italian was armed with a dagger.

"'If you come near me,' she said, 'I shall be compelled to plunge this blade into your heart. Go! you would despise me. I have conceived too great a respect for your character to abandon myself to you thus. I do not choose to destroy the sentiment with which you honour me.'

"'Ah!' said Sarrasine, 'to stimulate a passion is a poor way to extinguish it! Are you already so corrupt that, being old in heart, you act like a young prostitute who inflames the emotions in which she trades?'

"'Why, this is Friday,' she replied, alarmed by the Frenchman's violence.

"Sarrasine, who was not piously inclined, began to laugh. La Zambinella gave a bound like a young deer, and darted into the salon. When Sarrasine appeared, running after her, he was welcomed by a roar of infernal laughter. He saw La Zambinella swooning on a sofa. She was very pale, as if exhausted by the extraordinary effort she had made. Although Sarrasine knew but little Italian, he understood his mistress when she said to Vitagliani in a low voice:

"'But he will kill me!'

"This strange scene abashed the sculptor. His reason returned. He stood still for a moment; then he recovered his speech, sat down beside his mistress, and assured her of his profound respect. He found strength to hold his passion in check while talking to her in the most exalted strain; and, to describe his love, he displayed all the treasures of eloquence—that sorcerer, that friendly interpreter, whom women rarely refuse to believe. When the first rays of dawn surprised the boon companions, some woman suggested that they go to Frascati. One and all welcomed with loud applause the idea of passing the day at Villa Ludovisi. Vitagliani went down to hire carriages. Sarrasine had the good fortune to drive La Zambinella in a phaeton. When they had left Rome behind, the merriment of the party, repressed for a moment by the battle they had all been fighting against drowsiness, suddenly awoke. All, men and women alike, seemed accustomed to that strange life, that constant round of pleasures, that artistic energy, which makes of life one never ending *fête*, where laughter reigns, unchecked by fear of the future. The sculptor's companion was the only one who seemed out of spirits.

"'Are you ill?' Sarrasine asked her. 'Would you prefer to go home?'

"'I am not strong enough to stand all this dissipation,' she replied. 'I have to be very careful; but I feel so happy with you! Except for you, I should not have remained to this supper; a night like this takes away all my freshness.'

"'You are so delicate!' rejoined Sarrasine, gazing in rapture at the charming creature's dainty features.

"'Dissipation ruins my voice.'

"'Now that we are alone,' cried the artist, 'and that you no longer have reason to fear the effervescence of my passion, tell me that you love me.'

"'Why?' said she; 'for what good purpose? You think me pretty. But you are a Frenchman, and your fancy will pass away. Ah! you would not love me as I should like to be loved.'

"'How?'

"'Purely, with no mingling of vulgar passion. I abhor men even more, perhaps, than I hate women. I need to take refuge in friendship. The world is a desert to me. I am an accursed creature, doomed to understand happiness, to feel it, to desire it, and like many, many others, compelled to see it always fly from me. Remember, signor, that I have not deceived you. I forbid you to love me. I can be a devoted friend to you, for I admire your strength of will and your character. I need a brother, a protector. Be both of these to me, but nothing more.'

"'And not love you!' cried Sarrasine; 'but you are my life, my happiness, dear angel!'

"'If I should say a word, you would spurn me with horror.'

"'Coquette! nothing can frighten me. Tell me that you will cost me my whole future, that I shall die two months hence, that I shall be damned for having kissed you but once—'

"And he kissed her, despite La Zambinella's efforts to avoid that passionate caress.

"'Tell me that you are a demon, that I must give you my fortune, my name, all my renown! Would you have me cease to be a sculptor? Speak.'

"'Suppose I were not a woman?' queried La Zambinella, timidly, in a sweet, silvery voice.

"'A merry jest!' cried Sarrasine. 'Think you that you can deceive an artist's eye? Have I not, for ten days past, admired, examined, devoured, thy perfections? None but a woman can have this soft and beautifully rounded arm, these graceful outlines. Ah! you seek compliments!'

"She smiled sadly, and murmured:

"'Fatal beauty!'

"She raised her eyes to the sky. At that moment, there was in her eyes an indefinable expression of horror, so startling, so intense, that Sarrasine shuddered.

"'Signor Frenchman,' she continued, 'forget forever a moment's madness. I esteem you, but as for love, do not ask me for that; that sentiment is suffocated in my heart. I have no heart!' she cried, weeping bitterly. 'The stage on which you saw me, the applause, the music, the renown to which I am condemned—those are my life; I have no other. A few hours hence you will no longer look upon me with the same eyes, the woman you love will be dead.'

"The sculptor did not reply. He was seized with a dull rage which contracted his heart. He could do nothing but gaze at that extraordinary woman, with inflamed, burning eyes. That feeble voice, La Zambinella's attitude, manners, and gestures, instinct with dejection, melancholy, and discouragement, reawakened in his soul all the treasures of passion. Each word was a spur. At that moment, they arrived at Frascati. When the artist held out his arms to help his mistress to alight, he felt that she trembled from head to foot.

"'What is the matter? You would kill me,' he cried, seeing that she turned pale, 'if you should suffer the slightest pain of which I am, even innocently, the cause.'

"'A snake!' she said, pointing to a reptile which was gliding along the edge of a ditch. 'I am afraid of the disgusting creatures.'

"Sarrasine crushed the snake's head with a blow of his foot.

"'How could you dare to do it?' said La Zambinella, gazing at the dead reptile with visible terror.

"'Aha!' said the artist, with a smile, 'would you venture to say now that you are not a woman?'

"They joined their companions and walked through the woods of Villa Ludovisi, which at that time belonged to Cardinal Cicognara. The morning passed all too swiftly for the amorous sculptor, but it was crowded with incidents which laid bare to him the coquetry, the weakness, the daintiness, of that pliant, inert soul. She was a true woman with her sudden terrors, her unreasoning caprices, her instinctive worries, her causeless audacity, her bravado, and her fascinating delicacy of feeling. At one time, as the merry little party of singers ventured out into the open country, they saw at some distance a number of men armed to the teeth, whose costume was by no means reassuring. At the words, 'Those are brigands!' they all quickened their pace in order to reach the shelter of the wall enclosing the cardinal's villa. At that critical moment Sarrasine saw from La Zambinella's manner that she no longer had strength to walk; he took her in his arms and carried her for some distance, running. When he was within call of a vineyard near by, he set his mistress down.

"'Tell me,' he said, 'why it is that this extreme weakness, which in another woman would be hideous, would disgust me, so that the slightest indication of it would be enough to destroy my love,—why is it that in you it pleases me, fascinates me? Oh, how I love you!' he continued. 'All your faults, your frights, your petty foibles, add an indescribable charm to your character. I feel that I should detest a Sappho, a strong, courageous woman, overflowing with energy and passion. O sweet and fragile creature! how couldst thou be otherwise? That angel's voice, that refined voice, would have been an anachronism coming from any other breast than thine.'

"'I can give you no hope,' she said. 'Cease to speak thus to me, for people would make sport of you. It is impossible for me to shut the door of the theatre to you; but if you love me, or if you are wise, you will come there no more. Listen to me, monsieur,' she continued in a grave voice.

"'Oh, hush!' said the excited artist. 'Obstacles inflame the love in my heart.'

"La Zambinella maintained a graceful and modest attitude; but she held her peace, as if a terrible thought had suddenly revealed some catastrophe. When it was time to return to Rome she entered a berlin with four seats, bidding the sculptor, with a cruelly imperious air, to return alone in the phaeton. On the road, Sarrasine determined to carry off La Zambinella. He passed the whole day forming plans, each more extravagant than the last. At nightfall, as he was going out to inquire of somebody where his mistress lived, he met one of his fellow-artists at the door.

"'My dear fellow,' he said, 'I am sent by our ambassador to invite you to come to the embassy this evening. He gives a magnificent concert, and when I tell you that La Zambinella will be there—'

"'Zambinella!' cried Sarrasine, thrown into delirium by that name; 'I am mad with love of her.'

"'You are like everybody else,' replied his comrade.

"'But if you are friends of mine, you and Vien and Lauterbourg and Allegrain, you will lend me your assistance for a *coup de main* after the entertainment, will you not?' asked Sarrasine.

"'There's no cardinal to be killed? no—?'

"'No, no!' said Sarrasine, 'I ask nothing of you that men of honour may not do.'

"In a few moments the sculptor laid all his plans to assure the success of his enterprise. He was one of the last to arrive at the ambassador's, but he went thither in a travelling carriage drawn by four stout horses and driven by one of the most skilful *vetturini* in Rome. The ambassador's palace was full of people; not without difficulty did the sculptor, whom nobody knew, make his way to the salon where La Zambinella was singing at that moment.

"'It must be in deference to all the cardinals, bishops, and *abbés* who are here,' said Sarrasine, 'that *she* is dressed as a man, that *she* has curly hair which she wears in a bag, and that *she* has a sword at her side?'

"'She! what she?' rejoined the old nobleman whom Sarrasine addressed.

"'La Zambinella.'

"'La Zambinella!' echoed the Roman prince. 'Are you jesting? Whence have you come? Did a woman ever appear in a Roman theatre? And do you not know what sort of creatures play female parts within the domains of the Pope? It was I, monsieur, who endowed Zambinella with his voice. I paid all the knave's expenses, even his teacher in singing. And he has so little gratitude for the service I have done him that he has never been willing to step inside my house. And yet, if he makes his fortune, he will owe it all to me.'

"Prince Chigi might have talked on forever, Sarrasine did not listen to him. A ghastly truth had found its way into his mind. He was stricken as if by a thunderbolt. He stood like a statue, his eyes fastened on the singer. His flaming glance exerted a sort of magnetic influence on Zambinella, for he turned his eyes at last in Sarrasine's direction, and his divine voice faltered. He trembled! An involuntary murmur escaped the audience, which he held fast as if fastened to his lips; and that completely disconcerted him; he stopped in the middle of the aria he was singing and sat down. Cardinal Cicognara, who had watched from the corner of his eye the direction of his *protégé*'s glance, saw the Frenchman; he leaned toward one of his ecclesiastical aides-de-camp, and apparently asked the sculptor's name. When he had obtained the reply he desired he scrutinised the artist with great attention and gave orders to an *abbé,* who instantly disappeared. Meanwhile Zambinella, having recovered his self-possession, resumed the aria he had so capriciously broken off; but he sang badly, and refused, despite all the persistent appeals showered upon him, to sing anything else. It was the first time he had exhibited that humoursome tyranny, which, at a later date, contributed no less to his celebrity than his talent and his vast fortune, which was said to be due to his beauty as much as to his voice.

"'It's a woman,' said Sarrasine, thinking that no one could overhear him. 'There's some secret intrigue beneath all this. Cardinal Cicognara is hoodwinking the Pope and the whole city of Rome!'

"The sculptor at once left the salon, assembled his friends, and lay in wait in the courtyard of the palace. When Zambinella was assured of Sarrasine's departure he seemed to recover his tranquillity in some measure. About midnight, after wandering through the salons like a man looking for an enemy, the *musico* left the party. As he passed through the palace gate he was seized by men who deftly gagged him with a handkerchief and placed him in the carriage hired by Sarrasine. Frozen with terror, Zambinella lay back in a corner, not daring to move a muscle. He saw before him the terrible face of the artist, who maintained a deathlike silence. The journey was a short one. Zambinella, kidnapped by Sarrasine, soon found himself in a dark, bare studio. He sat, half dead, upon a chair; hardly daring to glance at a statue of a woman, in which he recognised his own features. He did not utter a word, but his teeth were chattering; he was paralysed with fear. Sarrasine was striding up and down the studio. Suddenly he halted in front of Zambinella.

"'Tell me the truth,' he said, in a changed and hollow voice. 'Are you not a woman? Cardinal Cicognara—'

"Zambinella fell on his knees, and replied only by banging his head.

"'Ah! you are a woman!' cried the artist in a frenzy; 'for even a—'

"He did not finish the sentence.

"'No,' he continued, 'even *he* could not be so utterly base.'

"'Oh, do not kill me!' cried Zambinella, bursting into tears. 'I consented to deceive you only to gratify my comrades, who wanted an opportunity to laugh.'

"'Laugh!' echoed the sculptor, in a voice in which there was a ring of infernal ferocity. 'Laugh! laugh! You dared to make sport of a man's passion—you?'

"'Oh, mercy!' cried Zambinella.

"'I ought to kill you!' shouted Sarrasine, drawing his sword in an outburst of rage. 'But,' he continued, with cold disdain, 'if I searched your whole being with this blade, should I find there any sentiment to blot out, anything with which to satisfy my thirst for vengeance? You are nothing! If you were a man or a woman, I would kill you, but—'

"Sarrasine made a gesture of disgust, and turned his face away; thereupon he noticed the statue.

"'And that is a delusion!' he cried.

"Then, turning to Zambinella once more, he continued:

"'A woman's heart was to me a place of refuge, a fatherland. Have you sisters who resemble you? No. Then die! But no, you shall live. To leave you your life is to doom you to a fate worse than death. I regret neither my blood nor my life, but my future and the fortune of my heart. Your weak hand has overturned my happiness. What hope can I extort from you in place of all those you have destroyed? You have brought me down to your level. *To love, to be loved!* are henceforth meaningless words to me; as to you. I shall never cease to think of that imaginary woman when I see a real woman.'

"He pointed to the statue with a gesture of despair.

"'I shall always have in my memory a divine harpy who will bury her talons in all my manly sentiments, and who will stamp all other women with a seal of imperfection. Monster! you, who can give life to nothing, have swept all women off the face of the earth.'

"Sarrasine seated himself in front of the terrified singer. Two great tears came from his dry eyes, rolled down his swarthy cheeks, and fell to the floor—two tears of rage, two scalding, burning tears.

"'An end of love! I am dead to all pleasure, to all human emotions!'

"As he spoke, he seized a hammer and hurled it at the statue with such excessive force that he missed it. He thought that he had destroyed that monument of his madness, and thereupon he drew his sword again, and raised it to kill the singer. Zambinella uttered shriek after shriek. Three men burst into the studio at that moment, and the sculptor fell, pierced by three daggers.

"'From Cardinal Cicognara,' said one of the men.

"'A benefaction worthy of a Christian,' retorted the Frenchman, as he breathed his last.

"These ominous emissaries told Zambinella of the anxiety of his patron, who was waiting at the door in a closed carriage in order to take him away as soon as he was set at liberty."

"But," said Madame de Rochefide, "what connection is there between this story and the little old man we saw at the Lantys'?"

"Madame, Cardinal Cicognara took possession of Zambinella's statue and had it reproduced in marble; it is in the Albani Museum to-day. In 1794 the Lanty family discovered it there, and asked to copy it. The portrait which showed you Zambinella at twenty, a moment after you had seen him as a centenarian, afterward figured in Girodet's *Endymion*; you yourself recognised the type in *Adonis*."

"But this Zambinella, male or female—"

"Must be, madame, Marianina's maternal great uncle. You can conceive now Madame de Lanty's interest in concealing the source of a fortune which comes—"

"Enough!" said she, with an imperious gesture.

We remained for a moment in the most profound silence.

"Well?" I said at last.

"Ah!" she cried, rising and pacing the floor.

She came and looked me in the face, and said in an altered voice:

"You have disgusted me with life and passion for a long time to come. Leaving monstrosities aside, are not all human sentiments dissolved thus, by ghastly disillusionment? Children torture mothers by their bad conduct, or their lack of affection. Wives are betrayed. Mistresses are cast aside, abandoned. Talk of friendship! Is there such a thing! I would turn pious to-morrow if I did not know that I can remain like the inaccessible summit of a cliff amid the tempests of life. If the future of the Christian is an illusion too, at all events it is not destroyed until after death. Leave me to myself."

"Ah!" said I, "you know how to punish."

"Am I in the wrong?"

"Yes," I replied, with a sort of desperate courage. "By finishing this story, which is well known in Italy, I can give you an excellent idea of the progress made by the civilisation of the present day. There are none of those wretched creatures now."

."Paris," said she, "is an exceedingly hospitable place; it welcomes one and all, fortunes stained with shame, and fortunes stained with blood. Crime and infamy have a right of asylum here; virtue alone is without altars. But pure hearts have a fatherland in heaven! No one will have known me! I am proud of it."

And the marchioness was lost in thought.

1. *Macédoine*, in the sense in which it is here used, is a game, or rather a series of games, of cards, each player, when it is his turn to deal, selecting the game to be played.

FACINO CANE

I ONCE used to live in a little street which probably is not known to you—the Rue de Lesdiguières. It is a turning out of the Rue Saint-Antoine, beginning just opposite a fountain near the Place de la Bastille, and ending in the Rue de la Cerisaie. Love of knowledge stranded me in a garret; my nights I spent in work, my days in reading at the Bibliothèque d'Orléans, close by. I lived frugally, I had accepted the conditions of the monastic life, necessary conditions for every worker, scarcely permitting myself a walk along the Boulevard Bourdon when the weather was fine. One passion only had power to draw me from my studies; and yet, what was that passion but a study of another kind? I used to watch the manners and customs of the Faubourg, its inhabitants, and their characteristics. As I dressed no better than a working man, and cared nothing for appearances, I did not put them on their guard; I could join a group and look on while they drove bargains or wrangled among themselves on their way home from work. Even then observation had come to be an instinct with me; a faculty of penetrating to the soul without neglecting the body; or rather, a power of grasping external details so thoroughly that they never detained me for a moment, and at once I passed beyond and through them. I could enter into the life of the human creatures whom I watched, just as the dervish in the *Arabian Nights* could pass into any soul or body after pronouncing a certain formula.

If I met a working man and his wife in the streets between eleven o'clock and midnight on their way home from the Ambigu Comique, I used to amuse myself by following them from the Boulevard du Pont aux Choux to the Boulevard Beaumarchais. The good folk would begin by talking about the play; then from one thing to another they would come to their own affairs, and the mother would walk on and on, heedless of complaints or question from the little one that dragged at her hand, while she and her husband reckoned up the wages to be paid on the morrow, and spent the money in a score of different ways. Then came domestic details, lamentations over the excessive dearness of potatoes, or the length of the winter and the high price of block fuel, together with forcible representations of amounts owing to the baker, ending in an acrimonious dispute, in the course of which such couples reveal their characters in picturesque language. As I listened, I could make their lives mine, I felt their rags on my back, I walked with their gaping shoes on my feet; their cravings, their needs, had all passed into my soul, or my soul had passed into theirs. It was the dream of a waking man. I waxed hot with them over the foreman's tyranny, or the bad customers that made them call again and again for payment.

To come out of my own ways of life, to be another than myself through a kind of intoxication of the intellectual faculties, and to play this game at will, such was my recreation. Whence comes the gift? Is it a kind of second sight? Is it one of those powers which when abused end in madness? I have never tried to discover its source; I possess it, I use it, that is all. But this it behoves you to know, that in those days I began to resolve the heterogeneous mass known as the People into its elements, and to evaluate its good and bad qualities. Even then I realised the possibilities of my suburb, that hotbed of revolution in which heroes, inventors, and practical men of science, rogues and scoundrels, virtues and vices, were all packed together by poverty, stifled by necessity, drowned in drink, and consumed by ardent spirits.

You would not imagine how many adventures, how many tragedies, lie buried away out of sight in that Dolorous City; how much horror and beauty lurks there. No imagination can reach the Truth, no one can go down into that city to make discoveries; for one must needs descend too low into its depths to see the wonderful scenes of tragedy or comedy enacted there, the masterpieces brought forth by chance.

I do not know how it is that I have kept the following story so long untold. It is one of the curious things that stop in the bag from which Memory draws out stories at haphazard, like numbers in a lottery. There are plenty of tales just as strange and just as well hidden still left; but some day, you may be sure, their turn will come.

One day my charwoman, a working man's wife, came to beg me to honour her sister's wedding with my presence. If you are to realise what this wedding was like, you must know that I paid my charwoman, poor creature, four francs a month; for which sum she came every morning to make my bed, clean my shoes, brush my clothes, sweep the room, and make ready my breakfast, before going to her day's work of turning the handle of a machine, at which hard drudgery she earned five-pence. Her husband, a cabinetmaker, made four francs a day at his trade; but as they had three children, it was all that they could do to gain an honest living. Yet I have never met with more sterling honesty than in this man and wife. For five years after I left the quarter, Mère Vaillant used to come on my birthday with a bunch of flowers and some oranges for me—she that had never a sixpence to put by! Want had drawn us together. I never could give her more than a ten-franc piece, and often I had to borrow the money for the occasion. This will perhaps explain my promise to go to the wedding; I hoped to efface myself in these poor people's merry-making.

The banquet and the ball were given on a first floor above a wineshop in the Rue de Charenton. It was a large room, lighted by oil lamps with tin reflectors. A row of wooden benches ran round the walls, which were black with grime to the height of the tables. Here some eighty persons, all in their Sunday best, tricked out with ribbons and bunches of flowers, all of them on pleasure bent, were dancing away with heated visages as if the world were about to come to an end. Bride and bridegroom exchanged salutes to the general satisfaction, amid a chorus of facetious "Oh, ohs!" and "Ah, ahs!" less really indecent than the furtive glances of young girls that have been well brought up. There was something indescribably infectious about the rough, homely enjoyment in all countenances.

But neither the faces, nor the wedding, nor the wedding-guests have anything to do with my story. Simply bear them in mind as the odd setting to it. Try to realise the scene, the shabby red-painted wineshop, the smell of wine, the yells of merriment; try to feel that you are really in the faubourg, among old people, working men and poor women giving themselves up to a night's enjoyment.

The band consisted of a fiddle, a clarionet, and a flageolet from the Blind Asylum. The three were paid seven francs in a lump sum for the night. For the money, they gave us, not Beethoven certainly, nor yet Rossini; they played as they had the will and the skill; and every one in the room (with charming delicacy of feeling) refrained from finding fault. The music made such a brutal assault on the drum of my ear, that after a first glance round the room my eyes fell at once upon the blind trio, and the sight of their uniform inclined me from the first to indulgence. As the artists stood in a window recess, it was difficult to distinguish their faces except at close quarters, and I kept away at first; but when I came nearer (I hardly know why) I thought of nothing else; the wedding party and the music ceased to exist, my curiosity was roused to the highest pitch, for my soul passed into the body of the clarionet player.

The fiddle and the flageolet were neither of them interesting; their faces were of the ordinary type among the blind—earnest, attentive, and grave. Not so the clarionet player; any artist or philosopher must have come to a stop at the sight of him.

Picture to yourself a plaster mask of Dante in the red lamplight, with a forest of silver-white hair above the brows. Blindness intensified the expression of bitterness and sorrow in that grand face of his; the dead eyes were lighted up, as it were, by a thought within that broke forth like a burning flame, lit by one sole insatiable desire, written large in vigorous characters upon an arching brow scored across with as many lines as an old stone wall.

The old man was playing at random, without the slightest regard for time or tune. His fingers travelled mechanically over the worn keys of his instrument; he did not trouble himself over a false note now and again (a canard, in the language of the orchestra), neither did the dancers, nor, for that matter, did my old Italian's acolytes; for I had made up my mind that he must be an Italian, and an Italian he was. There was something great, something too of the despot about this old Homer bearing within him an Odyssey doomed to oblivion. The greatness was so real that it triumphed over his abject position; the despotism so much a part of him, that it rose above his poverty.

There are violent passions which drive a man to good or evil, making of him a hero or a convict; of these there was not one that had failed to leave its traces on the grandly-hewn, lividly Italian face. You trembled lest a flash of thought should suddenly light up the deep sightless hollows under the grizzled brows, as you might fear to see brigands with torches and poniards in the mouth of a cavern. You felt that there was a lion in that cage of flesh, a lion spent with useless raging against iron bars. The fires of despair had burned themselves out into ashes, the lava had cooled; but the tracks of the flames, the wreckage, and a little smoke remained to bear witness to the violence of the eruption, the ravages of the fire. These images crowded up at the sight of the clarionet player, till the thoughts now grown cold in his face burned hot within my soul.

The fiddle and the flageolet took a deep interest in bottles and glasses; at the end of a country-dance, they hung their instruments from a button on their reddish-coloured coats, and stretched out their hands to a little table set in the window recess to hold their liquor supply. Each time they did so they held out a full glass to the Italian, who could not reach it for himself because he sat in front of the table, and each time the Italian thanked them with a friendly nod. All their movements were made with the precision which always amazes you so much at the Blind Asylum. You could almost think that they can see. I came nearer to listen; but when I stood beside them, they evidently guessed I was not a working man, and kept themselves to themselves.

"What part of the world do you come from, you that are playing the clarionet?"

"From Venice," he said, with a trace of Italian accent.

"Have you always been blind, or did it come on afterwards?"

"Afterwards," he answered quickly. "A cursed gutta serena."

"Venice is a fine city; I have always had a fancy to go there."

The old man's face lighted up, the wrinkles began to work, he was violently excited.

"If I went with you, you would not lose your time," he said.

"Don't talk about Venice to our Doge," put in the fiddle, "or you will start him off, and he has stowed away a couple of bottles as it is—has the prince!"

"Come, strike up, Daddy Canard!" added the flageolet, and the three began to play. But while they executed the four figures of a square dance, the Venetian was scenting my thoughts; he guessed the great interest I felt in him. The dreary, dispirited look died out of his face, some mysterious hope brightened his features and slid like a blue flame over his wrinkles. He smiled and wiped his brow, that fearless, terrible brow of his, and at length grew gay like a man mounted on his hobby.

"How old are you?" I asked.

"Eighty-two."

"How long have you been blind?"

"For very nearly fifty years," he said, and there was that in his tone which told me that his regret was for something more than his lost sight, for great power of which he had been robbed.

"Then why do they call you 'the Doge'?" I asked.

"Oh, it is a joke. I am a Venetian noble, and I might have been a doge like any one else."

"What is your name?"

"Here, in Paris, I am Père Canet," he said. "It was the only way of spelling my name on the register. But in Italy I am Marco Facino Cane, Prince of Varese."

"What, are you descended from the great *condottiere* Facino Cane, whose lands won by the sword were taken by the Dukes of Milan?"

"*E vero*," returned he. "His son's life was not safe under the Visconti; he fled to Venice, and his name was inscribed on the Golden Book. And now neither Cane nor Golden Book are in existence." His gesture startled me; it told of patriotism extinguished and weariness of life.

"But if you were once a Venetian senator, you must have been a wealthy man. How did you lose your fortune?"

"In evil days."

He waved away the glass of wine handed to him by the flageolet, and bowed his head. He had no heart to drink. These details were not calculated to extinguish my curiosity.

As the three ground out the music of the square dance, I gazed at the old Venetian noble, thinking thoughts that set a young man's mind afire at the age of twenty. I saw Venice and the Adriatic; I saw her ruin in the ruin of the face before me. I walked to and fro in that city, so beloved of her citizens; I went from the Rialto Bridge, along the Grand Canal, and from the Riva degli Schiavoni to the Lido, returning to St. Mark's, that cathedral so unlike all others in its sublimity. I looked up at the windows of the Casa Doro, each with its different sculptured ornaments; I saw old palaces rich in marbles, saw all the wonders which a student beholds with the more sympathetic eyes because visible things take their colour of his fancy, and the sight of realities cannot rob him of the glory of his dreams. Then I traced back a course of life for this latest scion of a race of *condottieri*, tracking down his misfortunes, looking for the reasons of the deep moral and physical degradation out of which the lately revived sparks of greatness and nobility shone so much the more brightly. My ideas, no doubt, were passing through his mind, for all processes of thought-communications are far more swift, I think, in blind people, because their blindness compels them to concentrate their attention. I had not long to wait for proof that we were in sympathy in this way. Facino Cane left off playing, and came up to me. "Let us go out!" he said; his tones thrilled through me like an electric shock. I gave him my arm, and we went.

Outside in the street he said, "Will you take me back to Venice? will you be my guide? Will you put faith in me? You shall be richer than ten of the richest houses in Amsterdam or London, richer than Rothschild; in short, you shall have the fabulous wealth of the *Arabian Nights.*"

The man was mad, I thought; but in his voice there was a potent something which I obeyed. I allowed him to lead, and he went in the direction of the Fossés de la Bastille, as if he could see; walking till he reached a lonely spot down by the river, just where the bridge has since been built at the junction of the Canal Saint-Martin and the Seine. Here he sat down on a stone, and I, sitting opposite to him, saw the old man's hair gleaming like threads of silver in the moonlight. The stillness was scarcely troubled by the sound of the far-off thunder of traffic along the boulevards; the clear night air and everything about us combined to make a strangely unreal scene.

"You talk of millions to a young man," I began, "and do you think that he will shrink from enduring any number of hardships to gain them? Are you not laughing at me?"

"May I die unshriven," he cried vehemently, "if all that I am about to tell you is not true. I was one-and-twenty years old, like you at this moment. I was rich, I was handsome, and a noble by birth. I began with the first madness of all—with Love. I loved as no one can love nowadays. I have hidden myself in a chest, at the risk of a dagger thrust, for nothing more than the promise of a kiss. To die for Her—it seemed to me to be a whole life in itself. In 1760 I fell in love with a lady of the Vendramin family; she was eighteen years old, and married to a Sagredo, one of the richest senators, a man of thirty, madly in love with his wife. My mistress and I were guiltless as cherubs when the *sposo* caught us together talking of love. He was armed, I was not, but he missed me; I sprang upon him and killed him with my two hands, wringing his neck as if he had been a chicken. I wanted Bianca to fly with me; but she would not. That is the way with women! So I went alone. I was condemned to death, and my property was confiscated and made over to my next-of-kin; but I had carried off my diamonds, five of Titian's pictures taken down from their frames and rolled up, and all my gold.

"I went to Milan, no one molested me, my affair in nowise interested the State.—One small observation before I go further," he continued, after a pause, "whether it is true or no that the mother's fancies at the time of conception or in the months before birth can influence her child, this much is certain, my mother during her pregnancy had a passion for gold, and I am the victim of a monomania, of a craving for gold which must be gratified. Gold is so much of a necessity of life for me, that I have never been without it; I must have gold to toy with and finger. As a young man I always wore jewellery, and carried two or three hundred ducats about with me wherever I went."

He drew a couple of gold coins from his pocket and showed them to me as he spoke.

"I can tell by instinct when gold is near. Blind as I am, I stop before the jeweller's shop windows. That passion was the ruin of me; I took to gambling to play with gold. I was not a cheat, I was cheated, I ruined myself. I lost all my fortune. Then the longing to see Bianca once more possessed me like a frenzy. I stole back to Venice and found her again. For six months I was happy; she hid me in her house and fed me. I thought thus deliciously to finish my days. But the Provveditore courted her, and guessed that he had a rival; we in Italy can feel that. He played the spy upon us, and surprised us together in bed, base wretch. You may judge what a fight for life it was; I did not kill him outright, but I wounded him dangerously.

"That adventure broke my luck. I have never found another Bianca; I have known great pleasures; but among the most celebrated women at the court of Louis XV I never found my beloved Venetian's charm, her love, her great qualities.

"The Provveditore called his servants, the palace was surrounded and entered; I fought for my life that I might die beneath Bianca's eyes; Bianca helped me to kill the Provveditore. Once before she had refused flight with me; but after six months of happiness she wished only to die with me, and received several thrusts. I was entangled in a great cloak that they flung over me, carried down to a gondola, and hurried to the Pozzi dungeons. I was twenty-two years old. I gripped the hilt of my broken sword so hard, that they could only have taken it from me by cutting off my hand at the wrist. A curious chance, or rather the instinct of self-preservation, led me to hide the fragment of the blade in a corner of my cell, as if it might still be of use. They tended me; none of my wounds were serious. At two-and-twenty one can recover from anything. I was to lose my head on the scaffold. I shammed illness to gain time. It seemed to me that the canal lay just outside my cell. I thought to make my escape by boring a hole through the wall and swimming for my life. I based my hopes on the following reasons.

"Every time that the jailer came with my food, there was light enough to read directions written on the walls— 'Side of the Palace,' 'Side of the Canal,' 'Side of the Vaults.' At last I saw a design in this, but I did not trouble myself much about the meaning of it; the actual incomplete condition of the Ducal Palace accounted for it. The longing to regain my freedom gave me something like genius. Groping about with my fingers, I spelled out an Arabic inscription on the wall. The author of the work informed those to come after him that he had loosed two stones in the lowest course of masonry and hollowed out eleven feet beyond underground. As he went on with his excavations, it became necessary to spread the fragments of stone and mortar over the floor of his cell. But even if jailers and inquisitors had not felt sure that the structure of the buildings was such that no watch was needed below, the level of the Pozzi dungeons being several steps below the threshold, it was possible gradually to raise the earthen floor without exciting the warder's suspicions.

"The tremendous labour had profited nothing—nothing at least to him that began it. The very fact that it was left unfinished told of the unknown worker's death. Unless his devoted toil was to be wasted for ever, his successor must have some knowledge of Arabic, but I had studied Oriental languages at the Armenian Convent. A few words written on the back of the stone recorded the unhappy man's fate; he had fallen a victim to his great possessions; Venice had coveted his wealth and seized upon it. A whole month went by before I obtained any result; but whenever I felt my strength failing as I worked, I heard the chink of gold, I saw gold spread before me, I was dazzled by diamonds.—Ah! wait.

"One night my blunted steel struck on wood. I whetted the fragment of my blade and cut a hole; I crept on my belly like a serpent; I worked naked and mole-fashion, my hands in front of me, using the stone itself to gain a purchase. I was to appear before my judges in two days' time, I made a final effort, and that night I bored through the wood and felt that there was space beyond.

"Judge of my surprise when I applied my eye to the hole. I was in the ceiling of a vault, heaps of gold were dimly visible in the faint light. The Doge himself and one of the Ten stood below; I could hear their voices and sufficient of their talk to know that this was the Secret Treasury of the Republic, full of the gifts of Doges and reserves of booty called the Tithe of Venice from the spoils of military expeditions. I was saved!

"When the jailer came I proposed that he should help me to escape and fly with me, and that we should take with us as much as we could carry. There was no reason for hesitation; he agreed. Vessels were about to sail for the Levant. All possible precautions were taken. Bianca furthered the schemes which I suggested to my accomplice. It was arranged that Bianca should only rejoin us in Smyrna for fear of exciting suspicion. In a single night the hole was enlarged, and we dropped down into the Secret Treasury of Venice.

"What a night that was! Four great casks full of gold stood there. In the outer room silver pieces were piled in heaps, leaving a gangway between by which to cross the chamber. Banks of silver coins surrounded the walls to the height of five feet.

"I thought the jailer would go mad. He sang and laughed and danced and capered among the gold, till I threatened to strangle him if he made a sound or wasted time. In his joy he did not notice at first the table where the diamonds lay. I flung myself upon these, and deftly filled the pockets of my sailor jacket and trousers with the stones. Ah! Heaven, I did not take the third of them. Gold ingots lay underneath the table. I persuaded my companion to fill as many bags as we could carry with the gold, and made him understand that this was our only chance of escaping detection abroad.

"'Pearls, rubies, and diamonds might be recognised,' I told him.

"Covetous though we were, we could not possibly take more than two thousand livres weight of gold, which meant six journeys across the prison to the gondola. The sentinel at the water gate was bribed with a bag containing ten livres weight of gold; and as for the two gondoliers, they believed they were serving the Republic. At daybreak we set out.

"Once upon the open sea, when I thought of that night, when I recollected all that I had felt, when the vision of that great hoard rose before my eyes, and I computed that I had left behind thirty millions in silver, twenty in gold, and many more in diamonds, pearls, and rubies—then a sort of madness began to work in me. I had the gold fever.

"We landed at Smyrna and took ship at once for France. As we went on board the French vessel, Heaven favoured me by ridding me of my accomplice. I did not think at the time of all the possible consequences of this mishap, and rejoiced not a little. We were so completely unnerved by all that had happened, that we were stupid, we said not a word to each other, we waited till it should be safe to enjoy ourselves at our ease. It was not wonderful that the rogue's head was dizzy. You shall see how heavily God has punished me.

"I never knew a quiet moment until I had sold two-thirds of my diamonds in London or Amsterdam, and held the value of my gold dust in a negotiable shape. For five years I hid myself in Madrid, then in 1770 I came to Paris with a Spanish name, and led as brilliant a life as may be. Then in the midst of my pleasures, as I enjoyed a fortune of six millions, I was smitten with blindness. I do not doubt but that my infirmity was brought on by my sojourn in the cell and my work in the stone, if, indeed, my peculiar faculty for 'seeing' gold was not an abuse of the power of sight which predestined me to lose it. Bianca was dead.

"At this time I had fallen in love with a woman to whom I thought to link my fate. I had told her the secret of my name; she belonged to a powerful family; she was a friend of Mme. du Barry; I hoped everything from the favour shown me by Louis XV; I trusted in her. Acting on her advice, I went to England to consult a famous oculist, and after a stay of several months in London she deserted me in Hyde Park. She had stripped me of all that I had, and left me without resource. Nor could I make complaint, for to disclose my name was to lay myself open to the vengeance of my native city; I could appeal to no one for aid, I feared Venice. The woman put spies about me to exploit my infirmity. I spare you a tale of adventures worthy of Gil Blas.—Your Revolution followed. For two whole years that creature kept me at the Bicêtre as a lunatic, then she gained admittance for me at the Blind Asylum; there was no help for it, I went. I could not kill her; I could not see; and I was so poor that I could not pay another arm.

"If only I had taken counsel with my jailer, Benedetto Carpi, before I lost him, I might have known the exact position of my cell, I might have found my way back to the Treasury and returned to Venice when Napoleon crushed the Republic—

"Still, blind as I am, let us go back to Venice! I shall find the door of my prison, I shall see the gold through the prison walls, I shall hear it where it lies under the water; for the events which brought about the fall of Venice befell in such a way that the secret of the hoard must have perished with Bianca's brother, Vendramin, a doge to whom I looked to make my peace with the Ten. I sent memorials to the First Consul; I proposed an agreement with the Emperor of Austria; every one sent me about my business for a lunatic. Come! we will go to Venice; let us set out as beggars, we shall come back millionaires. We will buy back my estates, and you shall be my heir! You shall be Prince of Varese!"

My head was swimming. For me his confidences reached the proportions of tragedy; at the sight of that white head of his and beyond it the black water in the trenches of the Bastille lying still as a canal in Venice, I had no words to answer him. Facino Cane thought, no doubt, that I judged him, as the rest had done, with a disdainful pity; his gesture expressed the whole philosophy of despair.

Perhaps his story had taken him back to happy days and to Venice. He caught up his clarionet and made plaintive music, playing a Venetian boat-song with something of his lost skill, the skill of the young patrician lover. It was a sort of *Super flumina Babylonis.* Tears filled my eyes. Any belated persons walking along the Boulevard Bourdon must have stood still to listen to an exile's last prayer, a last cry of regret for a lost name, mingled with memories of Bianca. But gold soon gained the upper hand, the fatal passion quenched the light of youth.

"I see it always," he said; "dreaming or waking, I see it; and as I pace to and fro, I pace in the Treasury, and the diamonds sparkle. I am not as blind as you think; gold and diamonds light up my night, the night of the last Facino Cane, for my title passes to the Memmi. My God! the murderer's punishment was not long delayed! *Ave Maria,*" and he repeated several prayers that I did not heed.

"We will go to Venice!" I said, when he rose.

"Then I have found a man!" he cried, with his face on fire.

I gave him my arm and went home with him. We reached the gates of the Blind Asylum just as some of the wedding guests were returning along the street, shouting at the top of their voices. He squeezed my hand.

"Shall we start to-morrow?" he asked.

"As soon as we can get some money."

"But we can go on foot. I will beg. I am strong, and you feel young when you see gold before you."

Facino Cane died before the winter was out after a two months' illness. The poor man had taken a chill.

PARIS, *March* 1836.

Z. MARCAS

To His Highness Count William of Wurtemberg, as a token of the Author's respectful gratitude.

De Balzac.

I NEVER saw anybody, not even among the most remarkable men of the day, whose appearance was so striking as this man's; the study of his countenance at first gave me a feeling of great melancholy, and at last produced an almost painful impression.

There was a certain harmony between the man and his name. The Z preceding Marcas, which was seen on the addresses of his letters, and which he never omitted from his signature, as the last letter of the alphabet, suggested some mysterious fatality.

MARCAS! say this two-syllabled name again and again; do you not feel as if it had some sinister meaning? Does it not seem to you that its owner must be doomed to martyrdom? Though foreign, savage, the name has a right to be handed down to posterity; it is well constructed, easily pronounced, and has the brevity that beseems a famous name. Is it not pleasant as well as odd? But does it not sound unfinished?

I will not take it upon myself to assert that names have no influence on the destiny of men. There is a certain secret and inexplicable concord or a visible discord between the events of a man's life and his name which is truly surprising; often some remote but very real correlation is revealed. Our globe is round; everything is linked to everything else. Some day perhaps we shall revert to the occult sciences.

Do you not discern in that letter Z an adverse influence? Does it not prefigure the wayward and fantastic progress of a storm-tossed life? What wind blew on that letter, which, whatever language we find it in, begins scarcely fifty words? Marcas' name was Zephirin; Saint Zephirin is highly venerated in Brittany, and Marcas was a Breton.

Study the name once more: Z. Marcas! The man's whole life lies in this fantastic juxtaposition of seven letters; seven! the most significant of all the cabalistic numbers. And he died at five-and-thirty, so his life extended over seven lustres.

Marcas! Does it not hint of some precious object that is broken with a fall, with or without a crash?

I had finished studying the law in Paris in 1836. I lived at that time in the Rue Corneille in a house where none but students came to lodge, one of those large houses where there is a winding staircase quite at the back, lighted below from the street, higher up by borrowed lights, and at the top by a skylight. There were forty furnished rooms—furnished as students' rooms are! What does youth demand more than was here supplied? A bed, a few chairs, a chest of drawers, a looking-glass, and a table. As soon as the sky is blue the student opens his window.

But in this street there are no fair neighbors to flirt with. In front is the Odéon, long since closed, presenting a wall that is beginning to go black, its tiny gallery windows and its vast expanse of slate roof. I was not rich enough to have a good room; I was not even rich enough to have a room to myself. Juste and I shared a double-bedded room on the fifth floor.

On our side of the landing there were but two rooms—ours and a smaller one, occupied by Z. Marcas, our neighbour. For six months Juste and I remained in perfect ignorance of the fact. The old woman who managed the house had indeed told us that the room was inhabited, but she had added that we should not be disturbed, that the occupant was exceedingly quiet. In fact, for those six months, we never met our fellow-lodger, and we never heard a sound in his room, in spite of the thinness of the partition that divided us—one of those walls of lath and plaster which are common in Paris houses.

Our room, a little over seven feet high, was hung with a vile cheap paper sprigged with blue. The floor was painted, and knew nothing of the polish given by the *frotteur*'s brush. By our beds there was only a scrap of thin carpet. The chimney opened immediately to the roof, and smoked so abominably that we were obliged to provide a stove at our own expense. Our beds were mere painted wooden cribs like those in schools; on the chimney shelf there were but two brass candlesticks, with or without tallow candles in them, and our two pipes with some tobacco in a pouch or strewn abroad, also the little piles of cigar-ash left there by our visitors or ourselves.

A pair of calico curtains hung from the brass window rods, and on each side of the window was a small bookcase in cherry-wood, such as every one knows who has stared into the shop windows of the *Quartier Latin*, and in which we kept the few books necessary for our studies.

The ink in the inkstand was always in the state of lava congealed in the crater of a volcano. May not any inkstand nowadays become a Vesuvius? The pens, all twisted, served to clean the stems of our pipes; and, in opposition to all the laws of credit, paper was even scarcer than coin.

How can young men be expected to stay at home in such furnished lodgings? The students studied in the cafés, the theatre, the Luxembourg gardens, in *grisettes*' rooms, even in the law schools—anywhere rather than in their horrible rooms—horrible for purposes of study, delightful as soon as they are used for gossiping and smoking in. Put a cloth on the table, and the impromptu dinner sent in from the best eating-house in the neighbourhood—places for four—two of them in petticoats—show a lithograph of this "Interior" to the veriest bigot, and she will be bound to smile.

We thought only of amusing ourselves. The reason for our dissipation lay in the most serious facts of the politics of the time. Juste and I could not see any room for us in the two professions our parents wished us to take up. There are a hundred doctors, a hundred lawyers, for one that is wanted. The crowd is choking these two paths which are supposed to lead to fortune, but which are merely two arenas; men kill each other there, fighting, not indeed with swords or firearms, but, with intrigue and calumny, with tremendous toil, campaigns in the sphere of the intellect as murderous as those in Italy were to the soldiers of the Republic. In these days, when everything is an intellectual competition, a man must be able to sit forty-eight hours on end in his chair before a table, as a General could remain for two days on horseback and in his saddle.

The throng of aspirants has necessitated a division of the Faculty of Medicine into categories. There is the physician who writes and the physician who practises, the political physician, and the physician militant—four different ways of being a physician, four classes already filled up. As to the fifth class, that of physicians who sell remedies, there is such a competition that they fight each other with disgusting advertisements on the walls of Paris.

In all the law courts there are almost as many lawyers as there are cases. The pleader is thrown back on journalism, on politics, on literature. In fact, the State, besieged for the smallest appointments under the law, has ended by requiring that the applicants should have some little fortune. The pear-shaped head of the grocer's son is selected in preference to the square skull of a man of talent who has not a sou. Work as he will, with all his energy, a young man, starting from zero, may at the end of ten years find himself below the point he set out from. In these days, talent must have the good luck which secures success to the most incapable; nay, more, if it scorns the base compromises which insure advancement to crawling mediocrity, it will never get on.

If we thoroughly knew our time, we also knew ourselves, and we preferred the indolence of dreamers to aimless stir, easy-going pleasure to the useless toil which would have exhausted our courage and worn out the edge of our intelligence.

We had analysed social life while smoking, laughing, and loafing. But, though elaborated by such means as these, our reflections were none the less judicious and profound.

While we were fully conscious of the slavery to which youth is condemned, we were amazed at the brutal indifference of the authorities to everything connected with intellect, thought, and poetry. How often have Juste and I exchanged glances when reading the papers as we studied political events, or the debates in the Chamber, and discussed the proceedings of a Court whose wilful ignorance could find no parallel but in the platitude of the courtiers, the mediocrity of the men forming the hedge round the newly-restored throne, all alike devoid of talent or breadth of view, of distinction or learning, of influence or dignity!

Could there be a higher tribute to the Court of Charles X than the present Court, if Court it may be called? What a hatred of the country may be seen in the naturalisation of vulgar foreigners, devoid of talent, who are enthroned in the Chamber of Peers! What a perversion of justice! What an insult to the distinguished youth, the ambitions native to the soil of France! We looked upon these things as upon a spectacle, and groaned over them, without taking upon ourselves to act.

Juste, whom no one ever sought, and who never sought any one, was, at five-and-twenty, a great politician, a man with a wonderful aptitude for apprehending the correlation between remote history and the facts of the present and of the future. In 1831, he told me exactly what would and did happen—the murders, the conspiracies, the ascendency of the Jews, the difficulty of doing anything in France, the scarcity of talent in the higher circles, and the abundance of intellect in the lowest ranks, where the finest courage is smothered under cigar-ashes.

What was to become of him? His parents wished him to be a doctor. But if he were a doctor, must he not wait twenty years for a practice? You know what he did? No? Well, he is a doctor; but he left France, he is in Asia. At this moment he is perhaps sinking under fatigue in a desert, or dying of the lashes of a barbarous horde—or perhaps he is some Indian prince's prime minister.

Action is my vocation. Leaving a civil college at the age of twenty, the only way for me to enter the army was by enlisting as a common soldier; so, weary of the dismal outlook that lay before a lawyer, I acquired the knowledge needed for a sailor. I imitate Juste, and keep out of France, where men waste, in the struggle to make way, the energy needed for the noblest works. Follow my example, friends; I am going where a man steers his destiny as he pleases.

These great resolutions were formed in the little room in the lodging-house in the Rue Corneille, in spite of our haunting the Bal Musard, flirting with girls of the town, and leading a careless and apparently reckless life. Our plans and arguments long floated in the air.

Marcas, our neighbour, was in some degree the guide who led us to the margin of the precipice or the torrent, who made us sound it, and showed us beforehand what our fate would be if we let ourselves fall into it. It was he who put us on our guard against the time-bargains a man makes with poverty under the sanction of hope, by accepting precarious situations whence he fights the battle, carried along by the devious tide of Paris—that great harlot, who takes you up or leaves you stranded, smiles or turns her back on you with equal readiness, wears out the strongest will in vexatious waiting, and makes misfortune wait on chance.

At our first meeting, Marcas, as it were, dazzled us. On our return from the schools, a little before the dinner-hour, we were accustomed to go up to our room and remain there a while, either waiting for the other, to learn whether there were any change in our plans for the evening. One day, at four o'clock, Juste met Marcas on the stairs, and I saw him in the street. It was in the month of November, and Marcas had no cloak; he wore shoes with heavy soles, corduroy trousers, and a blue double-breasted coat buttoned to the throat, which gave a military air to his broad chest, all the more so because he wore a black stock. The costume was not in itself extraordinary, but it agreed well with the man's mien and countenance.

My first impression on seeing him was neither surprise, nor distress, nor interest, nor pity, but curiosity mingled with all these feelings. He walked slowly, with a step that betrayed deep melancholy, his head forward with a stoop, but not bent like that of a conscience-stricken man. That head, large and powerful, which might contain the treasures necessary for a man of the highest ambition, looked as if it were loaded with thought; it was weighted with grief of mind, but there was no touch of remorse in his expression. As to his face, it may be summed up in a word. A common superstition has it that every human countenance resembles some animal. The animal for Marcas was the lion. His hair was like a mane, his nose was short and flat; broad and dented at the tip like a lion's; his brow, like a lion's, was strongly marked with a deep median furrow, dividing two powerful bosses. His high, hairy cheek-bones, all the more prominent because his cheeks were so thin, his enormous mouth and hollow jaws, were accentuated by lines of haughty significance, and marked by a complexion full of tawny shadows. This almost terrible countenance seemed illuminated by two lamps—two eyes, black indeed, but infinitely sweet, calm and deep, full of thought. If I may say so, those eyes had a humiliated expression.

Marcas was afraid of looking directly at others, not for himself, but for those on whom his fascinating gaze might rest; he had a power, and he shunned using it; he would spare those he met, and he feared notice. This was not from modesty, but from resignation—not Christian resignation, which implies charity, but resignation founded on reason, which had demonstrated the immediate inutility of his gifts, the impossibility of entering and living in the sphere for which he was fitted. Those eyes could at times flash lightnings. From those lips a voice of thunder must surely proceed; it was a mouth like Mirabeau's.

"I have seen such a grand fellow in the street," said I to Juste on coming in.

"It must be our neighbour," replied Juste, who described, in fact, the man I had just met. "A man who lives like a wood-louse would be sure to look like that," he added.

"What dejection and what dignity!"

"One is the consequence of the other."

"What ruined hopes! What schemes and failures!"

"Seven leagues of ruins! Obelisks—palaces—towers!— The ruins of Palmyra in the desert!" said Juste, laughing.

So we called him the Ruins of Palmyra.

As we went out to dine at the wretched eating-house in the Rue de la Harpe to which we subscribed, we asked the name of Number 37, and then heard the weird name Z. Marcas. Like boys, as we were, we repeated it more than a hundred times with all sorts of comments, absurd or melancholy, and the name

"WHAT IS TO BE SEEN?"

lent itself to the jest. Juste would fire off the Z like a rocket rising, *z-z-z-z-zed*; and after pronouncing the first syllable of the name with great importance, depicted a fall by the dull brevity of the second.

"Now, how and where does the man live?"

From this query, to the innocent espionage of curiosity there was no pause but that required for carrying out our plan. Instead of loitering about the streets, we both came in, each armed with a novel. We read with our ears open. And in the perfect silence of our attic rooms, we heard the even, dull sound of a sleeping man breathing.

"He is asleep," said I to Juste, noticing this fact.

"At seven o'clock!" replied the Doctor.

This was the name by which I called Juste, and he called me the Keeper of the Seals.

"A man must be wretched indeed to sleep as much as our neighbour!" cried I, jumping on to the chest of drawers with a knife in my hand, to which a corkscrew was attached.

I made a round hole at the top of the partition, about as big as a five-sou piece. I had forgotten that there would be no light in the room, and on putting my eye to the hole, I saw only darkness. At about one in the morning, when we had finished our books and were about to undress, we heard a noise in our neighbour's room. He got up, struck a match, and lighted his dip. I got on to the drawers again, and I then saw Marcas seated at his table and copying law-papers.

His room was about half the size of ours; the bed stood in a recess by the door, for the passage ended there, and its breadth was added to his garret; but the ground on which the house was built was evidently irregular, for the party-wall formed an obtuse angle, and the room was not square. There was no fireplace, only a small earthenware stove, white blotched with green, of which the pipe went up through the roof. The window, in the skew side of the room, had shabby red curtains. The furniture consisted of an armchair, a table, a chair, and a wretched bed-table. A cupboard in the wall held his clothes. The wall-paper was horrible; evidently only a servant had ever lodged there before Marcas.

"What is to be seen?" asked the Doctor as I got down.

"Look for yourself," said I.

At nine next morning, Marcas was in bed. He had breakfasted off a saveloy; we saw on a plate, with some crumbs of bread, the remains of that too familiar delicacy. He was asleep; he did not wake till eleven. He then set to work again on the copy he had begun the night before, which was lying on the table.

On going downstairs we asked the price of that room, and were told fifteen francs a month.

In the course of a few days, we were fully informed as to the mode of life of Z. Marcas. He did copying, at so much a sheet no doubt, for a law-writer who lived in the courtyard of the Sainte-Chapelle. He worked half the night; after sleeping from six till ten, he began again and wrote till three. Then he went out to take the copy home before dinner, which he ate at Mizerai's in the Rue Michel-le-Comte, at a cost of nine sous, and came in to bed at six o'clock. It became known to us that Marcas did not utter fifteen sentences in a month; he never talked to anybody, nor said a word to himself in his dreadful garret.

"The Ruins of Palmyra are terribly silent!" said Juste.

This taciturnity in a man whose appearance was so imposing was strangely significant. Sometimes when we met him, we exchanged glances full of meaning on both sides, but they never led to any advances. Insensibly this man became the object of our secret admiration, though we knew no reason for it. Did it lie in his secretly simple habits, his monastic regularity, his hermit-like frugality, his idiotically mechanical labour, allowing his mind to remain neuter or to work on its own lines, seeming to us to hint at an expectation of some stroke of good luck, or at some foregone conclusion as to his life?

After wandering for a long time among the Ruins of Palmyra, we forget them—we were young! Then came the Carnival, the Paris Carnival, which, henceforth, will eclipse the old Carnival of Venice, unless some ill-advised Prefect of Police is antagonistic.

Gambling ought to be allowed during the Carnival; but the stupid moralists who have had gambling suppressed are inert financiers, and this indispensable evil will be re-established among us when it is proved that France leaves millions at the German tables.

This splendid Carnival brought us to utter penury, as it does every student. We got rid of every object of luxury; we sold our second coats, our second boots, our second waistcoats— everything of which we had a duplicate, except our friend. We ate bread and cold sausages; we looked where we walked; we had set to work in earnest. We owed two months' rent, and were sure of having a bill from the porter for sixty or eighty items each, and amounting to forty or fifty francs. We made no noise, and did not laugh as we crossed the little hall at the bottom of the stairs; we commonly took it at a flying leap from the lowest step into the street. On the day when we first found ourselves bereft of tobacco for our pipes, it struck us that for some days we had been eating bread without any kind of butter.

Great was our distress.

"No tobacco!" said the Doctor.

"No cloak!" said the Keeper of the Seals.

"Ah, you rascals, you would dress as the postillon de Longjumeau, you would appear as Débardeurs, sup in the morning, and breakfast at night at Véry's—sometimes even at the *Rocher de Cancale*.—Dry bread for you, my boys! Why," said I, in a big bass voice, "you deserve to sleep under the bed, you are not worthy to lie in it—"

"Yes, yes; but, Keeper of Seals, there is no more tobacco!" said Juste.

"It is high time to write home, to our aunts, our mothers, and our sisters, to tell them we have no underlinen left, that the wear and tear of Paris would ruin garments of wire. Then we will solve an elegant chemical problem by transmuting linen into silver."

"But we must live till we get the answer."

"Well, I will go and bring out a loan among such of our friends as may still have some capital to invest."

"And how much will you find?"

"Say ten francs!" replied I with pride.

It was midnight. Marcas had heard everything. He knocked at our door.

"Messieurs," said he, "here is some tobacco; you can repay me on the first opportunity."

We were struck, not by the offer, which we accepted, but by the rich, deep, full voice in which it was made; a tone only comparable to the lowest string of Paganini's violin. Marcas vanished without waiting for our thanks.

Juste and I looked at each other without a word. To be rescued by a man evidently poorer than ourselves! Juste sat down to write to every member of his family, and I went off to effect a loan. I brought in twenty francs lent me by a fellow-provincial. In that evil but happy day gambling was still tolerated, and in its lodes, as hard as the rocky ore of Brazil, young men, by risking a small sum, had a chance of winning a few gold pieces. My friend, too, had some Turkish tobacco brought home from Constantinople by a sailor, and he gave me quite as much as we had taken from Z. Marcas. I conveyed the splendid cargo into port, and we went in triumph to repay our neighbour with a tawny wig of Turkish tobacco for his dark *Caporal*.

"You are determined not to be my debtors," said he. "You are giving me gold for copper.—You are boys—good boys—"

The sentences, spoken in varying tones, were variously emphasised. The words were nothing, but the expression!—That made us friends of ten years' standing at once.

Marcas, on hearing us coming, had covered up his papers; we understood that it would be taking a liberty to allude to his means of subsistence, and felt ashamed of having watched him. His cupboard stood open; in it there were two shirts, a white necktie, and a razor. The razor made me shudder. A looking-glass, worth five francs perhaps, hung near the window.

The man's few and simple movements had a sort of savage grandeur. The Doctor and I looked at each other, wondering what we could say in reply. Juste, seeing that I was speechless, asked Marcas jestingly:

"You cultivate literature, monsieur?"

"Far from it!" replied Marcas. "I should not be so wealthy."

"I fancied," said I, "that poetry alone, in these days, was amply sufficient to provide a man with lodgings as bad as ours."

My remark made Marcas smile, and the smile gave a charm to his yellow face.

"Ambition is not a less severe taskmaster to those who fail," said he. "You, who are beginning life, walk in the beaten paths. Never dream of rising superior, you will be ruined!"

"You advise us to stay just as we are?" said the Doctor, smiling.

There is something so infectious and childlike in the pleasantries of youth, that Marcas smiled again in reply.

"What incidents can have given you this detestable philosophy?" asked I.

"I forgot once more that chance is the result of an immense equation of which we know not all the factors. When we start from zero to work up to the unit, the chances are incalculable. To ambitious men Paris is an immense roulette table, and every young man fancies he can hit on a successful progression of numbers."

He offered us the tobacco I had brought that we might smoke with him; the Doctor went to fetch our pipes; Marcas filled his, and then he came to sit in our room, bringing the tobacco with him, since there were but two chairs in his. Juste, as brisk as a squirrel, ran out, and returned with a boy carrying three bottles of Bordeaux, some Brie cheese, and a loaf.

"Hah!" said I to myself, "fifteen francs," and I was right to a sou.

Juste gravely laid five francs on the chimney-shelf.

There are immeasurable differences between the gregarious man and the man who lives closest to nature. Toussaint Louverture, after he was caught, died without speaking a word. Napoleon, transplanted to a rock, talked like a magpie—he wanted to account for himself. Z. Marcas erred in the same way, but for our benefit only. Silence in all its majesty is to be found only in the savage. There never is a criminal who, though he might let his secrets fall with his head into the basket of sawdust, does not feel the purely social impulse to tell them to somebody.

Nay, I am wrong. We have seen one Iroquois of the Faubourg Saint-Marceau who raised the Parisian to the level of the natural savage—a republican, a conspirator, a Frenchman, an old man, who outdid all we have heard of Negro determination, and all that Cooper tells us of the tenacity and coolness of the Redskins under defeat. Morey, the Guatimozin of the "Mountain," preserved an attitude unparalleled in the annals of European justice.

This is what Marcas told us during the small hours, sandwiching his discourse with slices of bread spread with cheese and washed down with wine. All the tobacco was burned out.

Now and then the hackney coaches clattering across the Place de l'Odéon, or the omnibuses toiling past, sent up their dull rumbling, as if to remind us that Paris was still close to us.

His family lived at Vitré; his father and mother had fifteen hundred francs a year in the funds. He had received an education gratis in a Seminary, but had refused to enter the priesthood. He felt in himself the fires of immense ambition, and had come to Paris on foot at the age of twenty, the possessor of two hundred francs. He had studied the law, working in an attorney's office, where he had risen to be superior clerk. He had taken his doctor's degree in law, had mastered the old and modern codes, and could hold his own with the most famous pleaders. He had studied the law of nations, and was familiar with European treaties and international practice. He had studied men and things in five capitals—London, Berlin, Vienna, Petersburg, and Constantinople.

No man was better informed than he as to the rules of the Chamber. For five years he had been reporter of the debates for a daily paper. He spoke extempore and admirably, and could go on for a long time in that deep, appealing voice which had struck us to the soul. Indeed, he proved by the narrative of his life that he was a great orator, a concise orator, serious and yet full of piercing eloquence; he resembled Berryer in his fervour and in the impetus which commands the sympathy of the masses, and was like Thiers in refinement and skill; but he would have been less diffuse, less in difficulties for a conclusion.

He had intended to rise rapidly to power without burdening himself first with the doctrines necessary to begin with, for a man in opposition, but an incubus later to the statesman.

Marcas had learned everything that a real statesman should know; indeed, his amazement was considerable when he had occasion to discern the utter ignorance of men who have risen to the administration of public affairs in France. Though in him it was vocation that had led to study, nature had been generous and bestowed all that cannot be acquired—keen perceptions, self-command, a nimble wit, rapid judgement, decisiveness, and, what is the genius of these men, fertility in resource.

By the time when Marcas thought himself duly equipped, France was torn by intestine divisions arising from the triumph of the House of Orleans over the elder branch of the Bourbons.

The field of political warfare is evidently changed. Civil war henceforth cannot last for long, and will not be fought out in the provinces. In France such struggles will be of brief duration and at the seat of government; and the battle will be the close of the moral contest which will have been brought to an issue by superior minds. This state of things will continue so long as France has her present singular form of government, which has no analogy with that of any other country; for there is no more resemblance between the English and the French constitutions than between the two lands.

Thus Marcas' place was in the political press. Being poor and unable to secure his election, he hoped to make a sudden appearance. He resolved on making the greatest possible sacrifice for a man of superior intellect, to work as subordinate to some rich and ambitious deputy. Like a second Bonaparte, he sought his Barras; the new Colbert hoped to find a Mazarin. He did immense services, and he did them then and there; he assumed no importance, he made no boast, he did not complain of ingratitude. He did them in the hope that his patron would put him in a position to be elected deputy; Marcas wished for nothing but a loan that might enable him to purchase a house in Paris, the qualification required by law. Richard III asked for nothing but his horse.

In three years Marcas had made his man—one of the fifty supposed great statesmen who are the battledores with which two cunning players toss the ministerial portfolios exactly as the man behind the puppet-show hits Punch against the constable in his street theatre, and counts on always getting paid. This man existed only by Marcas, but he had just brains enough to appreciate the value of his "ghost" and to know that Marcas, if he ever came to the front, would remain there, would be indispensable, while he himself would be translated to the polar zone of the Luxembourg. So he determined to put insurmountable obstacles in the way of his Mentor's advancement, and hid his purpose under the semblance of the utmost sincerity. Like all mean men, he could dissimulate to perfection, and he soon made progress in the ways of ingratitude, for he felt that he must kill Marcas, not to be killed by him. These two men, apparently so united, hated each other as soon as one had once deceived the other.

The politician was made one of a ministry; Marcas remained in the opposition to hinder his man from being attacked; nay, by skilful tactics he won him the applause of the opposition. To excuse himself for not rewarding his subaltern, the chief pointed out the impossibility of finding a place suddenly for a man on the other side, without a great deal of manoeuvring. Marcas had hoped confidently for a place to enable him to marry, and thus acquire the qualification he so ardently desired. He was two-and-thirty, and the Chamber ere long must be dissolved. Having detected his man in this flagrant act of bad faith, he overthrew him, or at any rate contributed largely to his overthrow, and covered him with mud.

A fallen minister, if he is to rise again to power, must show that he is to be feared; this man, intoxicated by Royal glibness, had fancied that his position would be permanent; he acknowledged his delinquencies; besides confessing them, he did Marcas a small money service, for Marcas had got into debt. He subsidised the newspaper on which Marcas worked, and made him the manager of it.

Though he despised the man, Marcas, who, practically, was being subsidised too, consented to take the part of the fallen minister. Without unmasking at once all the batteries of his superior intellect, Marcas came a little further than before; he showed half his shrewdness. The Ministry lasted only a hundred and eighty days; it was swallowed up. Marcas had put himself into communication with certain deputies, had moulded them like dough, leaving each impressed with a high opinion of his talent; his puppet again became a member of the Ministry, and then the paper was ministerial. The Ministry united the paper with another, solely to squeeze out Marcas, who in this fusion had to make way for a rich and insolent rival, whose name was well known, and who already had his foot in the stirrup.

Marcas relapsed into utter destitution; his haughty patron well knew the depths into which he had cast him.

Where was he to go? The ministerial papers, privily warned, would have nothing to say to him. The opposition papers did not care to admit him to their offices. Marcas could side neither with the Republicans nor with the Legitimists, two parties whose triumph would mean the overthrow of everything that now is.

"Ambitious men like a fast hold on things," said he with a smile.

He lived by writing a few articles on commercial affairs, and contributed to one of those encyclopædias brought out by speculation and not by learning. Finally a paper was founded, which was destined to live but two years, but which secured his services. From that moment he renewed his connection with the minister's enemies; he joined the party who were working for the fall of the Government; and as soon as his pickaxe had free play, it fell.

This paper had now for six months ceased to exist; he had failed to find employment of any kind; he was spoken of as a dangerous man, calumny attacked him; he had unmasked a huge financial and mercantile job by a few articles and a pamphlet. He was known to be the mouthpiece of a banker who was said to have paid him largely, and from whom he was supposed to expect some patronage in return for his championship. Marcas, disgusted by men and things, worn out by five years of fighting, regarded as a free lance rather than as a great leader; crushed by the necessity for earning his daily bread, which hindered him from gaining ground, in despair at the influence exerted by money over mind, and given over to dire poverty, buried himself in a garret to make thirty sous a day, the sum strictly answering to his needs. Meditation had levelled a desert all round him. He read the papers to be informed of what was going on. Pozzo di Borgo had once lived like this for some time.

Marcas, no doubt, was planning a serious attack, accustoming himself to dissimulation, and punishing himself for his blunders by Pythagorean muteness. But he did not tell us the reasons for his conduct.

It is impossible to give you an idea of the scenes of the highest comedy that lay behind this algebraic statement of his career; his useless patience dogging the footsteps of fortune, which presently took wings, his long tramps over the thorny brakes of Paris, his breathless chases as a petitioner, his attempts to win over fools; the schemes laid only to fail through the influence of some frivolous woman; the meetings with men of business who expected their capital to bring them places and a peerage, as well as large interest. Then the hopes rising in a towering wave only to break in foam on the shoal; the wonders wrought in reconciling adverse interests which, after working together for a week, fell asunder; the annoyance, a thousand times repeated, of seeing a dunce decorated with the Legion of Honour, and preferred, though as ignorant as a shop-boy, to a man of talent. Then, what Marcas called the stratagems of stupidity—you strike a man, and he seems convinced, he nods his head—everything is settled; next day, this india-rubber ball, flattened for a moment, has recovered itself in the course of the night; it is as full of wind as ever; you must begin all over again; and you go on till you understand that you are not dealing with a man, but with a lump of gum that loses shape in the sunshine.

These thousand annoyances, this vast waste of human energy on barren spots, the difficulty of achieving any good, the incredible facility of doing mischief; two strong games played out, twice won, and then twice lost; the hatred of a statesman—a blockhead with a painted face and a wig, but in whom the world believed—all these things, great and small, had not crushed, but for the moment had dashed, Marcas. In the days when money had come into his hands, his fingers had not clutched it; he had allowed himself the exquisite pleasure of sending it all to his family—to his sisters, his brothers, his old father. Like Napoleon in his fall, he asked for no more than thirty sous a day, and any man of energy can earn thirty sous for a day's work in Paris.

When Marcas had finished the story of his life, intermingled with reflections, maxims, and observations, revealing him as a great politician, a few questions and answers on both sides as to the progress of affairs in France and in Europe were enough to prove to us that he was a real statesman; for a man may be quickly and easily judged when he can be brought on to the ground of immediate difficulties: there is a certain Shibboleth for men of superior talents, and we were of the tribe of modern Levites without belonging as yet to the Temple. As I have said, our frivolity covered certain purposes which Juste has carried out, and which I am about to execute.

When we had done talking, we all three went out, cold as it was, to walk in the Luxembourg gardens till the dinner hour. In the course of that walk our conversation, grave throughout, turned on the painful aspects of the political situation. Each of us contributed his remarks, his comment, or his jest, a pleasantry or a proverb. This was no longer exclusively a discussion of life on the colossal scale just described by Marcas, the soldier of political warfare. Nor was it the distressful monologue of the wrecked navigator, stranded in a garret in the Hôtel Corneille; it was a dialogue in which two well-informed young men, having gauged the times they lived in, were endeavouring, under the guidance of a man of talent, to gain some light on their own future prospects.

"Why," asked Juste, "did you not wait patiently for an opportunity, and imitate the only man who has been able to keep the lead since the Revolution of July by holding his head above water?"

"Have I not said that we never know where the roots of chance lie? Carrel was in identically the same position as the orator you speak of. That gloomy young man, of a bitter spirit, had a whole government in his head; the man of whom you speak had no idea beyond mounting on the crupper of every event. Of the two, Carrel was the better man. Well, one became a minister, Carrel remained a journalist; the incomplete but craftier man is living; Carrel is dead.

"I may point out that your man has for fifteen years been making his way, and is but making it still. He may yet be caught and crushed between two cars full of intrigues on the highroad to power. He has no house; he has not the favour of the palace like Metternich; nor, like Villèle, the protection of a compact majority.

"I do not believe that the present state of things will last ten years longer. Hence, supposing I should have such poor good luck, I am already too late to avoid being swept away by the commotion I foresee. I should need to be established in a superior position."

"What commotion?" asked Juste.

"AUGUST, 1830," said Marcas in solemn tones, holding out his hand towards Paris; "AUGUST, the offspring of Youth which bound the sheaves, and of Intellect which had ripened the harvest, forgot to provide for Youth and Intellect.

"Youth will explode like the boiler of a steam-engine. Youth has no outlet in France; it is gathering an avalanche of underrated capabilities, of legitimate and restless ambitions; young men are not marrying now; families cannot tell what to do with their children. What will the thunderclap be that will shake down these masses? I know not, but they will crash down into the midst of things, and overthrow everything. These are laws of hydrostatics which act on the human race; the Roman Empire had failed to understand them, and the Barbaric hordes came down.

"The Barbaric hordes now are the intelligent class. The laws of overpressure are at this moment acting slowly and silently in our midst. The Government is the great criminal; it does not appreciate the two powers to which it owes everything; it has allowed its hands to be tied by the absurdities of the Contract; it is bound, ready to be the victim.

"Louis XIV, Napoleon, England, all were or are eager for intelligent youth. In France the young are condemned by the new legislation, by the blundering principles of elective rights, by the unsoundness of the ministerial constitution.

"Look at the elective Chamber; you will find no deputies of thirty; the youth of Richelieu and of Mazarin, of Turenne and of Colbert, of Pitt and of Saint-Just, of Napoleon and of Prince Metternich, would find no admission there; Burke, Sheridan, or Fox could not win seats. Even if political majority had been fixed at one-and-twenty, and eligibility had been relieved of every disabling qualification, the Departments would have returned the very same members, men devoid of political talent, unable to speak without murdering French grammar, and among whom, in ten years, scarcely one statesman has been found.

"The causes of an impending event may be seen, but the event itself cannot be foretold. At this moment the youth of France is being driven into Republicanism, because it believes that the Republic would bring it emancipation. It will always remember the young representatives of the people and the young army leaders! The imprudence of the Government is only comparable to its avarice."

That day left its echoes in our lives. Marcas confirmed us in our resolution to leave France, where young men of talent and energy are crushed under the weight of successful, commonplace, envious, and insatiable middle age.

We dined together in the Rue de la Harpe. We thence forth felt for Marcas the most respectful affection; he gave us the most practical aid in the sphere of the mind. That man knew everything; he had studied everything. For us he cast his eye over the whole civilised world, seeking the country where openings would be at once the most abundant and the most favourable to the success of our plans. He indicated what should be the goal of our studies; he bid us make haste, explaining to us that time was precious, that emigration would presently begin, and that its effect would be to deprive France of the cream of its powers and of its youthful talent; that their intelligence, necessarily sharpened, would select the best places, and that the great thing was to be first in the field.

Thenceforward, we often sat late at work under the lamp. Our generous instructor wrote some notes for our guidance—two pages for Juste and three for me—full of invaluable advice—the sort of information which experience alone can supply, such landmarks as only genius can place. In those papers, smelling of tobacco, and covered with writing so vile as to be almost hieroglyphic, there are suggestions for a fortune, and forecasts of unerring acumen. There are hints as to certain parts of America and Asia which have been fully justified, both before and since Juste and I could set out.

Marcas, like us, was in the most abject poverty. He earned, indeed, his daily bread, but he had neither linen, clothes, nor shoes. He did not make himself out any better than he was; his dreams had been of luxury as well as of power. He did not admit that this was the real Marcas; he abandoned his person, indeed, to the caprices of life. What he lived by was the breath of ambition; he dreamed of revenge while blaming himself for yielding to so shallow a feeling. The true statesman ought, above all things, to be superior to vulgar passions; like the man of science, he should have no passion but for his science. It was in these days of dire necessity that Marcas seemed to us so great—nay, so terrible; there was something awful in the gaze which saw another world than that which strikes the eye of ordinary men. To us he was a subject of contemplation and astonishment; for the young—which of us has not known it?—the young have a keen craving to admire; they love to attach themselves, and are naturally inclined to submit to the men they feel to be superior, as they are to devote themselves to a great cause.

Our surprise was chiefly aroused by his indifference in matters of sentiment; woman had no place in his life. When we spoke of this matter, a perennial theme of conversation among Frenchmen, he simply remarked:

"Gowns cost too much."

He saw the look that passed between Juste and me, and went on:

"Yes, far too much. The woman you buy—and she is the least expensive—takes a great deal of money. The woman who gives herself takes all your time! Woman extinguishes every energy, every ambition. Napoleon reduced her to what she should be. From that point of view, he really was great. He did not indulge such ruinous fancies of Louis XIV and Louis XV; at the same time, he could love in secret."

We discovered that, like Pitt, who made England his wife, Marcas bore France in his heart; he idolised his country; he had not a thought that was not for his native land. His fury at feeling that he had in his hands the remedy for the evils which so deeply saddened him, and could not apply it, ate into his soul, and this rage was increased by the inferiority of France at that time, as compared with Russia and England. France a third-rate power! This cry came up again and again in his conversation. The intestinal disorders of his country had entered into his soul. All the contests between the Court and the Chamber, showing, as they did, incessant change and constant vacillation, which must injure the prosperity of the country, he scoffed at as backstairs squabbles.

"This is peace at the cost of the future," said he.

One evening Juste and I were at work, sitting in perfect silence. Marcas had just risen to toil at his copying, for he had refused our assistance in spite of our most earnest entreaties. We had offered to take it in turns to copy a batch of manuscript, so that he should do but a third of his distasteful task; he had been quite angry, and we had ceased to insist.

We heard the sound of gentlemanly boots in the passage, and raised our heads, looking at each other. There was a tap at Marcas' door—he never took the key out of the lock—and we heard the hero answer:

"Come in." Then—"What! you here, monsieur?"

"I myself," replied the retired minister.

It was the Diocletian of this unknown martyr.

For some time he and our neighbour conversed in an undertone. Suddenly Marcas, whose voice had been heard but rarely, as is natural in a dialogue in which the applicant begins by setting forth the situation, broke out loudly in reply to some offer we had not overheard.

"You would laugh at me for a fool," cried he, "if I took you at your word. Jesuits are a thing of the past, but Jesuitism is eternal. Your Machiavellism and your generosity are equally hollow and untrustworthy. You can make your own calculations, but who can calculate on you? Your Court is made up of owls who fear the light, of old men who quake in the presence of the young, or who simply disregard them. The Government is formed on the same pattern as the Court. You have hunted up the remains of the Empire, as the Restoration enlisted the Voltigeurs of Louis XIV.

"Hitherto the evasions of cowardice have been taken for the manoeuvring of ability; but dangers will come, and the younger generation will rise as they did in 1790. They did grand things then.—Just now you change ministries as a sick man turns in his bed; these oscillations betray the weakness of the Government. You work on an underhand system of policy which will be turned against you, for France will be tired of your shuffling. France will not tell you that she is tired of you; a man never knows whence his ruin comes; it is the historian's task to find out; but you will undoubtedly perish as the reward of not having the youth of France to lend you its strength and energy; for having hated really capable men; for not having lovingly chosen them from this noble generation; for having in all cases preferred mediocrity.

"You have come to ask my support, but you are an atom in that decrepit heap which is made hideous by self-interest, which trembles and squirms, and, because it is so mean, tries to make France mean too. My strong nature, my ideas, would work like poison in you; twice you have tricked me, twice have I overthrown you. If we unite a third time, it must be a very serious matter. I should kill myself if I allowed myself to be duped; for I should be to blame, not you."

Then we heard the humblest entreaties, the most fervent adjurations, not to deprive the country of such superior talents. The man spoke of patriotism, and Marcas uttered a significant "*Ouh! ouh!*" He laughed at his would-be patron. Then the statesman was more explicit; he bowed to the superiority of his erewhile counsellor; he pledged himself to enable Marcas to remain in office, to be elected deputy; then he offered him a high appointment, promising him that he, the speaker, would thenceforth be the subordinate of a man whose subaltern he was only worthy to be. He was in the newly-formed ministry, and he would not return to power unless Marcas had a post in proportion to his merit; he had already made it a condition, Marcas had been regarded as indispensable.

Marcas refused.

"I have never before been in a position to keep my promises; here is an opportunity of proving myself faithful to my word, and you fail me."

To this Marcas made no reply. The boots were again audible in the passage on the way to the stairs.

"Marcas! Marcas!" we both cried, rushing into his room. "Why refuse? He really meant it. His offers are very handsome; at any rate, go to see the ministers."

In a twinkling, we had given Marcas a hundred reasons. The minister's voice was sincere; without seeing him, we had felt sure that he was honest.

"I have no clothes," replied Marcas.

"Rely on us," said Juste, with a glance at me.

Marcas had the courage to trust us; a light flashed in his eye, he pushed his fingers through his hair, lifting it from his forehead with a gesture that showed some confidence in his luck; and when he had thus unveiled his face, so to speak, we saw in him a man absolutely unknown to us—Marcas sublime, Marcas in his power! His mind in its element—the bird restored to the free air, the fish to the water, the horse galloping across the plain.

It was transient. His brow clouded again; he had, it would seem, a vision of his fate. Halting doubt had followed close on the heels of white-winged hope.

We left him to himself.

"Now, then," said I to the Doctor, "we have given our word; how are we to keep it?"

"We will sleep upon it," said Juste, "and to-morrow morning we will talk it over."

Next morning we went for a walk in the Luxembourg.

We had had time to think over the incident of the past night, and were both equally surprised at the lack of address shown by Marcas in the minor difficulties of life—he, a man who never saw any difficulties in the solution of the hardest problems of abstract or practical politics. But these elevated characters can all be tripped up on a grain of sand, and will, like the grandest enterprise, miss fire for want of a thousand francs. It is the old story of Napoleon, who, for lack of a pair of boots, did not set out for India.

"Well, what have you hit upon?" asked Juste.

"I have thought of a way to get him a complete outfit."

"Where?"

"From Humann."

"How?"

"Humann, my boy, never goes to his customers—his customers go to him; so that he does not know whether I am rich or poor. He only knows that I dress well and look decent in the clothes he makes for me. I shall tell him that an uncle of mine has dropped in from the country, and that his indifference in matters of dress is quite a discredit to me in the upper circles where I am trying to find a wife.—It will not be Humann if he sends in his bill before three months."

The Doctor thought this a capital idea for a vaudeville, but poor enough in real life, and doubted my success. But I give you my word of honour, Humann dressed Marcas, and, being an artist, turned him out as a political personage ought to be dressed.

Juste lent Marcas two hundred francs in gold, the product of two watches bought on credit, and pawned at the Mont-de-Piété. For my part, I had said nothing of six shirts and all necessary linen, which cost me no more than the pleasure of asking for them from a forewoman in a shop whom I had treated to Musard's during the carnival.

Marcas accepted everything, thanking us no more than he ought. He only inquired as to the means by which we had got possession of such riches, and we made him laugh for the last time. We looked on our Marcas as shipowners, when they have exhausted their credit and every resource at their command to fit out a vessel, must look on it as it puts to sea.

Here Charles was silent; he seemed crushed by his memories.

"Well," cried the audience, "and what happened?"

"I will tell you in a few words—for this is not romance—it is history."

We saw no more of Marcas. The administration lasted for three months; it fell at the end of the session. Then Marcas came back to us, worked to death. He had sounded the crater of power; he came away from it with the beginnings of brain fever. The disease made rapid progress; we nursed him. Juste at once called in the chief physician of the hospital where he was working as house-surgeon. I was then living alone in our room, and I was the most attentive attendant; but care and science alike were in vain. By the month of January, 1838, Marcas himself felt that he had but a few days to live.

The man whose soul and brain he had been for six months never even sent to inquire after him. Marcas expressed the greatest contempt for the Government; he seemed to doubt what the fate of France might be, and it was this doubt that had made him ill. He had, he thought, detected treason in the heart of power, not tangible, seizable treason, the result of facts, but the treason of a system, the subordination of national interests to selfish ends. His belief in the degradation of the country was enough to aggravate his complaint.

I myself was witness to the proposals made to him by one of the leaders of the antagonistic party which he had fought against. His hatred of the men he had tried to serve was so virulent, that he would gladly have joined the coalition that was about to be formed among certain ambitious spirits who, at least, had one idea in common—that of shaking off the yoke of the Court. But Marcas could only reply to the envoy in the words of the Hôtel de Ville:

"It is too late!"

Marcas did not leave money enough to pay for his funeral. Juste and I had great difficulty in saving him from the ignominy of a pauper's bier, and we alone followed the coffin of Z. Marcas, which was dropped into the common grave of the cemetery of Mont-Parnasse.

We looked sadly at each other as we listened to this tale, the last we heard from the lips of Charles Rabourdin the day before he embarked at le Havre on a brig that was to convey him to the islands of Malay. We all knew more than one Marcas, more than one victim of his devotion to a party, repaid by betrayal or neglect.

LES JARDIES, *May* 1840.

AN EPISODE UNDER THE TERROR

To Monsieur Guyonnet-Merville.

Is it not a necessity to explain to a public curious to know everything, how I came to be sufficiently learned in the law to carry on the business of my little world? And in so doing, am I not bound to put on record the memory of the amiable and intelligent man who, meeting Scribe (another clerk-amateur) at a ball, said, "Just give the office a turn; there is work for you there, I assure you"? But do you need this public testimony to feel assured of the affection of the writer?

DE BALZAC.

ON the 22d of January, 1793, towards eight o'clock in the evening, an old lady came down the steep street that comes to an end opposite the Church of Saint Laurent in the Faubourg Saint Martin. It had snowed so heavily all day long that the lady's footsteps were scarcely audible; the streets were deserted, and a feeling of dread, not unnatural amid the silence, was further increased by the whole extent of the Terror beneath which France was groaning in those days; what was more, the old lady so far had met no one by the way. Her sight had long been failing, so that the few foot passengers dispersed like shadows in the distance over the wide thoroughfare through the faubourg, were quite invisible to her by the light of the lanterns.

She had passed the end of the Rue des Morts, when she fancied that she could hear the firm, heavy tread of a man walking behind her. Then it seemed to her that she had heard that sound before, and dismayed by the idea of being followed, she tried to walk faster toward a brightly lit shop window, in the hope of verifying the suspicions which had taken hold of her mind.

So soon as she stood in the shaft of light that streamed out across the road, she turned her head suddenly, and caught sight of a human figure looming through the fog. The dim vision was enough for her. For one moment she reeled beneath an overpowering weight of dread, for she could not doubt any longer that the man had followed her the whole way from her own door; then the desire to escape from the spy gave her strength. Unable to think clearly, she walked twice as fast as before, as if it were possible to escape from a man who of course could move much faster; and for some minutes she fled on, till, reaching a pastry-cook's shop, she entered and sank rather than sat down upon a chair by the counter.

A young woman busy with embroidery looked up from her work at the rattling of the door-latch, and looked out through the square window-panes. She seemed to recognise the old-fashioned violet silk mantle, for she went at once to a drawer as if in search of something put aside for the newcomer. Not only did this movement and the expression of the woman's face show a very evident desire to be rid as soon as possible of an unwelcome visitor, but she even permitted herself an impatient exclamation when the drawer proved to be empty. Without looking at the lady, she hurried from her desk into the back shop and called to her husband, who appeared at once.

"Wherever have you put?—" she began mysteriously, glancing at the customer by way of finishing her question.

The pastry-cook could only see the old lady's head-dress, a huge black silk bonnet with knots of violet ribbon round it, but he looked at his wife as who should say, "Did you think I should leave such a thing as that lying about in your drawer?" and then vanished.

The old lady kept so still and silent that the shopkeeper's wife was surprised. She went back to her, and on a nearer view a sudden impulse of pity, blended perhaps with curiosity, got the better of her. The old lady's face was naturally pale; she looked as though she secretly practised austerities; but it was easy to see that she was paler than usual from recent agitation of some kind. Her head-dress was so arranged as almost to hide hair that was white, no doubt with age, for there was not a trace of powder on the collar of her dress. The extreme plainness of her dress lent an air of austerity to her face, and her features were proud and grave. The manners and habits of people of condition were so different from those of other classes in former times that a noble was easily known, and the shopkeeper's wife felt persuaded that her customer was a *ci-devant*, and that she had been about the Court.

"Madame," she began with involuntary respect, forgetting that the title was proscribed.

But the old lady made no answer. She was staring fixedly at the shop window as though some dreadful thing had taken shape against the panes. The pastry-cook came back at that moment, and drew the lady from her musings, by holding out a little cardboard box wrapped in blue paper.

"What is the matter, citoyenne?" he asked.

"Nothing, nothing, my friends," she answered, in a gentle voice. She looked up at the man as she spoke, as if to thank him by a glance; but she saw the red cap on his head, and a cry broke from her. "Ah! *You* have betrayed me!"

The man and his young wife replied by an indignant gesture, that brought the colour to the old lady's face; perhaps she felt relief, perhaps she blushed for her suspicions.

"Forgive me!" she said, with a childlike sweetness in her tones. Then, drawing a gold louis from her pocket, she held it out to the pastry-cook. "That is the price agreed upon," she added.

There is a kind of want that is felt instinctively by those who know want. The man and his wife looked at one another, then at the elderly woman before them, and read the same thoughts in each other's eyes. That bit of gold was so plainly the last. Her hands shook a little as she held it out, looking at it sadly but ungrudgingly, as one who knows the full extent of the sacrifice. Hunger and penury had carved lines as easy to read in her face as the traces of asceticism and fear. There were vestiges of bygone splendour in her clothes. She was dressed in threadbare silk, a neat but well-worn mantle, and daintily mended lace,—in the rags of former grandeur, in short. The shopkeeper and his wife, drawn two ways by pity and self-interest, began by lulling their consciences with words.

"You seem very poorly, citoyenne—"

"Perhaps madame might like to take something," the wife broke in.

"We have some very nice broth," added the pastry-cook.

"And it is so cold," continued his wife; "perhaps you have caught a chill, madame, on your way here. But you can rest and warm yourself a bit."

"We are not so black as the devil!" cried the man.

The kindly intention in the words and tones of the charitable couple won the old lady's confidence. She said that a strange man had been following her, and she was afraid to go home alone.

"Is that all!" returned he of the red bonnet; "wait for me, citoyenne."

He handed the gold coin to his wife, and then went out to put on his National Guard's uniform, impelled thereto by the idea of making some adequate return for the money; an idea that sometimes slips into a tradesman's head when he has been prodigiously overpaid for goods of no great value. He took up his cap, buckled on his sabre, and came out in full dress. But his wife had had time to reflect, a reflection, as not unfrequently happens, closed the hand that kindly intentions had opened. Feeling frightened and uneasy lest her husband might be drawn into something unpleasant, she tried to catch at the skirt of his coat, to hold him back, but he, good soul, obeying his charitable first thought, brought out his offer to see the lady home, before his wife could stop him.

"The man of whom the citoyenne is afraid is still prowling about the shop, it seems," she said sharply.

"I am afraid so," said the lady innocently.

"How if it is a spy? ... a plot? ... Don't go. And take the box away from her—"

The words whispered in the pastry-cook's ear cooled his hot fit of courage down to zero.

"Oh! I will just go out and say a word or two. I will rid you of him soon enough," he exclaimed, as he bounced out of the shop.

The old lady meanwhile, passive as a child and almost dazed, sat down on her chair again. But the honest pastry-cook came back directly. A countenance red enough to begin with, and further flushed by the bake-house fire, was suddenly blanched; such terror perturbed him that he reeled as he walked, and stared about him like a drunken man.

"Miserable aristocrat! Do you want to have our heads cut off?" he shouted furiously. "You just take to your heels and never show yourself here again. Don't come to me for materials for your plots."

He tried, as he spoke, to take away the little box which she had slipped into one of her pockets. But at the touch of a profane hand on her clothes, the stranger recovered youth and activity for a moment, preferring to face the dangers of the street with no protector save God, to the loss of the thing that she had just paid for. She sprang to the door, flung it open, and disappeared, leaving the husband and wife dumbfounded and quaking with fright.

Once outside in the street, she started away at a quick walk; but her strength soon failed her. She heard the sound of the snow crunching under a heavy step, and knew that the pitiless spy was on her track. She was obliged to stop. He stopped likewise. From sheer terror, or lack of intelligence, she did not dare to speak or to look at him. She went slowly on; the man slackened his pace and fell behind so that he could still keep her in sight. He might have been her very shadow.

Nine o'clock struck as the silent man and woman passed again by the Church of Saint Laurent. It is in the nature of things that calm must succeed to violent agitation, even in the weakest soul; for if feeling is infinite, our capacity to feel is limited. So, as the stranger lady met with no harm from her supposed persecutor, she tried to look upon him as an unknown friend anxious to protect her. She thought of all the circumstances in which the stranger had appeared, and put them together, as if to find some ground for this comforting theory, and felt inclined to credit him with good intentions rather than bad.

Forgetting the fright that he had given the pastry-cook, she walked on with a firmer step through the upper end of the Faubourg Saint Martin; and another half-hour's walk brought her to a house at the corner where the road to the Barrière de Pantin turns off from the main thoroughfare. Even at this day, the place is one of the least frequented parts of Paris. The north wind sweeps over the Buttes-Chaumont and Belleville, and whistles through the houses (the hovels rather), scattered over an almost uninhabited low-lying waste, where the fences are heaps of earth and bones. It was a desolate-looking place, a fitting refuge for despair and misery.

The sight of it appeared to make an impression upon the relentless pursuer of a poor creature so daring as to walk alone at night through the silent streets. He stood in thought, and seemed by his attitude to hesitate. She could see him dimly now, under the street lamp that sent a faint, flickering light through the fog. Fear gave her eyes. She saw, or thought she saw, something sinister about the stranger's features. Her old terrors awoke; she took advantage of a kind of hesitation on his part, slipped through the shadows to the door of the solitary house, pressed a spring, and vanished swiftly as a phantom.

For awhile the stranger stood motionless, gazing up at the house. It was in some sort a type of the wretched dwellings in the suburb; a tumble-down hovel, built of rough stones, daubed over with a coat of yellowish stucco, and so riven with great cracks that there seemed to be danger lest the slightest puff of wind might blow it down. The roof, covered with brown moss-grown tiles, had given way in several places, and looked as though it might break down altogether under the weight of the snow. The frames of the three windows on each storey were rotten with damp and warped by the sun; evidently the cold must find its way inside. The house standing thus quite by itself looked like some old tower that Time had forgotten to destroy. A faint light shone from the attic windows pierced at irregular distances in the roof; otherwise the whole building was in total darkness.

Meanwhile the old lady climbed not without difficulty up the rough, clumsily built staircase, with a rope by way of a hand-rail. At the door of the lodging in the attic she stopped and tapped mysteriously; an old man brought forward a chair for her. She dropped into it at once.

"Hide! Hide!" she exclaimed, looking up at him. "Seldom as we leave the house, everything that we do is known, and every step is watched—"

"What is it now?" asked another elderly woman, sitting by the fire.

"The man that has been prowling about the house yesterday and to-day, followed me to-night—"

At those words all three dwellers in the wretched den looked in each other's faces and did not try to dissimulate the profound dread that they felt. The old priest was the least overcome, probably because he ran the greatest danger. If a brave man is weighed down by great calamities or the yoke of persecution, he begins, as it were, by making the sacrifice of himself; and thereafter every day of his life becomes one more victory snatched from fate. But from the way in which the women looked at him it was easy to see that their intense anxiety was on his account.

"Why should our faith in God fail us, my sisters?" he said, in low but fervent tones. "We sang His praises through the shrieks of murderers and their victims at the Carmelites. If it was His will that I should come alive out of that butchery, it was, no doubt, because I was reserved for some fate which I am bound to endure without murmuring. God will protect His own; He can do with them according to His will. It is for you, not for me that we must think."

"No," answered one of the women. 'What is our life compared with a priest's life?"

"Once outside the Abbaye de Chelles, I look upon myself as dead," added the nun who had not left the house, while the Sister that had just returned held out the little box to the priest.

"Here are the wafers … but I can hear some one coming up the stairs."

At this, the three began to listen. The sound ceased.

"Do not be alarmed if somebody tries to come in," said the priest. "Somebody on whom we could depend was to make all necessary arrangements for crossing the frontier. He is to come for the letters that I have written to the Duc de Langeais and the Marquis de Beauséant, asking them to find some way of taking you out of this dreadful country, and away from the death or the misery that waits for you here."

"But are you not going to follow us?" the nuns cried under their breath, almost despairingly.

"My post is here where the sufferers are," the priest said simply, and the women said no more, but looked at their guest in reverent admiration. He turned to the nun with the wafers.

"Sister Marthe," he said, "the messenger will say *Fiat Voluntas* in answer to the word *Hosanna*."

"There is some one on the stairs!" cried the other nun, opening a hiding-place contrived in the roof.

This time it was easy to hear, amid the deepest silence, a sound echoing up the staircase; it was a man's tread on the steps covered with dried lumps of mud. With some difficulty the priest slipped into a kind of cupboard, and the nun flung some clothes over him.

"Yon can shut the door, Sister Agathe," he said in a muffled voice.

He was scarcely hidden before three raps sounded on the door. The holy women looked into each other's eyes for counsel, and dared not say a single word.

They seemed both to be about sixty years of age. They had lived out of the world for forty years, and had grown so accustomed to the life of the convent that they could scarcely imagine any other. To them, as to plants kept in a hot-house, a change of air meant death. And so, when the grating was broken down one morning, they knew with a shudder that they were free. The effect produced by the Revolution upon their simple souls is easy to imagine; it produced a temporary imbecility not natural to them. They could not bring the ideas learned in the convent into harmony with life and its difficulties; they could not even understand their own position. They were like children whom mothers have always cared for, deserted by their maternal providence. And as a child cries, they betook themselves to prayer. Now, in the presence of imminent danger, they were mute and passive, knowing no defence save Christian resignation.

The man at the door, taking silence for consent, presented himself, and the women shuddered. This was the prowler that had been making inquiries about them for some time past. But they looked at him with frightened curiosity, much as shy children stare silently at a stranger; and neither of them moved.

The newcomer was a tall, burly man. Nothing in his behaviour, bearing, or expression suggested malignity as, following the example set by the nuns, he stood motionless, while his eyes travelled round the room.

Two straw mats laid upon planks did duty as beds. On the one table, placed in the middle of the room, stood a brass candlestick, several plates, three knives, and a round loaf. A small fire burned in the grate. A few bits of wood in a heap in a corner bore further witness to the poverty of the recluses. You had only to look at the coating of paint on the walls to discover the bad condition of the roof, and the ceiling was a perfect network of brown stains made by rain-water.

A relic, saved no doubt from the wreck of the Abbaye de Chelles, stood like an ornament on the chimney-piece. Three chairs, two boxes, and a rickety chest of drawers completed the list of the furniture, but a door beside the fireplace suggested an inner room beyond.

The brief inventory was soon made by the personage introduced into their midst under such terrible auspices. It was with a compassionate expression that he turned to the two women; he looked benevolently at them, and seemed, at least, as much embarrassed as they. But the strange silence did not last long, for presently the stranger began to understand. He saw how inexperienced, how helpless (mentally speaking), the two poor creatures were, and he tried to speak gently.

"I am far from coming as an enemy, citoyennes—" he began. Then he suddenly broke off and went on, "Sisters, if anything should happen to you, believe me, I shall have no share in it. I have come to ask a favour of you."

Still the women were silent.

"If I am annoying you—if—if I am intruding, speak freely, and I will go; but you must understand that I am entirely at your service; that if I can do anything for you, you need not fear to make use of me. I, and I only, perhaps, am above the law, since there is no King now."

There was such a ring of sincerity in the words that Sister Agathe hastily pointed to a chair as if to bid their guest be seated. Sister Agathe came of the house of Langeais; her manner seemed to indicate that once she had been familiar with brilliant scenes, and had breathed the air of courts. The stranger seemed half pleased, half distressed when he understood her invitation; he waited to sit down until the women were seated.

"You are giving shelter to a reverend father who refused to take the oath, and escaped the massacres at the Carmelites by a miracle—"

"*Hosanna*" Sister Agathe exclaimed eagerly, interrupting the stranger, while she watched him with curious eyes.

"That is not the name, I think," he said.

"But, monsieur," Sister Marthe broke in quickly, "we have no priest here, and—"

"In that case you should be more careful and on your guard," he answered gently, stretching out his hand for a breviary that lay on the table. "I do not think that you know Latin, and—"

He stopped; for, at the sight of the great emotion in the faces of the two poor nuns, he was afraid that he had gone too far. They were trembling, and the tears stood in their eyes.

"Do not fear," he said frankly. "I know your names and the name of your guest. Three days ago I heard of your distress and devotion to the venerable Abbé de—"

"Hush!" Sister Agathe cried, in the simplicity of her heart, as she laid her finger on her lips.

"You see, Sisters, that if I had conceived the horrible idea of betraying you, I could have given you up already, more than once-—"

At the words the priest came out of his hiding-place and stood in their midst.

"I cannot believe, monsieur, that you can be one of our persecutors," he said, addressing the stranger, "and I trust you. What do you want with me?"

The priest's holy confidence, the nobleness expressed in every line in his face, would have disarmed a murderer. For a moment the mysterious stranger, who had brought an element of excitement into lives of misery and resignation, gazed at the little group; then he turned to the priest and said, as if making a confidence, "Father, I came to beg you to celebrate a mass for the repose of the soul of—of—of an august personage whose body will never rest in consecrated earth—"

Involuntarily the abbé shivered. As yet, neither of the Sisters understood of whom the stranger was speaking; they sat with their heads stretched out and faces turned towards the speaker, curiosity in their whole attitude. The priest, meanwhile, was scrutinising the stranger; there was no mistaking the anxiety in the man's face, the ardent entreaty in his eyes.

"Very well," returned the abbé. "Come back at midnight. I shall be ready to celebrate the only funeral service that it is in our power to offer in expiation of the crime of which you speak."

A quiver ran through the stranger, but a sweet yet sober satisfaction seemed to prevail over a hidden anguish. He took his leave respectfully, and the three generous souls felt his unspoken gratitude.

Two hours later, he came back and tapped at the garret door. Mademoiselle de Beauséant showed the way into the second room of their humble lodging. Everything had been made ready. The Sisters had moved the old chest of drawers between the two chimneys, and covered its quaint outlines over with a splendid altar cloth of green watered silk.

The bare walls looked all the barer, because the one thing that hung there was the great ivory and ebony crucifix, which of necessity attracted the eyes. Four slender little altar candles, which the Sisters had contrived to fasten into their places with sealing-wax, gave a faint, pale light, almost absorbed by the walls; the rest of the room lay well-nigh in the dark. But the dim brightness, concentrated upon the holy things, looked like a ray from Heaven shining down upon the unadorned shrine. The floor was reeking with damp. An icy wind swept in through the chinks here and there, in a roof that rose sharply on either side, after the fashion of attic roofs. Nothing could be less imposing; yet perhaps, too, nothing could be more solemn than this mournful ceremony. A silence so deep that they could have heard the faintest sound of a voice on the Route d'Allemagne, invested the night-piece with a kind of sombre majesty; while the grandeur of the service—all the grander for the strong contrast with the poor surroundings—produced a feeling of reverent awe.

The Sisters kneeling on each side the altar, regardless of the deadly chill from the wet brick floor, were engaged in prayer, while the priest, arrayed in pontifical vestments, brought out a golden chalice set with gems; doubtless one of the sacred vessels saved from the pillage of the Abbaye de Chelles. Beside a ciborium, the gift of royal munificence, the wine and water for the holy sacrifice of the mass stood ready in two glasses such as could scarcely be found in the meanest tavern. For want of a missal, the priest had laid his breviary on the altar, and a common earthenware plate was set for the washing of hands that were pure and undefiled with blood. It was all so infinitely great, yet so little, poverty-stricken yet noble, a mingling of sacred and profane.

The stranger came forward reverently to kneel between the two nuns. But the priest had tied crape round the chalice of the crucifix, having no other way of marking the mass as a funeral service; it was as if God himself had been in mourning. The man suddenly noticed this, and the sight appeared to call up some overwhelming memory, for great drops of sweat stood out on his broad forehead.

Then the four silent actors in the scene looked mysteriously at one another; and their souls in emulation seemed to stir and communicate the thoughts within them until all were melted into one feeling of awe and pity. It seemed to them that the royal martyr whose remains had been consumed with quicklime, had been called up by their yearning and now stood, a shadow in their midst, in all the majesty of a king. They were celebrating an anniversary service for the dead whose body lay elsewhere. Under the disjointed laths and tiles, four Christians were holding a funeral service without a coffin, and putting up prayers to God for the soul of a King of France. No devotion could be purer than this. It was a wonderful act of faith achieved without an afterthought. Surely in the sight of God it was like the cup of cold water which counterbalances the loftiest virtues. The prayers put up by two feeble nuns and a priest represented the whole Monarchy, and possibly at the same time, the Revolution found expression in the stranger, for the remorse in his face was so great that it was impossible not to think that he was fulfilling the vows of a boundless repentance.

When the priest came to the Latin words, *Introïbo ad altare Dei*, a sudden divine inspiration flashed upon him; he looked at the three kneeling figures, the representatives of Christian France, and said instead, as though to blot out the poverty of the garret, "We are about to enter the Sanctuary of God!"

These words, uttered with thrilling earnestness, struck reverent awe into the nuns and the stranger. Under the vaulted roof of St. Peter's at Rome, God would not have revealed Himself in greater majesty than here for the eyes of the Christians in that poor refuge; so true is it that all intermediaries between God and the soul of man are superfluous, and all the grandeur of God proceeds from Himself alone.

The stranger's fervour was sincere. One emotion blended the prayers of the four servants of God and the King in a single supplication. The holy words rang like the music of heaven through the silence. At one moment, tears gathered in the stranger's eyes. This was during the *Pater Noster*, for the priest added a petition in Latin, and his audience doubtless understood him when he said: "*Et remitte scelus regicidis sicut Ludovicus eis remisit semetipse*"—forgive the regicides as Louis himself forgave them.

The Sisters saw two great tears trace a channel down the stranger's manly cheeks and fall to the floor. Then the office for the dead was recited; the *Domine salvum fac regem* chanted in an undertone that went to the hearts of the faithful Royalists, for they thought how the child-King for whom they were praying was even then a captive in the hands of his enemies; and a shudder ran through the stranger, as he thought that a new crime might be committed, and that he could not choose but take his part in it.

The service came to an end. The priest made a sign to the Sisters, and they withdrew. As soon as he was left alone with the stranger, he went toward him with a grave, gentle face, and said in fatherly tones:

"My son, if your hands are stained with the blood of the royal martyr, confide in me. There is no sin that may not be blotted out in the sight of God by penitence as sincere and touching as yours appears to be."

At the first words, the man started with terror, in spite of himself. Then he recovered composure, and looked quietly at the astonished priest.

"Father," he said, and the other could not miss the tremor in his voice, "no one is more guiltless than I of the blood shed—"

"I am bound to believe you," said the priest. He paused a moment, and again he scrutinised his penitent. But, persisting in the idea that the man before him was one of the members of the Convention, one of the timorous voters who betrayed an inviolable and anointed head to save their own, he began again gravely:

"Remember, my son, that it is not enough to have taken no active part in the great crime; that fact does not absolve you. The men who might have defended the King and left their swords in their scabbards, will have a very heavy account to render to the King of Heaven—Ah! yes," he added, with an eloquent shake of the head, "heavy indeed!—for by doing nothing they became accomplices in the awful wickedness—"

"But do you think that an indirect participation will be punished?" the stranger asked with a bewildered look. "There is the private soldier commanded to fall into line—is he actually responsible?"

The priest hesitated. The stranger was glad; he had put the Royalist precisian in a dilemma, between the dogma of passive obedience on the one hand (for the upholders of the Monarchy maintained that obedience was the first principle of military law), and the equally important dogma which turns respect for the person of a King into a matter of religion. In the priest's indecision he was eager to see a favourable solution of the doubts which seemed to torment him. To prevent too prolonged reflection on the part of the reverend Jansenist, he added:

"I should blush to offer remuneration of any kind for the funeral service which you have just performed for the repose of the King's soul and the relief of my conscience. The only possible return for something of inestimable value is an offering likewise beyond price. Will you deign, monsieur, to take my gift of a holy relic? A day will perhaps come when you will understand its value."

As he spoke the stranger held out a box; it was very small and exceedingly light. The priest took it mechanically, as it were, so astonished was he by the man's solemn words, the tones of his voice, and the reverence with which he held out the gift.

The two men went back together into the first room. The Sisters were waiting for them.

"This house that you are living in belongs to Mucius Scævola, the plasterer on the first floor," he said. "He is well known in the Section for his patriotism, but in reality he is an adherent of the Bourbons. He used to be a huntsman in the service of his Highness the Prince de Conti, and he owes everything to him. So long as you stay in the house, you are safer here than anywhere else in France. Do not go out. Pious souls will minister to your necessities, and you can wait in safety for better times. Next year, on the 21st of January,"—he could not hide an involuntary shudder as he spoke,—"next year, if you are still in this dreary refuge, I will come back again to celebrate the expiatory mass with you—"

He broke off, bowed to the three, who answered not a word, gave a last look at the garret with its signs of poverty, and vanished.

Such an adventure possessed all the interest of a romance in the lives of the innocent nuns. So, as soon as the venerable abbé told them the story of the mysterious gift, it was placed upon the table, and by the feeble light of the tallow dip an indescribable curiosity appeared in the three anxious faces. Mademoiselle de Langeais opened the box, and found a very fine lawn handkerchief, soiled with sweat; darker stains appeared as they unfolded it.

"That is blood!" exclaimed the priest.

"It is marked with a royal crown!" cried Sister Agathe.

The women, aghast, allowed the precious relic to fall. For their simple souls the mystery that hung about the stranger grew inexplicable; as for the priest, from that day forth he did not even try to understand it.

Before very long the prisoners knew that, in spite of the Terror, some powerful hand was extended over them. It began when they received firewood and provisions; and next the Sisters knew that a woman had lent counsel to their protector, for linen was sent to them, and clothes in which they could leave the house without causing remark upon the aristocrat's dress that they had been forced to wear. After awhile Mucius Scævola gave them two civic cards; and often and often tidings necessary for the priest's safety came to them in roundabout ways. Warnings and advice reached them so opportunely that they could only have been sent by some person in the possession of state secrets. And, at a time when famine threatened Paris, invisible hands brought rations of "white bread" for the proscribed women in the wretched garret. Still they fancied that Citizen Mucius Scævola was only the mysterious instrument of a kindness always ingenious, and no less intelligent.

The noble ladies in the garret could no longer doubt that their protector was the stranger of the explanatory mass on the night of the 22d of January, 1793; and a kind of cult of him sprung up among them. Their one hope was in him; they lived through him. They added special petitions for him to their prayers; night and morning the pious souls prayed for his happiness, his prosperity, his safety; entreating God to remove all snares far from his path, to deliver him from his enemies, to grant him a long and peaceful life. And with this daily renewed gratitude, as it may be called, there blended a feeling of curiosity which grew more lively day by day. They talked over the circumstances of his first sudden appearance, their conjectures were endless; the stranger had conferred one more benefit upon them by diverting their minds. Again, and again, they said, when he next came to see them as he promised, to celebrate the sad anniversary of the death of Louis XVI, he should not escape their friendship.

The night so impatiently awaited came at last. At midnight the old wooden staircase echoed with the stranger's heavy footsteps. They had made the best of their room for his coming; the altar was ready, and this time the door stood open, and the two Sisters were out at the stairhead, eager to light the way. Mademoiselle de Langeais even came down a few steps, to meet their benefactor the sooner.

"Come," she said, with a quaver in the affectionate tones, "come in; we are expecting you."

He raised his face, gave her a dark look, and made no answer. The Sister felt as if an icy mantle had fallen over her, and said no more. At the sight of him, the glow of gratitude and curiosity died away in their hearts. Perhaps he was not so cold, not so taciturn, not so stern as he seemed to them, for in their highly wrought mood they were ready to pour out their feeling of friendship. But the three poor prisoners understood that he wished to be a stranger to them; and submitted. The priest fancied that he saw a smile on the man's lips as he saw their preparations for his visit, but it was at once repressed. He heard mass, said his prayer, and then disappeared, declining, with a few polite words, Mademoiselle de Langeais' invitation to partake of the little collation made ready for him.

After the 9th Thermidor, the Sisters and the Abbé de Marolles could go about Paris without the least danger. The first time that the abbé went out he walked to a perfumer's shop at the sign of *The Queen of Roses*, kept by the Citizen Ragon and his wife, court perfumers. The Ragons had been faithful adherents of the Royalist cause; it was through their means that the Vendéan leaders kept up a correspondence with the Princes and the Royalist Committee in Paris. The abbé, in the ordinary dress of the time, was standing on the threshold of the shop—which stood between Saint Roch and the Rue des Frondeurs—when he saw that the Rue Saint Honoré was filled with a crowd and he could not go out.

"What is the matter?" he asked Madame Ragon.

"Nothing," she said; "it is only the tumbril cart and the executioner going to the Place Louis XV. Ah! we used to see it often enough last year; but to-day, four days after the anniversary of the twenty-first of January, one does not feel sorry to see the ghastly procession."

"Why not?" asked the abbé. "That is not said like a Christian."

"Eh! but it is the execution of Robespierre's accomplices. They defended themselves as long as they could, but now it is their turn to go where they sent so many innocent people."

The crowd poured by like a flood. The abbé, yielding to an impulse of curiosity, looked up above the heads, and there in the tumbril stood the man who had heard mass in the garret three days ago.

"Who is it?" he asked; "who is the man with—"

"That is the headsman," answered M. Ragon, calling the executioner—the *exécuteur des hautes oeuvres*—by the name he had borne under the Monarchy.

"Oh! my dear, my dear! M. l'Abbé is dying!" cried out old Madame Ragon. She caught up a flask of vinegar, and tried to restore the old priest to consciousness.

"He must have given me the handkerchief that the King used to wipe his brow on the way to his martyrdom," murmured he. "... Poor man! ... There was a heart in the steel blade, when none was found in all France ..."

The perfumers thought that the poor abbé was raving.

PARIS, *January* 1831.